BARGAINS AND BETRAYALS

ALSO BY SHANNON DELANY

13 to Life
Secrets and Shadows

BARGAINS AND BETRAYALS

Shannon Delany

St. Martin's Griffin
New York

BARGAINS AND BETRAYALS. Copyright © 2011 by Shannon Delany. All rights reserved. Printed in the United States of America. For information, address St. Martin's Press, 175 Fifth Avenue, New York, N.Y. 10010.

www.stmartins.com

ISBN 978-0-312-60916-0

First Edition: August 2011

10 9 8 7 6 5 4 3 2 1

Dedicated to my son, Jaiden.
Regardless of how insane things get,
no matter whether my work is
appreciated, ignored, or despised,
looking at you I know I brought at least one
amazing thing into this world.

BARGAINS AND BETRAYALS

PROLOGUE

Curled in Pietr's arms, her knee aching from her ex-boyfriend's brutal attack, Jessie Gillmansen knows monsters come in all shapes and sizes. She rests her head against Pietr's fiery chest, appreciating the heat that's the aftermath of his change even more now that she doesn't know when she'll feel it next. Listening to the staccato rhythm of his heart, her pulse races to match it as shadows fall over them in the barn, throwing them into darkness.

"Pecan Place—*where the nuts gather*," she mutters, shaking her head as Pietr pulls her closer as if his body can shield her from this sudden betrayal. "The mental institution?" It's only been a few months since her mother's sudden death and the reality is she's not handling things well. But beyond the heartache of losing her mother, Jessie is struggling with much stranger things. "No," she insists, voice rising. "No, no, no!"

Pietr steadies himself. His breath stirs the chestnut-colored strands of hair that curl slightly by Jess's ear and he says, "I won't let them take you, Jess. I promise. I won't let you down."

Some seventeen-year-olds might make promises hastily. Might not be prepared to back them up. Jess has done her share of that.

But Pietr wasn't made that way.

Pietr doesn't take promises lightly.

Clutching his arm, she whispers, "Please—*puhzhalsta . . .*"

Her breathing calms. The thrumming of her heart slows as she feels a subtle shift in the muscles sliding just below his skin.

Pietr is her hero.

Capable of amazing things.

A growl builds softly in his gut, clawing toward his chest. "Don't touch her," he warns.

Looking at Jess's father, Leon, Dr. Jones's lips purse in a distinct, nonverbal cue.

"Now, Jessie," Leon says, watching Pietr's eyes flick from person to person as he weighs his options. "This is the best thing we can do for you." He rubs a hand across his forehead. "I want you to cooperate. Pietr. Let her go."

"*Nyet.*" He bites the word off. "I will not let you take her. She does not want to go."

"Pietr, let go of her."

"*Nyet,* Wanda," he snaps. His breathing hitches when he looks at Jess, so often so strong and now so frightened.

Dr. Jones steps forward, speaking in low, measured tones. "It's okay," she consoles him. "This occasionally happens." She glances at Leon and Wanda. "That's why we bring extra help."

Car doors groan open and two sets of heavy feet approach.

"Let her go," Dr. Jones suggests gently, stepping back as the darkness shrouding the teens deepens.

Jess looks up, eyes widening. It would take three of Pietr to make one of the giant who thickens the shadows. And he's the smaller of the two approaching men.

"Do it," Wanda encourages him. "Just let her go."

From the hay bale where he cradles his girlfriend, Pietr looks up. And up. His head finally stops, neck craning, when he locks eyes with one of the giants. "*Nyet.*"

For a moment time stands still—for everyone except Jess.

She knows how fast it rushes by, based on the thundering gallop of Pietr's heart.

The shadows shift, the men's arms blurring as they tear the couple apart.

Stretching toward each other, Jess and Pietr's fingertips brush and she whispers a single word in warning: "Witnesses."

He roars. She's right. He can't change—can't shift—can't let the wolf inside free to fight. His expression twisting with rage, he struggles to keep from showing what's really inside: his fear that he finally can't keep a promise to her.

And this may be his most important promise yet.

Ten minutes before they were ready to face the truth, tell her father everything. Stop the lies. Face the consequences.

Together.

But now?

Pinned, Pietr goes wild, writhing. Then, as fast as the rage comes, it disappears. He lies there. Still. The only clue to his inner turmoil is how his eyes hold Jess's, glowing a furious red.

"No," Jess whispers, voice catching. The goliath clambers away and Pietr springs forward and grabs her, nearly pulling her free before he's slammed to the ground again.

Her father barely gets a word of objection out before the women silence him. They've already discussed this possibility.

Teenagers can be stubborn.

And Jessica needs protection.

Pietr's nose streams blood and a fresh gash spills red into his blinking eyes. His cheek is ragged, abraded raw. He's not nearly as beautiful as he was just fifteen minutes ago.

"Pietr," Jess whispers, choking back a cry as she's dumped onto her feet and the pain in her knee explodes like fireworks caught beneath her skin.

The other giant sits up again, watching as Pietr staggers to his feet, swaying. With one more burst of strength Pietr shoves him aside and goes for Jess.

"Stop fighting!"

The biggest grabs Pietr by the shoulders and hurls him to the earth. Jess winces. The *crunch* of bones carries.

Clutching his head, Pietr groans, his eyes filled with Jess. Only Jess. And he struggles to rise. He reaches for her, arms trembling.

The giant snarls and Leon shouts for everyone to stop as he grabs at the doctor's clipboard.

But she holds her ground. "Unless you want me to call Social Services and have them reconsider your youngest's living arrangements . . ."

Pietr's head cracks against the hard-packed dirt as Dr. Jones calmly continues. ". . . you'll follow through with the treatment plan we've agreed upon for Jessica."

Pietr's body shudders, but he tries to pull himself back up.

"Stay down! God, Pietr . . . please, please stay down. . . ." Jess begs. "I'll go with you," she swears to Dr. Jones, grabbing her sleeve. "Hurry. Before he tries again."

Car doors open and slam shut again and the car's engine growls back to life.

For one long, horrified minute Leon and Wanda stand in the dirt-and-gravel driveway, autumn's leaves teasing their shoelaces as the car lurches forward, heading down the drive. Leon moves first, shaking off the immobilizing power of shock to reach for the boy lying crumpled on the ground.

Wanda follows, crouching beside the battered boy as Pietr groans and struggles to drag his hands closer toward his chest. One arm is clearly broken. Wanda tries not to imagine how many other parts of him are fighting to mend.

He's survived bullet wounds that would have killed far bigger men; he's killed murderers and mobsters—monsters who wore nothing but human skins. He's proven himself a fighter when he must be, a gentleman when he can be. For all the wolf inside him, he still has moments when he's an absolute lamb. A warrior with a gentle heart.

Regardless of all the blood and battling, no one's really sure at what point one of his kind can no longer make it back from death's door.

And Wanda realizes she doesn't want to be around when they finally learn how much is too much.

Her ex-partner—her superiors—they were right. She has gotten too close to all this. Which means the pressure's on to keep things looking as normal as possible. "Stop fighting," Wanda whispers, reaching for his shoulders.

He grunts and tries to pull his arms under himself. He struggles to rise.

Just.

Once.

More.

His broken arm buckles beneath his weight and with a howl equal parts frustration and pain he falls back to the dirt.

Leon reaches for Pietr, his eyes still fixed on Wanda. "Call the ambulance," he suggests.

But she looks at him blankly as if the word *ambulance* is no longer within the scope of her vocabulary.

"Let us help you." She slips a hand under Pietr's arm and something inside him rattles, the noise rising a moment before it slips into a wheeze. Pietr coughs, spattering the ground by his head with spit and blood.

Leon takes his other arm. "Here we go . . . careful now . . ."

They pull him up, supporting him between them. He raises his head and winces—not at the physical pain that threatens to consume him but at the sight of the car flashing away out of the driveway. Out of his reach.

Pulling out of their grip, he stumbles forward a single step before his legs give out and he crashes to his knees. Wanda drops beside him, looping an arm around his waist. "Let us help you," she insists.

He shakes his head. "Help me?" he whispers between the wheezing of his lungs. "You took her from me." He looks at her, his eyes fierce, mismatched in the intensity of the red that betrays the firestorm raging within.

Head trauma, Wanda realizes, reaching out to examine his face, his skull.

"You made a liar out of me," he snarls, pulling back from her touch. "God," he moans, quivering beside her, his head down, shoulders shaking. "I couldn't keep my promise. . . ."

Her hand slips away from his cheek. Her fingers trembling before her, Wanda marvels at the moisture glistening on their tips. "Oh, Pietr," she whispers. "Oh. God. Pietr. Please. Don't cry."

But hearing her use his name after ignoring that any of his people *had* names only makes tears come faster.

"Leon. Help me get him inside," Wanda orders.

"Shouldn't we call the ambulance first?"

"NO." The answer comes in unison. An ambulance manned by uninformed public servants is precisely the type of *help* Wanda and Pietr must avoid.

"Okay," Leon concedes, stooping.

Arms linked around his waist, they help Pietr limp to the house. Inside they start to set him down on the couch, but he protests. "*Nyet.* I'm bleeding."

"We need to call the ambulance," Leon tries again.

"*Nyet*," Pietr whispers. "Old towels, sheets?"

"I do not understand you, boy," Leon admits, and he leaves Pietr, supported by Wanda.

"You can set the bones?" Pietr asks her, grinding the words out between startling spasms of pain. "It's too difficult with only one working arm."

"I'll set them. But first I'm calling Max."

Pietr nods. He winces as she shifts, withdraws her cell phone, and makes the call. Returning with an armful of sheets Leon follows Pietr's haltingly given directions and covers the couch. With a groan and some help, Pietr lowers himself onto the protected surface.

"Hey, that cut above your eye's not bleedin' so bad," Leon mutters. "And your face . . ." He looks at Wanda.

Her complete lack of surprise does not reassure him. Neither does her lengthy silence.

"Let's set your arm," she grumbles, looking away from Leon as she grabs Pietr's wrist.

Leon scrubs a hand across his face. "You know how to—"

Wanda doesn't answer, but braces a foot on the side of the couch and yanks until Pietr snarls. "Better?"

He tests the arm with his other hand, fingers sliding along the edge of muscle and tendon to prod at bone. He grunts approval.

"We should splint it. Don't want it healing wrong," she points out. "Max would break and reset it, right?"

Pietr pales at the thought. She's right. Internal organs mend decently when left alone, but broken bone crawls toward its mate regardless of awkward angles.

And Pier's brother Max is not the gentlest of nursemaids.

"Leon . . . ," Wanda begins, but he's already gone in search of something to serve as a splint.

At what point, Wanda wonders, must she tell Leon the truth? That she's not a reference librarian—not *only* a reference librarian? That she works for a company she thought was CIA but now . . . Their willingness to murder some children and cage others has her asking questions she doesn't dare voice aloud.

Not quite yet.

"What about your legs?" Wanda asks. "You didn't seem able to keep them under you on your own."

Pietr closes his eyes, taking a mental accounting of the injuries he still feels—things not ready to mend or not ready to mend right.

Outside, a car races up the gravel drive and stops short.

"What now?!" Leon shouts as Max bounds through the doorway.

Shoving the curls that shadow his glinting blue eyes back from his face, Max glares at Wanda. "Step back." He rounds the couch, taking her place, his eyes narrowing. Silent, he peers down at his younger brother, his jaw so tight it twitches.

Pietr opens his mouth, but Max simply says, "Explain things later. All I want to know is what's broken. And if they shot you."

They both remember the drama of the last fight far too freshly.

"What?" Leon's eyebrows tug together. "Shot?"

"Wanda," Max snaps.

Wanda moves over to Leon's side, taking his arm and drawing him toward the kitchen.

"What's going on here? People have *shot* at them? And Pietr—he's looking a helluva sight better than just minutes ago. . . . What's happening here, Wanda?"

CHAPTER ONE

Alexi

My cigarettes called to me, urging me to step outside, to light one smooth cylinder and suck down the richly tainted air before the autumn wind could tug it away. To breathe deep the poison that calmed me. My hand shook, fingers raking through my hair; overanalyzing our current predicament rattled my nerves.

Max, Pietr, and Cat remarked on my smoking once: how could an oborot be a smoker? How could anyone with a werewolf's nose stand such a stink? I was, briefly, a puzzle to them.

Did I not disappear at all the right times to run beneath a moonlit sky? Did I not learn to pick out subtleties of sound and oddities of scent like the rest of them? Was I not quick on my feet and strong as a beast when I had to be?

Of course I was. I was trained by the best. Our parents built me up to be a perfect fraud—a fine work of fiction.

On the balls of my feet I descended the stairs as soft-footed as any full-blood Rusakova. At the bottom of the steps I turned, breathing deep. The mix of scent and sound told me Pietr and Cat were cloistered together in the sitting room, deep in discussion.

We lived, as my Russian predecessors would have said, *like a cat and a dog*—suitable in some ways but frequently quarreling and snapping at one another. I, once the domineering alpha, was now the too-human interloper skulking at the fringes of conversation until someone realized a need for my expertise.

Time spent working the black market came in handy, though I'd closed those doors as firmly as I could.

"I need to get her out," Pietr complained. Stating the obvious was only one of his ample gifts. Still bruised, battered, and with bones reset by Wanda, the very woman we'd been going head-to-head with over Mother's imprisonment, Pietr was healing more slowly than ever before. Faster than a simple human might, but at a pace unbearably slow for an oborot—*one transformed*.

We did not discuss the fact he almost died trying to keep his girlfriend free. That was the main rule Pietr, as the current and yet understated alpha of the family, enforced.

"*Da*, Jessie should be out," Cat agreed, and I peered around the door frame to watch a moment, patting my shirt pocket to make the cigarettes cease their insistent call.

Cat leaned over, a slender shadow stretched across the freshly repaired love seat's arm. What any of us bled on or tore up or warred across—as a result of Pietr's or Max's past reckless actions or our attempts to free Mother—Pietr made sure was cleaned or repaired. He knew appearances mattered to our sister most.

Cat patted his hand. "She is only to stay there what?—a month?"

Pietr groaned and sat back in the chair, his eyes narrow as he gazed at his twin. "*Da*. A month. More, if she does not behave."

"Then let her behave. Do not interfere."

He groaned again.

"Think, Pietr." She nudged his knee with her foot and laughed. "Think with the more *proper* part of your anatomy," she teased.

He snorted.

"Do not become like Max, salivating over a girl." Though I could not see them, I knew she rolled her eyes dramatically as she waved a hand to dismiss the idea altogether. "A month is not so long."

"Not to you," he said, cocking his head to examine her heart-shaped face. "Not now."

Did she seem different to him since she'd taken the cure? Was she somehow less now she had more years to her life span? To me, she was still and always Ekaterina—*Cat*—beautiful and troublesome as ever. A danger to young men's hearts . . . and anyone willing to try her cooking. Was there something about her my simple human senses overlooked? Something in her complexion, her carriage, her gait, her scent?

I drew back, slinking around the banister to head to the rear of the Queen Anne house we still called home, and the solitude of the back porch.

Each child in a family had a role to play; the eldest was often the leader—the alpha. For a while the role was mine. When it was necessary I shouldered the heaviest responsibility, took the greatest risks. I learned the ins and outs of the dark side of commerce. I sold my soul as much as anything on the black market to make ends meet once our parents were gone and our safety was at risk.

Everything I did, I did for *them*. My brothers. My sister. *My family*.

But the night of the twins' seventeenth birthday—the night the Mafia came for them—they learned the truth behind all my years of deception: Although I was their brother in name, I was never their brother in blood. Therefore my usefulness was limited and officially at an end except as their legal guardian. That usefulness might yet conclude when Maximilian turned eighteen.

I froze at the back door, my hand upon the knob; the lace of the small window's curtain teased across my fingers like an ant traipsing over the mountains my knuckles formed.

Seated on the porch, Max hung his right leg over the edge, his left tucked beneath him, so he sat near enough to shadow Amy. Her feet swung back and forth, beating an angry rhythm into the cool air, her fingers curled around the edge of the decking. Beneath the thin gloves she wore I imagined her knuckles were white in frustration.

In the yard beyond them, leaves flew and splintered in the snapping wind of approaching winter. No snow had fallen yet, but the clouds threatened daily. The earth was brown and crisp, the bright colors of autumn's leaves dulled.

Max spoke. Amy heard, her head nodding at appropriate intervals. Max believed she was listening, but I knew better.

From her closed body language I realized he was back to the same words that had so recently made her storm away and slam the basement door in his face.

It was the discussion survivors of abuse dreaded. A discussion Max tried to have with the very best of intentions, but . . . how could he understand? He was the hero. She was the victim. There could be no even footing between them until she found her place in the story of her own life. Stood on her own.

Max was new; she and her abuser, Marvin Broderick, shared a past. Max had chosen to give her an option beyond her abusive boyfriend: *him*. She had taken it, but still she and Marvin had a connection: They shared a town, a school, and acquaintances. Her life was a daily mix of stressful decisions.

Max had difficulty understanding that. He made his choice. He did not realize she had to continue making choices moment by moment and day by day.

I considered leaving my spot inside the back door, knowing well the ground being retread.

A breeze snatched at Amy's auburn hair, lifting it up and away from her face in snapping angles. Her eyes closed and she turned to face Max, her mouth opening to bite off a reply just as her hair struck out and blinded him.

He choked, flailed.

And made a greater ass of himself.

From the door I nearly made my presence known by snickering at him—my idiotic little brother.

Amy laughed, seeing him so off balance. She gave him a little shove, her hands flying up and shaking between them as if to say, *If you weren't sitting on top of me, you gigantic oaf . . .*

Or perhaps that was merely my interpretation.

In the time it took to blink an eye, the heated discussion had fallen to the wayside and they had returned to what they did best together—flirting and teasing. It seemed years were added to his life just being around her.

He said something. Stupid, no doubt, and she slapped him playfully—how did she phrase it?—*upside the head*. I would have gladly helped put words in Max's mouth, but it was always awkward fitting them around his foot.

He sputtered, seizing her wrist to drag her hand slowly across his stubbled jawline. In that singular moment, that heartbeat when she shivered and he straightened ever so slightly to watch her reaction, in that moment alone was more intimacy and passion than in all the flings and one-night stands he'd ever reveled in.

Priding myself a scientist of sorts, I watched their body language: her leaning toward him, falling into the shadow he cast, him rolling his shoulders forward to envelop her more completely without even raising his arms. A subtle slide of movement, a gentle curve to her posture and the rays and angles—the lines their bodies drew—the very math that existed between their two separate figures, spoke more accurately than any words in either of our first languages.

This was something stronger than anything he'd ever known—ever felt—before. Something deeper. Something new to both of them. It was love, made clear in geometric terms.

Once, in Moscow, I had been able to measure the distance

from a girl's heart to mine simply by noting the few degrees of separation between our forms, the dimensions devising our expressions. I loved that girl.

And I realized *this* might yet be the death of us. Not the werewolves—neither the mafiosos who called themselves werewolves nor the oboroten, living the abbreviated and violent life span that would eventually kill my siblings. *Nyet.* It has never truly been about werewolves, has it?

It has always been about life and death. About choices. About love and loss.

I made my choice and left Moscow. Left Nadezhda. My brothers have made theirs, so we stay in Junction.

Someday soon all our most dangerous decisions, all these choices, will catch up to us and we will drink what we have brewed—reaping and sowing not being nearly as fashionable.

Clutching the dry comfort of the cigarettes nestled in their box, my hands trembled and the doorknob squeaked.

Without even turning to face the door, Max rolled out words underpinned with the growl that had become his normal tone when mentioning or addressing me. "He's watching us again."

Amy peered over his shoulder and winked at me as I stepped past them on the porch and headed down the stairs to light up. "Then let's give him something to watch," she suggested.

Behind me, I heard him growl. She giggled when he pounced.

Perhaps leaving Nadezhda in Moscow had been a bigger mistake than I'd ever imagined. Time would surely tell, as it did in all things.

CHAPTER TWO

Jessie

Trapped in Dr. Jones's office at Pecan Place for another session, being asked the same questions and getting none of mine answered, I was becoming frantic.

"What does it matter?" she asked. Leaning back in her leather chair she watched me from behind her wide desk. "You are *here*. Safe. You're already making progress with your therapy."

It might have been congratulations, but it rolled out of her mouth through a sneer.

"Just tell me," I whispered—*implored*—bending forward to narrow the distance between us. "Tell me how he is."

"No."

My eyes pressed shut and I clamped my teeth together to bite back a shout. Three days and no word about Pietr. No message from Dad. Nothing from beyond Pecan Place. Nothing to anchor me to my past or to the people I loved. "Damn it." The words squeezed out from between my lips.

Dr. Jones pitched forward and jotted a note on her clipboard. "You need to stay in control. Remember our facility's rules against profanity."

Against profanity, contact with the outside world, and freedom of thought.

Dr. Jones stood. "I'd hate for you to be placed on restriction."

Words curled up in my throat, spiraling around as uselessly as dry leaves. There were a few things I'd learned over the three days since I'd agreed to come to the institution to keep Dr. Jones's guards from killing Pietr . . .

. . . from *killing* Pietr . . .

I struggled for focus. Of the things I'd learned in the sparsely populated Pecan Place, when to keep my mouth shut was the most vital lesson.

But that lesson was being tested.

"Pietr Rusakova's situation has nothing to do with your mental health."

"His situation has *everything* to do with my mental health." The chair was suddenly too confining, so I stood. "*I'm* the reason he was attacked."

"I disagree," Dr. Jones said, her tone level and cool while her eyes flicked down and forward. I followed her gaze to my hands—gripping her desk so hard my fingers were splotched red and white. "He is the only one responsible for his behavior and the results of that behavior."

"His behavior was an attempt to protect me."

"*Protect* you? From what? From achieving better mental health? He was obviously obsessed with you."

I twitched. Obsessed? Hardly. In love? I hoped. But the word that bothered me most in that sentence? *Was.*

As if Pietr was firmly in the past tense.

"Put me on restriction—I don't care! Just tell me if Pietr's okay. Is he alive, or did your guards—*my* guards—did they kill him?" With a growl I pried my fingers from the lip of her desk long enough to clear it with one violent sweep of my arms. Files and papers of all shapes and sizes flew off its surface and snowed down around us in deceptively slow and gentle arcs.

She grinned and took one hard step forward, her shoe slapping the floor.

An alarm sounded.

Behind me the door burst open and a nurse rushed in, flanked by my mountainous guards.

The nurse paused, eyed me—judged and weighed me and pulled a hypodermic needle from behind her back. She nudged the syringe's thumb rest slightly so a brief trickle of amber liquid dribbled down the needle's sharp tip before slipping onto the syringe's transparent shaft.

"No!" I dodged to avoid the guards' grip, but their fingers hooked into my arms like icy sausages. "Just tell me," I begged, throat tightening, tears fuzzing my vision as they burned free of my eyes. "Tell me if Pietr's alive!"

But the needle was in, the plunger was down, and everything wobbled in my sight like heat waves hovering above blacktop.

"Tell me." My tongue slow, the words were thick, as blurred as my vision. I fought to focus, desperate for an answer . . .

"What does it matter? You'll never see him again."

And the darkness chewing at the edge of my failing vision finally stole my senses away.

Alexi

In the foyer, Pietr readied to again sneak off into the night, to hope for still winds and calm air and a few precious minutes to press his face to the thick glass that separated him from the girl he adored. To stare at her a mere moment before the dogs caught his scent. "What good comes of this? Does she want to see you—like *this*? Knowing the danger you put yourself in? Does she even know you visit?"

He turned away, unmoved by my question except for the

telltale rise of a single vein near his temple. *"I know I'm there. Jess needs me."*

"Jessie, even locked away in an insane asylum—did you not say she's been *sedated*? *She* makes more sense than you," I stated. "She would not want you there if it meant you risked your safety."

His hand was already on the door, his mind made up. "Maybe I'm not doing this just for her," he said, his eyes a cool blue though I knew he seethed within, "maybe I'm doing this for me."

"Then you've finally succeeded in combining stupidity with selfishness," I congratulated him. "You know pining over her does nothing for any of us. It is a distraction—not a solution."

"Why don't *you* focus on the solution, then, brother," he snarled, whipping around, "rather than your *multitude* of distractions?" He grabbed the pocket of my shirt and, with a quick squeeze of his fingers, crushed the box of cigarettes resting there.

The front door slammed shut behind him.

I dragged the crumpled box out and examined its bent and broken contents.

Little brothers were so difficult.

Sliding the paper from its normal place between the cigarettes and my heart, I unfolded it carefully so as to not drop the small photograph nestled within. In my grasp the letter quivered, the flowing Cyrillic script of Nadezhda's uncompromising hand wobbling until it became nearly impossible to decipher. But I knew the words by heart.

Part Pushkin's "Night" and part her own words of love, the letter was a perfect example of the superiority of longhand correspondence to the stale vanilla of e-mail and text.

She and I had been apart too long, because I did what Pietr never would. I broke a promise. A promise to the daughter of one of the most dangerous men in Russia—head of one of the largest districts of the Russian Mafia. A promise to take her away from the danger, the drug lords, the whores and violent criminals, to settle with her in a modest *dacha* all our own.

To wipe clean the slate of our violent and destructive pasts and build a future—our own happily ever after.

Together.

What if the happily ever after we both wanted only existed in fairy tale stories? Or what if the choices that set one on the path to becoming a deserving hero had already passed me by? Perhaps I deserved nothing better than what I had.

Just one of my "multitude of distractions."

Pietr had no idea.

Jessie

My body ached. My eyes, sticky with sleep, peeled open with a sound like masking tape being pulled from the roll. Vision hazy, I struggled to get a handle on my location. Something creaked beneath my hip as I rolled up into a seated position. A mattress. I concentrated on keeping whatever contents my stomach still held where they belonged.

"Nice of you to join us, Jessica."

I squinted at the woman in the chair before me, searching the cottony mess of my brain for a name. "Dr. Jones?"

"Very good. How are you feeling today?"

"Groggy."

"That happens when we have to sedate a patient so frequently."

"Sedate?" My arm stung. I looked at it, seeing tiny puncture marks marring the tender skin of the crook of my elbow.

"Yes. You kept getting yourself so worked up. . . ." Dr. Jones shook her head. "You were dangerous to the staff. And to yourself."

My eyes slammed shut and I wondered what could have upset

me that much. Me? *Dangerous?* I rubbed my eyes. My head hummed, but nothing stepped out of the shadowy recesses of my brain with an answer. "Really?" I muttered. "I'm sorry."

"That's okay, Jessica." She glanced at the two tall men flanking her. They wore the same long-sleeved uniform my guards had, but . . .

Tilting my head to view them from a different angle was a big mistake. I clutched at the bed and waited for my vision to stop swimming. Slowly I raised my eyes from the concrete floor to the stalwart men.

They *looked* like my guards but *weren't* my guards.

Dr. Jones's mouth moved and I struggled to understand the words coming out of it. "Is there anything you'd like to ask me about?"

I felt like I was back in Latin level one. I ran my tongue along my teeth. My mouth seemed as fuzzy as my vision.

"Go ahead. Ask me anything. Do you have any questions?" She peered at me. "Any questions at all?"

Although it sounded distinctly like a challenge, there was nothing I had to know—no question pounding inside my skull. I shrugged. "No."

"Excellent." She stood and looked at the two giants. "I believe we can finally take Jessica off restriction. Give her a few minutes and let her shower and change. Then take her to the common room to join the others."

Mute, they nodded.

Dr. Jones turned to the shadows behind the guards. "Nurse."

A woman stepped forward, the muted light of my room making her white uniform glow.

"Prep her for chores tomorrow. She can at least help with the laundry."

The nurse gave me a fleeting look before returning her gaze to the doctor. "Are you—?"

"—sure?" Jones nodded. "She's under guard. She should at least be useful while she's here. In two days your father visits."

Her voice lowered along with her eyes. "He's a stubborn man when it comes to his children." Rising, she brushed her hands across her slacks. Her cell phone sounded, and, tugging it out of her pocket, she glanced at it, a smile stretching her lips. "Excellent. The thing we've been looking so forward to receiving is finally on its way in. I need to gather some paperwork and get ready to meet the shipper," she informed the nurse. "Is room twenty-six prepped?"

"Yes." The nurse waited until the door closed behind the doctor before addressing me again. "Can you stand?"

I nodded with more certainty than I felt.

"Good. Shower. Breakfast. Tomorrow: chores."

The door clicked shut and I was alone in my room. With a groan I rose and steadied myself, holding the cold metal bed frame. *Shower.*

Bathroom.

There.

A door.

I shuffled to it and timidly bent to start the water running. Slipping out of my top and pants I stepped into the shower and let my head hang, slowly waking under the pelting sting of water.

Beneath its roar, my mind began to clear.

Was there a question I should have asked? I shook my head, water rolling down along my ears, threatening to plug them. "Ugh." No answer—or, more appropriately, no question—came. Between the ache in my elbow and the emptiness in my skull, I realized there was no question I needed answered, no curiosity gnawing at my gut.

I dried my hair, dressed in a nondescript blue shirt and pants, and joined my guards.

"You two. You aren't my regular guards. What are your names?" It was something I'd never figured out about their predecessors.

A moment passed as they exchanged a slow look. Their

meaty skulls swung back on their tree-trunk necks and they blinked in unison. One jerked his chin toward the common room.

We trudged in that direction, down the hall lit with hissing fluorescent bulbs. Past the nurses' station and the room with its whirring refrigerator locked and filled with chemically based support for almost any behavior deemed abnormal, all in handy vials and bottles with names so long they wrapped all the way around their labels.

I took a seat at a round white table while one guard got my food. There were only a dozen other people seated throughout the broad space, but I realized that was twice as many as had been here before my forced sedation.

Something strange was definitely going on.

The nurse rolled a cart in, the platter on its top lined with tiny crimped paper cups, black numbers on their sides. The daily meds. I stretched up as tall as I could as she stopped the cart beside my table. Most of the cups appeared to have the same selection of pills inside. The nurse glanced at the cup numbers briefly before selecting one for me.

Mine wasn't like the others. "Umm? What's so different about me?"

"Just consider it proof that what your parents always said was true." Handing me the cup, she reached over and, folding my sleeve, swabbed my arm with alcohol. "You're *special*." She lined up a syringe and jabbed me, slowly pulling back the plunger so the shaft filled with red.

"*Ow.*" I twitched. "And drawing my blood? That's new."

"Get used to it," she suggested. "Consider it our little way of seeing just how special you are."

My stomach did a little flip. The Rusakovas knew my blood was part of the cure for the werewolves and we were pretty certain the CIA knew, too, since Officer Kent tried to kill me at the shooting range. Was it possible Dr. Jones was somehow tied in with them?

The nurse withdrew the needle, put a cotton ball and Band-aid over the spot, saying, "Press down a minute," and went on her way.

Could they all be in cahoots? I squeezed my eyes shut. No. That'd be crazy. Opening my eyes, I sighed. Maybe crazy was to be expected in an asylum.

My guard returned, sliding a tray of food across to me, his long sleeve slipping up to briefly expose the underside of one wrist.

"Wait," I commanded, seeing something strange. But he didn't obey. "Fine." I poked at the stuff daring to be defined as food and even ate some. It was like eating the love child of cardboard and Styrofoam.

While faking interest in eating I tried to get a look at the guard's wrist. There was a mark—a tattoo?—that seemed familiar. I glanced at his other wrist. The edge of a matching something peeked out from beneath that sleeve, too.

"I'm full." It was one of the easiest lies I'd told in the past few months. "I want to go back to my room."

In unison they rose, one taking my tray while the other watched me with dull eyes.

"If you don't tell me your names, I'll just make something up." They didn't react, just kept walking.

"Fine," I announced. "Thing One"—I turned to the one on my left—"and Thing Two," I dubbed the one on my right.

Still no reaction.

Heading back, I noticed a young woman in a straitjacket and leg irons latched to a bench, her escort standing by, warily watching the length of the hall, his arms folded, eyes only briefly pausing on her.

Or me and my guards as we approached.

The most interesting thing in the vicinity, she didn't look much older than me. Her complexion made me think she'd been tanning recently; she definitely wasn't the happily stuck indoors type. Her shoulder-length hair was brown, with narrow highlights of blond and red, and as we passed her I thought I saw her nostrils flare. I craned my neck, dragging down my already slow pace to watch another moment. Her gaze flicked toward me and I stumbled, catching a reflection of red in her eyes. She blinked, looking away, just another normal girl.

In an asylum.

I regained my balance and, untangling my feet, turned back toward my room, ignoring the creeping prickle as the fine hairs on my arms rose in warning.

Dr. Jones's voice behind me made me spin around once more. "Excellent. Here are your papers." She leaned toward the girl, who leaned away, baring her teeth in response. "We've been greatly anticipating your arrival, Harmony. You've had quite the journey."

The creeping prickle turned into a full-body shudder before I could turn away again. Exhaling, I wondered if Harmony was the *thing* they'd been looking forward to receiving.

Three-quarters of the way down the hall we stopped outside room 39. A white metal door with a narrow window of reinforced glass near eye level marked the entrance to my private room.

Homey.

Thing Two took a card from his shirt pocket and slipped it into the electronic lock, waiting until the light blinked green to twist the handle. Considering his size and strength I bet the door would open whether locked or not.

Stepping inside, the door shut, bolting behind me and separating me from my Goliath guards.

Spectacular in its solitude, room 39 was so silent my ears wanted to bleed just to hear the rhythmic drip of blood.

I spent the rest of the day there, seated on the edge of my bed, flopped across the middle of my bed, staring at the walls surrounding my bed. I closed my eyes briefly and imagined my mother sitting on the bed's edge, brushing the hair off my forehead like she used to do when I was home sick from school.

A breeze tickled my face and my hair was swept back from my eyes with a soft caress. I sat up. The room *looked* empty, but considering the weird things happening around Junction, I knew seeing and believing didn't equate. "Mom?" My bed-sheets fluttered and I caught the scent of sunlit summer fields. Although the air stilled as quickly as it had stirred, flopping back down on the bed, I didn't feel quite as alone.

When my guards gave up on me going out again and eventually brought my lunch, I ignored them.

When they returned a few hours later with my dinner and a small notebook, a pen tucked in its spiraling spine, I still ignored *them*.

But ignoring the notebook was impossible.

Inside there were no instructions, just page after page of beautifully blank, lined paper.

I poked at the cube of gelatin glimmering cheerily beside a carton of milk. The journal was far more enticing to a would-be writer than food would ever be.

Tapping the pen on its cover, I enjoyed the echoing sound.

But I got the feeling I was missing something. Like the thing I'd forgotten was so important it should have been impossible to forget.

A question that begged—*begged* . . . I paused. A question that *begged* asking.

It felt as if somehow I'd woken up to find an arm or a leg missing. Only it went deeper, like someone had carved into my chest and left a hollow spot where my heart should have been.

What question had frustrated me so much I needed sedation?

Rolling over on my mattress, my hand landed on my elbow and I looked at the pink-and-tan puncture marks there. Counted them. If I'd been dosed once a day . . .

I'd been sedated—blind to experience and blunted to emotion—for . . . one, two . . . three days. I rubbed at my eyes. What happened four days ago? What should I remember that I couldn't?

And as the world outside my room's thickly glassed window grew dark I heard it: the undulating call of an animal in the woods beyond the rolling, manicured lawns of Pecan Place.

Something inside me unfurled and fluttered, remembering and filling the empty space behind my ribs.

My heart pounded, restarting in recognition.

Pietr.

And everything came crashing back to me: the question I should have still wanted an answer to, the reason I'd let myself be locked away . . .

Pietr.

I rushed to the window to catch a glimpse of him and heard the camera, high on the wall and safe in its cage, turn to follow me.

Yes, everything came back to me then—but the last four days of my life. But I'd gladly bargain them away knowing Pietr was alive—and free.

An alarm sounded and the noise of dogs—hunting hounds—rose to me. A flash of movement blurred across the gathering gray of nightfall and I knew Pietr was on the run.

More importantly, I knew there was still hope.

Jessie

When the next day dawned I was aware enough to notice. I tugged the journal out and paused before jotting down my thoughts. I wanted to use it—I was desperate to write—but I didn't want my writing used against me later.

I wouldn't write about werewolves. Or the Mafia. Or the CIA.

I'd write about the farm. About my horse Rio and my dogs, Maggie and Hunter. I'd try some fiction: poems and short stories like I used to write before Pietr showed up and made all fiction pale against a few amazing facts.

Gone was my desire to write about vampires; now my head was full of Pietr, of wolves and darkness, danger, blue-eyed Russian boys and—

If I only wrote about Pietr in his human skin . . .

My door swung open and my guards stepped in.

I closed the journal and got ready to drag myself to breakfast. It was on the horrendously normal trek to the common room that I heard the request.

"I'm here to see Jess Gillmansen."

My head snapped up at the sound of his voice, every nerve in my body jangling in response to the richness of his faintly Russian purr. I froze. My pulse jumped, heart stuttering.

In unison, my guards turned, identifying Pietr.

A threat.

I grabbed at their arms, but they didn't notice.

The nurse flipped through some papers, unaware of the tension rising in the hall behind her. "I'm sorry. You aren't an approved visitor."

My throat tight, a sigh still slipped loose and Pietr's eyes, blue and stormy as a distant sea, rose and caught mine. My knees softened under his powerful gaze.

"Jess." He vaulted over the nurse's desk and had me in his arms before the giants could block his path. His lips on mine, arms tight around me, I realized what Pietr Rusakova was doing even as the guards bent to pull us apart.

Pietr was counting.

How long did we have before they grabbed him? I clutched his T-shirt's collar, slipping my hands around his neck to hold on as long as I could. . . . How soon before they threw him out?

Pietr would know soon enough.

I kissed him back. *Hard*.

His eyes snapped open for a moment, but I knew the clock was quickly running down on our little rendezvous.

But by counting the time between his arrival and the

guards' reactions he'd be better prepared next time. Prepared for whatever that beautiful brain of his was already plotting.

I had never appreciated simple numbers so much as when we counted the moments together with our kisses. . . .

The taste of Pietr's lips lingering on mine, he was heaved up by one giant's massive hand to dangle before me. His spiky hair obscuring his right eye, he winked for only me to see and it was then I noticed the still-healing cut on his face.

To not be healed more than a week after a fight . . . My heart clenched and I reached out to him, fingertips brushing his jaw.

For a moment everything was quiet, everyone still, the few wandering patients of Pecan Place frozen in speculation. The world faded away and there was only Pietr.

And me.

The guards moved as if thawing out after independent thought had stunned them. Pietr glanced at the tattoo exposed on the guard's wrist and then at his face.

Pietr's jaw tightened.

He knew something.

The nurse, hands on her hips, glared at Pietr as he did the finest display of passive resistance I'd seen short of school DVDs about the civil rights movement.

The guard lumbered toward the door with his more-than-human burden. He pushed one door open, inside the first set of reinforced glass doors, bracing it with a huge booted foot. He pulled back his arm and tossed Pietr unceremoniously out.

Anyone but a Rusakova would have landed badly. But the grace and strength of the wolf within—that wildest part of Pietr—was ever-present.

Especially when he stared down into my eyes and crushed his lips to mine.

The few patients in the hall near me went wild with whooping and cheering—for which side, I couldn't tell. And babbling.

Both the patient who obsessed over ceiling fans and light switches and the nurse who was taken totally by surprise.

"Gonna have to up everyone's meds this afternoon," she snapped, shuffling her papers back together.

"It's love! It's love! Crazy, crazy love!" a woman shouted as she danced in circles.

I tried not to agree with the already medicated population of Pecan Place, Junction's one and only mental institution. But, watching the woman dancing her loose-legged jig, I thought she just might be right.

Crazy, crazy love.

My guards took a single step toward the thin but rebellious crowd and everyone fell silent, eyes wide. Patients hugged the wall, slinking back to their rooms.

Terrified.

And the list of questions slowly developing in my mind doubled.

Jessie

When my door opened and the nurse appeared, standing beside a laundry cart, emotions battled just below my skin. Having seen Pietr made me itch for activity. The journal rested under my bed, page after page filled by my thoughts after having seen—and *kissed*—him. But there were strange things going on here. Maybe staying in the solitude of my room was the best bet.

"Laundry detail's really simple," the nurse encouraged me. She patted the stack of folded clothing. All the same lifeless shade of blue—the one color Pietr's eyes never became. "You'll deliver the laundry to our clients with your guards nearby, of course."

I touched a shirt on the top of the stack. "Color theory. It's supposed to keep us subdued, right?"

"Same reason the walls are painted eggshell or ecru," she said with a shrug.

Oddly like Junction High's decor. I rubbed at the goose bumps dotting my arms.

She pulled the cart to the first stop. "Sheets have all been changed, so don't worry about that. Clients on this wing are currently either in the common room or in private sessions. All you do is—" She pulled out a card that dangled from a lanyard around her neck and slid it through the lock.

A twist of the handle and a push and we stepped inside, the cart's wheels squeaking. The room looked exactly like mine. Sterile. Indistinct. Dull, dull, dull.

"Here." She withdrew another lanyard and electronic key from her pocket and hung it around my neck. "Don't get any ideas," she warned. "It only works on interior client doors."

"Ideas? Me? Not at all. Absolutely no ideas."

She sighed. "Just look at the list and take two sets of pants, two shirts, and a single pair of socks and lay them on the bed. The doors lock automatically, so you'll have to slide your key to open it."

"What if I wedge the cart in the door?"

"An alarm triggers. Extra paperwork for all."

"So let the door close. Got it."

"Your guards have a master key in case there's a problem."

"Are there usually problems doing laundry? I mean, other than mixing reds and whites, which"—I tapped the stack again—"obviously isn't an issue here."

"No problems to date," she remarked, "but it seems you have a knack for getting into trouble."

I couldn't disagree. At least not honestly.

"Don't take too long. Some clients get aggravated if they realize someone was in their room. So in and out."

I nodded, put a checkmark on the list, and took the cart. It wasn't a difficult job and it reminded me of my service learning assignment at Golden Oaks Adult Day Care and Retirement

Home, a place I'd met many great older people dealing with issues my mother never had the chance to face and fight. My fingers tightened on the cart and I pushed out a breath, refocusing.

Except for the checkmarks that differentiated patients by number—not name—everything mercifully began to blur.

It was as I was setting clothes on yet another nondescript bed that I heard movement behind me—

—too late.

The bathroom door opened the rest of the way and the occupant of room 26, the odd import named Harmony, stared at me, narrowing her eyes. "You will *not* take me back."

I dropped my gaze—totally nonconfrontational. "I'm not—"

"Liar!" Enraged, she lunged at me, snarling. With a savage kick she knocked my feet out from under me, taking me to the ground. My left knee burned so hot I cried out and my breath snared in the back of my throat, rattling.

Bent over to straddle me, her mouth frothed, and she drew an arm back, rolling her fingers into a fist.

I raised my hands in front of me. "Sorry, sorry," I said, trying to avoid direct eye contact, hoping submitting might work. But as my gaze flicked back to her raised and quaking hand I saw something in her change.

"Guards!" I shrieked. Reaching up, I grabbed her upper arms and rocked back onto my shoulders hard, throwing her off balance and over my head.

She hit the floor, but even as I screamed again for the guards and jumped to my feet, she scrambled to hers. She was fast and she was strong.

Crazy strong.

Spittle foamed at the corner of her mouth as she worked her jaw, an eerie red light rising in her eyes, and I stumbled backward, slamming against the door as she came at me. "Sorry," I whispered, narrowly avoiding her charge. "I thought you were out. Guards!"

There were plenty of times I wanted to be right. But recognizing the instinct that had stuck with me since first seeing Harmony in the hall—that identified her as a werewolf—recognizing it and realizing it was right was *not* what I wanted.

"You will not take meee . . . ," she roared, rushing me.

I swung my key through the lock but didn't quite connect with the magnetic strip—someone might have anticipated the problems that could arise by giving a girl who struggled with hotel swipe keys a similar system to get in and out of rooms housing the insane. . . .

She swung around at me and we circled each other until I was again with my back to the door. I thumped my knuckles against it, kicked it with my heel . . . slid the card again just as the door opened and she charged, grabbing the lanyard, bowling me over and into the hall, where she tried to strangle me.

"Help!" I shouted at the mountainous men who were supposed to be protecting me. I broke her grip on the lanyard and shrugged out of it to give her one less way to kill me.

Out of the corner of my eye I saw my guards turn to each other.

"Not time for a conference!" Our hands locked, we rolled, and I gained the advantage.

I heard a *pop*. Her eyes glowed. And her teeth lengthened.

"Oh, *crap!*"

My sentiment was echoed by the nurse.

"Separate them!"

My guards finally moved, peeling us apart as easily as a kid separated sections of string cheese. I grabbed the arm of the closest guard and wrapped it in front of me like a shield. Pressed as close as I was to Gigantor, my pulse thumped so loudly in my skull I couldn't even hear his huge heart beat.

Barely ten feet ahead of me, the woman twisted and howled in midair, gnashing sharp teeth and swinging her arms wildly, restrained by Thing One. Or was it Thing Two? *Crap.* There was so much to figure out.

Like: *Why is there a werewolf in Thing Whichever's grip?*

The nurse pulled out a syringe and jabbed the woman, depressing the plunger with one quick push.

The red faded from her eyes, the first pop echoed by a second sickly sound as joints refit into more human sockets and her teeth returned to normal. She hung suspended by my other guard's fist, strangely like Pietr had in his show of passive resistance.

Stomach twisting at the comparison, I heard the nurse say, "Take her back down to room seven. I'll treat her there."

My breathing only steadied when Thing Whatever disappeared down the hall and the nurse again turned her attention to me. I stepped away from the remaining guard, glaring at the nurse. "A: Did you *see* her? *That's* not normal."

"Of course not. She had a fit."

"A f—" My brain rioted.

I needed to think before opening my mouth and challenging her with the truth: A werewolf tried to kill me in a place I was supposedly sent to for the improvement of my mental health. *So* not good for the successful completion of my therapy.

Quaking, I tamped down my anger. "B: I thought the patients were out of their rooms."

"Sorry about that."

My jaw swung open, loose. *Sorry?*

"She must have been brought back early for problem behavior."

"No sh—" Think. "No *kidding.*"

"No one signed her back in," she justified herself.

I blinked at her.

"Heads will roll for this."

"Mine almost did."

"Sometimes a situation seems more dangerous in the heat of the moment than it really is." She set a hand on my shoulder. "Come on, let's get you back to your room."

I shook out of her grip. "Fine. Don't bother me until my father comes to visit."

"I can arrange that."

When my door closed behind me, I curled onto my bed, hugging my knees to my chest. She was a werewolf, wasn't she? Could I have imagined the way her eyes flashed . . . and her teeth and claws . . . Was there an oborot living only a wing away in Pecan Place?

Wrapping my arms more tightly around myself, I totally understood why some patients spent most of their time at Pecan Place seated, muttering and rocking.

Jessie

The tap on my window made me jump out of bed. Face masked in the gathering gloom, his eyes bright, Pietr stood outside my room.

Remembering the camera in the corner, I walked to the window. Slowly. As if my reason for going was nothing more than simple curiosity.

His eyes brightened at my approach and something in my stomach did somersaults in reply.

Face-to-face, he opened his mouth and breathed out a single syllable, fogging the glass between us. I didn't need to hear what he'd said. I read it in his eyes and across his lips.

Jess.

Closing my eyes, I tried to hold tight to the memory of how it sounded when he said it. There was a quality to even that simple syllable that couldn't be duplicated by anyone else.

My eyes opened, wet. With the back of a trembling hand I wiped at them and steadied myself. I couldn't touch him and he couldn't hold me. But he was here when he could have been so many other places.

His eyebrows lifted, eyes so much more than sad.

I shook my head, smiled bravely, and reached a hand out, stroking the glass like I'd trail my fingers across the strong line of his jaw. His eyes fluttered shut, and he leaned his cheek to the glass as if he could feel me through it. He pulled back suddenly, eyes flashing as the red that heralded the wolf inside rimmed his irises. He took a deep breath and fogged the entire window.

On it he wrote backward in awkward, tilting letters:

I'll get you out.

He cleared the words away with a sweep of his hand, nodding for approval. Grinning at the challenge.

I shook my head *no*. As much as the weird stuff going on inside Pecan Place had shaken me, I was okay. Besides, being on the inside might help me figure out what was going on. And Pietr, well, he needed to focus on other things. I'd be okay. As long as I was careful.

Things One and Two might not be the same guards who beat him *bloody*—him, a nearly indestructible werewolf—but they seemed their equals.

He mouthed my name again, drawing it out with an imploring look.

No. I shook my head. He had to know I wanted to be with him, but the idea of him facing off with Dr. Jones's gigantic guards . . . the idea of him getting hurt or . . . I swallowed hard.

Or worse.

My freedom at his expense was too high a price to accept. I shook my head once more, so hard I had to push the hair out of my eyes when I finished.

His eyes narrowed, but he nodded once, just a curt dip of his head. Not pleased, he'd still do what I said. He placed his hand on the glass, stretching his palm and fingers flat. I mirrored the move, imagining I could feel the ripple of his heat reach through the layers of cool glass.

The baying of hounds rolled across the darkening landscape, seeping through the window. Patrols had stepped up. I looked over my shoulder at the camera, then back at Pietr. "Go."

The noise of dogs grew louder and he glanced to his left before mouthing three final words and racing into the deepening dark.

I love you.

CHAPTER THREE

Alexi

I groaned, rolling over in my bed and covering my head with my pillow. It did no good. The pounding on my door only increased in volume.

"Alexi!" Pietr roared.

The clock on the nightstand read 6:15. Why did morning feel the insistent need to arrive so early every day?

"Alexi!"

"I don't know why you bother." *Max*. "He doesn't want to drive. And I don't want to go." His voice became a low rumble. "There're much more interesting things I could study here."

Amy giggled. "Some of us need to learn more than biology and chemistry," she scolded. Playfully.

I suddenly doubted it was last night's vodka souring my stomach this morning. What day was it, anyhow? I rolled onto my back and thought about it.

"Come on," Amy said. "I'll make everyone some breakfast."

Reluctant footsteps faded down the hall.

I groaned again, remembering. I'd been betting on American

football last night. Tonight I'd know if I'd won. That made today—Monday?

Again.

It seemed every week was determined to have a Monday in it. This, I feared, would be a six-cup Monday. I breathed deeply. Coffee was already on. Amy certainly had redeeming qualities.

I threw the pillow against the wall and sat, drumming my feet on the floor. The drumming echoed in my skull. I stopped, scratching my chest and rubbing my head, yawning the whole while.

Pulling open the nightstand's drawer, I withdrew Nadezhda's photograph. *"Dobray den*, beautiful," I said, skimming my thumb across the flawless surface of her face. As I rose in Junction, she continued a day started hours earlier in Moscow—time and distance only being two things standing between us.

Gently returning her photo to the drawer, I tried not to think about the other thing that kept us apart, but it scurried into view of my mind's eye, anyhow.

The oboroten.

Moyeh semyah. My family.

"Garr." I scrubbed my fists against my forehead. Nadezhda probably wanted me dead. One did not break a promise to the daughter of such a powerful man—even if it was a promise that went against his dictates. He doted on her and would gladly have me killed if she asked. I should wipe her from my mind, get her out of my head.

And yet the drawer could not close tightly enough to lock her image away from my heart.

Growling, I grabbed some clothing and headed to the bathroom for a quick shower and an opportunity to clear my head.

Minutes later I was downstairs in the dining room, poking at the food on my plate and working through my second cup of coffee, left black as my mood.

"My cooking's fine," Amy said, looking at me. "Don't you start acting like Pietr, just pushing food around the plate."

Across the table Pietr collected dishes for the kitchen. Amy was right. It was as we sometimes said: He had eaten so little *it was like underfeeding a worm.*

"Your cooking is fine. My stomach is simply unsettled."

"You're too young to be developing digestive issues," Amy complained. "What are you, Alexi? Twenty-two? Twenty-three?"

I held up two fingers. It seemed so young numerically, and I had no right to complain being surrounded by the internally aging oboroten.

"Let's go, old man," Pietr called from the foyer.

"Go where?" I retorted, turning my two raised fingers to him in a distinctly rude gesture.

Amy missed it.

Max smacked my hand down and laughed.

"Drive us. To school," Pietr demanded.

"Ask our brother, Max."

The tension in the room became palpable. Max's playful mood shifted hearing me use the term *brother* to relate to them. If we pretended to simply be roommates we were usually okay.

"*His* brother Max," he corrected, his voice low, "knows he hates my driving." Max shook out coats, holding them for both Amy and Cat.

"Pietr hates mine, too." I flooded my mouth with coffee. The taste coating my tongue remained a foul reminder I was out of bed and didn't want to be. I fought to swallow. "The fact you haven't pursued getting a permit and preparing for your license is hardly my fault."

Pietr opened his mouth to protest.

I stuck a hand up. "*Nyet*, you are correct," I admitted, thinking back to the obstacles I had placed in front of my sometimes erratic little brother, a little brother who had gotten himself nearly killed testing his dramatic healing abilities again and again.

And paying more attention to girls than driving even his ATV.

Pietr's brows lowered to shadow his eyes.

"It *is* my fault." I barely kept the pride from my voice. Keeping Pietr from controlling an even bigger vehicle than the ATV that nearly tore his head off during a recent jump didn't seem like a bad idea most days.

Just inconvenient most mornings.

He'd never drive illegally—Jessie would not look at him the same way since her mother had died in an accident with a car whose driver wasn't legal. The fact Jessie had done so much to remake and forgive the girl—twisted, but somehow admirable.

"Take the bus. It seems capable of taking you to your destination. And the driver—relatively competent, *da?*"

"Come on, Pietr. The bus isn't so bad," Amy tried.

Pietr's eyes darkened.

"It's a status thing, isn't it?" Amy jabbed him in the ribs. "You don't want to be seen as a bus rider."

"I don't see why we have to go in the first place," Max complained.

Dear. God. They could be so utterly annoying. "You do know why attending school is important. None of us should be left looking a fool, *da?*"

Max's lips pressed together, drawing a grim line. He knew. It wasn't for the sake of education anymore, though I wanted that for my family—I knew enough history to know education equated with freedom—but it was to maintain the appearance of normalcy. And it seemed odd things frequently occurred at Junction High, so being there was like placing our family's hand on the pulse of the town.

I rallied a sense of what once allowed me to dominate the family—*rule the roost*, as Amy sometimes quipped—and said, amazingly firmly: "Ride the bus or have Max drive. I do not care. But I will not waste my time dragging your ass back and forth to school."

Pietr's eyes flared and Max's hand settled on his shoulder, acknowledging the challenge to the family's alpha.

I raised my mug in a salute and looked flat at Amy.

Pietr read my warning clearly.

Amy knew we were odd. She realized there were things vastly different about us. Most she probably equated to our Russian heritage and travels in Europe. But she didn't want to know how different we were. And if Pietr changed just to show me who was boss in the Rusakova household, it'd ruin every tenuous thing holding Max and Amy together.

As much as Pietr and Max argued, Pietr would never ruin Max's chance at a real relationship. He understood just how precious they were now.

We all did—especially in the absence of one in particular.

There was a noise outside.

"Crap. That's the bus. Come on." Amy grabbed Max by the hand and pushed past Cat and Pietr, swinging the door open.

The chill of autumn woke me further and damped down the heat burning in Pietr's eyes. With a frown, he turned and followed the others from the house.

Alexi

I was headed to the kitchen with my empty plate and coffee mug when someone knocked on the door. "It's open." I no longer bothered to lock the door since the CIA and Russian Mafia knew where we lived. If they wanted us badly enough a single deadbolt surely would not keep them out.

Luckily the one thing all sides seemed to want even more than our capture was the illusion of normalcy. Breaking down our door and dragging out a bunch of good-looking teens (and myself) would certainly draw attention to what was going on in and around Junction and Farthington.

So we had an uneasy peace.

Or a stalemate.

Either was more nerve-wracking than a full-out onslaught.

It was like having a quiet neighbor digging up his backyard. You wanted to believe it was in the name of gardening, but you never understood the depth of your unease until people started going missing.

Wanda found me in the kitchen. "Morning, sunshine."

I grunted, looking her up and down. Even Wanda, with her brutally pulled back blond ponytail and all-business-like attitude, was beginning to appear almost feminine.

I needed to get out more.

"Is it wise for you to be seen here?"

"I took some precautions."

"Hmm." Refilling my coffee mug, I asked, "So how goes it for a guard of the order?" The steaming black stuff couldn't be made strong enough to help me tolerate a morning visit from her.

"Ever get the feeling you're being lied to?"

My sipping grew cautious. "I dealt with lies frequently when I was alpha."

"But were *you* ever lied to?"

"Must I explain the nature of teenage siblings—or, better yet, the black market, to a member of the CIA?" I sat.

She moved to the counter and helped herself to a mug and coffee, emptying the pot.

Cruel woman.

"I get the feeling things aren't what they seem at my job."

"Do you refer to the cover job you hold as a research librarian or your actual job?"

"Actual."

"And you thought the CIA would be honest with its employees—an organization that deals regularly with liars of all nationalities?"

"You wonder why your phone is tapped."

"*Nyet.* I do not."

"What if the CIA branch I work for . . ." She paused, staring into her coffee cup. "What if . . ."

"The very best fiction starts with a simple 'what if.'"

"What if it's not the CIA at all, but something else entirely?"

I set down my mug. "That would be a fascinating bit of—"

"Don't say fiction," she warned, her tone dangerously flat. "I'm starting to think it's fact."

"Why?" I slugged back a swallow of coffee, needing the acrid heat to sharpen my senses. "And why tell *me* this?"

"I don't know who else to tell. I need to work it all out. Puzzle the pieces together. Hearing it out loud might help."

"Is there not a mirror in your flat? Say it there." I licked my lips. Mentally I measured the angle of her eyebrows, the dimension of her eyes, the set of her mouth, the width of her nostrils, trying to find the truth in the mathematics of expression. Either she believed what she was saying or she was an actor of the finest caliber. "So tell me. How is the CIA not like the CIA?"

"When I was transferred out here, it wasn't a promotion."

"But Junction's such a thriving metropolis," I scoffed.

She ignored me and plowed forward. "There had been problems with my boss. . . . We had been . . ."

". . . in a situation that made you appear to be a woman of loose morals? Of easy virtue?" I interjected. I was beginning to enjoy my morning after all.

"His wife objected to the intimacy of our relationship."

I blinked. Wanda seemed the stoic type. The never-break-a-law-or-moral-code type.

"So I *can* make you shut up." She was not proud of the realization. "He transferred me out here. I figured I'd be digging through bogus Cold War paperwork at the warehouse forever."

I raised my hand. "Why do we have a warehouse of important government-type files in this region?"

"Cheaper real estate. Our government makes cuts in strange areas. So I was excited to get out of there—even on a wild-goose chase—well, a wild-werewolf chase. Even if I—who never understood the Dewey decimal system—was sentenced to spend time as a research librarian. I took a pay cut, another transfer, but other agents were losing their jobs back at headquarters. I couldn't imagine *that*."

"You didn't ask questions."

"No. I even felt lucky." She looked up from the cup. "But with all this—me having to tell my superiors so often we couldn't bust down your door and drag your asses out—"

"Thank you for that. What may at first appear a ballsy, self-confident move often equates with shortsightedness and stupidity. And Cat seems to like the door attached and the upholstery not so bloodstained."

But she rambled on, "And with Kent gunning for Jessie at the pistol range—"

I opened my mouth to ask after Kent. His sudden disappearance had not slipped my mind completely.

But she ignored me. "And the way I'm being told I need to keep you away from Mother right now . . ."

"What? Why?" Kent, and the very real possibility the woman sitting across the table from me had left his body in a shallow grave, was not nearly as important.

"Things are ugly, Alexi."

"Is Mother—well?"

"She's still aging rapidly. I don't think they really know what to expect. How long she's got."

"You need to get us in there."

"I'm working on it."

"Actions speak louder than words."

She nodded. She knew. "So all that and the royally weird beat-down Pietr took when they crated Jessie away . . ."

"That was the doing of Pecan Place."

"What if they're fingers on the same hand? One organization manipulating different things?"

"For a CIA agent—"

"Maybe I'm not."

"You're quite a conspiracy theorist." I shrugged and tipped

my chair back. "Why does this matter to me? From my perspective, my family has a few specific goals and they appear to contradict yours. We want Mother out. We want Jessie out. We want our family healthy, whole, and sane. I want to be done with all of this."

"I want to be done with all this, too."

It sounded like a confession.

"Until I met Leon, I couldn't imagine life outside the CIA—or whatever organization it is I really work for."

"Tired of playing at being a cloak-and-dagger knight?"

"Tired of running the risk that lies are going to screw up something that could be really great."

"You're in love," I accused her, kicking my legs up to rest my feet on the table's edge. "I could ruin you with Leon."

"You won't. You know exactly what I'm dealing with. Lies."

I raised an eyebrow.

"There's been some chatter."

"Terrorist chatter?" I suddenly felt off balance.

"It's *all* terrorist chatter if it might screw up my country. Someone's looking for you. A woman, from what we've gathered."

I slid my feet back off the table and set the coffee mug down to make it less obvious my hand trembled. "Does this woman have a name?"

"Just a handle. The White Crow."

I blinked, my most frequent tell, and the reason I was no longer allowed to bet at poker. White Crow was certainly a name Nadezhda would choose for herself. Part of a flock, but set apart. Different in more than plumage.

"You know her."

My throat tightened until words only squeezed out in a whisper. "What intelligence do you have on her?"

"Very little, but the chatter's intensifying. She's planning a visit. She seems anxious to be reunited with you."

I glared at the table.

"So. Love and lies." She stood. "Maybe we could each do a favor for the other. I'm looking for answers. And the best folks at speculating and researching the supposedly dastardly dealings of the U.S. have traditionally been our old Cold War rivals. You get me info from your contacts and I'll keep you in the loop about the White Crow."

"*Nyet*. The only favor I want from you relates to my mother."

"From what intel's passing on to me, your mother—a *Mrs. Hazel Feldman*—is quite available for visits at the Golden Oaks Adult Day Care and Retirement Home. She'll gladly read your future with some weird sort of tarot cards, too." She smirked and, taking a sip of coffee, made a face. "Though it seems her memory about all things oborot is faulty." She looked at me for confirmation.

I kept my face free of expression. So the old woman was clever even if she'd been heartless, giving me—her only child— away as a baby to grow up living a life full of lies. I doubted she wondered why I'd never yet visited. I raised and lowered one shoulder.

"And her lockbox is empty."

Because she'd handed over the thirteenth journal to Pietr. "The only favor I want relates to *our* Mother. Tatiana Rusakova." The woman who gave us all her last name because Father's came with a more high-profile and dangerous history. And how many other Americans would know enough to ask about boys and a girl with Russian heritage and the same exact last name? It had been enough to keep our Russian hunters off our trail until I sought them out personally. "I want Mother healthy and *out*."

"You know that's beyond my control."

"Then get us in. Soon."

"That, I think I can do." She dumped the remaining coffee into the sink. Barely touched.

Such a cruel woman.

She strode from the room and I heard the door open and close. And open again.

"You really should lock your door," Wanda advised. "'What may at first appear a ballsy, self-confident move often equates with short-sightedness and stupidity,'" she quoted me.

Da, it definitely felt like Monday.

Alexi

"Why are you still here?" I asked when I spotted him curled on the love seat, alone. Cat had taken the evening to go to the mall with Amy and one of Jessie's stranger friends, Sophia—maintaining the illusion of normalcy, she claimed. As if it was quite the sacrifice. I, however, had noticed the advertisement for the season's hottest new sweaters and suspected she was window shopping—or more.

Max was running—hunting—like Pietr should have been.

Pietr shrugged.

"When was the last time you hunted?" I asked, realizing I could not recall. Was it the night before our raid on the CIA bunker, when we first tried to free Mother? That was . . . I ran the tally through my head—weeks ago.

Again, he shrugged.

"How are you keeping your calorie count up?"

"I'm fine."

"*Nyet*. If you don't hunt and—I've seen how little you eat . . . Your system's stressed already. When was the last time you turned?"

He looked straight at me, the alpha in his nature sparking for a moment. But his eyes were dull and narrow with disinter-est. "Do you realize that if I'd been . . . *normal*"—he tore the word away from the rest of the sentence—"there would be no reason for Jess to be locked away?"

"If you'd been *normal*"—I quoted with my fingers, the way I'd seen Amy and Jess do before—"Jess would have never connected with you in the first place."

"Wrong. Even when I didn't wear my chain she showed remarkable self-control."

"She said you acted like an arrogant prick that first day. Her not throwing herself at you wasn't a demonstration of remarkable self-control. It simply proves she exhibits an occasional bout of common sense."

His eyes narrowed further, becoming small blue marbles. "The point is: I acted normal around her. We bonded. If I'd just been able to do more than *act* normal—if I could have *been* normal . . ."

I wanted a cigarette. Wasn't *I*, as the family's Judas Iscariot, destined to be the king of self-loathing? Did he need to take that title from me, too? "You *are* normal, considering your genetic makeup."

He looked away.

"Pietr," I urged, "you need to accept who you are. Embrace it. Jessie would approve of nothing less."

He examined the design of the love seat's recently repaired upholstery. "I doubt that," he murmured. "She has this need to have me *cured* so I live longer. Would that be normal for me, Alexi—*given my genetic makeup?*" He whispered the words, but they still snapped out and stung. "Would it be a cure, or the destruction of my self?"

I hesitated.

"That's the problem. You can't have it both ways. I can't cure—*remove*—the very part of me that makes me unique, the part you want me to *embrace*. What would it mean, living longer but not as myself?" He shook his head. "It can't work that way."

My fingers twitched and my heart sped just enough that the call of the cigarettes grew louder in my ears. "Go. Hunt," I insisted. "War with me about this once you have a full belly and a clear mind." Turning, I stalked out of the house, leaving him.

I had to agree with his logic, though I'd never say so out

loud. He could not have it both ways, unless I could admit that the oboroten's abbreviated lifespan was truly a mistake.

And admitting yet another way my biological family had made a mistake—bringing more shame to my grandfather and myself? I wasn't sure I was selfless enough to do that.

CHAPTER FOUR

Jessie

"What about a chess set?" I asked the nurse in the common room when she delivered my daily meds and again drew my blood. I recognized the tranquilizers that had been added to my numbered cup.

Following my second day off sedation, Dr. Jones confessed a worry I was too anxious—already asking questions. Asking questions wasn't *my* job, it was hers, she said. So she prescribed meds to "take the edge off."

After being totally out of it one day and missing Pietr's regular nightly visit, I figured out how to cheek my pills. I wasn't slick at it, but I was competent. Besides, how did it help me deal with my myriad issues if I was too tired to think?

"No, Jessica," she said. "We've found issues associated with the societal differences between kings, queens, and pawns frustrate our patients. And knights and bishops raise subliminal concerns about violence and a lack of acceptance by religious authorities."

"Wow. So what can I do? Are there books? What about schoolwork?" I was bound to be falling further behind in all my classes.

"It's Thanksgiving break. Didn't you notice the cranberry gelatin and turkey gravy yesterday?"

"Not so much." *Crap.* Thanksgiving break already? Well, it wasn't like I had much to be thankful for at the moment, anyhow.

She tilted her head, speculating. "Are you journaling?"

"I journal all the time. But it's tough to find stuff to write when there's nothing to do. It's pretty dull: Woke up. Ate. Won bingo. Went to sleep." I didn't tell her about the other things I wrote.

About Pietr. My outrageously hot boyfriend.

She nodded. "Could your father bring a book you'd like? Nothing taxing. Not too stimulating."

Well, there went all my YA paranormal novels. And the few romances I'd squirreled away, that I'd *never* ask Dad to touch. "Maybe."

"I'll put a request in. Dr. Jones and parents respond well to things like that."

There was a commotion in the hallway just beyond the common room's open doors and the nurse grabbed her cart, heading toward the trouble. I rose and followed her at a distance, Thing One and Thing Two flanking me.

"Really, it's important you don't get too worked up. . . ."

Recognizing the voice, I tried to look around the nurse blocking my view. Was it really Ms. Harnek, my old middle-school counselor who'd come to my defense and taken over my case after I'd kicked two cheerleaders' butts?

I bent down, searching for her signature shoes. Yep. Bright red heels. I straightened again. I'd overheard a conversation between Harnek and Derek at school that cemented her connection to some company he was part of—something tied in with what we'd presumed was the CIA. Having her here—the nurse dodged around the cart to help and my view cleared—with Dr. Jones—connected them all.

On a stretcher between two EMTs a girl was strapped down.

"We appreciate you opening your doors to the hospital's overflow," one man said to Jones as they moved down the hall slowly. "I never would have thought we'd have so many kids rolling in with so many weird symptoms."

Jones shook her head. "Yes. Who would have ever imagined?" She shot a look at Harnek.

I dodged around the cart and followed, nearly keeping pace with them and not worried they'd notice me because of the way Harnek and Jones focused on each other across the stretcher.

Harnek's hand clutched the girl's as she writhed. "Really, sweetie, you need to relax. You're swelling up because you're freaking out."

The EMTs exchanged a glance.

The girl looked at them both, noting their confusion.

"Relax. Trust me. No," Harnek urged. "There's no reason to panic. . . ."

Her hand fell away from the girl's, no longer able to hold it as it swelled so large.

Jones stepped back from the stretcher. So did the nurse.

"What the—" The EMT struggled to disconnect the fluids bag he held above his head and stared at his partner.

"Relax," Harnek soothed the girl, patting her hand. "Count backward with me from twenty. Twenty, nineteen, eighteen . . ."

Her head swollen to an impossible size, the girl's bloated lips moved, but the sound was more of a hiss than a word and with a final fearful thrash came a noise like fabric ripping. Pieces of her flew free in a bloody spatter.

Harnek and the EMTs were slick with gore and blood.

I covered my mouth and shook back the trembling terror that rattled through me.

Leaning away at a more comfortable distance, Jones flicked something unrecognizable off her shoulder and withdrew a handkerchief from her pocket to dab at the blood freckling her face.

Harnek wiped at her eyes as the EMTs cursed and slipped backward in gore.

"We need decontamination!" one exclaimed, panic edging into his voice.

"No," Harnek insisted. "Breathe. The girl was clean—there's no contagion."

"Like the others—the symptoms don't transmit?"

"Exactly. Everything's self-contained." Harnek sighed, a shudder shaking through her as she slid her hands across her dripping face to clear it. "God, poor girl . . . What am I going to tell her parents?" Her body shook with a sob before she straightened and noted the distance Jones and the nurse had managed to keep between themselves and the exploding girl. "You *knew . . .*"

Jones's hands rose. "No. How could we possibly *know?*"

But Harnek's eyes grew small. Although I was no longer sure I could trust Harnek, I knew *she* didn't trust Jones, so I wouldn't, either. "Point us toward the showers." She dug keys out of her pocket and threw them at Jones. "Get my overnight bag out of my car. I was going to stay with her. . . ." she said, strangling on the sentence. "I guess I'll need my clothes, anyhow."

Jones flipped the keys to the nurse and pointed down the hall, away from me. Quietly I turned, heading back toward the common room. But not before I realized someone was watching me.

Looking up, I caught the eyes of a new addition to Pecan Place—a guy a few years older than me, with brown hair and hazel eyes. He smiled as I dodged past to reclaim my seat at the round white table. But there was no warmth in his smile, just a cool slide of lips and the mimicry of a friendly expression that got lost somewhere between his mouth and his eyes.

Silent and still except for the anxious drumming of my fingers on the tabletop, I sat with my back to the common room's doors, waiting until I thought it was safe to head back to my room. A glance over my shoulder proved the hall was clean, the stretcher and EMTs gone, the dead girl just a grim memory.

"Back to my room," I instructed the Things.

Nearly there I heard arguing as Jones and Harnek rounded the corner and stepped into view in the hall not far ahead of me. Hair still damp from her shower, Harnek startled when she spotted me.

"Jessie," she breathed. "That's right. You're here now." Her face fell.

"Not for long, I hope," I replied.

She nodded and faced Jones. "You do know how special this girl is, don't you?"

Jones's expression stiffened, her eyes narrowing. "I'm aware there are unique things that caused Jessica to be under my care."

Harnek nodded. "So you'll take very good care of her. I won't have to worry about her having trouble while she's here."

Jones licked her lips. "As long as she doesn't create any trouble, she won't get into any trouble."

Nodding again, Harnek placed her hand on my shoulder. "You hear that, Jessie? Do the right thing and you won't have any trouble."

Watching the two leave before I slipped into my room, I got the sinking feeling I'd just been warned.

But really. What were the odds I'd stumble into some sort of trouble? An unexpected sob bubbled out of me, and I collapsed on my bed, trying to forget the exploding girl and the strange new guy who watched me with such open interest.

Jessie

Sleep was hard to come by, and I woke exhausted and began my day doing everything by habit. It was as I loitered by the nurses' station, shadowed by the Things and waiting for the laundry checklist that the newspaper on the counter rustled. Goose bumps rose on my arms and I realized there was no draft to cause the movement. The smell of fresh hay washed over me and I shivered, thinking of Mom. I focused on the headlines:

VISITING WRESTLERS STILL MISSING

THANKSGIVING BREAK SIGNALS MORE TESTS FOR JUNCTION STUDENTS

But the one that made my heart jump was:

LOCAL FOOTBALL STAR DIES

My stomach did a little flop and for a moment both hope and fear fought in me, tightening my throat around my suddenly misplaced heart as I briefly hoped the headline was about Derek.

Guilt swamped me. To hope someone was dead . . . even after he'd done so much . . .

That wasn't who I wanted to be.

I adjusted my position to get a better view as the nurse rearranged pages on the laundry clipboard.

> Jack Jacobsen of Junction High School died tragically Saturday afternoon on the train tracks outside Farthington. Deemed another in the growing rash of Train Track Suicides, the local community is stunned.
>
> "Jack had so many things going for him," Mr. Richard Maloy, head guidance counselor for the high school, reported. "The football team has been really shaken up by these last two suicides," Maloy admitted. "We've brought in additional counselors like Dr. Sarissa Jones to help handle any questions the students may have."
>
> Junction Jackrabbits quarterback and team captain, Derek Jamieson refused to comment, though friends have mentioned their concern over his recent absences.

"It's obvious we're all very shaken up," Sarah Luxom,
the recently returned captain of the cheerleading squad,
said.

The clipboard slapped down on top of the newspaper. "Here,"
the nurse said. "New day, same concept. Now made even simpler
for your safety."

"You make it sound like I was to blame. I was *attacked*."

She wheeled the cart over to me. "You shouldn't waste your
time reading that stuff. The news can be disturbing."

"Ignorance may be bliss, but I'd rather be aware than blindly
blissful."

"Whatever. Go on, the laundry doesn't do itself."

Pushing the cart along, I let its wheels chatter, fighting me a
few minutes. Things One and Two paid no attention. I finally
relented, turned the cart correctly, and headed down the hall.

Laundry detail was blessedly uneventful, giving me plenty
of time to add to my ever-growing list of questions.

Jessie

Again under guard, I headed to the common room for visitation.

I was spotted by the strange guy a moment before I noticed
my father. Hazel eyes followed me as I entered the room.

"Dad," I said, careful not to shout. If something like chess or
laundry delivery could upset the regularly maintained balance
at Pecan Place, what would an exclamation of relief do?

Things One and Two led me to the table where Dad waited.

He eyed them warily. "Jessie," he said, wrapping me in his
arms and choking me with a bear hug. He glared up at my hulk-
ing guards and said, "Dr. Jones said I'd be allowed the privilege
of speaking to my daughter in private because Jessie has done
such a good job recently."

I waited until my guards backed away before I raised an eyebrow at my father in question. He pulled out chairs for us and winked.

"You've been good, but not that good."

"Yeah." I agreed, not bold enough to mention the sedation. Or the fight. How bad would Dad feel knowing he'd sentenced me to spend time in a place I got attacked delivering clothes?

"That boy of yours is drivin' himself crazy with guilt."

I stared at my hands resting loose on the table between us. Dad reached out for them. "I don't want him doing anything stupid."

"Love makes you do all sorts of stupid things, Jessie," Dad muttered. "He says he loves you. Makes no bones about it."

"Dad, you saw what they did to him when he tried to keep me from coming here." Leaning in, I whispered. "He's showing up here, outside my window every night."

Dad let out a low whistle. "I don't know what to make of him, Jessie," he admitted. "He's really worried about you. And . . ." He licked his lips and looked around the room.

"And what?"

His gaze settled on me again. "Nothin'. Nope," he assured me. "I'm really worried about you."

"Then get me out of here."

He glanced away. "I wish it was that simple. I've spoken to Dr. Jones. But the paperwork I signed . . . it's for one solid month of treatment. Here." He looked at me, his eyes dark. "I don't know how to get around that. Legally."

My fingers twitched under the warm weight of his hands. I doubted we had money for a lawyer to combat someone as savvy as Dr. Jones and I hated even bringing it up. "I wouldn't ask you to do anything that wasn't legal."

"Well, you're the only one," Dad said, pulling his hands away from mine to drum on the table with his fingers. "Pietr's already made some interesting suggestions. And Wanda? She's almost of the same frame of mind as that boy."

"Wanda and Pietr, agreeing?"

"Yep. He's a little weird . . . don't you think?"

I snorted. "How, Dad?"

"Well, he's been hanging around the house a bit. I figured it was a good idea, you know, so I could rub off on him a little. Talk to him about this issue with fightin' he has—"

Yeah, he gets into rumbles whenever somebody attacks his girl-friend.

". . . you know, give him some sort of strong moral influence since he's dropped that Sarah and is *crazy* for you."

I glared at him.

"Sorry. I guess I shouldn't say the 'c-word' here." He rubbed his forehead. "I don't want some guy who's constantly in trouble being around you. So he's helpin' out. A lot."

"And?"

"And . . ." He leaned forward until our noses nearly touched. "You should see him throw hay bales. Not like any other guy who's helped out on the farm. This boy can throw hay. And he's fast doin' chores," he marveled. "And." Dad glanced away.

"And?" I bit the inside of my cheek, remembering the other things Pietr excelled at when *we* were in the barn alone.

"And that's not nearly the oddest thing about him, Jessie."

Time to steer the conversation away from the absolute weirdness of my boyfriend. "He's really something, Dad. Has he taken Rio out for a ride?"

"Nope. That's weird, too," Dad muttered. "Rio's okay with him—shy at first, but he refuses to take her out. I offered to teach him a bit, get him up to snuff, but he said you'd teach him everything he needs to know."

"And he told you he loves me?"

"In no uncertain terms. I think—"

"Please don't tell me we're too young to feel that sort of way about each other."

Dad shook his head. "I don't think it'd matter if I tried. The boy lives and breathes everything about you. He's full of questions. All the time." He paused, scrunching his eyes up and searching my face. "He stops by—every night?"

"Yes."

"Should I be worried he's . . . a stalker?"

I'd only worry about Pietr stalking me if I was some small forest creature out late. "No, Dad. He's no stalker. He just . . ." I heaved in a long breath. "He just . . ."

"Loves you."

"I guess." Resting my head in my hands, I stared at the table.

"Jessie, if you don't love him—"

I dropped my head to the table.

"You should let him know."

"I *do* love him. That's why I wish he didn't love *me* so much."

Dad leaned back and studied his hands a moment. "Your mother always said we'd have problems understanding teenage girls. This was easier when she handled it."

"Pietr could get into huge trouble sneaking around here. They've got dogs. He could get hurt."

Dad started to open his mouth and then shut it again.

"Pietr needs to keep clear of here."

"I don't think there's anything I can say that'll keep that boy away from you. Even if it puts him in danger."

"Tell him I *want* him to stay away. Tell him it's . . ." My face heated. I wanted to tell Pietr in person, not pass my message through Dad.

"What?"

"Tell him—oh, crap. It's so cheesy."

Dad chuckled. "Love is cheesy sometimes. Give me the message."

"Tell him it's—it's not like he's not with me every moment of every day, because he is. He's in my heart. I don't have to *see* him." I closed my eyes and shook my head. "See? Cheesy."

Dad put his hand on my shoulder and gave me a gentle shake. "I'm sure he'll understand," he assured me in the same tone he used when he tried to bolster my spirits before a math exam. He was just as convincing about the odds of success.

I needed to believe it. "He'll be smart—stay away?"

He folded, snorting. "No guarantees. Love makes people crazy."

"Look around. I've got plenty of crazy. What I need is *smart*."

Jessie

But Pietr seemed more capable of delivering crazy. Maybe it was like his brother Max had said: Smart didn't come easy to a seventeen-year-old guy with a girlfriend.

That night he tapped on my window again. Hadn't Dad delivered my message? I raced over, ignoring the all-seeing eye of the camera. It meant nothing the way the wind howled. There would be only moments between Pietr's appearance, the scattering of his scent, and the warning call of the dogs as they barreled after their quarry, my guards on their heels.

Dammit.

I tore a sheet of paper from my journal and scrawled a note, which I pressed to the glass.

I love you, but run and DON'T come back!

Thank goodness for werewolf night vision. I tugged the paper away.

His mouth moved, carefully, as he enunciated each word.

"You *love* me?"

Oh, holy crap! Smart—I needed *smart*! I tore the paper away and scribbled.

YES! Don't be stupid—RUN!

I underlined *"DON'T come back!"* and flattened the paper out. He stood there, puzzling at it. I flipped it around, wondering how soon the dogs would be on him. My writing was barely legible. Trembling I circled the key words.

YES! and DON'T come back!

The dogs began their keening cry. When I finally pulled the paper back down I saw Pietr's reply—his handprint wanting mine—pushed into the fog left by his breath.

I rested my hand against the print and leaned my forehead on the glass until all sign of his visit had faded away.

CHAPTER FIVE

Alexi

True to her belief she could get us in to see Mother soon, Wanda arranged a meeting time for us and so we found ourselves retracing a path we were beginning to know well.

After promising to hand over the single baby tooth the family had kept, we were allowed entry to the bunker that looked, from all outward appearances, to be a Colonial farmhouse with a rapidly failing border of aromatic herbs.

In. Down. The numbers were the same: the same number of steps. The same number of doors, locks, and cameras, but still I counted them to better burn them into my memory, to make their existence second nature so that when we came to free Mother we would not trip over ourselves or tangle and fall in the dark, victims of our own feet and some misstep.

The only thing that seemed to change was the code they typed into the door at the bottom of the stairs. I'd caught it, memorized it, played it back in my mind, but each time we visited, it was new. If I could determine a pattern, then I could predict the next round of numbers. But it seemed some things were truly random. Perhaps sometimes there was no pattern—no way to anticipate an opponent's next move.

The concept frustrated me beyond all logic.

I understood that when we came to free her we would need a way past the interior doors, a way I could not yet provide.

We walked through a long fluorescent-lined cement hall of a buried tractor trailer and through the cubicle-filled office area that branched into the underground science lab and the broad room where Mother was kept in a clear-walled environment that offered no privacy and made the rarely occupied office cubicles look inviting.

Behind me—because they still insisted I go first, like some substandard bodyshield—Pietr's breathing wavered as the final door opened.

Our escorts continued forward, but we paused, noting a difference so subtle many would not have considered it.

They were down a guard.

"Mother?" Pietr asked the figure in the seamless glass cubicle.

She turned, saw him—saw *us*—and let out a little cry of relief, tears shining on her face. My heart hammered in my chest and I felt my brothers bristle beside me, saw how Catherine's spine straightened, all of us thinking the same thing at once. Something else had changed—something beyond one less guard. Something deeply disturbing.

Mother *never* cried.

We walked to the transparent door, limbs stiff with stress as we exchanged glances. Pietr and I entered first, the warning call of "Red-Red-Red" coming just as the nearly invisible door slid open.

Max and Cat watched the guards, though Max's wolf senses and all of Cat's sadly muted human ones were trained on us.

"Mother." Pietr reached a tentative hand out to stroke her hair.

She leaned into him, resting her head on his chest and the

look he gave me spoke more than words could as he tenderly lifted and dropped a long curl of her hair back to join the rest, sweeping down to obscure her face.

I nodded. I saw. The hair that had been so recently auburn and copper was shot full of silver. I slid my hand down her slim arm and subtly pinched for a pulse. Too fast.

Everything was moving way too fast.

My eyes locked with Pietr's and he suddenly realized what I knew—what I'd read was inevitable. When the end came, it came suddenly.

Mother may have been dying since she first started to change—to evolve into an oborot at age thirteen—but now she was sliding down the slope toward sudden death.

And no matter how powerful in life an oborot was—no matter how fierce in their wolf form—they were helpless as any human when death came hungering to their door.

We stayed there with her for the allotted time. I tried to absorb her every word, reminding myself this might be the last chance. . . . But every time I fought harder for focus, her words retreated further into a fog and I lost every thought except the one that made me angriest: We had to find a way to free her—there had to be a bargain that could be struck—and that I had no idea how to do it or what it would take.

Max and Cat switched places with us, and standing outside mother's unyielding environment, I glared at Pietr and wished Grandfather had somehow endowed the oboroten with telepathy so we could take advantage of one less guard and, even unarmed as we were, somehow break Mother out.

In a very few minutes the thought became an obsession of dizzying power.

So it was only logical, in an extremely illogical way, that when the door to the cubicle next hissed open to release Max and Cat and Mother was so near the opening—

I took a chance.

Grabbing Mother so suddenly, I yanked her free of the cubicle, stunned by how light she was in my grasp.

Max and Pietr only stared at me a moment—a single heartbeat between fascination and horror—before they pulled free of their clothes and shook into their wolfskins.

Cat tried to look threatening as we began to move to the door as a unit, the wolves snarling and snapping at the guards, lunging so they forced their guns' muzzles up as the agents tried to gain control without harming the assets they still needed intact—my werewolf siblings.

Mother stumbled, tucked against me, and I took her negligible weight, my back nearly at the exit when I felt a draft and realized the door had slid open before I was ready.

Safeties clicked off three guns behind me and their snouts bit into my head. I froze, steeling myself against the possibility that this was the last thing I'd ever do.

And probably by far the finest.

If I could throw my body at my killers and let go of Mother at the right moment, they might all still make it out. . . .

"Let go," I urged Mother, her fingers claws in my arms.

"*Nyet*," she replied, eyes flaring with red and filling with moisture as, searching my face, she discovered my intent. "*Nyet*, Alexi!" With a brutal shove she threw herself back from me, past her other sons, ruffling the crests of their furs as she landed at the feet of her guards.

And gave herself up.

The wolves whined, Catherine crying out at her choice. Their shapes shuddering, Max and Pietr regressed to their human forms, crouched, damp with sweat and stunned to the marrow.

"You will not die forrr me," she roared, the words growing guttural. "I am dead alrrready, do you not see?" Shaking out her long mane of hair she stood and tugged at the silver filling so much of it now. "My clock rrruns down too quickly."

Her voice a hoarse whisper, its intensity never lessened. "Hear me clearly. If they will not release me—if they intend me to die here, so be it. I will not have you sacrifice yourself for me. I will not have my family made into martyrs." She inhaled sharply and bent over, fighting for control.

"Heart-Rate-Is-Elevated," the computerized monitor called.

Mother growled her response.

A pop sounded and her hands twitched, shifting as they rested on her slender legs just above her knees. Hair shot up from one in a dramatic display of the wolf's growing power.

Mother shook, pushing back the change.

When she straightened to address us again, her eyes were bright with unshed tears. Taking a deep breath she said, "I will not watch my children die as my husband did."

Turning her back to us, she led her guards to her cell and waited obediently for the door to open and let her in once more. A guard picked up Pietr and Max's shed clothing and threw it at my brothers, grinning at our failure.

Behind me, the agents withdrew their guns and stepped aside to let us out.

"This was both unexpected and disappointing." *Wanda.*

The agents flanked us, fingers by their trigger guards.

"You know what this means, of course," she stated crisply, but in her eyes I read something soft, like pity. "Mother's now under restricted access. You'll have to earn your way back into our good graces—and into her environment. And"—she measured the weight of her words, trying to lighten the impact with her tone. But no change in volume or pitch could stop the inevitable pain of hearing—"that will take time."

Dazed, we were led away from the bunker's bottom section, where Mother lived and might very well die, and up the stairs.

Still stunned, I would not have noticed him if it were not for Pietr's sudden lunge toward a dimly lit room.

"Whoaaa—easy, fella," an agent said, pressing the end of his gun into Pietr's gut and pushing him back into our midst.

Blind with rage at whomever lurked in the shadows, Pietr roared and Max grabbed him, wrapping his arms tight around Pietr's chest to haul him away as the agent and the person he guarded joined us in the narrow hall.

I'd never met the boy, but I knew him immediately from the descriptions Cat, Max, and Pietr had shared.

He stood nearly the same height as Pietr, but where Pietr had dark, unruly hair that often hid one eye, Derek's hair was golden blond pushed back from classic American features. A square and powerful jaw framed Pietr's crisp cheekbones, where Derek's jaw was mildly blunted and somehow less threatening. Where Pietr had an edge and wildness to him, Derek had refinement and polish. An artist could have compared the two and viewers would have still argued who was more handsome.

But after what had happened between Derek, Pietr, and Jessie there could be no doubt of who was more dangerous. And it only made his boy-next-door charms more ironic.

"Youuu," Pietr seethed, pulling against Max so he was inches from Derek's smiling face. And less from the gun barrel of Derek's smiling guard.

"Hello, Pietr. How's Jess?" His eyes unfocused and he looked somewhere beyond us. "Yep. Still hot." He blinked, his vision returning to where we all stood. He grinned at Pietr.

Pietr went wild and Max's arms were suddenly filled with a snarling, snapping werewolf clawing toward his antagonist. To Pietr's credit, his sudden loss of control made Derek jump back. The smile fell off his face and from the dim room behind him someone reached forward and took his arm.

"Don't be stupid," a dark-haired woman with fine features advised Derek. Slender and well dressed, she didn't carry herself like an agent. Catching a glimpse of her tailored outfit and high heels I doubted she was a normal feature in the bunker. "Come away now. We have a session."

Tight-lipped, he spared us one more look, then raised his chin arrogantly and followed her back into the dim room.

Snapping and thrashing in his wolfskin, Pietr struggled in Max's grip, his brilliant red eyes never leaving his ex-rival. I doubted he'd even seen the woman ghost in and away.

With a grunt, Max dragged himself and his more than human burden toward the door.

My mind racing, I ushered Cat out ahead of me, scooping up the remnants of Pietr's jeans with my shoe.

Household expenses would again be on the rise, it seemed.

By the time we'd gotten out the front door, Pietr had changed back and slipped into his shredded pants, holding them together at his waist with a clenched fist. He didn't say a word, just sat in the car, staring grimly ahead.

Max dug into the glove compartment and handed him a belt to twist through his tattered waistband.

We drove home in silence, each of us surely thinking of how we'd alone been responsible for our joint failure.

Pietr was brooding.

I was allowed no such luxury. Now was a time for action, not sorrowful introspection. If only I knew what action to take. . . .

Pietr was the first out of the car, throwing his door open with so much force its hinges groaned and Max shouted. We shadowed him up the stairs, onto the porch, and inside the house.

There, hidden from the potential curiosity of nosy neighbors, Pietr let loose.

He tore through the house, filled with a white-hot anger, kicking door jambs, punching walls, and cursing. *Bilingually.* Cat followed, a banshee wailing for him to stop—to *think* . . . I reached for my cigarettes and trailed them like a ghost.

What could I say or do? My grandfather's science was what had brought us all to the realization that Mother was dying. And we couldn't free her—couldn't save her.

When Pietr cleared the small, marble-topped table at the sitting room's edge, sending the pieces of the family's *matryoshka* flying, Max took him to the ground.

Pietr snarled and spat, cursing beneath Max's greater bulk. Quaking with rage he was as helpless as any of us—and as helpless as Jessie had been the day her mother burned to death in their family car.

When he turned his glowing eyes away from mine I realized he knew that, too.

I knelt beside Pietr.

"How long, Alexi?"

The breath thickened in my throat, wedged beneath a lump.

"How long does she have?"

"Pietrrr . . . ," Cat whined.

Max raised his chin and sucked his lips between his teeth, pinning them. His nostrils flared and he looked away.

"I don't know," I admitted. "Months?"

Pietr's eyes squeezed shut. "Not even years," he said, his tone clipped and brutal. He nodded. "Months."

"Maybe less."

He nodded again, taking it like a blow to the gut he'd somehow anticipated. "We're not enough to get her out."

Max grunted and, rocking forward, stood. His hand out to help Pietr up, he said nothing. His macho posturing was gone, deflated by fact. He did not bull his way through the conversation. Shoulders slumping, he pulled Pietr to his feet.

"What if there are more like us?" Max asked suddenly.

"What? More Russian-Americans in Junction?" Amy asked, rubbing her workout towel around her damp ponytail, fresh from a run. "Shi—oot. What happened here?" she asked, her eyes shooting from the wreckage of the room to each of our faces—masked against emotion as they were.

"*Da*," Max whispered, dragging the syllable out, turning so his eyes latched onto mine. "*Da*. Russian-Americans in Junction. *Near* Junction." He gathered Amy to him, linking his arms around her and sighing as he buried his face in her hair.

"Dude!" she protested, wriggling out of his grip. "I'm soaking wet, like gross beyond belief."

He shook his head, sighing. "*Nyet.* Come here."

Some force between them, like an undeniable gravity, pulled her back into his arms, and they both relaxed.

I returned to the question. "In Junction? We would know."

"Yeah," Amy agreed. "You guys are hardly subtle. You'd be easy to spot."

Pietr nodded. "*Da.* She is right."

"*Near* Junction . . ." I tried to imagine another pack close enough to make a difference. "How near is near?"

Max's eyes narrowed and he snorted. "Good question."

Amy again wormed free and started helping Cat pick things up. "Seriously," she whispered. "What happened?"

Cat just shook her head.

Amy paused a moment, watching Cat's body language—a victim trying to recognize another victim and not coming away with an easy answer. Straightening, she looked at Max as he and Pietr spoke Russian in low tones.

For a heartbeat it seemed everything was open to interpretation and Amy wasn't sure if she'd been overlooking a danger just like the one she'd so recently escaped.

She exhaled, finally determining the danger she had known was still worse than what was before her and unknown. Max needed to tell her the truth soon or risk losing her forever because there was no other way to truly understand my family.

"Perhaps we should try to find them?" Max again turned to Pietr and me for input.

"Too many of us in one place makes things difficult."

Max glared at me over my use of *us*, but kept quiet.

"There ain't room enough in this here town for a new bunch of Ruski"—Amy blinked—"Russian-Americans," she said, lightening the mood.

Max snorted.

Though she had no idea just how right she was, Amy's words gave us pause. Oboroten were territorial. We were a small family—a small *pack*—at best. Inviting another pack in was asking for trouble. Trouble we had plenty of. We needed allies.

And trustworthy allies for a group so often hunted and so eagerly wanted under control were hard to come by.

CHAPTER SIX

Jessie

"It's good to see you, Jessica," Dr. Jones said.

I refused to pay her a similar compliment.

She flipped back a few pages in the set of papers curled around the clipboard's top. "Fred and Jeremy reported that you've had an unapproved visitor several times."

"Fred and—?"

"Jeremy. Your guards."

"Thing One and Thing Two? Wait. They've"—I air-quoted—"*reported* to you. Huh. I was seriously starting to doubt they were capable of speech."

Her pen scratched out something else. "The boy who insists on visiting you is putting himself in danger."

"I know. I told him to stay away."

She peered at me a moment. "You *told* him . . ."

"Wrote an insistent note," I clarified. "I want Pietr safe way more than I want Pietr *here*."

"That's what I thought. So it's Pietr Rusakova."

I blinked at her.

"He's the only Pietr in your records. He tried to drop this off for you." She held up a book.

The classically inspired cover was titled: *Bisclavret*.

"Have you read it?"

"No," I said. "It's his."

"I took the liberty of screening it for you."

My jaw was so tight I thought my teeth would pop.

"It doesn't end well—did you know? The hero, this disillusioned warrior and werewolf, destroys the woman he loved."

"That's a pretty crappy romance."

"Do you think young Mr. Rusakova is trying to send you a message? Perhaps threatening you?"

The prospect of catching Pietr threatening me seemed like it was as good as finding out Christmas was coming early.

"No," I insisted. "He's no threat to me."

"The other day Fred and Jeremy mentioned that he vaulted over a desk and grabbed you moments before they got the two of you apart. Was he hurting you?"

"No!" I glared at her. "He was kissing me."

"In a violent way?"

"No—in a firm and French way, if you must know. If you take a peek at your history I'm sure you'll agree the French have developed an unfortunate reputation for not being much as fighters. So. Not violent. Just a French kiss. No threat unless we consider potential germ warfare," I grumbled. "May I have the book? Please."

"No. I'm afraid not. It might incite mood swings in you."

"So it's a pretty good book."

"You've already gotten into trouble here, Jessica. You've been on restriction and you were caught fighting."

"I was *attacked*."

"We don't know who started it—"

"There's a camera in every room. Check the tape."

"Unfortunately it went off-line right after you walked in with the laundry. I've examined the tapes myself."

"Come on," I groaned. "I was attacked. I defended myself."

"I see." Pages on her clipboard uncurled to lie flat on the other papers. "I'm trying to help."

"If you really want to help me, give me the book, let me have more visitors, and remove the camera from my room. It'll do me a world a good to not be wondering if Thing One"—I caught myself—"*Fred* and *Jeremy* are watching me undress each night."

She looked at me, weighing my resolve. "We'll talk soon."

I stood. "Can't wait."

Jessie

Laundry detail gave me a mobility other patients didn't have. I'd done the same routine just often enough that one morning, when the regular nurse was absent and Fred and Jeremy were not at their standard place guarding my door, I decided not to ask questions but instead take advantage of the situation.

In school we'd been told to be proactive.

"Jessica Gillmansen, reporting for laundry duty."

"Oh. Um. Yes. Hold on." The substitute nurse fumbled with the papers and finally found the clipboard. She glanced at the clock. "You know, laundry's not up yet—a few of the staff called in sick today. . . . Everything's running behind schedule. Hold on." She unlocked a drawer and produced a swipe key and lanyard. "Here you go."

"Thanks."

She believed I knew my way. Not ready to correct her, I smiled, took the lanyard, and headed to the elevator.

Not up yet, she'd said. I needed to go down.

I swiped the key, stepped inside the metal box that for some reason smelled faintly of urine—I always wound up in the nicest places—and pressed the button for the next floor down: BASEMENT. The doors groaned closed. "Breathe, Jess," I said. "But not too deep. Geez. Just going to get the laundry. Maybe poke around. A little. Not a big deal."

The elevator rocked, stopping in the basement.

"See? Not dead yet. No big deal." The doors wheezed open and I stepped out into a brightly lit hallway. "Well, this is . . . clean." Goose bumps rose on my arms.

Above me, long banks of fluorescents hummed.

Doors lined the long hall; some had labels, many did not. There was no sign pointing the way for a laundry room—no sound of machines whirring as blue clothing tumbled in industrial driers, no scent of fabric softener or water other than the dampness that pervaded the building's lowest level.

It appeared the poking around I had hoped to do would be necessary just to find the laundry cart. It'd seem legitimate because, sadly, it was. I wouldn't get labeled as rebellious, proactive, clever, or stealthy as a result of this.

Maybe *domestic.*

Not high on my list of goals.

Slowly I made my way down the hall, glancing in each of the thin windows set in each metal door.

The sound that stopped my progress made my goose bumps reappear and the hair at the nape of my neck tickle.

Someone screamed.

Instinct shouted at me to race to the elevator and head back up as fast as the rickety thing could carry me.

But I crept forward, toward the noise. If I'd been Sarah Luxom, ex–best friend and reestablished mean girl and Queen Bee of Junction High, my word of the day would've been: *counterintuitive.*

Dogs growled and the screamer, a woman by the pitch, let out another cry. The screech became a howl. Without words it was only a primal announcement of pain.

What if she just needed help? What if she . . . my mind

stuttered through possible scenarios and mercifully paused on the least gruesome . . . was pinned under a pile of freshly folded blue shirts and was terrified of wrecking the stack by wiggling out without help?

Refolding laundry *was* awful.

It was plausible, I justified, remembering my boyfriend.

The werewolf.

Anything was possible. Like this—not ending badly. My stomach quivered, and I continued forward.

One door away, I heard voices rise above the screaming.

"Sedate her!"

Dr. Jones?

"Damn it! Must I do everything myself?! Give me the syringe!"

"Doctor, she's—"

There was another howl of terror, a *rrrip* and *pop* and several somethings—small and metal?—clattered to the floor.

"Damn it!"

The dogs went wild.

"—she's *free*," the other woman stated.

The doorknob rattled and the howler burst into the hallway, the placid blue of our uniforms hanging loosely from a fur-covered body that shivered somewhere between wolf and woman. Tubes hung, dripping, from her arms. She looked down the hall, chest heaving and, turning, she spotted me.

She convulsed, one paw re-forming into a hand, one side of her face sinking into human features as the other half stayed long and narrow and furred, stretching her skin and testing her bones until she shrieked at her transformation.

Falling to the floor she shuddered, her backbone whipping her torso and head so hard I heard a *crack*. She whined and, mostly human, clambered to her feet.

Hair a wild tangle, and her eyes as red as Pietr's had ever been, I recognized her instantly. Harmony—my attacker on the first day I did laundry detail.

So not good.

She staggered one step forward. One ear still pointed, one hand still curled and sharp with claws, Harmony flared her nostrils, sucking down my scent.

Still inside the room she'd torn out of, dogs whined, clawing and pushing at the door, eager to run.

"Pull them back so we can open it—" Jones shouted.

Collars and chains rattled.

I turned to the door at my back and tried the knob. Locked. Dodging across the hall I tried another.

"Push them out of the way!"

Dammit.

"Get *between* them—"

Harmony watched as I charged up the hall to the next set of doors. I twisted another knob. Locked. But as I slid across the floor to move on, I heard a *click* behind me. My heart hammered and the scent of summer drifted past. "Mom." I tried the knob again and it squealed open. Jumping inside, I shoved the door shut, pinning it closed with my body as I slid down, the clipboard clattering to the floor.

Outside, the door down the hall opened. Claws clicked on the hall's floor as the dogs scrabbled after their quarry.

Climbing to my feet I stood snug to the door to peer out the narrow window.

She was on the ground, eyes closed, belly up. Throat exposed, she was still except for the flash of a pulse in her throat and the rise and fall of her chest as she fought panic.

Submitting.

"Wait for it," Jones commanded. "We should know in just another minute . . ."

"You really think there's a cure—you've found it?" This close the other voice sounded distinctly like my regular nurse.

"Yes. The girl Rusakova—*Cat.* I'd stake my reputation she's been cured. Why else wouldn't you fight as an oborot when trying to free your mother? And if we have the cure, we know what things we can't let them near. The other office may be working on *making* them—"

BINGO. They *were* part of the same company.

"But if we can assure they can't be *unmade* once the deed's done . . ."

I trembled, the tiny spots on my arm where they drew daily blood samples bit into me with cold. They were using me to undo werewolves so they could discover how to work beyond a cure. The changes they intended would be permanent.

The dogs stood, hair spiking along their shoulders and backs. Mouths open and tongues trembling, their snouts were ridged with wrinkles. Their teeth glinted, slick with saliva. They were huge—big brutes. And there were—one, two . . .

. . . *seven* I could see, more than I'd imagined prowling the grounds.

Hunting people like Pietr.

Harmony screamed again, thrashing, her body racked with tremors, hair sprouting in thick and sudden patches. She clawed at herself, frantic, eyes wide. Her face distorted, pulling into a snout and she shouted, words garbled as her vocal cords changed and her body stuttered, choosing one shape or another.

Tight to the dogs' broad chain collars thick leashes were attached. They rattled in anticipation.

With a final cry she kicked out, her foot cracking against a dog's jaw.

There was no more barking. No snapping. Only a growing, rumbling growl.

Harmony grew still, only the occasional flutter of her chest showing she lived, her form stuck between the two warring sides of her twisted genetics.

Just beyond the scope of my vision, Dr. Jones cursed. "This isn't working. I'm not exactly sure where we went wrong, but this subject is a total loss."

"She's strong—she popped the straps and sent those buckles flying. Maybe it just doesn't work on half-bloods."

"Perhaps. Or perhaps we're missing a component. She's worthless either way. She submitted," Jones pointed out. "More flight than fight. And that? *That* doesn't look like a cure—stuck between. Disgusting. We'll need another subject. I'd love to get my hands on a full-blood. The Rusakova alpha. Now *he* would be a prize specimen."

"What do we do with *her*?"

"Look away."

Fingers snapped. "Fred. Jeremy."

My eyes went wide as I caught a glimpse of a wickedly scarred arm repaired with awkward-looking stitches. Its hand moved to detach the leashes.

The wrist turned and I spotted the odd tattoo.

My guards?

"We've made a dog's breakfast out of this," Jones said, more a command than a comment.

There was no more growling.

But the screaming made up for it as the dogs attacked.

I barely kept from jumping back, gasping in horror. She'd submitted! Given up!

For a moment the writhing bodies of the dogs parted. Harmony struggled to rise, slipping in her own blood, her hand reaching for my door's knob . . .

And then they pounced and tore her to pieces.

I slid down the wall, covering my head with my arms.

The frenzy of noise rose in volume for the space of a few heartbeats and then the sounds changed.

Gnawing.

The lapping up of liquid . . . *blood.*

I was going to be sick.

The quiet sounds of the aftermath of murder were deafening.

"See?" Dr. Jones asked. "Just a little additional cleanup."

The nurse gagged.

"Stop that," Jones scolded. "We must be pragmatic about all

this. We are on the verge of changing—*recharging*—the abilities of evolution itself."

Eyes wide, I clutched my discarded clipboard, crushing it to my chest.

The nurse reasoned, "If we include werewolfism in humanity's new evolution, don't we, the previous generations, slip down the food chain?"

"Oh. See? You've already recovered your sense of humor."

"I wasn't . . ." The nurse fell silent.

"If only dealing with that Gillmansen girl was this simple. But she's off the menu."

"She's his pet," the nurse reminded.

"It seems she's the pet of a few. You wouldn't expect it, looking at her, would you?"

I blinked.

"But Derek does get a charge out of strange things."

The nurse chuckled—almost on cue. "*Charge*. He calls her his favorite battery."

"He's made such a mess of things," Jones muttered. "But to realize his potential—it's as amazing as finally finding these werewolves." There was a pause. "Fred. Jeremy. Get a mop and a bucket."

Heavy footsteps clumped away.

"Your stitching's clumsy," Jones confided.

Stitching? Like, the stitches I'd seen on the arm?

"Jeremy's new bit will work just fine. We're not stitching for cosmetic improvement."

"Touchy, touchy. As long as they wear long sleeves and long pants it isn't really noticeable, I guess. They run through replacement parts quickly."

Replacement *parts?*

"Must be bad circulation. Their systems gum up easily."

"These are still functioning a lot better than the first."

My head snapped up. By first pair did she mean—my original guards?

"Jessica's still too self-absorbed to notice much of anything outside herself, anyhow," the nurse pointed out.

Crap. Murder and multiple insults.

"At least there's no shortage of parts."

"Quality would be better than quantity. And frankly he needs to be trained to feed on the living. And let them *keep* living," Jones clarified. "Good, Fred and Jeremy. Mop that up. I mean, injecting some misery into people's lives to get something back—it's nothing more than our own government does every April fifteenth. But the way he finishes . . ." Her words trailed off.

"Everyone's following the Teen Train Track Suicides story. It makes us a little more high-profile than I like." Jones paused. "But it's worth it. The werewolves . . . no. Jeremy. Get a fresh bucket. We're not trying to *paint* the floor, but clean it." There was a *clunk* and a *slosh*. "We're close to replicating the code that makes them so changeable. But Jamieson is a stranger cocktail of capabilities. He makes his parents look like nothing."

Derek's parents?

"That goes down on my list of things I never thought I'd hear," the nurse admitted. *"The high school football star's more amazing than Soviet-created werewolves."*

"His services are invaluable. If we can just get him to only feed from *her* . . . or better yet, some other battery altogether. Then if she's troublesome we can eliminate her. Everything's set for that possibility."

"What about that Sarah being his battery?"

"She's too stable. Too happy being nasty. But Gillmansen? She's a roller coaster of emotions."

Niiice. I was officially less stable than my psycho ex-BFF.

"Nice job, boys. We should spray the hall so it doesn't smell. Now where did we—"

I forced myself into a crouch. They were going to search for disinfectant spray. I needed to hide. The room was nearly empty except for an industrial-sized refrigerator that took up most of it. Great choice, Jess. Hide in the one room with no closets.

"I'll check here—"

I sprinted to the fridge, staying low, and pulled the massive door open to slide inside. I snatched the papers off my clipboard and stuffed them between the two lock sections so the door appeared closed but didn't seal me in.

Taking a step deeper inside, I decided to wait them out. Not registering closed, the light remained on. The fridge puffed out a fresh round of cold air, fogging my surroundings.

The chill caught up to me, and I rubbed my arms and moved my feet. Maybe if I walked in a tight circle . . .

I paused at the first set of shelves.

A black bag—a *long* black bag—stretched most of its length. I knew of no produce needing a bag that size.

Cold as I was, my heart pounded faster as the doctor's and nurse's words came back to me: *replacement parts.*

No shortage.

My hands trembled. It was official. I was living a nightmare. Still, I reached out—needing to know . . .

Fingers quivering with cold and dread, the bag—so much like the leaf bags lining Junction's suburban lawns this time of year—rattled under my touch, noisy and stiff as it opened.

I stepped back and fought my rebelling stomach.

In the thick, black plastic bag, in the huge refrigerator, lay the train-bludgeoned remains of Jack Jacobsen.

Frozen on his bruised and waxy face was a smile. Like he'd just won Homecoming, not like he was ready to embrace an iron horse on a short ride to death.

I swallowed hard. Okay. Jack's body was in cold storage in the local asylum. "Get a hold of yourself, Jess."

I could do this. I could figure out what was going on and help . . . somehow. I made myself step forward and reclose the bag over Jack's euphoric face.

Derek was feeding. On his friends. He'd definitely gotten a charge out of me and made me believe things I shouldn't have with just a simple touch. . . . What if . . . ?

The thought disconnected and spun, loose, in my head.

I'd forgiven a lot of people's mistakes recently. And some I'd *tried* to forgive. . . . Maybe in Jack's last moments he believed he *had* won Homecoming.

At what point did we become unforgivable?

I wanted to tug at my hair, urge my sluggish brain to go faster, but I couldn't stand the thought of touching myself with the same hands that had just opened that bag.

I paced.

We had a group trying to cure the werewolves and one trying to replicate them. We had my guards—slow to function and needing replacement parts of the human variety. How much could you get out of a body that had been partially pulped by a train?

"Oh."

Quality would be better than quantity.

My gaze skimmed the other shelves. Filled with black bags. Different sizes, with different volumes of—contents.

Parts.

I looked at the door. How soon could I leave? How long had I already been here, stunned? Taking in a deep breath, I realized I had no answers. Except the most disturbing ones.

Slumping, I slid down into a seated position and rested my head on my knees. I couldn't leave yet. But I wanted nothing more than to get away.

Away from the refrigerator from Hell, the bloodstained basement hall and zombie Fred and Jeremy.

Away from all of Pecan Place.

Maybe from Junction itself.

Curled in on myself, I stayed there until my breath no longer steamed as brightly from my mouth and my body threatened to shake apart with cold. Finally I rose and went to the door, opening it slowly—partly because my joints were stiff and partly to retrieve the papers I'd used to stop the lock.

I grabbed the clipboard and shouldered the door open, slipping out and crawling to the room's door, beneath the view of the single window. The papers on the clipboard rustled and I clamped them down with my fingers.

Peeking out the window I noticed the hall was scrubbed clean—absent of doctors, nurses, dogs, zombies, body parts, and blood. No noise echoed in the clean white space, nothing to alarm me and keep me in the room.

Carefully I opened the door and stepped into the hall. The overpowering scent of disinfectant spray hung in the air.

It was as if there had been no experiment performed on a patient. No murder—no bodies in the basement. Like everything was normal and scented with lavender.

It seemed healthy.

And that's how I had to appear, too.

Healthy. Normal. Unrattled.

Straightening my back, I squared my shoulders and set off down the hall in search of the laundry cart.

And there it was. Like a beacon of hope and normalcy, stacked high with pants and shirts.

"You can do this." I grabbed the cart and headed to the elevator. I swiped the key and thrust the cart inside. "Normal. You wanted normal, right?" I was babbling. But I was willing to excuse myself this time. Extenuating circumstances. "What's that philosophy? Act like you already have something and the universe will provide it for you? Yeah. Go normal."

Deciding whistling a cheerful tune would be pushing it—especially since I was nearly tone deaf—I waited for the elevator to open and shoved the cart into the hall with a grunt.

I set the clipboard on top of the stack, hurried to the first room, and laid the change of clothes on the patient's bed.

In.

Out.

I could almost forget what I'd just witnessed. . . . Besides, I was *untouchable*, they'd said.

As long as I didn't screw up.

I reached for the clipboard to put down my customary check mark showing successful delivery.

The page was missing.

Out of order?

I flipped through the stack.

The page I needed wasn't there.

My gaze skated over the cart.

No.

Not there, either.

I glanced toward the elevator, stomach churning. I could—

"Miss Gillmansen!"

The substitute nurse had spotted me.

I waved. "Sorry. Moving slowly this morning."

"Just hurry up."

"Yes, ma'am," I said. Fear sped my steps.

Finishing quickly I tucked the swipe key and lanyard in my bra. Maybe I could sneak down and retrieve the missing paper. . . .

I handed over the clipboard and cart and shuffled away—right into Fred. Or Jeremy. "Oh. Hey." I glanced over broad shoulders at the clock hanging on the wall. "Lunchtime, isn't it?" Looking down I noticed dark red speckling their shoes. I tried to swallow the rock in my throat. "I'm not—really—hungry. Home," I said, wanting it more than ever. They, of course, led me to my room.

"Miss Gillmansen," the substitute nurse called. "I think you forgot something. . . ." She hurried toward me.

I gave her a blank look.

"The key."

"Oh. Ohhh. Sorry." Damn it. I snaked a hand down my shirt and pulled out the lanyard. "Must've—gotten caught in—"

"Your ample bosom?" the sub asked, scoffing.

Crap. People were just mean here. *Mean*. And murderous. Priorities, Jess. Priorities. Murderous was worse than mean. "Boobs," I confided. "They get us all in so much trouble."

She snorted and took the key—and my hope at recovering the paper—away.

I spent the rest of my day seated on my bed, doing what so many patients did.

Rocking and muttering to myself I realized the person I wanted closest was the one in the most danger from Jones's desired experiments and the nightly patrols of killer dogs.

I wouldn't risk Pietr's safety any longer.

Jessie

He was at the window, tapping for my attention. One heartbeat before the dogs caught his scent, a moment beyond the rush of the guards.

They might catch him. Hurt him worse than the day he failed to keep his promise, or hold him long enough to restrain him, cage him . . . tie him down and shoot him up like Harmony. . . .

Beat the wildness from his eyes . . .

I'd love to get my hands on a full-blood, Jones had said. *The Rusakova alpha. Now he would be a prize specimen.*

They'd make him think even his brief life was far too long.

I kept my back to the window. There was nothing Pietr could do for me right now and at least seven ways I risked him by encouraging his presence. It was better this way—me on the inside, caged, him with a hope of freedom.

Even if it meant freedom without me.

The noise of the dogs rang out, turning on the night's breeze, my stomach twisting in echo.

Pietr slammed his fist on the glass; even his power, his anger, resulted in only a dull thud.

Like my heart made in my chest.

I stared at my useless hands, my fingers knotting.

Another insistent thud.

Why didn't he run?

Please. Please . . . run . . . , I begged, squeezing my eyes tight against the sound of the approaching dogs.

Down the hall from my room a door slammed. I wanted to shriek, "They're coming!" But I didn't react in case it gave him one more heartbeat's worth of hesitation. . . .

I needed Pietr safe. And that meant far from here. From me. I hardened my heart against the glowing eyes cutting into my back.

And when I heard the approaching dogs turn and race off, following their retreating prey, I fell to the floor and cried my heart out at my betrayal.

Jessie

"Jessie," Dad greeted me.

Fred—or Jeremy—stood, followed by his mute companion. They lumbered away from the table, giving Dad and me some privacy. We hugged, me holding on a little bit longer this time and definitely a little tighter.

Dad finally broke away, his face full of worry.

He slipped something into my hand.

A cell phone.

It buzzed, vibrating.

"Sit down," Dad instructed. "Act normal. Alexi sent it. Looks like a piece of junk, but he said it's exactly what's needed in these circumstances."

Realizing any phone Alexi provided was probably untraceable, I obeyed.

"It's Pietr," he explained. "He's upset about last night."

Thank God he was okay. Upset, I could deal with. Hurt. Dead? I fought for focus.

Dad pulled out chairs and I slipped my hands under the table, slouching for a view of the phone, and opened it. "I'm going to give you an update on my favorite sports teams and you just nod and react, okay?"

I nodded. "Sounds absolutely . . . purgatorial." I typed in my message.

RU safe?
Da. I <3 you.
I <3 U 2. Don't come here again. *Promise*.

No response. I tried again.

Promise u won't come here again.
I try 2 keep promises. Failed b4. Don't make me promise 2 stay away. = 1 more failure.

My stomach knotted. Even though they were tiny letters on a poorly lit screen, they meant huge things to him.

U did ur best. U always do ur best 4 me.

Nothing.

Do ur best 4 u. Stay safe.
She's dying.

His last sentence was so simple and clear it seemed he'd whispered it in my ear, stealing my breath away.

Dad raised his voice, extolling the virtues of some football team's kicker.

Have u seen her?
Da. Last x went badly.
Srry . . .

God! Why couldn't I help him with this thing? Why was I so—*helpless?*

Can u get 2 her?
Nyet. Heavy guards. Derek's inside. Watching.

"Damn it," I snapped. Out loud.

"Now, Jessie," Dad reprimanded in his jolly way, "just 'cause they didn't win that game doesn't mean we should get upset."

U have 2 get her out.
No good unless ur out 2.

Even texting, Pietr had a gift for pointing out the obvious. They'd need my blood to make the cure.

Focus on ur mother. I focus on me. Do what u have 2 to get her out.

Nothing.

Do what u have 2. It will work.
Has 2.

I imagined the set of his jaw, the way his eyes would pinch near the bridge of his nose realizing there were no other options and so little time.

Time was running out so fast. For almost all of them. The distinct advantages of being an oborot were balanced cruelly with a huge disadvantage. They were stronger, faster, more nimble. They could hear, scent, and see better than someone like me—simply human. But the canine aspect of their DNA meant strength, agility, and superior senses as much as it meant shorter life spans.

By human standards, Pietr's mom appeared to be middle-aged. But internally, her liver would be hardening, her heart racing even faster than its normally rapid rhythm, her arteries toughening. She'd be fighting an even harder battle to keep the wolf that always longed to claw its way out of her deep inside. If she hadn't been dangerous before, she'd be a gun with a hair-trigger now.

Pietr and his siblings—well, not Cat, she'd sucked down the cure like it was nothing—might live even shorter lives because they were the offspring of two full-blooded oboroten. No one really knew what would happen as the generations progressed and the genetics compounded. Both powerful and poisoned by their own DNA, the oboroten were victims of their genetic code.

I love you, I concluded.
I want to hear it.
U will. Soon.
g2g

I snapped the cell shut and nudged it against Dad's leg, obscuring the sight of the phone with my hand.

He shook his head. "Well, I just wanted to update you on the sports world. I know how you *love* that sort of stuff."

"Thanks, Dad. I really appreciate it."

"I better get back to the farm," he said, rising.

"Uh, yeah. Geez, is it hot in here?" I asked, tugging at my neckline just enough to pop the cell into my shirt, resting it in my bra.

Ha. An *ample bosom* wouldn't have left room for such a clunky phone. Score one for the averagely endowed.

"Yeah," Dad said. "It is a little toasty," he agreed, swabbing at his forehead as if it were dotted with perspiration. He hugged me. "I've got us a lawyer. He's going to push that I was under duress when I signed those papers. He says if court goes quickly, he'll have you out in a little more than a week."

My heart leaped, trying to lodge in my throat. "How much will that cost?" I asked, but he squeezed me tight.

"Freedom always comes at a cost, but no price is too high. God, Jessie, I'm sorry I put you in here."

"You did what you thought was best," I admitted begrudgingly.

"I had the very best of intentions," he agreed. "I'll get you out soon. It'll all work out." He pulled back from me, blinking rapidly as he looked into my own damp eyes.

I nodded sharply. "It has to."

Jessie

Back in my room, I hugged my journal and thought things through. Dad would work from a legal angle to get me out, Pietr would work on getting his mother out, and I would try to be the best little patient I could and hope nobody knew where'd I'd been or, more importantly, what I'd seen.

It was official: We had something that passed for a plan.

But what Pietr had mentioned about Derek's involvement, the way he was tucked safely away and watching things from a distance, worried me. I'd known Derek since I was in middle school and had crushed on him starting around then, too. He was Junction's golden boy: fast on the football field, smart, smolderingly hot with all-American good looks. Very popular.

But I'd known all that before the Rusakovas moved in.

I'd lived in a comfortable bubble before the werewolves moved in and Pietr showed me what he really was the night of his seventeenth birthday. I accepted things I could see and prove—although I researched things that defied explanation.

I expected to find werewolves in high school just as much as I'd expected to meet the love of my life there.

So meeting Pietr blew my mind doubly.

But the world got even stranger.

If the company had Derek in their underground bunker, he could watch the werewolves coming. He'd done it using my eyes and we'd dug poisoned bullets out of Max and Pietr as a result.

Derek's abilities made him a huge threat. He'd manipulated more than me with just a touch, implanting and fuzzing memories. And he juiced up when people got emotional—making me a prime target of his attentions since the death of my mother. He could even transfer energy from one person to another in a pinch so he was hard to take in a fight. But what the company wanted him most for was his remote viewing—his ability to see what was going on some place he wasn't near.

He had the abilities spies dreamed of and a hunger that made him doubly dangerous.

The physical connection Derek made with me when we dated amped up his viewing power. Having me as a direct and—my stomach twisted, remembering, *touchable*—link to Pietr had been like giving Derek super-creepy 20 / 20.

I needed to get out of here, and Pietr's mother needed to get out of *there*. Eliminating Derek might be a necessity.

CHAPTER SEVEN

Alexi

We were gathering for breakfast when Pietr leaned over the table to speak to me. He glanced back toward the hallway, making it clear he knew Amy was nowhere near enough to overhear.

"We cannot wait any longer. We need help to free her."

I resisted the urge to reach up and choke him for thinking I was waiting. That because things appeared normal, no progress was being made. "I am examining options."

"Not good enough," he said. "We need help. Now."

"And where would you suggest we get help, little brother?" Max scraped his chair back from the table.

Pietr ignored him. "There's only one group that has the firepower we need."

Our eyes met and I read his intentions clearly. Desperate times. Desperate measures. "*Nyet.* Absolutely not."

"What?" Cat had leaned in over my shoulder. "Pietr—who?"

"Think, Cat," Max said, which I found amazingly ironic.

Her eyes widened, reading the stern expressions we all

wore. *"Nyet*, Pietr. The Mafia?" She shook her head, disbelieving. "Why would *they* help us? They want—"

"They want something we have," he said with deceptive simplicity.

"Pietr—no. You cannot," Cat replied.

"This discussion is over. We'll find some other way." Max stood.

"Sit down," Pietr commanded.

Max sat, grumbling. He glanced toward the hallway, watching for Amy as well.

"Be reasonable," Cat urged. "They'll want more than you—more than any of us—can give."

"When did we determine a limit to what we're willing to sacrifice to free Mother?" He stood and picked up his chair just to slam it back down. "Didn't you see her? Were you not in the same room with me?" He swung around, facing each of us separately for a moment, his face filled with turmoil.

"So you would do what," Cat whispered to her twin, "bargain away your freedom to earn their help and set Mother free?"

"Da," he said.

A simple word, it was laced with all Pietr's conviction.

"They can't be trusted," Max reminded him.

I stood, stepping back from the table—my appetite for breakfast gone before any food was offered. Tired of the posturing, I had trouble believing what I was about to say. "Max is right. This conversation is over. We will find another way."

Alexi

Approaching my room, dread stabbed me in the gut. I'd closed my door, but a narrow band of light shone from around it. Inside, someone rustled through my belongings. I held my breath, careful not to give warning of my presence. My training served me well as I crept with my back to the wall and rested my shoulder against the doorjamb.

This was a part of being a displaced alpha that I hated—no longer having rights in my own home. "What are you doing?"

Pietr jumped, caught.

I fought back the smile tugging at my lips. I had surprised an alpha. Funny how that perked my failing ego.

He closed my bureau's drawer.

"If you needed to borrow socks . . ."

But we both knew what had brought him here. It was not my sense of decor, nor my reading material, though a selection of my magazines was scattered boldly across the bed.

Catherine would have thrown a fit had she seen them, preaching to me about the exploitation of women, not believing that I, of course, read such magazines for the articles. The beautiful women inside merely broke the text in an appealing fashion. Pietr read less Russian than I did, so he surely suspected the magazines had another use.

My eyes rested on the mess he'd made. I cleared my throat. "Or if you needed to borrow something else . . ."

He followed my gaze and, seeing the magazines, blushed.

I snorted. *Virgin* was more than a powerful British company.

"I need information, Alexi."

I could not resist, having him on the ropes. I leaned forward and held a magazine out to him. "I thought they taught the birds and the bees in school."

His eyebrows lowered. I bit the inside of my cheeks to keep from laughing at how uncomfortable a simple magazine made him: the Rusakova alpha.

Around a catch in his voice, he said, "I need a name."

I threw the magazine down, ruffling pages. *"Nyet."*

"Who else can we turn to?" he asked, tilting his head to examine me in his canine way. "What other option do we have?"

"We will find another option." I jabbed a finger at the door and pulled up every ounce of alpha I had in me. "I will not let my brother indebt himself to the mob."

His nostrils flared and he raised his chin in defiance, but he left my room, slamming the door behind him.

"*Allo*, ladies," I whispered, gathering the magazines up carefully and replacing them in the box underneath my bed: a box again starting to accumulate dust. As I closed them away once more in their cardboard tomb I realized, as beautiful as they were, they paled to nothing but aging paper beside Nadezhda.

Alexi

While I hurriedly researched options and contemplated the ulcer probably festering in my gut, Max had taken some initiative.

"Come on, beautiful," Max coaxed from the door that opened into the Queen Anne foyer.

I looked up from the newspaper in a mix of curiosity and disgust. Watching Amy and Max together was a reminder I had the full legal right to get blind-drunk on cheap vodka and crawl into a dark corner in my own home. Full legal right and frequent motivation, the way they went at it.

I snapped the newspaper up to block my view of their flirting. And kissing. And inevitable pawing.

"CIA RECORDS SHOW EXPENDITURES DOWN—PUBLIC APPROVAL UP"

Expenditures down? How was that possible if they'd expanded operations with things like the bunker they'd built in Junction? Maybe Wanda was right.

What if . . .

"I don't know why we had to go so far out of Junction just for me to run," Amy complained. "I like the trail that goes out by the college."

"Your ex knows that course. He used to run it, *da?*"

"Daaa. Yesss," she hissed. "But that doesn't mean he still does." Her jacket rustled as she hung it up. "I want to be able to run in my hometown."

"I want you to be able to run safely."

"Jesus, Max! You're making this into such a big deal. Yes. I dated Marvin. Yes. He hit me—"

Max hunched his shoulders, glowering at the thought.

"But I *know* that. I was there!" Her foot stomped against the rug. Not loud enough, she took a step and stomped it again on the bare hardwood.

I shook the paper again, a reminder I was still present. Even trying to read.

They ignored me, pressing on.

"I don't know what you expect, but you need to stop dragging me farther and farther from town just to get my running in." A telltale creak warned the basement door was opening. "And," her voice lowered. "I have no frikkin' clue why you felt the need to pee every couple hundred yards—"

I bit my lip, realizing why Max was dragging Amy out so far from our normal perimeter.

"But maybe you need to—*uhm*—get that checked. There may be something—*wrong*."

I choked.

The door closed and she retreated down the stairs, alone.

Folding the newspaper, I glanced at Max. "When are you going to tell her the truth?"

He crossed his arms over his chest and widened his stance.

"You are going to tell her the truth. *Da?*"

He collapsed into a chair across the table from me. "I can't find a trace of any others," he confessed. "We've followed the main road out of Junction. I even took her to our old hunting grounds. There's no scent. No sign."

I forced myself to keep looking in his eyes. "We knew it was a very good possibility there'd be no more of us."

His eyes narrowed.

"Of *you*," I corrected. "With all the news coverage of the Phantom Wolves of Farthington I would have thought if others *wanted* to find you . . . maybe none want to find you because that equates to *them* being found."

"We need backup. We can't do this alone."

"You think I don't know this?"

"What other options do we have?"

My brow wrinkled. "None I want to consider." I had been thinking a lot about options, wild possibilities, and dramatic failures resulting in multiple deaths. The one option I still toyed with in the darkest hours of early morning was the one I was least willing to utilize. Numerically it was plausible. But to win with the numbers meant losing something irreplaceable.

Mother would never agree if she knew.

"No connections spring to mind. . . ."

He was testing me.

"What would you have me say? Who would you see me sacrifice?" My thumb smudged the newsprint. "I am no longer worthy—you understand? They don't want *me*." I raised my eyes to his again, heart hammering as we locked gazes. "And you, *dear brother*, are not known to be the self-sacrificing type."

The silence between us hung thick as the mist that cloaked Junction's hills each late autumn morning.

Max looked away.

I took a breath, not realizing I'd been holding it. "You understand. There is no answer to give."

His brow lowered, giving his features a brutal edge.

"She thinks something's wrong with you."

"And you did me a great service by not agreeing."

"What are brothers for?"

He snorted.

"We are brothers, Max."

He stood. "You can change your"—he wrinkled his nose—

"your cologne. Now that we all know, the imitation of our natural scent only annoys me."

"I like the scent. It reminds me of our parents."

"None of it's yours to like." He turned and left, stomping up the stairs as angrily as Amy had stomped down the others.

It was as our people said: *It takes two boots to make a pair.* And they were quite a match.

CHAPTER EIGHT

Jessie

Pietr didn't visit that night. As glad as I was that he was safe, I missed seeing him. So as soon as I could stretch and yawn enough to seem convincing, I curled up with my back to the camera and, shimmying the cell phone out from under my pillow, turned it on.

With no charger, I felt a glimmer of what Pietr must have felt regularly. Time was short. I had to make each moment count.

Pietr, I texted. I <3 u. Miss u. Don't come here. But know I'll dream of u.

I turned off the cell and flipped it shut, slipping it back beneath my pillow and curling into a ball, ordering sleep to give me dreams of Pietr.

Jessie

The forest was dark, cold, strangling in the grasp of an unseasonably cold autumn unwilling to commit to winter's snowy and muffling blanket. I stumbled forward, heading for the few creaking swings that spun off the old park's swingset's belly, twisting and squealing in the wind.

I grabbed a swing and sat; the seat creaked beneath me. I waited. My heart pounded in my chest, recognizing the fact but unable to define what I waited for in words that could drift to my brain, carried by my pulsing blood.

Something skimmed the shadows, something dark and grim and beautiful, ghosting along and teasing the dappled moonlight as it stayed just beyond reach—just beyond the brush of starlight's subtle fingers.

"Pietr," I breathed, something deeper than physical recognition pushing his name from my lips as it pushed my heart into my thickening throat.

And then he was before me, lean and lovely, cloaked in night's skittering shadow. At once too beautiful and wild for moonlight to dare touch him and yet so proud and powerful, how could even cool moonlight resist? Before me, his image stuttered; one moment wolf, the next moment not—his spirit equally both and none at the same time.

I stood, releasing the swing's chains, my hands numb from where my fingers had pressed the links so deep they'd engraved my palms.

Behind me the swings screamed, metal grating and howling as chains twisted in the same breeze that tugged my hair out around my face, teasing my vision with Pietr's image and then nothing. I wrenched the hair back from my eyes, hunting and hungry for another glimpse of him.

He filled my vision and I gasped at his nearness, heat washing across me, radiating off his smooth skin. The frigid sting of fall was forgotten, winter but a weakly whispered rumor as Pietr wrapped me in his arms and crushed his hungry lips to mine.

Jessie

The morning shuffle to breakfast was agonizing. My head throbbed and my mind raced. I cheeked my pills, got jabbed for blood, and my stomach rebelled when faced with what passed for food. I pushed it around my tray, building strange shapes with it.

"So. Jeremy. Fred," I addressed the silent hulks. "Fred. Jeremy." I switched the faces the names corresponded with. Not so much as a blink of reaction. Did names matter to zombies? They were like—undead, right?

Maybe living impaired? Life-abled? There was bound to be a politically correct, self-affirming term for every brand of strange thing prowling Junction.

The fact I wondered made me even more certain I needed to get out of Pecan Place. Fast.

But who else was there to talk to—uh—talk *at*?

"Are you happy? I mean, seriously happy? When you look at your life—erm—your *existence*—do you say—yep. This is where I want to be right now? Because, honestly, this"—I waved the bastardization of a spoon and a fork around to symbolize encompassing the entire facility—"was not a stop I'd scheduled on the agenda of my life."

"You neither, huh?" A tray clinked down on the table.

Fred and Jeremy bristled a moment, then relaxed. The same guy I'd seen watching me stood just across the table from me. "May I?" he asked, motioning to the seat.

"Yeah. Whatever. I'm almost done."

"That's too bad," he said. "I was hoping to talk." He looked around the room, eyes pausing on the gradually increasing number of people who sat, either tranq-ed up or restrained, aides spooning almost the same amount of food in that spilled out of their slack-jawed mouths. "You seem most likely to be capable of holding up your end of a conversation."

I blinked at him.

"I'm Christian."

"Congratulations. I'm Undecided."

He chuckled. "My *name's* Christian."

"Ah. I wondered why you were announcing yourself according to religious affiliation but here"—I glanced around the room meaningfully—"you never know exactly *what* people think's most important."

His smile widened into a grin. He appeared nearly sane.

Appeared. Appearances weren't everything . . . and I still got that vibe that something just wasn't quite right with him.

Go figure. It was like I was in an asylum or something. So should I adjust my standards based on location? I paused, listening to the warning buzzing in the back of my head.

"I'd say nice to meet you," I concluded, "but I'd prefer to reserve judgment on that until the statement seems justifiable. Jessica."

"Charming," he said with obvious sarcasm. "But very logical considering location and circumstances. I'll bridge the gap and give you the benefit of the doubt. It's nice to meet you, Jessica. I'll even go so far as saying I hope to see you later today."

"That's only because I don't drool on myself. Normally."

He shrugged. "We all adjust our standards here."

I narrowed my eyes at him. No. Not me. Adjusting my standards felt like letting my guard down.

"Let's go, boys," I said to Fred and Jeremy and we headed down the hall so I could start laundry detail.

Jessie

Back in Dr. Jones's first-floor office—I had to presume she had something similar in the basement, too—I was bored with the same line of questions every session. More than some therapeutic retreat, Pecan Place felt like a holding tank of some sort.

"How are you doing today, Jessica?"

I stuck with our plan, behaving and waiting on Dad's

lawyer. "Pretty well. I've been trying to think things out better. To have more faith that what people are trying to do is in my best interest."

Dr. Jones nodded.

"I've been journaling. Since there's nothing to read," I hinted, thinking about the fact she still had the book Pietr had intended for me, *Bisclavret*.

She scribbled down a note.

"You've been quite prolific with your writing." She pulled something out of her drawer. "Jeremy and Fred brought this from your room."

My journal. "Okay," I said slowly. "Did you read it?"

"Of course." She paused, looking up from my journal to stare straight into my eyes. "You don't like me."

I paused. "If you actually believed my writing you'd figure I don't like many people."

"Except Pietr."

Oh. God. Every bit of my exposed skin turned sunburn red. I'd been very—liberal—colorful—*passionate*—about expressing my feelings for Pietr. "I love Pietr," I said, justifying my writing with the blanket admittal.

"Are you missing mental stimulation here?"

"Yes. And my family. And friends."

She slid the journal out of her way and flipped a page on the clipboard. "Fred and Jeremy also reported that you spoke to one of our newest clients: young Mr. Christian Masterson. What are your impressions of him?"

"Why? Are you looking for a new diagnosis?"

"Sometimes clients who aren't a good mix will mix, anyway. It's best if we identify potential problems immediately."

"I don't foresee us mixing."

One of her perfectly sculpted eyebrows rose. "Hmm. Here's the book the boy left for you. And your journal. I want you to write about your feelings regarding the death of your mother for a few entries. Since *that* is our focus here."

"Fine," I said, taking *Bisclavret* and the journal and heading for the door.

"And Jessica, if you do well these next few days, I'll arrange for you to have a more private room."

"Without a camera?"

"Yes, Jessica. Camera-free."

Jessie

That evening I sat on my bed, closed my eyes, and visualized shooting, rolling Wanda's weapon advice around in my head. I would be out of here soon. And we'd put the plan to free Pietr's mother into action. Whatever the plan was now. I needed to be ready to help the people I loved.

I changed for bed—a pretty ridiculous idea considering the same fashion options were available both day and night. Slipping into my bed, I pulled the covers up and grabbed the cell. I dialed Pietr's number, wanting to hear his voice. Straight to voice mail.

"Pietr, I'm sorry. I know things are crazy." I paused, noting the irony. "I just wanted to hear your voice. So it's okay that I'm going to ring straight through to your voice mail again in a moment. At least it's something. I love you."

I redialed.

"You have reached the voice mail of Pietr Rusakova," the recorded voice purred. "Leave a message."

I slid the phone away, holding the sound of his voice in my head as long as I could before sleep snatched it from me.

CHAPTER NINE

Alexi

Pietr had drifted into my room several times already to carefully pick through my belongings and nearly as carefully put them back. He grew increasingly slicker with his ability to leave things looking untouched, but I had an eye for details—and knew how to set things to see if they'd been disturbed.

He'd been working his way methodically in a clockwise manner so I knew what remained for him to search.

And I knew he'd never find what he was seeking.

One didn't leave a Mafia contact's number sitting out.

But he had no way to get it from where the information was truly stored—in my brain. And I didn't want to wait for him to grow desperate enough to realize and try to find it there.

Being a coward had saved my life before.

He was so young at such a dishonest game. But as young and new as he was, he was also right.

We could not free Mother by ourselves. And there was no other group willing to help us.

As I tucked the small black notebook into a section of my closet yet untouched by Pietr I prayed that being a wretched brother willing to sacrifice Pietr to the mob I might yet become a better son—able to free the only mother I'd ever truly known. And the only person still living who'd ever truly known *me*.

Jessie

I woke to the buzzing of the cell phone as it trembled beside my hand. I couldn't remember turning it on. Wary of the camera, I opened the cell and put it between my ear and the pillow.

"Jess."

"Oh, God, Pietr!" I nearly sat up, but fought down any reaction that might telegraph the truth to the camera. "I love you."

"You have an odd way of showing it," he returned, "turning your back to me so the dogs nearly caught me." I heard the corner of his mouth turn up, the smile unmistakable in his tone. He'd already forgiven me, knowing why I'd done it. "I love you, too," he said with a sigh. "I had to call. Jess . . ."

"What?"

"There's nothing Max and I can do to free her. . . ."

"Alexi and Cat," I reminded him.

"*Nyet*. There's no other choice. I'm going for help. I shouldn't be long. . . ."

"What? Where?"

"Not far. But I may be out of touch. . . ."

"No, Pietr. Don't cut me out."

"I could not cut you out if I wanted to," he said, his voice tight. "How would I live if I cut out my heart?"

My breath caught.

"You've done well without me. You're a survivor. Even when things seem impossible, you hold on to hope. I need you to have a little more faith in me—"

"I have all the faith in the world in you," I confessed.

"*Horashow*. Good. Then have faith in my choices and trust I'll come back for you. Soon."

And then there was just the echo of silence coming back to me. *Dammit.* I tossed and turned the rest of the night, imagining a multitude of horrible scenarios. The worst always ended with Pietr dead.

And all my hopes of happiness died alongside him.

CHAPTER TEN

Alexi

I was not surprised when Pietr announced he was going hunting late that evening; I was pleased.

I watched him leave, saw Max slink off after Amy was asleep, and caught the smell of popcorn.

Cat emerged with a bowl brimming with the stuff, light on butter but heavy with salt. Though she no longer hunted and no longer changed, she still craved the occasional late-night snack, especially when she knew her brothers were roaming the old abandoned park and nearby woods looking for prey.

I couldn't be sure if it was a psychological need or a physical one still linked to her tweaked genetic code. I only knew she complained about it frequently.

"Studies have shown people tend to put on more weight if they snack after seven in the evening." She settled onto the couch beside me. "And here I am, seventeen and starving at nearly midnight! I am too young to have my body ruined by the tinkering your grandfather did."

"*Da*," I said. Nodding, I changed the channel.

"I am getting fatter."

"To get fatter you must first be *fat*," I pointed out, switching channels again. "You are not even approaching plump."

"What are we going to do, Alexi?" she asked.

"You are going to pass me the popcorn and we are going to watch some horrible infomercial on a channel that has embraced capitalism beyond all reason," I said, reaching for the bowl.

"*Nyet*," she said.

I looked at her.

"What are we going to do about Mother?"

The couch felt suddenly too soft to be comfortable, so I tugged myself free of it and handed her the remote.

"Alexi."

"I do not know, Catherine. I do not know." I left the room and headed for my own instead. I straightened some things—trinkets and junk—and then thought of the small notebook I had left intentionally in Pietr's way.

I opened the closet and moved a shoebox aside.

Gone.

Hunting, he had claimed.

Pietr had lied.

I sat down with a sigh on my bed, playing with my lighter and waiting for his inevitable, and angry, return.

Alexi

"You knew," Pietr accused me from my bedroom's open door.

I flipped the lighter closed and looked at him. "*Da*. Of course I knew. I have played this game far longer than you have." I studied him, noting the bruises healing on his face.

I hardened my heart. If their initial rejection could change his mind I would know I had at least gone as far—pushed as hard—as *I* could.

It would be Pietr who stopped the insanity.

"You were not welcomed," I said coolly, touching a finger to my cheek so he knew I saw his battered one.

"Of course I was not welcomed," he snapped. "You knew that, too, though, didn't you?"

"*Da.*"

"Why, Alexi? Why waste my time?"

"In hopes it is enough to save your soul. This is no game these men play. If they want you, they will want to keep you until you're no longer of use. Or until you betray them. And then they'll still want you—but *dead.*"

"My *soul?* What about our mother's *life?*"

I winced. *Our* mother's. It was odd how different he and Max could be. Same bloodline, same genetic code and upbringing, and yet—there were things science could not account for.

"What if we can still save her?"

"What if. What if!" I stood, anger straightening my spine. "We don't know the cure will do her any good. And we don't have any more blood to make the cure. What if she finds out what you're thinking? What then, little brother? You saw what she thought of *me*—the Rusakova *outcast*—taking a bullet for her. It turned her stomach! What would she think of a plan including her youngest son and the Mafia?"

"I don't know," Pietr barked. "But at least we'd have time to ask her and find out!"

"Damn it, Pietr."

"I need a proper introduction, don't I?"

"*Da.*"

"Then arrrange it," he commanded, rolling the words into a seamless growl.

The little black book struck me in the chest as he strode out the door.

Jessie

I did laundry detail and returned to my room to read until it was time for my session. Then I returned and read some more. Reading *Bisclavret* I gained a better understanding of Pietr's desperation to be understood, to be accepted although he struggled to accept himself.

Bisclavret was every bit the tragedy Pietr hoped to avoid. And whereas the hero in *Bisclavret* had years to win his wife's trust and love, it took moments for her to decide to betray him.

Pietr'd never had the luxury of such a lengthy time line to find someone to understand him. His life was destined to be cut short if he continued to refuse the cure.

And he would continue to refuse until his mother was free.

So to feel so deeply for me so quickly and risk his heart by showing himself—a move that might have made most girls agree he was nothing but a monster—took real guts.

That night, with only a few chapters left to read in *Bisclavret*, I chose to try and be as brave as Pietr. I set aside the novel, picked up my journal, and wrote about losing my mom.

About the last time I'd seen her before the accident.

The fight we'd had.

And the fact I really believed obeying her the very last time I'd seen her had been the biggest mistake of my life.

When I finished, my eyes stung. Exhausted, I crawled into bed and checked the phone. No message. But I was certain that whatever Pietr was doing, wherever he was, he was okay.

He had to be.

CHAPTER ELEVEN

Alexi

I had consumed so much vodka between Pietr's rejection, my request of an introduction, and the actual event I was amazed I was not yet blind. My head ached and even the scent of food sent me into heaves. I patted the cigarettes again in my pocket. So sleek, small, and potentially deadly. What was better when choosing one's death, I wondered, the hacking and wheezing of ruined lungs or the hardening of a vodka-soaked liver?

Peering through the windshield into the dark I realized at the rate things were going, I wouldn't live to see either choice take its final toll.

Riding shotgun was Pietr, the sole reason I was here, sober and sickened—by my own willingness to sacrifice him at least as much as by any drink.

I turned the steering wheel and we headed down a pockmarked dirt road. Our destination loomed ahead—an old dumping ground for far more than the wrecks of cars that towered haphazardly throughout the dump.

"Any advice?" Pietr asked me.

"*Da*. Tell me to turn the car around."

"I can't do that."

"I do not think you know what you're getting into, little brother," I whispered, reaching across to open the glove box.

Pietr barely twitched when I pulled out the gun. "If they find that on you—"

"I guess we're both taking some risks." I popped out the gun's clip, slid my finger along the slot windowing the rounds, spinning each a quarter turn, reassuring myself. This was all about things going smoothly. I chambered the first round. "They'll want a show. Things will get bloody."

From the corners of my eyes I noticed the way his Adam's apple slid in his throat as he swallowed, taking in my words. Nervous. If I noticed, they might notice, too.

It would be like blood in the water.

"Tell me to turn the car around."

But we both knew what his answer was going to be—what it had to be. And I was enough of a bastard I was ready to sacrifice my youngest brother to gain even a thin chance at freeing my mother.

"*Nyet.*" His eyes closed.

He was thinking. Of what? Or whom? Jessie? "There are some things—some alliances and choices, you may not ever be forgiven for. Regardless of how forgiving the girl seems."

"I'll deal with the fallout after Mother's out. I have to . . . prioritize. There are always other girls, aren't there?" he asked, his lips twisting in a cynical smile that mirrored the one I turned so often on the world.

A car pulled into the area ahead of us from a different entrance. It stopped, still a distance off, and faced us. Its headlights blinked twice. Then three more cars joined it.

I kept my voice steady. "*Nyet,*" I confided. "Sometimes there is only one girl."

He glanced at me. But only briefly. "I thought this was to be a small meeting." He motioned with his chin to the waiting cars.

I flicked our lights off and on, answering their summons, as my stomach roiled. "A small meeting about a big deal," I muttered. "It's not every day the Mafia gets exactly what it's been wanting." There were more cars than even I'd anticipated.

"Then let's give it to them. Get this over with. Let's make this deal."

I nodded. "Follow my lead and stay cool." Opening my door, I slid out of the car.

Briefly blinded by the glare of headlights, I realized if this didn't go just right it meant the end of the both of us. Quickly. And without us the Mafia would feel even less reason to pause in going for Max and Cat. . . . A kidnapping would be quieter without the threat of an alpha in the house.

There were things I hadn't dared tell Pietr. He needed to be as natural as possible. If I'd told him how I expected this to go down he'd have overanalyzed things. And one moment free of pure instinct—a heartbeat's worth of thought—of recalling what you'd believed was the right decision when you ran the scenario through your mind: It became the difference between life and death.

Pietr mustn't hesitate when it came down to it.

My contact, Ivan, according to the name he most frequently used, met us in the intersection of the awkward spotlight the cars' headlights cast, his face dripping with shadow. I put my game face on. "Where's Dmitri?"

"In the car. He wants to see your boy before he bothers getting out."

"Pietr." I snapped my fingers.

Pietr snarled at the insult, but came around from behind me, eyes glowing and jaw set grimly.

Ivan looked him up and down.

Pietr spread his arms wide and threw his head back. Slowly, as a testament to his easy animal grace, he took a turn, showcasing his long lines—all muscle and sinew held together by a nearly perfect bone structure. In the stark light he was a young god emblazoned by the headlights cutting through the cold and dark. He stopped, cocked his head, and glowered at the much shorter Ivan. "I don't do pirouettes."

I heard a door open. Someone clapped.

Other doors opened and my heart sped, knowing what came next. We would both be tested. I managed to keep my hand from instinctively going to the gun hanging in my jacket pocket. I'd seen the drama played out before—been one of the players once.

Proving *my* loyalty.

"Impressive, but I need to see more. The form is splendid, but form without function? Nothing but dead meat. Perhaps something more directly applicable to your unique skill set?" The clapping man, Dmitri, if my guess was right, stepped into the circle of light, keeping his face to us so his most telling features fell into hard shadow. I could make out short-cropped hair, a lean, medium build, but if I ever needed to identify him in daylight I would surely fail.

Not Pietr, though, I knew.

Pietr had his scent.

Pietr turned, hearing what I knew was inevitable. Someone was at our car. Our headlights flicked off.

Pietr snarled and he widened his stance, lowering his center of gravity.

I stayed perfectly still, tamping down my fear. Panic did no good, gained us no advantage. And this was all about advantage and bluff—there would be no fair play.

All but one set of headlights blinked off.

We knew they wanted his stealth, his speed and strength, but those came in his human form as much as any other. But what else they wanted to see, I wasn't sure of. I could only guess.

I stepped back, mirroring Dmitri, and Pietr drew up to his full height, peering into the surrounding darkness, eyes catching fire as he heard the whisper of footsteps circling.

They came at him slowly at first, two at a time.

Shadowy figures slipped in and out of the headlight's glare, taking swipes at him, pulling his attention different directions as they tried to get the advantage, to get him unbalanced and judge his raw potential, his natural state as a fighter.

Dmitri ringed the action until he stood beside me. "He's holding back," he muttered, disgusted. "That will get him killed." He slapped his hands together. More mafiosos joined in.

I saw the flash of a knife and heard Pietr's snarl of surprise.

"I have no use for men who hold back. What did you bring me, Alexi? An oborot, or a boy trying to be an oborot? Faster!" Dmitri yelled. "Don't you *dare* hold back. He's no boy—he's a *beast! A monster!* Remind him of what he is!"

More men dove for him, more knives flashed, and Pietr's snarl deepened and thickened and though he no longer faced me, I knew his eyes were bright as fresh blood—the beast readying to rip free.

They ringed him now, knives flicking out, taunting and tearing at his human-looking flesh, an attack on every side meant to take him down a piece at a time and break his control. To force the change he seemed determined to hold back.

There was a *rrrip*, a startled howl. His clothes hung in tatters, and his flesh became a pin cushion.

Pacing off a slow circle they dodged in and out, each contact eliciting a snarl or a snap from Pietr. And still, he did not change.

Dmitri looked at me. "Cigarette?" he asked, looking meaningfully at the lump in my shirt pocket.

"Of course," I replied, pulling out the box instead of the gun I so desperately wanted. I kept my hands steady as I shook a cigarette free, ignoring my brother's sudden yelp of pain.

"You could still find a home with us, Alexi. Light."

As I pulled the lighter loose, Nadezhda's letter tumbled out, her picture fluttering free.

Dmitri plucked it from midair and took my lighter. In the yellow glow the lighter sparked he examined the photo a moment. He lit his cigarette. "She has not forgotten you, either," he mentioned, letting the picture fall between us.

He said it as if Nadezhda's remembering me was far worse than her forgetting me.

And I knew it was.

I watched the photo hit the ground, roll across the dirt of the junkyard, and I didn't reach for it, didn't dare. No distractions. No connections. So instead I watched Nadezhda's image stolen away by the chilling breeze and returned my gaze to a sight that tore at me almost as much as it tore at him—Pietr's proving.

Dmitri's attention refocused, too. His boredom obvious, he snapped, "Finish it!"

The last headlights blinked out and all of the men rushed Pietr at once.

Above us a spotlight flashed on, dangling from a wrecking ball and illuminating the writhing hell a hundred feet below it.

Pietr was gone, a mound of men punching, slicing, and kicking weighing him down. I heard his strangled cry and reached for the gun, my eyes on Dmitri, fear a distant memory. This was suicide. I didn't have the ammunition to kill them all. Maybe not even enough to save Pietr.

But if I could get some of them off him—scatter them so he had a second chance . . . a chance to run . . . a way to know I hadn't just mutely *watched* him die. . . .

It would be worth death. My hand closed around the gun's cool grip.

Then, as fast as Pietr had fallen, men began flying back.

And Pietr, furred in his wolfskin, clambered to his hind legs, flinging men back with the best of his inhuman strength and all of his uninhibited animal rage. Mobsters screamed as they flew. And as each of them crashed into the rubble of the junkyard with sickening crunches, Pietr stood taller.

Fought fiercer.

Dmitri smiled as my gut twisted and I released the gun again.

Suddenly it was just Pietr, bathed in blood with glowing red eyes under the spotlight like some beast from the most brutal of Russia's ancient myths. His furred hand, half-turned, clutched his remaining attacker, twisting his head at such an angle. . . . One stroke of Pietr's claws and the man's neck would open, spilling blood; one snap of Pietr's wrist and his neck would break.

Dmitri clapped, thrilled to see his soldier so close to a sudden end.

Pietr, his face far more wolf than man, growled at Dmitri, his lips pulled back to reveal his massive line of teeth.

"Bravo, Pietr!" Dmitri commended. "Now release him."

Pietr tossed his head and howled his defiance.

"Release him."

I nodded at Pietr, but high on the adrenaline rush that came from surviving—and, I shuddered, realizing, high on the blood-lust—he growled at me, too, muscles quivering with something between rage and thrill.

Pietr released the man, letting him slide limply in to the dust and dirt at his feet. Muscles and tendons yanking at bone and jerking his limbs, his body spasmed as Pietr resettled into his more familiar human form.

Covered in grime and bleeding from dozens of knife wounds, Pietr crouched, his eyes still glowing hot and red.

"You have potential," Dmitri admitted as Pietr panted before him. "Your fighting is sloppy. You have trouble committing to action. You overthink." He shook his head. "You'd need time to be trained for what we want." He looked at his own bedraggled and beaten soldiers. "And from what I understand, time is a commodity you do not have."

"What?" Pietr popped to his feet, his muscles still quivering from stress and exertion. "Are you—are you rejecting my offer?"

"*Da, bratàn*. I am," Dmitri said, reaching a hand out to shake Pietr's.

"I almost kill your men—because you want me to prove something—and then you say *no?* Do not call me *bratàn* if you reject what I am willing to give. We are certainly not brothers." Pietr smacked Dmitri's hand away and the older man bristled. "I offer you my services and you turn me down because I'm raw? Untrained?"

"Pietr," I warned.

"Stop now, boy, before you say something you'll regret." Again Dmitri stuck out his hand.

Pietr looked at me.

My jaw stiffened. I nodded.

Reluctantly Pietr took Dmitri's hand. Something subtle about the light in his eyes changed. His fingers stayed curled as his hand dropped back to his side. He held something Dmitri wanted him to have.

Something I shouldn't know about.

I looked away.

"Come, Pietr," I said, clipping my tone. "There might yet be another way."

"Alexi," Dmitri said as I turned to the car and was blinded briefly when all the other headlights flared back on. "Remember what I said."

Nodding, I opened the car's door and climbed in, starting the engine and wondering if he meant I should remember what he said about Nadezhda or finding a home with the mob.

With my bleeding brother nearby, I thought it didn't matter either way. Some bridges needed to be burned.

"Here." I tossed Pietr a pair of jeans.

He looked at me—in that moment realizing I'd known they'd force him to change into the very thing he regretted being, that they'd make him a monster, tear him down bit by bit until that was all he *could* be.

He knew I'd held back from telling him everything.

Again.

He winced, getting into the jeans, and fell into the seat beside me. He seemed not to notice he was bleeding all over the car's expensive leather interior.

Or perhaps he longer cared.

Alexi

The weekend's arrival meant very little in a household consumed with thoughts of betrayal and impending battle. I wanted guns and ammunition far more than the fluffy pancakes—the American version of our Russian *blini*—and bacon Amy served up and Max greedily devoured. I poked at my food, still sickened by what I'd allowed the night before.

I needed to make a shopping list.

Feeling eyes drilling into me, I peered across the table at Cat. She too merely moved the things on her plate around, only pensively nibbling a bit here and there. Her eyes darted from Amy to me and back again. She needed to talk, but it concerned something Amy should not hear.

Even in our own house we were liars. Cat trailed me into the kitchen and when she was sure Amy was nowhere to overhear, she asked me about Pietr's whereabouts.

"He's not sleeping in?"

"*Nyet*. His bed's still made up."

I was more astonished by the fact that at his age he made his bed every morning than hearing what I'd feared was inevitable. "Bags?"

"One's gone—and a lot of clothing—a mix of things."

A mix of things. *Da*. It took more than a tracksuit to be a member of the modern Mafia.

"Shhh. Shhh," I soothed, running my hand slowly across her back. "He is not stupid." Perhaps not *stupid*, but dangerously ignorant. "He is probably taking time to think." More likely taking time to have his ass handed to him by the Mafia. "He'll be in contact soon."

"You are lying." Tears trembled at the edges of her thick eyelashes. "Alexi," she wheezed, pushing herself into the shelter of my arms, "where has my brother gone?"

I gave her a squeeze, my lips brushing her forehead. "Where has *our* brother gone?" I corrected her, shaking her gently. "I am not sure, Ekaterina. But we will know soon—of that, I am certain."

With a sniffle she pulled out of my grasp and bounded up the stairs and to her room. She cranked her music so that Linkin Park echoed through the Queen Anne.

Alone in the kitchen, I remembered introducing my baby brother to the mob. I had not seen the note Dmitri slipped Pietr during their reluctant handshake, but I was sure there had been one. I'd expected another test, but the amount and variety of missing clothing spoke of a more permanent arrangement.

Alexi

On the second day of Pietr's absence, Amy had to swallow a new lie. I left its construction to Cat. I was so deep in lies I could barely keep them straight anymore. The steady stream of vodka didn't help.

My shopping list of weapons and ammunition was only half-finished. We were all going to die eventually, anyhow.

Cat somehow threw Amy a red herring—leading her off the strange trail of clues that, if put together correctly, would show Jessie in an asylum, Pietr with the Mafia, and Max as a werewolf. After Amy seemed satisfied, Cat found me.

"I don't know where he is, Ekaterina," I insisted. Technically true. "All I know is, he's not captured and not dead. Yet."

She wrestled with a box of some sort of supposedly idiot-proof food. "Damn it, Alexi. Pietr's disappeared and you act as if it's no big deal!"

"I don't know what you want me to do. Track him? Oh. Wait. I'm not an oborot, remember?" I slugged back the shot of vodka that sat before me on the table. "And, come to think of it, neither are you. If you want someone to trail him, ask Max." I rolled the empty glass between my hands and contemplated the bottle. "I don't know what you expect me to do."

She grabbed the bottle before my fingers could close around its slender neck and slammed it into the sink, shattering it. "I expect you to stop whatever this self-destructive bent is and find a way to find our brother."

"*Your* brother, you mean?" I had grown tired of fighting just to prove I had a right to a family I had worked so hard to keep together.

"*Nyet*," she whispered, leaning so close the sting of alcohol on my breath made her nose scrunch up. "I meant what I said. *Our* brother. Mine. Max's. And *yours*," she snapped before slamming down a piece of paper and pen. "And you know I'd prefer a Glock," she noted, drawing a line through one of the items on the list. "Sober up. We need you sharp." And she turned on her heel and left, assured I'd obey.

It seemed everyone in the family had a bit of alpha in them.

Alexi

The phone woke me and I knocked the cup of water off my nightstand reaching for it. "Who the hell is this?"

I recognized immediately the voice crackling across the airways, though the phone number was new. I leaped to my feet in the dark, demanding, "Pietr?! Where the hell are you?"

Ignoring my question, he replied, "I need the benefit of your expertise. There's a situation . . ." His voice trailed off, leaving me wondering if he was being listened to. So I filled in the blanks.

"A situation *you* cannot handle?" I flipped on a lamp and stared at the knickknacks spread across my bureau that had all been bits and pieces of my years of cover-up. The specially designed cologne that made my scent a close match to theirs. The red dye I used to highlight my plain dark brown hair so it was comparable to their natural color. The vitamins and minerals that helped increase my strength and stamina. The things that made me a weak imitation of what they naturally were.

What situation could an alpha oborot not handle? What expertise did I have . . . ?

It hit me like a sock full of nickels.

"*Vwee pohnehmytyuh menya?*"

"Shit. *Da, yah pohnemyoo.*" Of course I understood. "But I cut those ties when they came for you and your siblings. I have avoided the darker side of commerce ever since."

"*Otkrojte dveri snova. Sdelajte eto eshhe raz.*"

"Opening that door again could get someone killed—"

"I'm in too deep, Alexi," he admitted.

I fell back onto my bed. For him to admit he was in over his head—my brilliant little brother—it was like Max asking me for advice about girls. Unheard of.

"It's hard to explain. It'd all be Greek to you."

Jesus. It was never good when we needed to speak Greek to cover our tracks. It meant only one thing: The people Pietr was keeping secrets from were Russian. And the only other Russians we'd ever known were Mafia. He'd been with the mob less than three days and already he needed help circumventing them.

This was not a conversation to have over the phone, so I suggested, "*Den boroume na meelahme ap toe teelefono.*" Maybe if I knew where he was, we could meet. "*Pooh eese?*"

"*Den pyrazee afto.*"

Wonderful. He didn't even want me to worry about his current location.

"*Avryo. Rantevou stees paleaes apothykes steen othos Praseenee.*" He paused. "*Kseereetee tee thesee?*"

"*Da.*" I could meet him tomorrow at the warehouses on Green Street. "*Ne,*" I assured him. "*Tha sas seenanteeso ekee.*"

The call ended, leaving my jaw hanging open. Perhaps Pietr had found us help, but it seemed he'd found himself a nest full of trouble in the bargain. And I realized that the only type of trouble too big for Pietr to handle was probably way out of my league, too.

CHAPTER TWELVE

Jessie

Dad's next visit did not start on an encouraging note.

"I don't know what else to do, Jessie. The lawyer's doing his best, but things are being held up in the local court. It's looking like at least another week," Dad said, his eyes full of disappointment. "Pietr's gone AWOL—nobody'll say what he's off doing, like he's on some secret mission."

My stomach trembled knowing that was just it. And knowing that was all I knew, too.

Dad sighed and continued. "Amy and that boy Max have started coming over to help with the horses, but I'm surprised they get anything done the way they keep lookin' at each other and kissin'." Dumbfounded, he asked, "She's livin' over there with them?"

"Dad, it's not what you think."

"The way they act around each other I can't imagine it being anything else."

I sighed. "Dad, I really need to get out of here."

"I'm doing all I can, Jessie."

"What if I said it's a matter of life or death?"

His eyebrows shoved together. "Are you in danger?" He leaned closer.

"Uhm." *Untouchable*, they'd said. "It's someone else. And I'm the only one who can help."

"You start talkin' like that and I might start to think you need to stay longer."

"Okay, okay." I waved my hands. "Never mind. It'll work itself out. Somehow."

"Dr. Jones said you're doing better. She's thinkin' about giving you a better room. Without a camera."

"That would be so awesome."

"And I brought you something." He passed me something beneath the table.

I shoved it into my waistband. "Another one?"

"Longer battery life, since I can't sneak you a charger, and there's a ringtone on it programmed with Pietr's number—a ringtone nobody over age twenty can hear."

"Cool."

"Ain't technology grand? You're obsolete at twenty-one."

I snorted. "Thanks, Dad."

We both stood and I hugged him. Tightly. "Think about what I said. About life and death."

"And you think about what I said about maybe you need to be here longer if that's what you believe," he repeated.

"Fine."

He left and I flopped into the chair and the back of my neck tickled as I realized someone was staring at me.

Christian.

Shivering at the uncanny way he watched me, I stood and returned to my room, guards trailing behind me.

Inside I sent Pietr a quick text, saying I missed him and avoiding the weird and frightening things going on that I might have mentioned. I resigned myself to sleep, my fingers wrapped around the phone and tucked beneath my pillow.

The next morning I woke and called Pietr. Straight to voice

mail. I readied to hear his standard message, but his words and tone had changed.

Tremendously.

"Leave a message, but don't expect me to return your call promptly."

I hung up and hit the number again. Definitely Pietr's voice. But it was the voice he'd used with me when he'd dated Sarah in a misguided attempt to keep me safe. The cool, matter-of-fact voice made me shiver. It was like his mouth, his brain and his heart had somehow disconnected.

Pietr was in trouble.

And there was nothing I could do about it.

I just hoped someone else could help.

Alexi

Parking the car on a nearby side street, I walked the perimeter of the abandoned property looking for an easy way past the chain-link fence and the razortape crowning it. I hadn't dressed for climbing. From the graffiti-tagged buildings inside, I knew kids had wormed their way in before.

And since only serious taggers came to a site prepared to cross razortape I paused, looking beyond the chain links to study the craftsmanship of their lettering.

Amateurs.

There had to be a hole in the fence easy enough for potheads and slackers to find.

Nearly around the property's back I found the hole and slipped through. I picked my way around the rows of buildings, coming to the one Pietr had mentioned.

I glanced at my cell. Two minutes late. Not needing to rely on a watch or cell phone Pietr would be inside already and waiting impatiently.

Testing the door, I shouldered it open and let my eyes adjust to the dark. An open window flooded a section of the old warehouse with light, illuminating piles of pigeon droppings and shards of dusty broken glass. I passed a worn mattress dotted with a variety of stains, a large baby doll missing its right arm and head, the same doll's hollow ceramic head with an attached handle making it a fine drinking vessel . . . I rubbed the chill from my arms near a discarded pair of children's sneakers and finally found my way to him.

"You have certainly discovered a location where no one in their right mind would meet," I congratulated him, stepping over the rotting body of a rat. I balled up a handkerchief and pressed it to my nose. "How can you stand it?"

His back to a wall, he stood cloaked in shadow. "Sometimes you must adjust your standards, *da?*" He took one small step forward, into the light where dust motes danced. This was not my little brother, the idealistic boy who tried to rescue kittens from trees not realizing how easily he tripped their prey-versus-predator senses.

This Pietr's eyes never stayed still, never quite settled on me though we were not far apart. They danced all around us, searching shadows and watching all possible entrances and exits.

"I've made a deal," he confirmed. "We'll have the manpower we need to free Mother." His eyes now simply avoided mine and although a smile slipped across his lips, it fled as quickly as it appeared. "But—"

"There's a price you cannot quite pay."

"I can pay the price—I'm more than capable of delivering on the promises *I* make," he said. The words landed hard, smacking across my face. "But I don't *want* to pay this particular price."

"Jesus, Pietr." I rubbed a hand across my brow. "What sort of bargain have you struck? And with a devil I know, or another?"

"The less you know, the better. I just need a couple things—consider it a morbid shopping list." He handed me a folded paper. "*Nyet.* Don't open it here."

"Delivery: When and where?"

"It's on the paper."

"So that's it? I'm your personal shopper?" It seemed I'd be shopping for us both.

"And research assistant," Pietr said with a dark grin. "Tell me, Alexi, can you—can regular people—tell the difference between the scent of pigs' blood and human blood?"

"If there's no flesh attached . . ." I said, my stomach churning at the reasons Pietr might need such information to begin with. "It depends on amounts, but probably not."

"*Horashow*. It only needs to buy me time . . ."

"You're always trying to buy time, Pietr."

"*Da*. Beg, barter, buy . . . maybe steal," he whispered more to himself than to me. "I just need a little more—otherwise, time'll be up for us all faster than we imagined."

I grabbed his arm, but he shook me off. "Pietr. Tell me what's happening."

"You'll know soon enough." He tapped the paper I still held stiffly in my hand.

And then he turned and slid back into the shadows of the old warehouse.

Exiting a different way than I came in, my instincts—or my training—still echoed in the back of my head. Never take the same path twice. Never let someone anticipate your next move and get the drop on you.

I never wanted this life—this lifestyle—but what choice did I have? I was raised in it. It was like breathing—second nature. Eventually I'd understood you couldn't easily live without it, like breathing.

Diving into the black market again to run our shopping errands would most likely bring me closer to Nadezhda—my White Crow. And most likely closer to death.

Perhaps breathing would not be so very necessary for long after all.

Jessie

"Good news, Jessica," Dr. Jones announced even before I'd settled on the couch for my session. "You'll be getting moved into your new room tomorrow. No camera, additional privileges . . . You've earned it."

"Great. Should I mention it's tough to not make a comment like, 'Thank goodness I have a whole day to pack my things'?"

She didn't blink, didn't scribble down my quote on the clipboard. Like it didn't matter. "Change—even change for the better—can be difficult at first, Jessica. I cannot fault a sarcastic response at this stage in your therapy. Besides, you've gone above and beyond in helping with laundry detail for your hall."

I blinked.

"Though there was the little matter of one of your checklists not being on your clipboard." She leaned toward me. "Do you remember that day?"

Crap. The missing paper from the day I found the bodies in the basement. "Was that the day my regular nurse was absent?"

"Mmhmm," Dr. Jones confirmed.

"The substitute nurse did seem flustered," I tried, my stomach knotting as I struggled for a viable lie. "I'm sure she just made a mistake—misplaced it." I shrugged. "I know everyone got fresh laundry every day I worked, though."

She studied my face. "Well, that's the important part." She flipped a page on her clipboard. "How has your journaling been going?"

I sat. "Fine. I tried to take your advice and write about Mom. Well, losing Mom."

"And how did it make you feel?" she asked softly.

"Like absolute crap," I admitted.

"Excellent."

CHAPTER THIRTEEN

Alexi

It was shortly after Pietr, Max, Amy, and Cat had allowed the bus to again drag them to school that the knock sounded from our front door. I'd locked the door, marking Wanda's words, and rose, coffee in hand, to see who was on our porch.

Lifting the curtain, I nearly dropped my mug, going for the gun under my shirt.

The blond boy—Derek—from the bunker stood on the porch, watching the road in front of our house.

Gun in my right hand, mug in my left, I gingerly unlocked the door and gave the knob enough of a twist and a tug that the door slowly opened and I spilled little of my drink.

He looked at me, smiling so deeply his face dimpled.

I kept the gun pointed at him, just below the door's modest window, and stopped the door with my foot. "How can I help you?" I asked, more mindful of his hands than his expression. Jessie's brain had been fried several times when she'd let him get his hands on her. A social manipulator of sorts, Derek Jamieson had the ability to change a person's perception with a touch and a little time. Whereas the oboroten were created, some more monstrous things, like Derek, were merely born. A simple human, there was little simple about him.

"You're so much more polite than your brothers," he commented. His eyes unfocused for a moment and he shook his head. "Except for that gun." His eyes cleared. "But you don't get fangs or claws, do you? That must be quite a disadvantage in the Rusakova household."

"Consider me differently abled," I stated, moving the pistol up to tap its snout on the glass. "What brings you here?"

"We share an asset," he said. "A brown-haired girl currently residing in an asylum."

Jessie.

"And it seems as much as I want to keep her, some others in my company—"

"Is that what it is, then—'some company'?"

"Finally you're catching on." He cleared his throat. "Others see her as a liability. They haven't told me why specifically, but it appears"—he winked—"that there's something even more special about her than I thought." The smile dropped away from his face along with any hint of charm. "They're going to kill her."

"When? Where?"

He shrugged. "Soon. The asylum."

My vision narrowed as I read his very open expression. Shouldn't this be a trap? "And you're telling me this because?"

"Because you have no idea how badly I want to get my hands on Jessica one more time. For old times sake," he said. "And I'm used to getting what I want—one of the drawbacks of being spoiled as a child with absentee parents. Both Pietr and I want her out of the asylum—alive. I can't get her out; Pietr can."

"He won't *give* her to you."

"That doesn't matter," he assured me as if he expected Jessie to just come to him. "Just pass along the message."

A Mercedes pulled up.

"Ah. My ride's here."

He strolled off, down my sidewalk and to his waiting car.

I closed the door, locked it, and put my gun away. Our situation had all the makings of a Russian tragedy: a young woman torn between two men—neither of them truly good for her—a battle over family and life itself . . .

The train sounded. *Da*, there were even trains and horses.

And so much hung in the balance. If Jessie broke, then it would all be for nothing. Without her blood there was no cure, no way to fix the damage already done to Mother. Of course, we'd never tested anyone else's blood. Would it not be but one more cruel twist of fate to find out the cure lingered in everyone's blood—that it was as common and as simple as humanity itself?

Peering into my coffee cup I wanted something much stronger to drink.

But Cat was right. They needed me sharp.

Alexi

The wonderful thing about the black market—if anyone dared string such a phrase together—was that the black market was never where most people expected it to be. People working in the shadows also indulged themselves in bright lights and odd comforts.

The contact I needed to tap for information and supplies was rumored to have a love of carriage rides through big city parks. So I took the money I had squirreled away thanks to hustling an occasional pool game and understanding American football better than most other Americans, drove a distance, and hunted down the correct horse and carriage at the appointed time.

After, of course, I had delivered Derek's message to Pietr.

Waiting in a line with others, the carriage nearly disappeared against the growing evening oozing across the rolling park's cobblestone paths. Its dark horse stomped impatiently, nearly as black as the carriage it was hooked to.

The convertible black top up, it shielded my contact from view. Whereas most of the carriages had low doors, if doors at all, my appointed carriage had doors that rose high enough no one from the outside could see what bargains were made within.

A small and mean-looking driver examined both me and the case I carried. *"Strasvoytcha."* I waved. He nodded and reached behind him to open the door.

I stepped up into the carriage, its interior even darker than the falling night outside.

Before my vision had cleared and my ass had even hit the seat, there was a gun to my head.

She reached around me, tugging the door shut, her perfume like flowers blooming in Russia's wild forests. "Sit," she commanded, kicking the seat ahead of her.

The carriage jolted forward and I sat.

Even holding a gun to my head, Nadezhda was undeniably hot. God. I needed to get out more. I sank into the seat, holding the case to my chest.

"You're not Boris," I mentioned, peering openly at her. My eyes traveled the length of her sleek form. She was so definitely *not* Boris.

No black catsuit for this Russian femme fatale, Nadezhda sat straight and stiff beside me; dressed in the finest European fashions, her long blond hair wrapped elegantly up and away from her slender neck.

I gave her a look—but the same look that landed Max invitations to flats from Moscow to Paris to New York City played differently across my sharper features and could potentially get me slapped with a harassment complaint.

She was a princess, not a mobster, I thought. Hoped.

But something seemed wrong—something was just a bit *off*.

"Do not look at me," she snapped. "You have no right to look at me after what you've done."

This was going badly.

I looked straight ahead and rested the case on my lap. I needed to think of anything other than the beautiful woman seated beside me. *Da.* Like the reason I was here.

"You promised to return for me. And then—what? What, Alexi? You drop off the face of the planet. You disappear into the backend of the American nowhere." The gun's muzzle jabbed my temple as the carriage turned.

Down an even more isolated pathway.

"I—"

"Shut up! Did I ask you a question?"

"Actually—"

"Shut up!" She drew down a deep breath. The gun poked me again. "You turned on the family," she murmured. She sniffed, pouting. "Alexi, I understand why you did what you did. There is no good life with this family—it is so splintered, so filthy, as bad as the CIA and common street gangs."

I couldn't help it: At her mention of the CIA, I blinked.

She sighed, stretching the sound out. "You did what you did out of love, Alexi. *Yah pohnemyoo.*"

"*Da.* It is good you understand."

"Then why did you not finish things? Out of love? Why did you not come for me?" she asked softly. "Did you not love *me?*"

I sat as still as the jostling carriage allowed, my spine fused.

"Tell me the truth, Alexi."

"Uh . . ."

"Oh." She set the gun down between us. "The truth."

So I turned in the seat and told her everything that had happened since I'd left Moscow. That I still wanted her. And that a declaration of love seemed ill-timed when she might question the authenticity of the emotion, wondering if the sentiment had been influenced by the presence of a gun.

She chuckled.

"And you, White Crow," I whispered, finding it hard to believe I was smiling at her and she was smiling at me, "why are you here?"

"I needed to know," she said. "And I thought I might kill you for sport."

"Is honesty not wonderful?"

"I wish I could be completely honest with you. But so much has changed. I made some hard decisions." She ran her tongue across her lips and my mind drifted to a much warmer place and time.

In Moscow.

In Nadezhda's room.

No matter how many ways I took apart her expression, measured the aspects and points creating her face, I couldn't break it down far enough to forget that this woman was the one I still loved.

"We all make bargains, *da?*" she confided. "Little moves to secure our own happiness—and safety. And sometimes we make big moves. Betray those closest." She shook her head and straightened in her seat. "But this is not all pleasure. You came for business. There are things you requested. There is information you need."

"And you?"

"—are what we shall call an enabler." She smiled.

Oddly, the least amount of time spent in that carriage was spent on guns, passports, and getting the name of places to purchase pigs' blood.

"Oh. Alexi, be careful. We have news there is someone in your area who may be getting ready to make a big move of his own. He wants an oborot for a captain."

My heart dropped into my gut.

"Watch out for him."

I nodded. "*Da*. And you," I whispered, stepping out of the carriage. "Watch out for you."

She smiled and pulled the door closed, but not before I got

one more glimpse of her shoes. The red soles were unmistakable. But so was the amount of wear on them.

Nadezhda had been doing far more than walking comfortable red carpets and hanging with the trendy friends who used to take up most of her time.

The carriage took off, leaving me to find my way back to the more brightly lit areas of the park and transportation home.

I jumped when I heard something in the bushes groan, and my hand went to my gun.

"Uhhh. Crazy bitch."

I stepped back, hugging the shadows as Pietr and Max did so expertly and watched a man crawl backward out of the bushes and struggle to his feet.

He dusted off his tracksuit and reached back under the shrubs, looking for something. Dragging his cell phone free of the park's dirt and debris, he made a call. He plucked a leaf from his slicked-back hair and then returned his hand to his head, his face twisting in pain. "*Da*. Your baby's here. But she's not your baby anymore. *Da*. She reeks of Interpol."

Nadezhda? *Interpol?*

Bargains and betrayals, she'd said.

I looked down at the case I held. As long as the merchandise worked, I did not care who was selling it. I needed it to free Mother.

And probably to save Pietr.

CHAPTER FOURTEEN

Jessie

Although the new room looked nearly identical to my old one, there were significant perks that kept me hanging out inside it more frequently. No camera equated to less paranoia—at least as long as I stayed in. And the fact I could press a button that buzzed the nurses' station to let me out made it seem like I had a *choice*. Fred and Jeremy seldom shadowed me anymore, but it seemed they were kept busy by the continuing population boom at Pecan Place.

I tried to steer clear of all of it. I kept my head down, my eyes and hands to myself, and waited on my rescue. When it finally came, I was unprepared. But when I heard Dad's voice raised in anger, I headed straight out of the common room and toward the commotion. "I was told when her room got changed her visitation privileges were upgraded."

The nurse muttered a response.

"So call Dr. Jones," he demanded.

Hand on the phone, the nurse said, "Dr. Jones isn't in the office, sir. She's unavailable."

And that was when I saw Pietr. I froze, motionless as a deer spying its hunter, my heart racing at least as fast. He looked at me and Dad's words faded to a jumbled mess of nothing. . . .

"Then you need to make the right decision. I don't want to drive all the way home. . . ."

. . . like background noise—static.

And before I really understood what was happening, Dad had somehow gotten the nurse to open my room and let the three of us, Pietr, Dad, and myself, inside.

"Oh-god-oh-god-oh-god!" I launched myself straight into Pietr's arms.

He held me for a long, quiet moment, his face in my hair, breathing in the scent of me as the stress left his back and shoulders little by little. "Shhh," he soothed. "Jess, we don't have much time."

"Dammit, Pietr, we never have much time. Kiss me."

Dad cleared his throat.

"It's not like you haven't seen people kiss before," I protested.

"Not my daughter."

Grumbling, I moved away from Pietr's embrace, letting my hand slip into his.

I held on.

Dad sat on the edge of my bed, the springs groaning faintly. "This boy of yours," he muttered, "is saying some pretty crazy stuff. He would not take no for an answer when he showed up on our doorstep this morning. And he would not tell me where he's been all this time."

"Where were you?"

"Later." He grabbed my other hand and stared down into my eyes. "You're in danger, Jess."

I blinked. "Seems it's my normal."

"Pietr insists someone in here is trying to kill you," Dad said with a snort. "I told him the food's probably awful and I'm sure not Dr. Jones's biggest fan right now, but kill you?"

"There've been some—*dangerous*—situations," I confirmed. "But I thought I had it under control."

Dad gaped. "Why didn't you say . . . ?"

"There's only so much guilt a body can handle, Dad," I explained, keeping my focus on Pietr. "You're at your limit. And I wanted to believe I was safe. . . ." *Untouchable.*

"Well, why the hell would anyone want to kill my girl?" Dad muttered, running his hands through his hair. "I don't understand. . . ." He shook his head. "And why now?"

"No camera," Pietr said, glancing back toward the door. "They could make it look like a suicide. No one would know the truth." He paced slowly around the room, his eyes pausing on the ceiling's heavy lighting fixture.

I saw what he was wondering: How they'd do it. Hanging? Damn fluorescents. There were even more reasons to hate fluorescent lights.

Pietr saw my journal on my bed and picked it up, examining the pen first. His thumb flicked the metal spiral holding it together, his features registering *sharp.*

He looked at my arms. My *wrists.* I rubbed them frantically, looking away from Pietr's cool and grimly assessing gaze. His eyes were somehow different, more calculating and distant.

I wondered if Derek was in the loop about the plans they had for his pet and favorite battery? Was he—even now— arguing to save me out of his own twisted sense of need?

I shivered at the thought and reached out for Pietr's hand again, turning back to face Dad.

"But, why?" Dad pushed. "Have you done something, Jessie?"

"No, Dad. I *am* something." I tried to choose my words carefully. "What if I said there's something in my blood that can help certain people"—I squeezed Pietr's hand—"and other people don't want them to get that help?"

Dad looked up, bleary eyed. "I'd need—I'd need more than that, Jessie. Something in your blood? You aren't even O negative, and that's the one everyone wants for blood drives . . . universal donor . . ." He began to babble.

So *that* was where I got it from.

I dragged Pietr forward and crouched before Dad, unwilling to release Pietr now he was here but feeling the need to set my hand on Dad's knee, to reassure him.

Pietr crouched beside me.

"Dad. Dad."

He looked at me again.

"There's something you don't know . . . something big. I never wanted to drag you into this, but . . ." I shook my head and looked at Pietr. Lost.

Pietr let out a long, slow breath. "Mr. Gillmansen. You know there's something different about me."

Dad blinked.

"I've seen the way you watched me doing chores. I wasn't completely careful," he admitted to me apologetically.

Dad nodded. Slowly. Mute.

"My strength and agility are the results of a Cold War experiment the USSR did several generations ago."

Dad snorted. "We're a long way away from April Fool's, don't ya' think?"

"He's not joking, Dad."

"They tampered with our DNA—toyed with our genetic code until our predecessors became something. . . ." Pietr paused and shook his head.

"No," I whispered to him. "It's not the right word."

Pietr looked at me. "But it's the clearest one."

"Wait," Dad broke in. "You became something *what*?"

"Something monstrous," Pietr said so levelly a chill stroked my spine.

"Look. You're fast. You're strong," Dad admitted. "But there's nothing monstrous about you," he insisted, his jaw set.

Pietr and I exchanged a look. Some people needed to see to believe. Pietr let go of my hand and stood, peeling off his shirt.

"What the hell is he doin'—" Dad asked, each word hanging in the air like a bad smell.

"I'll show you," Pietr volunteered, his hands working the button on his jeans.

Dad grabbed me, placing his hands over my eyes. His fingers trembled and he blustered on. "Look, boy, I played sports in high school—"

I heard the zipper go on Pietr's pants.

Dad was rambling. "I've seen all sorts—"

Pietr's jeans rustled, hitting the cool concrete slab floor.

"—of things guys thought were *monstrous*—"

And then there was the sound of two more things falling softly to the floor and Dad's hands yanked away from my face just as Pietr's front paws touched down.

Wolf, he shook out his coat and padded over to me.

Stunned to silence, Dad pulled me away from Pietr and yanked me haphazardly onto the bed beside him.

Pietr's eyes glittered in his wolfskin, watching and worried.

"Holy. *Shit*."

"Dad!"

"No, Jessie. Your mom would allow me this one," he guaranteed.

I slid off the bed and crouched down, reaching out to Pietr. He padded forward on silent feet and let me wrap my arms around his furry neck and draw his head in to rest on my chest.

"Hey!" Dad warned. "None of that stuff."

I chuckled.

Pietr whined, but I adjusted our position.

Dad was back.

"Okay. Maybe I just suffered an aneurism or stroked out," Dad muttered. "There's a rational explanation for this. Maybe I'm lying in a coma somewhere and this is all just part of it. Weird stuff happens on farms all the time. When was I last messin' with that combine?"

"Dad. Dad!" I stood, taking his hands in mine. "You're fine. I'm fine. Pietr's—" I glanced at the wolf.

He had cocked his head to the side, listening intently.

"Pietr gives *fine* a whole new definition," I declared.

Dad looked from me to the wolf. "Can he—?" Dad jumped, his fingers tightening on mine, and I knew that behind my back Pietr had become human again.

"Pants?" I asked, trying to be mindful of Dad's fragile state and the fact I could wind up grounded as soon as I was out of the asylum.

My normal.

"*Da.* Pants."

Pietr was always a moment slow with human logic and re-membering appropriate social behavior after he'd just shed his wolfskin. Things like pants were occasionally forgotten in the first moments after the change. I knew. I'd noticed that fact (along with other things) several times. I blushed just thinking about it.

Dad blinked.

Pietr came to stand beside me, shirt still in his hands.

"Shirt, too," I admonished, though I really didn't want to. I could spend hours staring at Pietr bare-chested . . . Pietr grinned in direct opposition to my father's expression.

"Put your shirt on, boy."

Pietr reluctantly obeyed.

"Okay. What just happened here?" Dad asked out loud.

Pietr started removing his shirt again, but I placed a hand on his arm. Just touching him made my nerves tingle and my blood rush.

"You sure are quick to strip, boy," Dad said, clearly disapprov-ing. "Lemme get this straight. He's a werewolf, and your blood . . ."

"—is part of the cure."

Dad stood. "How'd you figure that out?"

"Catherine volunteered to try a concoction . . ."

"So what? You kids are over at his place one day—after I re-lease you from being grounded—and he says, *Hey, I'm a were-wolf, but I'd like to be fixed*—"

Pietr blinked.

"Oh. Sorry," Dad muttered, shoving his hands into his jean pockets. "Probably not the words you wanna hear. *But I wanna be just human* and so you—Jessie—what? You open a vein?"

"No, Dad," I sputtered, trying not to laugh. "It's not anything like that."

He started to pace. "I always wondered what you teenagers would be doin' together," he admitted. "But this . . . I figured, underage drinkin'—Jessie'll say no. Drugs? Jessie'll turn 'em down flat," he said with assurance. "Premarital sex?" Dad spun on his heel, staring us both down.

Pietr shifted his weight from foot to foot, staring at the floor. My alpha male had just been reduced to a puppy who'd imagined piddling indoors.

"She'd. Say. No." Dad ground out each word. "But bloodletting? That's a new one. Hadn't given it a moment's thought." Dad shook his head and paced some more. He froze.

"Were you in his room to do this?" he asked, deceptively softly. I imagined smoke pouring from his ears as the gears in his brain sputtered off track a moment.

Dad sometimes got like this, not seeing the forest for the trees. As sole guardian of two daughters—and an admitted "red-blooded American male" back in the day—Dad focused on location so much sometimes he should have gone into real estate.

To be in a guy's room—alone—was a huge taboo. Right up there with setting crosses on fire and leaving the milk out.

My normal.

I sighed.

I looked at Pietr. Absolutely no help. Was I in his room to do the bloodletting? Why, no, I wasn't. I was in his room several other times—even slept in his bed one night (while Pietr sprawled on the floor)—but I wasn't there for the bloodletting.

"No. I wasn't." Sweet, sweet honesty. So rare recently in my life.

Dad sighed. "So your blood's part of this cure and someone doesn't want them cured, so they want you out of the mix."

"Literally," I added.

"Who?"

I wasn't sure what to say. I mean—which lines had blurred and which were crossed while I'd been inside? If Wanda was agreeing with Pietr about getting me out . . . "It's complicated."

Pietr nodded. "More now than ever," he said, a new note of regret in his voice.

Dad looked at us. "I just keep thinking this is all some strange dream. Any minute I'll wake up and everything will be back to normal."

"Try defining *normal* sometime, Dad. I can't find any suitable words to do it myself anymore." I closed my eyes a moment, taking it all in and knowing all I wanted was *out*. "So how do I get out of here?"

"I can't get you out today. Dr. Jones isn't here and she'd need to sign any legal stuff I could get the lawyer to fudge. But I can't leave you here, either. Wait," he whispered. "If your blood's part of a cure . . . what about Anna's?"

The blood turned to an icy slush in my veins. My snooping and far-too-smart-for-the-good-of-her-social-status little sister Annabelle Lee was a logical second choice, considering we shared the same genetics. If they wanted me because my blood could screw up their experiments, when would it occur to them to check her, too?

"Call Alexi. Have him run a test," I urged. "And watch her, Dad. Watch everyone around her."

"Thank God Christmas break's just around the corner," he said. "We can try and figure all this out together then—watch each other's backs."

Pietr nodded. "When do the nurses change shifts?"

"In about twenty minutes," I answered.

"Mr. Gillmansen. In twenty-five minutes you'll walk out of this door and head to the nurses' station, ready for home. When they ask where I am, tell them I left a few minutes ahead of you. They'll check the sign-out sheet. Tell them I was in a hurry and the nurse was pretty scattered from an earlier situation. Be apologetic. Explain Jess broke up with me before I stormed out. It broke my heart," he concluded, his eyes drifting back to mine.

"Pietr," I whispered, astonished. "You're lying." I couldn't believe my ears. Lying was almost the one thing Pietr Rusakova couldn't do.

"I've had to learn a few things since I last saw you." Guilt again crept into his voice.

Dad nodded. "And you?"

"Will sleep here tonight," Pietr said simply. Like it was the most obvious thing in the world.

"In. Her. Room?" Dad snapped.

Oh boy.

"Seriously, Dad, let's prioritize, okay? Someone wants to kill me. Pietr's my best chance at protecting me. There's no other place to stash him but here. In my room."

Pietr eyed my bed.

"I don't like the way you're lookin' at that," Dad mumbled.

Pietr ignored him and stepped over to the mattress, playing with the sheets so they hung down to the ground. He crouched, sweeping the sheets back up and eyeing the space underneath the bed as if measuring it. "I'll sleep there," he said so firmly there could be no argument.

Dad glared at him.

"I'm here to protect Jess," he assured. "Don't worry."

"I won't—about *anything*," Dad repeated, stressing the final word.

"No, Mr. Gillmansen," Pietr reassured. "Not anything."

I sighed and Dad's glare shifted to me.

"Young lady," he warned. "Don't you even *think* . . ."

I rolled my eyes. "Fine, Dad. Like Pietr said. You won't have anything to worry about."

"I'll journal the rest of the day and tomorrow until you arrive, Dad. I'll just stay here."

"The nurses should be switching now," Pietr announced, his internal clock freakishly accurate.

"You'd better go, Dad. You," I said to Pietr, "under the bed in case they peek in the window."

He did as I suggested and I arranged the sheets so he was completely hidden. For once my sloppy housekeeping skills would pay off as the accepted routine.

I hugged Dad and walked him to the door, pressing the button. The door buzzed and with a click the lock released. "It'll be fine," I assured. "I'm the safest I've been in days."

He shot a look at the shadowy space beneath my bed.

"If he tries . . ."

"Dad. Pietr's a puppy dog," I whispered, though I knew werewolf ears would hear.

The door shut behind him, and my back against it, I let out a sigh.

"Were you ever frightened growing up?" Pietr asked.

"Of what?"

"The monster under your bed?"

"You're no monster, Pietr," I admonished, crossing the room to get my journal and do my best to appear normal. Bored.

He sighed and shifted in the darkness, waiting for me to tell him when the coast was clear. "Things change, Jess. People change."

The silence that followed his words was heavier than it had ever been.

Jessie

"It's been ten minutes," I whispered.

"Thirteen. But who's counting?" Pietr responded dryly.

"They would have checked by now if they were going to."

"So I'm allowed out?"

I flipped back the sheets. "Come out."

He slid out from under my bed, staying toward the wall farthest from the window's view. He stretched, joints popping.

"A little cramped down there?"

His lips curled in a teasing grin. "We wind up in the nicest places."

"At least you can't complain about the company." I jabbed his ribs and raised my face for a kiss.

"*Nyet*. No complaints there." Eyes glowing, he leaned down to kiss me.

The knock on the door startled us both, and Pietr slid with an accuracy a baseball pro would envy, right under the bed again. I tugged at the sheets and crossed the room.

Christian.

I buzzed the door open.

Christian wheeled in the laundry cart and clipboard. "Sorry this is so late. I just found out I've been sentenced to laundry duty. Rumor has it you're on your way out."

I grinned. "Finally a rumor with truth behind it!"

He looked me up and down. "That's too bad. I was really hoping to get to know you. I guess I should've taken a chance earlier on." The smile he showed me was far more wicked than anything that had ever twisted Pietr's lips. "Ah well, there's no time like the present—" He grabbed my face and kissed me.

I yanked back with a squeak. "*That* wasn't a good idea. Go. Now." I stepped back, closer to the bed, and felt the heat rolling off of Pietr as he held his animal instincts back. This was bad. "I'm telling you. Go now."

"Fine." He grinned. He put up his hands and backed toward the door. "Can't blame a guy for trying."

"Yes, I can."

He scowled. "Will I see you at dinner?"

"No. I've totally lost my appetite."

As soon as the door closed behind him I rushed to the

bathroom—past Pietr, who was out from under the bed and bristling in the corner—to grab my toothbrush.

He glared after me the whole way as I stepped into the tiny bathroom and loaded my toothbrush with toothpaste and scrubbed the flavor of Christian's mouth away from mine.

"I see you've made new friends," he said, slinking in and filling the bathroom's other side. He cast a menacing shadow.

"Not. Friends. Obviously." I spewed foam into the sink. "Grrr!"

In the mirror I saw him startle.

"Don't glare at me." I spewed more foam as I shook my toothbrush in the mirror at him. "God!" I spit. Rinsed. Brushed some more. "This is your fault."

His eyes widened at the accusation and the rage fell away from his face. "How is it *my* fault?"

"Until you started showing an interest in me there were very few guys trying to ram their tongues down my throat. I was fine like that," I pointed out, bending to spit again. "Now it seems I'm getting some funky oral exam by every guy I meet. Gross!"

Pietr chuckled, gently prying both the cup and toothbrush from my trembling hands to set them on the sink. He turned me to face him. "Why can't you accept that guys wanting you is because of *you*? Not me. You're beautiful, Jess."

I snorted.

"Even when you do that," he whispered, pulling me close to nuzzle his face into my hair. He sucked my scent into his lungs with a rattling breath and my knees trembled.

"Stop," I whispered, breathless.

"What?" He glanced at his hands and, closing his eyes, ran his fingers lightly down my back. Pausing at my waist he fumbled and pulled me closer.

The raw power of his body heated the length of mine. I shook my head to clear it and although I didn't want to, I said, "Stop," and pulled back to look up at him.

His eyes opened, now a shade of near violet, the red and the blue warring passionately. He touched my cheek with a trembling hand and I clutched his wrist, grabbing his attention.

"We promised my dad he had nothing to worry about leaving us here together."

His hand pulled free of mine and moved down the side of my face, along my neck, his eyes following its path. Both his hand and his gaze paused at the same spot, just above my left breast. He looked up at me. "Does this worry you?" he whispered, his voice husky.

I smacked his hand away and watched his eyes flare. "Yes. You and I made a promise. A *promise*, Pietr."

He groaned, a sound halfway between pain and pleasure. His eyes half-lidded, he reached for me again. "Jess."

I stepped away, backing into the sink.

"People break promises every day."

"No," I insisted. "Not you, Pietr."

He took a single step forward.

I'd never realized how big he could seem, how powerful and imposing. I stepped back, but had no place to go.

His hand rested heavily again on the same spot, below my collarbone but above my breast. He froze a minute, mesmerized, one finger following the raised outline of my bra strap just beneath my top.

"How could you forget?" he wondered, his hand retracing its agonizingly slow path to my face just before he tenderly pushed a strand of hair back from my eyes, tucking it behind my ear. "I promised I wouldn't let them take you. That afternoon at the barn," he clarified, as if I didn't know. "But they did. I've broken promises. Even to you."

"They would have killed you. You didn't *let* them take me— you were standing up to go another round. *I* let them take me. I negated your promise."

He blinked at me.

"Do you understand? *You* didn't break the promise, Pietr. You've never broken a promise that I know of." I moved closer to him and this time I was the one to reach out. "Although I get the feeling a lot of people have broken promises to you."

He looked down. "Jess, I—"

"Stop torturing yourself. You're a good guy." Grabbing his shoulders I gave him a little shake. "You've always done everything right by me. You've done everything I ask, even when I asked for stupid, stupid things."

"I have," he agreed. "And you did."

I ignored how willingly he agreed and went on. "So relax. You don't need to push. I love you."

His eyes squeezed shut at the words. "I don't know if you should say that. . . ."

"What?" My hands on either side of his face, I turned him to look at me. "I love you. You wanted to hear it. Now *listen* to it, because I've never meant anything as much as I mean this. I love you, Pietr Rusakova."

I waited, watching him watching me, his eyes flashing through the color spectrum as if his brain was trying to make sense of the words I'd spliced together. And I held my breath.

"It's your turn," I finally sputtered. "Unless you don't . . ." My throat tightened.

His eyes widened. "I do. I do love you, Jess. Why would you even wonder?" he marveled, reaching out and gathering me to him. "I don't take a breath without thinking of you. I can't sleep. I barely eat. . . . I do more stupid, reckless things than ever. If that's not love . . ." He stroked my head. "I love you, Jess. And," he pushed me back suddenly, "you're making me crazy."

He ran his hand through his hair, muttering something in Russian. "I'm seventeen in human years and older as an oborot. I'm in my prime and . . ." He muttered something else and although I didn't understand the words, I recognized the frustration.

Very clearly.

"I'm sorry, Jess." He shrugged like that would soften the reality. "I want you. Like . . ."

"You think I don't want you?"

His lips tightened into a thin, pale line.

"I do. *Ugh*. Boy, do I. But not here. Not in this place. We deserve the right place. The right time. Don't you agree?"

"I don't know if I'm so picky." He laughed, rubbing at his forehead.

I tilted my head and looked at him.

"But for you, Jess—anything."

"Pietr. We're here. Together. Safe. We love each other. That's so much already. A little more time. I know what it means to ask that."

He nodded and the end of his lips twisted up into a slow smile. "Okay," he agreed. But I noticed a strain shadowing his normally bright eyes. He sighed, straightened, and stretched, brushing past me to reach for the shower's faucet.

"Shower?" I asked.

He nodded, mute. He swung his head to the side, looked at me darkly, and cranked the faucet as far as it'd go to the right.

Cold.

"A little more time," he said with a sigh.

Laughing, I left the bathroom, leaving Pietr to his privacy.

CHAPTER FIFTEEN

Jessie

It wasn't long before Pietr was out of the shower, back in his shirt, socks, and jeans and sitting cross-legged at the foot of my bed, hair damp and spiked in all directions in a wild tousle. I loved the soft wild pine forest scent that naturally marked Pietr, but I realized I loved him even more fresh from the shower. I'd probably be turning the faucet to cold at this rate, too.

"Feeling better?" I asked.

"*Da.*" He shook his head, spraying water at me, a devilish look lighting his eyes.

I smacked him playfully and suddenly found myself pinned to the bed, Pietr's wet head mopping across my face. "Hey!" I yelped, struggling and giggling until I finally held his face in my hands.

He grinned wickedly at me as he rested just above me, propped on his elbows and knees.

"You pain," I muttered, kissing him once before shoving him away. Something I couldn't have done if he hadn't let me.

He fell beside me on the narrow bed, bouncing my heart into

my throat, and curling one of his lean and powerful arms under his head so he could peer at me more easily. "Talk to me, Jess."

I rolled to face him. "Whatcha' wanna talk about?"

His eyes ran the length of my body and I blushed.

"Expectations."

"Oh. Like . . ." I was suddenly an absolute idiot. "Oh. You want to talk about *sex?*" I squeaked out the last word.

"I don't ever want to disappoint you, Jess."

"You won't," I assured him.

"Uh, statistically speaking . . ."

"Down, boy. *What* were you doing while I wasn't around?"

He sputtered. "I read some statistics. . . ." He covered his eyes with his other arm and peeked out at me.

I laughed. "What did the statistics say?"

"Chances are . . . you'll be disappointed," he confessed, flopping onto his stomach on the bed.

I snorted. *My alpha.* "And you didn't read anything that said it'll be perfect?"

He turned his head to look at me and blinked. Pietr, with his defenses down, just tore at my heart.

I pointed to my face. "Well, read *this*, Pietr Andreiovich Rusakova. It will be perfect because it will be us. You. Me. Because we love each other and are being smart."

"*Da?*"

"*Da,*" I assured. "Because I believe in us more than I believe in anything. Go to sleep. We're getting out of here as soon as Dad picks up the lawyer."

Pietr shifted beside me.

"Where are you going?"

"To bed," he said, confused.

I pushed on his shoulder. "You're already there. Sleep. Nobody ever bothers to check on us until breakfast," I yawned. "I'm off to take a shower," I said, carefully picking my way over him and off the bed.

I felt his eyes on me the whole way to the bathroom, curious and hungry.

Jessie

In the middle of the night I curled in the bed, resting my head on Pietr's warm chest. He stiffened beneath my touch, his breath catching, and suddenly I heard his heart race forward, beating frantically. "Shhh," I soothed, snuggling closer with a sigh.

He put a tentative arm around me. "Jess," he murmured sleepily.

"Mmhmm."

His heart rate slowed and his arm became a warm weight across my shoulders.

I drifted off.

I started awake to the sensation of eyes on me. "Oh," I whispered. "Pietr."

His eyes, bright and red as warning, blinked at me in the thin light radiating from two beams that cut the room in two, the scant moonlight meeting the light from the small window in the hall and leaving a strange splotch of white, like spilled milk, on the concrete floor.

His breathing hitched at the sound of his name.

"Jess," he whispered. He grabbed my hand and ran it down his shirt, groaning at my hesitant touch. When my hand paused at the top of his jeans his grip on me tightened, his hand trembling around mine. His eyes slitted so I only glimpsed the thinnest glare of red, he mumbled, "I need . . ."

"What, Pietr?" But I knew, my body responding with a heat of my own even with the cool night air like a narrow wall between us.

He sat bolt upright, dropping my hand. "I need to sleep on the floor," he snapped, dragging in a breath. "Sorry," he muttered as he clambered off the bed, the mattress squeaking in protest. "Mad at myself. Not you."

I stayed perfectly still until I heard him settle onto the cold concrete slab with a rumbling sigh of self-loathing. My body electrified by his proximity, and at war with the promise we'd made, I pulled the pillow from beneath my head, pressed it tightly to my face, and screamed.

Pietr didn't say a word.

He understood.

Jessie

"Mmm." Pietr adjusted his position, balanced on the edge of my bed, careful to keep a distance between us, though he'd crawled up onto the bed at some point in the night while I dozed.

"Tomorrow you're getting out of here, one way or the other. And when we're ready to leave, if things go badly, you need to trust I can handle the guards." He must have seen my eyes fill with panic because he reached out and took my hand, carefully spreading my fingers and examining each one. "Trust me, Jess."

"Pietr," I protested, wrapping my fingers around his. "Things are—*wrong*—here."

"You're getting out tomorrow," Pietr said. "Unless they're making werewolves in the cellar or storing bodies in the basement, I don't care about anything else going on here—other than you getting out."

Very slowly I touched my finger to the tip of my nose and tapped it twice. "Almost. They're trying to *cure* werewolves."

He blinked, realizing what my signal implied. "Werewolves? Bodies in the . . . ? Crrrap, Jess! What sort of town do you live in?"

"A typical hot dog- and hamburger-eating, football- and baseball-loving, werewolf-wanting small-town American sorta town." I took a breath. "Where everyone thinks they know everything about everyone else. So, just as typically, no one knows anything about what's *really* going on."

"It doesn't matter," he insisted. "You can tell me all about it later. We have a schedule to keep. Things are happening. Fast. Everything's finally lining up." He sighed. "Tomorrow you're out of here. Trust me."

"I can't stop thinking about that day. . . ." My voice faded into a whine and he looked down, a muscle in his jaw jumping.

"Things will be different this time," he assured me. "I know what they are—monsters." He nodded bleakly. "Something that shouldn't exist. Like me."

I squeezed his hand. "If I had a gun . . . I want to be able to take care of myself. I used to handle things pretty well."

"Even if you had a gun—and you're an amazing shot—" he added, "it would barely matter to your guards."

"So you'll *kill* Fred and Jeremy . . . ?"

"*Nyet*. They aren't technically alive."

"Right. Zombies."

He shrugged at the word. "That research was also done during the Cold War."

I leaned toward him. "People researched how to make zombies during the Cold War? Weren't there enough problems without making new ones?"

He snorted. "Alexi says they researched reanimation of dead tissue as early as the forties. Rat brains reacted like they were still alive for eight minutes after true death," he explained. "That was done with simple electronics and a clumsy understanding of the brain." He held my gaze.

"Imagine what's being done now. Oh. Wait, I don't have to," I said grimly. "So their tattoos mean . . ."

"*Life*. In Hebrew. Someone had a sense of humor designing the electronics that keep them moving. Here." He tugged me close, bold again. "Think of the tattoos as key parts of tiny circuit boards. The circuitry runs through most of their bodies at a subdermal level, deep enough to trigger muscle control and some sense of coordination. They don't feel anything, so they don't get hurt."

"They're like high-tech strings pulling on oversized puppets," I realized, rolling over to curl my back into his chest and stomach. My toes crept between the bottom of his pants legs and the top of his socks, tickling the hair on his legs. He twitched, stiffening at the contact. "For people without ink of our own we sure are learning a lot about tattoos."

His heart sped, thrumming in his chest. "What else do you know about tattoos, Jess?" His whispered breath stirred the hair at the top of my head.

"Some stuff about which tatts mean what in the Russian Mafia."

He rested his chin on my head and sighed.

"Church spires and steeples count for one murder apiece, spiderwebs are about addiction, and captains in the organization get stars on their chest. It would be so much easier to spot the bastards if they went around shirtless."

Pietr was silent.

I nudged him. "So zombie Fred and Jeremy. Their tatts," I prodded.

"In traditional Hebrew lore—"

I twisted around in his grasp to kiss the point of his jaw, the tender spot right beneath his chin. "By the way," I whispered. "I'm very proud you've become research-boy in my absence. I knew you'd be fine without me."

Again he sighed. "In traditional Hebrew lore there are stories of golems—things crafted out of clay to appear like men and brought to life through magic and prayer. Part of the magic was in the letters of the word. Together the symbols gave life. But remove one and—dead again."

"A very good movie."

"What?"

"Sorry. Being a little random. Zombies—uhm. Golems. It's a bit much to take in."

He held me by the shoulders and moved me back from where I rested so he could search my face. "I don't want to ever push your limits. If you don't want to know something, tell me. About anything. About me—whatever."

I reached up, taking his face in my hands. "I want to know everything about you, Pietr. Everything." I rubbed my hand along his jaw, feeling the subtle scratch of stubble across my palm and then my fingertips.

His eyes fluttered shut.

"What did you do while I was here?" I whispered, still petting him. "Where did you go? What did you do?"

There was a tightness around his eyes, a subtle shift in his expression. "I learned a few things," he whispered noncommittally. "Made a few friends." And then his eyes popped open and he grabbed my arm, tugging me off the bed. "Here. Let me show you what I learned."

"As long as it's nothing to do with trigonometry."

He sighed, exasperated. "*Nyet*, it has nothing to do with trig. I am so far behind in classes . . . ," he growled. "But it does have to do with geometry . . . and physics," he said with a grin.

"Oh?"

He stood me before him and stepped back a couple paces, bending his knees and lowering his center of gravity.

"Uh. What did you say you learned?" I asked, my voice rising as I noticed the glint in his eyes.

"A little of this and a little of that," he teased, shifting his weight and studying me. "Some Sambo, Systema—rukopashka, really."

"What?"

"Rukopashka," he repeated. "Hand-to-hand." He nodded. "Come on. Attack me."

"Er . . ." Totally counterintuitive.

"Come on, Jess." A growl rose up and folded into a purr, teasing me.

I lunged at him and was on the ground in a heartbeat, pinned by Pietr, his hand cradling my head to protect it from the concrete floor. "Ow."

His eyes peered into mine. The heat of him warred with the cool floor beneath my back, my body a battleground of hot and cold. "You okay?" he whispered.

"Mmm," I said, taking a quick mental inventory. Yep. Still okay. "That was . . . impressive. Whatever that was," I admitted, still stunned.

He laughed, his body so close it shook me.

I reached to the bottom of his T-shirt, my hands running along its edge, and I started to pull it up, but he glanced at the window over his shoulder—at the moonlight pouring through to illuminate us—and tugged free of my grip on his shirt, pulling it back down.

"What?" I said as he stood and pulled me back to my feet.

He stepped away, his back to the window.

I lunged and he took me down. Again.

This time he looked at me coolly. "In Systema, you learn to distract your opponent." He kissed my cheek and I rolled my head to try and catch his lips with mine. But he'd already moved on, peppering my face with quick kisses. "And"—he said between pauses to brush his lips across me—"you learn to use your opponent's body and momentum against them."

"Mmm. Like Judo, right?"

"In some ways, *da*," he agreed. And then he was on his feet again, his hand reaching down for me.

My body again warred with my mind and the promise I was determined to keep and yet so ready to break. I sighed, sat, and stuck my hand out, letting him pop me to my feet.

"You'd better get some sleep."

I nodded. "Yeah. Come here first." I motioned to the bed. "Curl up beside me for a couple minutes. Till I drop off."

He was torn, looking at the bed as if it was some new challenge to surmount. He nodded and lay down, as close to the bed's far edge as he could get.

"I don't have cooties."

He remained where he was, a study in control and tension.

"For God's sake, relax, Pietr," I whispered, rolling my head across the pillow to watch him, daring him to obey. My eyes fluttered and I heard myself sigh a moment before things went black.

I didn't even feel the mattress shift when he carefully removed himself from the bed and disappeared beneath it. It was only when my arm flopped out and my hand hung limp and cool in the nothingness over the bed's edge that I realized he'd moved.

Jessie

"Only a few more hours," I whispered, hanging over the edge of my bed to peer at Pietr, curled under it.

He growled.

"Hey. Come out of there." I snaked a hand beneath the bed.

He looked away, rolling back to avoid my touch.

"What's wrong? Other than the fact you slept on a cold floor most of the night," I added, swinging around so my bare feet touched down.

Pietr said nothing.

With a sigh I lay down on the concrete just beyond the shadowy recess under the bed.

Pietr watched me with narrow eyes.

"Are you hungry?" I asked, knowing guys got crabby if there wasn't something to eat.

His eyes went even narrower and he bit off the single-syllable reply. "*Da.*"

"Okay then. I'll go for breakfast—just long enough to bring some stuff back for you."

His hand reached out to me, stroking along the soft part of my wrist. I shivered. "That may not do it," he admitted softly.

I stood up. "Get up. Now."

With a growl he obeyed, keeping to the shadow and farthest from any view someone pausing by the hall window might have.

"I don't want any complaining from you. We agreed to stick to the promise we made. We kept it. If you think it's easy for me to keep you at bay—well, it's not. The arguments against doing it are on constant repeat in my brain and yet the moment you look at me—the moment you touch me . . . the words all fall away." I shifted from foot to foot. "Stop it," I commanded. "You're looking at me that way again."

He looked down.

"As much as I want you—and I do want you, Pietr, believe me," I said with a strained laugh, "I want even more for us to be smart about this. This is big," I emphasized. "There's no going back once we do this thing, you know?"

"I know," he snapped. "In my head, I understand. I get it. Waiting is logical. Smart. Maybe waiting a long time," he said with a suddenly crazed expression. "But I get close to you and . . ." He growled out his frustration. "And my brain stops working and everything else . . . kicks in instead."

I avoided mentioning that I had noticed.

"You know why I love you?"

He blinked. "*Nyet*. I have absolutely no idea. But I can name the reasons you shouldn't."

"I can, too."

He blinked again, stunned.

"But they're nothing compared to why I do love you. They can't stand up against that."

"So why, Jess?"

"Because of your brain." I reached up and gave his forehead a playful thump with my fist. "Because of your heart and your soul." I tapped his chest. "Your body—that thing throwing your brain off-line? It's ahh-mazing," I admitted. "But it's like the icing on a cake that's already too good."

I held his gaze with my own. "Keep your body in check, Pietr. It's the rest of you I'm after." I reached up and stroked his jaw, then dropped my hand, stepping back. "Just a little more time."

"A little more time," he agreed, rubbing the heels of his hands into his eye sockets. "I'll give you time, Jess," he assured me. "All the time I have."

I touched his arm and headed to the door.

With a sigh he slipped back under the bed.

Jessie

That morning Christian was buzzed into my room from the outside.

"Put that over there." I kept to the room's perimeter, the single chair between us. "It's early for laundry," I complained, glancing out the window. The sun was still low in the sky, shadows slanting.

He ignored my comment, instead looking at the assortment of food on the chair's seat. "Having a little celebration since you're leaving?"

"Sort of," I said, keeping my eyes on him as he set the laundry down on the chair's edge. For a moment my focus shifted and I looked at the clothes. "If they've accepted that I'm leaving, why the laundry?"

"Nurse says it's become standard procedure now that there's nearly constant hospital overflow."

I set down the muffin I was peeling the paper from, having lost my appetite at the thought of the people still coming in as I was on my way out. I sighed. "At least they believe I'm on my way out, too."

"That's the great thing," Christian stated, his eyes beady

and fixed on me. "Anyone can get out of here if they're just willing to work for it." He took a step forward, dragging the chair
out of his path, its feet chattering on the concrete.

I glared at him. "Don't start with me." I'd handle his ad-
vances better this time. I picked up a cup of orange juice. "You
try to ram your tongue down my throat one more time and
you'll get a face full of orange juice. And citric acid in the eyes?
Burns like a bitch."

Grabbing me so fast I yelped, he squeezed my hand until the
cup crumpled. Between my fingers orange juice ran, dripping
onto the floor.

"You've got the wrong idea, Jessica," he said, eyes shining.
"My signing myself out only relates to you so much."

I tried to pull free from his hand. I smacked at him with my
left.

"If you die peacefully, I get my fee and walk."

"What?"

He grabbed the stack of clothes and gave them a shake.
They unfurled to reveal a knotted length of sheets tied into a
cruel-looking rope. "Make it look like a suicide, Jones said. But
no spilling of blood." He tilted his head and looked at me,
speculating. "Why did she specify that? What's so special about
your blood that someone wants it to die in your veins, choked
of oxygen?"

"Christian," I whispered, casting a look toward the bed, "Let
me go. Now."

He hooked a foot around the leg of my chair and dragged it
forward a pace, glancing up at the light fixture in the ceiling.

Stunned, I opened my mouth.

"Wanna scream?" he suggested. "You know it doesn't do any
good in these upgraded rooms. Crazy, isn't it? More privilege
means more danger." He pulled me tight to him and growled in
my ear. "Come on," he suggested. "Try and make a deal with me.
What'll you give up to live? What's your life worth?"

"Yours and a dozen morrre," Pietr snarled, bursting from

beneath the bed to grab Christian by the back of his neck and pull me free.

I tumbled to the ground with a cry and stared up at Christian, hanging in Pietr's grip.

Christian definitely looked surprised.

I recognized the familiar pop of Pietr's joints as they slipped and slid, readjusting as the wolf clawed out from his heart and filled up his skin. His hands changed first, enlarging, settling somewhere between paws and human hands, nails lengthening to wicked claws as tremors shook along Pietr's arms and shoulders.

The wolf raced through his blood, strengthening him with its wildness and he fought it for control, holding his change at something terrifyingly between man and beast—something nature never intended but man was eager to make.

Pietr panted, his eyes strange, feral and somehow new. Different and more dangerous than the eyes he'd always turned toward me. And I realized what I was watching glint and form in them—murder.

"Don't kill him," I begged.

"Why?" Pietr growled.

"Because that isn't you. You aren't a killer."

His eyes blinked shut for a fraction of a heartbeat. When they reopened they sparked with greedy hellfire. "He'd gladly kill *you*. You'd let him live so he can come against us again? Learn from his mistakes?" He shook Christian. "Make allies?"

"He won't, Pietr, he won't!" Christian's sneakers scraped in slow arcs across the floor as he strangled in Pietr's powerful grip. "Say you won't, Christian! *Promise!*"

Christian mumbled something and Pietr adjusted his hold so he could get a few words out from under the press of Pietr's powerful fingers. "I promise . . . ," he choked, eyes bulging.

"Look away, Jess," Pietr commanded. "Look away now."

My heart crashed to a stop. "Oh, god—what will you do?"

"What I failed at before. I'll protect you. I've learned a few things, Jess," he whispered. "*You* are my life. My light. What matters."

I remembered the picture he'd given me for my birthday, the one that now hung over my bed at home—*Vassilissa in the Forest*. The girl holding the glowing skull to light the path ahead.

"Nothing else," he whispered, "*almost* nothing else matters."

I threw myself at Pietr's feet. "He promised, Pietr . . . please . . . for *me* . . ." My eyes begged even after my voice failed.

The red drained from Pietr's eyes as the wolf left him and the things that were most monstrous, most cruel, about him tucked themselves away once more beneath a soft and sleek human hide. His fingers peeled back from Christian's neck and he dropped him to the ground in a heap.

A still-breathing heap.

I grabbed Pietr's leg, wrapping my arms around it in gratitude. "Thank you."

His voice was thick as he reached down to pull me up. "I hope we don't regret this," he muttered. "Grab your things."

Knocked suddenly to the ground, I barely heard Christian's snarl above the roar of my pulse as Pietr again pulled him off me and grabbed him by the neck, arm quaking with rage.

Utterly human and utterly brutal, Pietr peered into my attacker's eyes.

This time I looked away until I'd heard the crunch of bones and the pop of flesh and knew the deed was done. Dropped to the floor like a worthless doll, nothing about Christian gave the impression of life any longer.

My voice wavered in a whisper. "Is that one of the things you learned while you were away . . . to show no mercy?" Pietr's image blurred before me as tears streamed down my face.

"*Da*," he whispered, his eyes changing from red to purple to a blue so cold I trembled beneath the bite and burn of it.

"What else did you learn?"

He pulled me to my feet, his fingers fierce on my arms.

"That everyone breaks promises. Everyone lies. He chose *then* to lie," he added. "To bargain for his life and then betray it—to try to kill you *again*. Bad idea." He grabbed my wrist and I flinched back in fear.

This was not my Pietr. . . .

He pulled off his pants and thrust them into my hands. There was no modesty or hesitation in his movements. "Your guards will be coming. He should have been back out by now. Stay behind me and be ready."

The guards burst through the door, leaving it hanging awkwardly off one hinge with the force of their entry.

Pietr flashed into his wolfskin, teeth sharp as knives. He rushed the nearest one, biting into his wrist and tearing the electronic tattoo away so flesh hung in a chunk, suspended by oozing tubes and thin wires that popped, flared, and flickered.

The guard looked as close to startled as he could and crumpled to the floor. His mirror image, staring, moved to cover its matching wrist tattoos somehow—

—moments too late.

In a heartbeat the second guard was reduced to a heap of poorly stitched body parts, too.

The wolf spun to face me and I reached under my pillow for the cell phone and my journal but noticed the phone on the floor. I didn't have time to wonder before the wolf dodged behind me and slipped his snout between my ankles, bouncing me onto his back.

I snagged hold of his furry back and leaned in as he bolted through the door to the hallway, sliding on the polished floor as he scrabbled toward the main doors leaving nothing in his wake but startled faces and shrieking patients.

His stride lengthened and he quickly carried me out of the building and to the far end of the parking lot nearest the trees and the road. He paused, lifting his head to catch a scent, and I tumbled off him, snapping the cell open to call Dad.

"Jessie?"

"Grab the lawyer and be prepared. I'm out, but . . . it's gonna take some damage control, Dad," I said as Pietr slipped back into his pants. "Pietr stopped the guy from killing me, but . . ."

Pietr's gaze flicked to me, cool as steel.

". . . the guy wasn't so lucky. And there are additional bodies. But—they've been dead awhile. No. Think zombies."

Pietr turned away, crossing his arms over his chest.

"Oh," Dad mumbled.

"I'm calling Max to get us," I said, as much to Dad as to Pietr. "Can you handle this, Dad?"

"I'll have to."

Pietr looked at me. "We're going. Now." He swung his head back toward the front doors of Pecan Place.

An alarm blared and nurses and guards, human-seeming guards, flowed out of the building.

Pietr put his arms out for me. To carry me.

Spotlighted by the glowing light of morning something dark stained his outstretched hand.

Blood.

Nearly dry. Nearly just a memory. *Nearly.* I stepped back. Unwilling to let him carry me, I wondered how long I could run on a knee that was still occasionally weak from Derek's previous assault.

I called Max.

Pietr reached for me and I stepped back, eyes still locked on the blood on his hand.

I shook my head at Pietr.

His gaze dropped away from my face, realizing why I hesitated. Staring at his bloody hand, he crouched, rubbing it clean in the frost that sparkled on the browning blades of grass.

Pietr stood, reaching for me again, and I flinched away. His expression darkened, eyes stormy, lips thin and tight.

I shook my head, *no.*

Pietr slid something from his pocket and held it over his head, glowering at me. He pressed a button.

"Allo?"

"Max. I need you to pick us up."

"In the car," Max rumbled. "Pecan Place?"

A vein rose by Pietr's hairline as I opened my mouth to say *yes* to Max. He turned his back to me and watched the milling of the staff back by the building's opening.

Kicking at the grass lining the parking lot, every muscle in his back and arms went tight. He dropped into a crouch, scrubbing his hands across his face and head.

He wanted to shout—maybe curse—but didn't dare because it'd draw unwanted attention. So Pietr worked out his aggression silently for our safety—*my* safety—while I watched.

I heard the squeal of tires and a small dark car pulled up beside us, the passenger door flinging open. Pietr rose and in one fluid move threw me in, pushing in beside me and yanking the door shut.

We sped away.

"Jessie?" Max's growl reverberated in the receiver.

I looked at the driver. Short hair, sharp features, slightly graying around the temples. Strong, tough and sure.

Ex-military?

His posture spoke of authority—leadership material of some sort.

He and Pietr were engaged in a heated conversation. In Russian.

"Jessie!"

"A ride's already here, Max." I snapped the cell shut and wondered what I'd fallen into this time.

CHAPTER SIXTEEN

Jessie

Cat and Amy grabbed me the moment Pietr shoved me through the door at the Rusakovas' house. They murmured and stroked my hair and hugged me again and again, but I couldn't focus on them at all. No matter where he paced, the older man behind him, railing on in Russian, my eyes focused only on Pietr.

"What's really going on here, Cat?" I whispered. "Who's that guy?"

"*Uncle* Dmitri." Her eyes tugged free of mine to follow him. Her words stiff, she said, "He's come to help."

Amy shrugged. "Glad you're back."

Cat took my hand and led me to the kitchen. "You need to make a phone call," she said. "To your father."

Instantly I knew what she meant. As hard as it was going to be for him to accept, the Rusakovas would be better able to protect me than Dad could. Besides, any attempt he made to protect me would simply place him in the line of fire.

"Give me that first," Pietr said, his hand out for my cell.

"What?"

"Consider it insurance," he muttered, heading for the computer. I followed him.

He connected the cell phone to the computer and downloaded a brief video file.

"Hey," I said, seeing Christian unfurl the makeshift rope in my room back at Pecan Place. The perspective was strange. . . . I looked at Pietr. He'd shot the clip from under the bed. While I thought I could still handle things, he was handling them in a different way.

Pietr tapped a few keys. "The audio's not crisp, but it's understandable."

I clutched the back of his chair, the memory doubling in intensity as the video rolled.

"Now . . ." He pulled up the website for Pecan Place and hit the staff button. It took a moment, but he opened an e-mail account I didn't recognize, typed in Dr. Jones's address, and attached the file, his message only reading:

> You've been named in this video. Keep your distance or everyone will see it.

He tapped send and, disconnecting the phone, handed it back to me. "Call your dad."

Mute, I nodded, watching as Pietr strode from the room, Uncle Dmitri close behind.

Dad picked up on the first ring and I wandered into the kitchen.

"Dad," I said before he even finished his hello, "I'm not coming home. It's safer this way. The Rusakovas can protect me. Alexi's coming over now to draw some of Annabelle Lee's blood. This'll all be over soon."

He was very quiet and I imagined him working it all out in his head. "Okay, Jessie. You be careful."

"Don't worry, Dad. I will. About everything."

"Good girl. I love you."

"I love you, too, Dad." I set the cell phone down, my hand trembling.

Alexi leaned into the kitchen. "I'm going now."

Cat nodded and pulled out a pot.

"Er—can I help with anything, Cat?"

She looked at me, lips twitching into a smile. "I have it, Jessie," she said. "You have been gone quite a while, really. My cooking has improved. Alexi and Max are coping. . . ." She paused and her eyebrows drew together. She shot a worried look at Amy.

Amy shrugged.

"And Pietr?" I prodded.

Amy glanced over her shoulder toward the window that looked out over the backyard. I pushed past her to see Pietr and Dmitri circling each other. My heart settled back into its normal pace realizing they were sparring, not fighting. *"Rukopashka,"* I realized aloud.

"Da," Cat answered as if I'd asked a question.

"Uncle Dmitri's wicked fast for an old guy," Amy commented, watching Dmitri dodge Pietr, block an attack, and land a kick in his gut.

I winced, but Pietr took it in stride, falling back a half pace and watching for an opening, an advantage before he lunged in and connected with Dmitri. A hit that should have knocked Dmitri on his ass only pushed him back a few paces. "Strong, too," I muttered, turning back to Cat.

She continued mixing and stirring.

I continued wondering just who Dmitri was. Uncle? I doubted the title was accurate.

Watching fearfully as Cat stirred the now bubbling something on the stovetop, I said, "Hey, your clock . . ."

Cat shook her head.

"What?" I asked, looking at Amy.

"Beats me. Max says it's bad luck to mention anything about it. Must be a Russian thing."

"Huh." It wasn't a Russian thing last time I'd been here. . . .

I took a moment and looked back into the sitting room. The clock there was wrong, too. "Seriously?" The dining room . . . No downstairs clock held the actual time, and all were different. I stepped back into the kitchen, confusion clear on my face.

Cat shut me down. "*Nyet*, Jessie. Do not mention it."

They were all set at least two hours ahead of time. I paused by the calendar. There were no marks, no notes, no dates after the day I'd been forced to enter the hospital. It was like time—the very thing the Rusakovas were most closely attuned to—was being ignored.

There was no timing instrument more accurate than an oborot's internal clock, so maybe to them the rest meant nothing. But to a simple human like Amy or me or—I glanced out the window and saw Dmitri deliver a startling blow—okay, not Dmitri, then, but to simple humans, it would . . .

I blinked, thinking back to Pietr's words. "They have Derek and he's watching. . . ." To a remote viewer like Derek, it might be enough to confuse what he was seeing with real time. . . . Was Derek arrogant enough to think that given his amazing set of abilities he might also occasionally get a glimpse of the future?

Yes.

His arrogance might even be enough to make him believe there was more time to react to a Rusakova attack on the CIA bunker. Lull him and the agents into a false sense of security so their reaction came too late.

It was a strange idea—a long shot, but who knew? "One of Pietr's new philosophies?" I finally asked Cat.

"*Da*," she said softly, realizing I'd caught up.

She set a bowl before me and I ate a delicious concoction I would have never imagined Cat being able to put together. And I realized, glancing out the window again at Pietr and Dmitri circling each other, a lot had changed while I was gone.

Jessie

Amy dragged me down to the street corner to buy a newspaper out of the metal-and-glass dispenser. Sitting together on the curb, the first headline we spotted announced another Teen Train Track Suicide. "So how many is that now?" I asked her. "Five?"

"I think it's six. Garr. It's all grim news. Students getting sick. Those visiting professional wrestlers who disappeared right around the time you headed—*away*."

Fred and Jeremy? They were big. Wrestler big.

"And the moratorium on burials—"

"Moratorium?" I said.

Amy was breaking out some big words.

"Yep. A special environmental police rep put an end to burying people because of some issues with shifting waterways. Can you believe it? Jack Jacobsen was cremated."

"No." I thought back to Jack's body in the refrigerator, in line to be used for zombie parts. "I can't believe it." Holy crap. Environmental police covering up disappearing bodies? How deep did this weirdness run? Was everyone in Junction in on this?

I looked at the photo and caption partway down the page. "Hey. Mark Millford?" I tapped it. "Wasn't he second string on the football team? One of Derek's cronies?"

She nodded and leaned her head on my shoulder.

Derek. *Feeding.* Murdering to get one last good jolt out of his prey.

"Oh, please, Jessie. Forget all the wacky crap going on around here for a minute or five. Pass me the comics."

"I don't think there are—"

"Of course there are comics. They're the only redeeming feature to the newspaper. Without comics, newspapers would just be crap, crap, and more crap."

"And sports," I said.

She rolled her eyes and said, "*See above.* Crap."

"You're in a precious mood."

"Sorry. I missed you gobs. You're my best friend."

I wrapped an arm around her. "You're my best friend, too."

"They told us you were away at some writers' camp," she said. "I didn't believe it. You would have totally blabbed if you'd been selected for something that cool."

I smiled. "True."

"Max finally broke and took me to see you, but they wouldn't let us in," she said. "But I knew you hadn't gone off to some camp. Pietr's here. You wouldn't ditch him to learn some new writing technique."

I shifted on the curb, uncomfortable with her assessment. I would have skipped off to anywhere to learn something new about writing. Before Pietr. "A new writing technique?"

"Yeah. What'd they call it? Oh. The fast-draft technique."

"Never heard of it."

"I looked into it," she said.

"What? You did research while I was gone? That's very . . ."

"Unlike me? Yeah. Pietr and I have become nerds in your absence. Maintaining the brainy quota around here without you."

"What'd you learn?"

"Some people can write a whole frikkin' book in two weeks." My jaw dropped. "No."

"Yes. They use this fast-draft method to crank it out. Some pretty darn good books have come out of it, too."

"Well, look at you, saying *frikkin'* and *darn*," I marveled. "Cat's really been cleaning up your language."

She stuck up a single finger.

"But not your attitude. Niiice." I leaned back and let the wind tease my hair out from under my knit hat. "A book in two weeks. I'd like to try that. After all this craziness is over. If it's ever over."

"Maybe I'll write a book, too," Amy suggested.

I rolled my head to look at her, awed. "You could totally do it. You have a very creative mind."

She snorted. "We should both have pen names. But we have time. Like you said: *after* this craziness is over."

"Yeah. What do you know about this craziness?"

"Enough to know when to walk out of the room."

"And you don't want to know any more?"

"Not unless I have to. Look. I'm going back to the trailer tomorrow night."

I realized she hadn't called it *home.* From what I'd seen the morning after my birthday party—her dad hung over so bad, he didn't even know she was gone—it probably hadn't felt like a home for a while.

"Max insisted," she explained. "I'll stay a couple nights, clean the place up, and check on Dad. When you guys say I can come back, I will."

"I've heard worse ideas."

"Max says whatever you guys are doing will work out."

I nodded, watching the way she crushed the newspaper, wrapping her arms around herself. "But Max is ballsy. I don't think he really plans stuff out. . . ."

I chuckled. So some things *hadn't* changed since I'd left. "It'll work out. I'm sure Pietr's been rolling ideas around in his mind a lot."

Amy relaxed, smoothing the newspaper out on the curb between us.

The autumn wind tried to snatch it away but only managed to flip a few pages. "Hey!" I exclaimed. "You're right. There are comics."

"You can learn two lessons from that," Amy sniped. "A: I'm always right, and B: Things are looking up already."

CHAPTER SEVENTEEN

Jessie

Alexi returned with a sample of Annabelle Lee's blood, and a belated—*very* belated, considering we were almost entering Christmas vacation—birthday present for me. He looked at me carefully as he handed it over, setting it in my arms so I felt the weight and recognized the size of it.

Amy leaped up, looking at the package expectantly. "Well, aren't you going to open it?" she said, shifting her weight from side to side. "Who's it from?"

Without even glancing at the poorly affixed tag, I guessed, "Wanda and Dad?"

Alexi nodded.

"I'll open it later," I assured Amy (who immediately looked disappointed). "Now's not the right time."

Alexi nodded again and took the present back. "I'll put it with the others."

Others. Other weapons. There were only so many guns one girl could carry. . . . Just how many beyond us was *Uncle* Dmitri including?

"Your father says he's worried, he loves you, and he knows

you're in a bigger mess than you're saying," Alexi continued his message. "He also said something about an old song, about wanting to send lawyers, guns, and money, but there's little of the latter and the former's scared to death now, so the other will have to be enough."

I smiled. Dmitri looked from Pietr to myself and muttered something. In Russian.

"Stop," I said. "You want to say something? Say it in English. If it's something that shouldn't be said, don't frikkin' say it at all."

His eyes narrowed, "Little girl," he began, his voice heavily accented, "this is no game we are playing. You are a liability. How can Pietr focus when he worries about you?"

Amy stood, placed her hands firmly over her ears, and began singing "Happy Birthday" as she exited the room. She didn't want to know.

"I'm doing my best to make sure he has nothing to worry about." My gaze flicked to where the package from my father and Wanda rested. Guns. *My* guns.

"You must be one hundred percent when we go in, Pietr," Dmitri said. "You cannot worry about her."

Pietr weighed Dmitri's words.

"Send her home," Dmitri insisted.

"Pietr," I growled his name out.

He raised an eyebrow, but his eyes stayed on Dmitri.

"*You* are the alpha," Dmitri said.

"*Pietr.*"

Max began a slow yawn—

Dmitri snapped, "You let your bitch speak to you that way—?"

Which was cut short when Pietr sprang to his feet, knocking down the chair he'd just been sitting in.

"She is no *bitch!*" he roared, so close the ends of Dmitri's short hair quivered in the wake of Pietr's rage.

Dmitri was unmoved. "We see things differently." He shrugged. "Send her home. Watching out for her was not part of our deal."

"Our deal," Piter snarled, "includes everything involved in freeing my mother." He hissed. "She"—he stabbed a finger in my direction—"is involved!"

Dmitri looked at me.

"I've done my part in this bargain," Pietr said, his volume growing soft and even more dangerous. "Do yours."

Dmitri rubbed his chin. "*Da*. You have. Mostly." Dmitri shrugged. "Fine. I will arrange for her to go with some of my men for her part in this."

"I will go with her as well," Cat volunteered.

Pietr nodded, but Dmitri's eyes narrowed. "Will anyone else slow us down?"

Alexi grinned. "We simple humans also have a stake in this event's success. I am going."

Dmitri puffed out his breath in exasperation.

Pietr looked at me, eyes guarded. "Your father?"

"And Wanda." I stared at Alexi, realizing we'd said her name in unison.

He nodded and Dmitri growled. "Will the whole of Junction know of our efforts?"

Pietr chewed his lower lip. "It will be a large party."

"The more the merrier," I said, my voice grim as I tried to catch Pietr's eye.

Dmitri rose from the table and stormed away.

Alexi

The call from Wanda was something none of us expected, but Jessie, Pietr, and I got into the car and headed to Jessie's horse farm, where Wanda waited with files. Jessie's dogs, Maggie and Hunter, rushed the car and Jessie briefly tumbled to the ground with them, letting them lick her face and nuzzle her neck. Pietr and I were far less interesting to them.

Pietr scanned the area, scenting and looking for trouble, his back rigid. This place was Jessie's home—perhaps knowing trouble had come here, too, was more unsettling to him.

The last time they had been here together things had gone very badly. I tried not to think about it.

"Stop, stop." Jessie laughed, one minute batting at the dogs playfully, the next tugging them close.

Pietr paused in his scan, his focus snapping once more to her and his features both hardened and softened at the same time. "Come now," he whispered, reaching down to help Jessie out of the dust.

"Leon's in the barn and will be for a while," Wanda greeted us from the small porch, opening the door and waving us inside. "He's seen this already."

Jessie didn't bother hiding her surprise.

"I—*reconnoitered*—these files from the bunker, thought they might be useful. It was easier than I expected since I'd been an employee at the warehouse before and it seems everyone in the—let's call it the company—prefers data files to file folders."

I nodded. "So you grabbed a paper trail." I was beginning to almost like her.

Almost.

"Yes. Always grab anything labeled with your own name and at least one coworker." She flipped open a file. "The problem is I have nothing that proves the actual CIA—our government—is directly involved. In any way. Because it winds up I'm no longer working for our government. I haven't been since I was transferred here."

"You lied. . . ."

"No," she assured Jessie. "I was absolutely under the impression my employer hadn't changed. I was given no reason to assume otherwise. I continued receiving my pay in the same fashion from what appeared to be the same institution." She pulled out two paystubs.

They looked identical except for the dates.

"One before my transfer. One after."

I nodded.

"But here's the deal. The company I'm a current employee of is the same company that hired *these* people." She flipped open another file, scattering pictures across the tabletop. Some names were different from who I thought the people were, but each face I recognized.

"Our vice principal," Jessie announced, tapping a photo of a friendly looking African-American man, "Perlson. My favorite counselor, Ms. Harnek," she said of a smart-looking blonde. She slid the next one aside.

"Officer Kent," I said, looking at Wanda soberly, "wherever *he's* gotten to."

"I doubt it's much farther than where I left him," Wanda responded crisply.

So she had killed him to protect Jessie. That, I could respect. Liking Wanda became more of a possibility.

"The boy, Derek," I said, seeing the next photo.

Jessie glanced at me.

"We had the dubious pleasure of meeting the last time we were at the bunker."

Wanda broke in. "I wanted to . . ." She stumbled to a stop and tried again. "I'm so sorry I had to close down visitation to Mother. I had to keep up appearances."

"Water under the bridge." I looked at the remaining pictures. "Ah. And this lady was with Derek," I said, seeing the fine-featured brunette.

"Dr. Sarissa Jones," Jessie said.

"Is she not helping the students come to grips with the Teen Train Track Suicides?" I asked.

"Probably lining them up for Derek to feed from. What a screwed-up jerk. . . ." She touched Derek's picture again and Pietr stiffened, watching her.

"That screwed-up jerk warned us about—" But Pietr cut me off with a pained look.

"Warned you about what?" Jessie asked, turning on me.

I put my hands up and deferred to Pietr. He was alpha, let him admit it.

She swung to face him. "Warned you about what?"

"He warned Alexi that you were in danger in the asylum. That they were going to kill you. And he told Alexi to tell me."

Jessie sat down hard. "He warned you to make sure I was safe?"

I leaned into her view. "For his own twisted reasons. Maybe for this—to make you doubt how sick he is."

Pietr stepped back from the table and crossed his arms, watching us with cool eyes.

"It's not enough, is it?" Jessie mumbled.

"What? What isn't enough?"

"Saving me isn't enough to wipe away everything else he's done, is it?"

I stayed still, letting her work it out.

Pietr turned away to look out the window.

"There's a point, isn't there," she asked, "a point we can't come back from? A moment we're no longer redeemable?"

I held my breath.

"*Da*," Pietr replied from the window. "There comes a mo-ment," he agreed, his voice flat.

"Geez, my teenage years weren't this damn dramatic," Wanda muttered, collecting the photos. "Sooo . . . I made some phone calls to an old friend and asked some questions. Being too much trouble at my old job—shut up, Jessie—" she warned, see-ing Jessie briefly brighten, a smart comment at the ready. "So my old boss *auctioned* me off to this company. They run quite an or-ganization. I haven't begun to find all the tendrils. They act just like the CIA, except with different funding. And expectations."

Jessie and I stared at her.

"And they really want your werewolves. Because the guy who helped design them, the one who was second in command to Alexi's grand—whatever—he's alive. They're his pride and joy. He never got full credit on the project and tried a redo years later but was made a laughingstock. So he did other things, chemical engineering and ingestibles, all while still looking into the freaky stuff. He's got his fingers in everything. Guess what one of his sidelines is?"

"No idea," Jessie and I admitted simultaneously.

"Institutional food production and delivery."

"The school food?" Jessie's eyes lost their focus.

Wanda tapped her nose twice. "So what's in the food that most every kid in Junction's eating? Whatever it is, you can bet it's not something good." She flipped the files shut and restacked them.

" 'A stronger, better youth for tomorrow,' " Jessie whispered. "Harnek said something like that to Derek."

"*Nyet*. Not good. You have more files," I said, seeing the stack and the empty file box.

"Yes." She spread them before us.

Jessie seemed to recognize one and opened it immediately. "Sophie. They know what she can do. . . ." She ran her finger down the text of the file. "Senses energy fields and impressions, kirilian photography . . . They don't know she sees ghosts."

Pietr and I looked at her.

She shrugged. "My mom's hanging around. She follows me pretty often, watching."

"*Watching?*" Pietr asked. He swallowed hard.

I snickered at Jessie's expression.

"Yeah," she said. "We're totally grounded when we die for—*ample*—public displays of affection."

Pietr groaned and Wanda cleared her throat. "Well. That certainly falls into the realm of too much information." She closed the file, putting the folders back into the box and kicking it under the nearest chair.

Jessie tapped the table. "So what now? If they're as big as you say, won't they just keep coming and coming?"

"Unless the werewolves are cured, or dead, or they can catch at least one to use for DNA. Or breeding."

"They're not *animals*," Jessie said, recoiling.

"Yes, they are, Jessie. Just like the rest of us," Wanda assured her. "Beasts below the skin. It only matters why we let our inner beast out."

Jessie

Back at the Rusakovas' house Dmitri took the place of honor at the head of the table for dinner and Pietr sat at the opposite end of the table. The food Cat had prepared was remarkably good and although I tried not to, I sounded surprised when I complimented her.

It was as Dmitri tore open a roll that he began to speak. "There is an amazing Russian legend you should hear—about a man who cheated death many times because he knew how to control his heart." He glanced at Pietr.

I leaned forward, intent.

"He was called Koschei the Deathless."

Alexi's glass rattled as he set it down, but he swallowed the drink in his mouth and listened to Dmitri's retelling.

"He had amazing abilities—so great that some claimed they were magical," he said, waving the roll and butter knife dramatically. "And no matter what anyone did to him, no matter what trouble came, no one could hurt him. Why?" He leaned forward, looking at Pietr. "He was *invincible*."

Rocking back in his chair, Dmitri continued, knowing Pietr was enthralled. "But—ah, Dmitri, you say, how is such a thing possible? How can a man become invincible? When Koschei the Deathless was young he removed his heart from his body and set it aside, hidden in a chest on an island far away. *Da*, swords might rip into him, spears might pierce his body, but he had no heart for them to break—"

Pietr's eyes fell on me. So did Dmitri's.

"And so he took his wounds in stride—they were not so

much, only bites into his body. His heart—his soul—was untouchable. He won many fights over . . ."

I saw him pause.

"The years—"

And I realized he'd avoided saying "many."

"And he became a famous character in Russian legends. Because, like a true warrior"—his eyes fixed on Pietr—"he knew
his heart and soul had their place."

Pietr's jaw tightened.

Ohhh. So there was a moral to his little tale. A jab aimed
right at me.

"So how did he finally die?" I asked boldly.

Dmitri paused and then bit into his roll.

"How did he die?" I repeated.

Pietr cocked his head, watching Dmitri.

Dmitri swallowed. Hard. "Eventually someone learned
where he had kept his heart and destroyed it. Tragic."

"So he was never in love?" I prodded.

"What?" Dmitri sputtered.

"He never knew love," I proposed.

Alexi snorted.

"Because if he had," I reasoned, "he would have entrusted
his heart to the woman he loved instead of burying it in some
chest, alone. And a good woman would have protected it. With.
Her. Life." I ripped into my own roll. "Your precious Koschei
the Deathless might have gone on forever if he'd been wise
enough to trust in hope and work for love."

Dmitri was speechless.

Alexi said, "If you study your Slavic mythology, *Uncle* Dmitri, you'll find Koschei was not one to emulate. He was—at
best—a jerk. Having a long life may have been good for him,
but it made many people miserable. Because of the same thing
that kept him alive—the fact he was heartless."

"And being heartless would make even the shortest life mean-
ingless," I concluded.

Amy clapped and Max bit his lips to keep from laughing.

At my side Pietr turned and looked at me with astonished eyes. The hope I saw reflected there, so different from the glow of murder when he'd killed Christian, made me turn away.

I needed time. No matter how I approached it in my head there wasn't enough of that most precious commodity to go around. So I pulled out my chair, excused myself from the table, and dragged Amy away to the basement to talk.

Jessie

Awkward. Amy didn't want to know half of what I did about the Rusakova weirdness, but I needed her generally sharp common sense to help me sort out my heart. I snagged the old office chair from the corner and spun in it, kicking my legs out.

She grabbed the armrests, yanking me to a stop so sudden my head snapped to the side. "You don't drag me away from dinner just so I can watch you get dizzy."

"Sorry."

"Something's eating at you."

"I thought I'd come down here and just spill, but . . ."

"Okay," Amy said. "You ask me a question first. Maybe that'll help." She gave the chair a hard yank and I spun in a slowing circle.

"How's Max?" I asked when the room realigned and there was only one Amy. One was plenty to deal with.

"Oh. My beautiful disaster?"

"Um. Yes?"

"I don't know. I can't read him." She shrugged, shoulders nearly at her ears.

Instead of asking when there'd been subtext about Max to read, I tried, "What's he doing?"

"It's . . . oh, God. Can we just not talk about this? Let's try your problem again."

"Not if you're—like *this*." I mimicked the way she shifted uncomfortably on her bed. "You're not the only one who's changed since I went away. I want to pay better attention. Be a better friend."

"That's a sucky revelation to have when I wanna be ignored."

"Timing. So what's Max gone and done?"

"It's what he's—what we're—*not* doing." She peeked up at me and blushed.

"Pretend I'm stupid, Amy." At the moment it didn't seem far from the truth. My brain had stumbled to a stop. "Tell me what you two *aren't* doing."

"*It.*"

"Oh. Kay." I froze, suddenly very aware of why so many parents avoided talking to teens. "What's it?"

She hesitated.

"Oh. Ohhh. *That* it." There were few things I was uncomfortable hearing about. *It* topped the list. "You two aren't doing *it.*" I ended the sentence with air quotes. *Be a better friend.* Okay. "Talk to me."

"Look," she said, "it's just this—relationship stuff—is different with Max than with Marvin."

"It darned well better be," I replied. "If I ever find out Max's treated you anything like Marvin did, I'd have Pietr and Alexi beat the crap out of him."

She sniffed. "Whatever happened to that theory of forgiveness you were so keen on?"

"I believe in forgiveness," I stated. "And redemption. But people who do bad stuff—like beat on their girlfriends—need to *want* forgiveness and redemption, need to *want* to change."

BINGO. I straightened in my seat, recognizing my epiphany. Pietr wanted redemption. Pietr wanted to do the right thing. But Pietr kept getting thrown into situations where black and white weren't any clear part of the visual spectrum and everything was a murky and dangerous sludge of gray. And some choices— horrible choices—were the only means to a better end.

Desperate times. Desperate measures.

"It doesn't matter how badly *I* want those things for them." She nearly sidetracked me alluding to my mistakes with Sarah. "But this isn't about me. Has Max done anything?"

"No," she insisted. "That's what has me so confused."

"What do you mean?"

She crossed her arms over her chest and tried to look as tough as when she'd first started dating Marvin. Amy against the world. Amy, whose best friend's head was so filled with her own issues she'd forgotten everyone else had issues, too.

Her tough-girl act no longer came as naturally.

"Sleeping over here is different from sleeping over at Marvin's," she began. "With Marvin, certain things were expected. He made everything very clear. I never had to second-guess."

"Because if you did something he didn't like he hit you."

Focusing on a spot over my shoulder, she avoided my eyes. "Yes."

Realizing *she* felt shame because *he* hit her, I felt awful. She believed she'd *let* him hit her. My throat constricted. I wanted to find Marvin and knock his teeth in. "What are Max's intentions?"

"Max hugs me, kisses me, strokes my hair so gently . . . He nearly purrs my name—even though it doesn't have a single *r* in it," she said, puzzled.

"Mmm. Russian boys," I said with a smile.

"Daaa. Russian boys." She allowed herself a giggle. "It's great, but when Marvin did something like that it was a signal."

"For what?"

"Sex."

"Seriously?" Blinking, I recalled how many *signals* I'd seen pass between them at school. "Wow. So if he hugged you—"

"Sex."

"Kissed you—?"

"Definitely sex."

"Petted your hair—?"

"Do I seriously need to repeat myself?"

"Every nice thing he did . . ."

"Got him sex. Yeah. Stupid me."

I shrugged. "There was nothing stupid about the choices you made. You didn't think you had any other ones."

She looked at me, smiling slowly like she was beginning to find an epiphany, too. "Max is . . ." She tried to explain. "Well, he does nice things and you know . . ."

I shook my head. "Not exactly."

"Oh. You and Pietr haven't . . ."

"Nooo." My face felt like it had caught fire, the blush was so hard.

"Smart girl," she congratulated. "If I could have I think I would have stayed a virgin longer. You know. Hindsight?"

"Yeah. It's always twenty-twenty. But don't give me too much credit," I said. "I'm seriously thinking about it. A lot."

She grinned. "Wow, Jessie. There's finally something about you that's really, frikkin' normal." She leaned forward to whisper, "You kinda distanced yourself from normal with the competition shooting stuff, you know. . . ." She winked, having no idea just how far from the norm I'd gone.

But I'd adjusted my standards and broadened my definition of normal. You had to, living in small-town America.

"You're thinking about having sex," Amy teased.

"*Thinking* about it," I stressed.

"A lot?"

"Enough," I admitted. "Not as much as he does!" I cleared my throat. My cheeks still stung from answering Amy's questions. "And Max isn't trying anything with you?"

"Nope. And it's not because he isn't interested. In sex. And not because he hasn't ever done it before."

"Yeah. Definitely not that."

She arched an eyebrow at me.

"Just ask him about Europe. Why do you think he's not trying anything? Wait. Do you *want* him to try something?" God. Sex was confusing and I wasn't even having it!

A slight smile lifted the edges of her mouth. "I guess I worry maybe he just doesn't like me as much as I like him. Maybe I'm with him as a favor to Pietr and you. Like, to make me comfortable."

"Yee-aahh. No way. You may have been blinded by his boyish good looks, or his rugged good looks—whichever, because he is certainly good-looking. . . ." I snorted. "But I know enough about Max to know he's not doing anything with you as a favor to us."

"I guess if he wants me around but doesn't want to go at it like rabbits . . . maybe he's playing the good boy for once."

"You deserve a good guy," I pointed out.

She leaned in, guarding her mouth with a cupped hand. "Don't tell anyone, but I think we may *both* have good guys."

Sighing, deep down I knew what I said next was true. "You're right." I just needed to remind Pietr of the fact.

Jessie

I closed the door behind me and Pietr spun around, coming away from the single round window that held a place between his packed bookshelves. "Jess."

He looked down at the bed between us, looked at me, and then away. He licked his lips and swallowed.

"Who is he, Pietr?" I asked.

"He's the one man who can help us get Mother out." The reluctance in his tone was tempered with challenge.

"That's not enough information and you know it." I avoided the elephant in the room, hoping "Uncle Dmitri" was not the thing that filled my stomach with fear. "He hates me."

"It's not like that," Pietr muttered. "He's looking out for me.

He saved our asses at Pecan Place and knows I would have never done that if it weren't for you. You're the chink in my armor. My Achilles' heel." He looked at me, his voice tight. "If you would have let me carry you . . ."

I shook my head. "No, Pietr, I couldn't. I—" I swallowed.

He sat down heavily in a chair by the window, his face obscured in shadow blanketing the corner of the room. "I've done it, haven't I?" he whispered. "Ruined everything. Alexi always said if you chase two rabbits you lose them both." His voice broke and he stumbled to finish his thought. "I've been trying so hard to get you both . . . you and Mother . . ."

I don't know why I hesitated as his heart was breaking, when everything in me said to run to him. . . . But my feet were suddenly stuck in place by the image of him squeezing the life out of Christian. Not as a wolf. Not as something between man and beast, but as Pietr.

My so often gentle Pietr.

"Oh, *shit*." His chest rose and fell in a sudden flutter. He coughed. His hands twitched on the arm rests, fingers exploring the way they curved. He sighed. "You better just say it then, Jess. Say it and go."

"Say what, Pietr?"

He exploded out of the chair with a volley of pops, to stand before me, his shadow thrown across me, as huge and menacing as he could be, the wolf's head on his quaking shoulders, breath steaming across my face.

I stood my ground.

"Ssay you cannot love a monsterrr," he growled. "Ssay it! You *can't* love me!"

I glared up at him. He was so hungry for forgiveness. I smacked him. *Ow.*

He looked at me, dazed. "Ssay it . . ."

I grabbed his arms and turned with him, the power of my momentum magnified by how unstable his emotions made him. I knocked him onto the bed, climbed up, and straddled his

chest. Leaning forward, I wrapped my fingers around his wolf-
ish snout. "You listen to me, Pietr . . ."

"You shouldn't love meee . . ." His words fell into a whine.
"You don't knooow . . ."

I gave his snout a shake and the whining stopped.

"You don't get to tell me who I love or why. You are *my*
choice, Pietr Andreiovich Rusakova. I love you for *my* reasons!"
I released his snout and sat back. Pondering a moment, I said, "I
think sometimes you don't want anyone to love you. That you
don't think you deserve it."

I arched over him, stroking the wolf's furry cheek until I
heard the pop of the beast releasing its hold, and Pietr's human
face reemerged. And still I petted him, running my fingers gently from his temple to his chin and back again. "I don't know
why you'd want that, Pietr. . . . Loving you is so easy to do. . . .
But you're different," I conceded. "Somehow harder and colder
one moment, then soft and warm the next. Everyone here is
different. You've all moved forward without me."

He closed his eyes and his body shuddered beneath me.
"Jess," he said, like a prayer.

"Yes, Pietr?"

"*Pocelujte menyah.*"

So I took his face in my hands and I kissed him until his eyes
sparkled and my lips tingled and he was Pietr—*my* Pietr—again.

Jessie

In front of the bus stop by the Rusakovas' house, I hopped up
and down to stay warm. Pietr finally grabbed me, tucking me
beneath his jacket with him.

"So tell me again why we're going to school three days
before . . ."

Pietr grinned at me, snuggling tighter against me, his breath
hot on my face. "Because I know your ex likes keeping an eye

on you even more than he wants to watch anything here," he said, motioning back to the house with a toss of his head. "You're our decoy. How do you feel about that?"

"Glad to contribute," I said. "Besides, I have a little sister. I've been called way worse than *decoy*." I smiled and burrowed into his side.

Max huddled with Amy, using his body as a wind block. He carried a duffel bag and backpack. A sad look overrode his normally devil-may-care expression.

"He's going to really miss her," I commented softly, but of course Pietr heard.

"*Da*. He was going to keep her here if she wanted to know the truth, but she doesn't," Pietr explained. "It's not like we can just live a lie forever, you know? At some point she'll choose to know the truth and he'll have to let her go."

"You didn't really give me much of a choice about knowing," I pointed out. "You tied me to a tree and, poof"—I flicked my fingers—"my secret boyfriend's a wolf."

"That's not how I remember it. I told you that you could go. You had a choice."

"Oh, be real, Pietr. I'm an editor for the school newspaper, a research junkie. You seriously thought if you gave me a choice to learn some crazy secret about how you tracked down Annabelle Lee *or* just head back to the house that I would have trotted off?"

"I hoped not."

The bus squealed to a stop and we climbed in, Cat following slowly behind.

I curled up against Pietr, content at the sound of his rapid heartbeat and the warmth of his body. For once the bus ride was too short. And for once I didn't care who saw us together.

All that changed when Sarah, Macie, and Jenny met us inside Junction High.

"Back so soon?" Sarah called out, glaring at me. Her gaze

dropped from my face, trying instead to burn a hole in my hand as it held Pietr's.

Sophie slipped into the midst of our bristling group, addressing me. "Nice to have you back. The place has totally gone into the crapper since you took your little leave of absence. And the school newspaper? It's a hell of a job to do your part and mine at the same time."

"Good to be back, Soph," I said hesitantly. As a group we headed to my locker.

Sarah, Jenny, and Macie followed us, sniping just out of earshot. I sensed a crowd gathering. This wouldn't be good. From the pit of my stomach dread uncurled and I remembered the crowd that had gathered to watch the smackdown between Pietr and Derek.

I looked up at Pietr. He remembered, too. "He's not here. They're nothing."

I pulled my books out and Amy helped shove them into my backpack. I glanced at what I'd expected to be a large group, but really it was just some curious stragglers.

Hospital overflow. Junction High had become a ghost town.

And there was still math class. Paranormal ground zero plus math class seemed like the equation from hell.

Across the hall, Sarah watched me, looking me up and down, her eyes taking in my worn sneakers, last year's off-the-rack jeans, and the T-shirt Annabelle Lee had printed for me that read:

IMPRESS ME WITH YOUR CLEVERNESS.
(NOT GOOD ENOUGH. TRY AGAIN.)

Behind the others I saw Marvin, Amy's ex-boyfriend, and one more of my previous attackers. His eyes dark and circled by shadows, he looked bad. But he wasn't watching me. Or Pietr.

He was watching Amy. From time to time his gaze would

flick to Max, his jaw would tighten—the vein near his temple raised to throb in anger. Then he'd stare at Amy again with anger, disgust, and hunger—a frightening mix.

I got stacks of make-up work. So. Much. Math. Did no one realize I had an integral role to play in the freeing of my were-wolf boyfriend's dying mother from an organization parading around as a legitimate branch of the CIA?

Jessie

I hugged Amy, giving her a reassuring squeeze before I watched her board the bus, heading back to the trailer where her father still lived. "It'll be okay. Soon this craziness'll be all over, we'll be writing our novels"—I said with a wink—"and life'll be normal."

She nodded, wanting to believe, and boarded the bus. It was as I walked away I noticed Marvin standing there, watching me board the bus with Pietr and Max, Amy alone.

"What is it?" Pietr asked, watching as I stared at the figure on the sidewalk following the buses with his eyes.

"Marvin. He's been watching Amy and Max all day."

Max leaned across Stella Martin. "He does that constantly. I told the little creep to back off. I'm tired of him gaping at us. She should have never dated him."

"Hindsight, Max. She thought he was somebody much different from who he really was. She saw *man*, he was *monster*," I said in Amy's defense. "You see a pretty package and you expect what's inside it is good. It's human nature."

Max looked at me, doubtful.

"But now she gets a pretty package and a good deal on the inside, too," I assured him, reaching across to chuck his chin.

He snorted and sat back in his seat, focusing out the window.

CHAPTER EIGHTEEN

Jessie

That night I headed to the basement early with my make-up work. I'd fallen asleep on Amy's abandoned bed when I heard the distant call of wolves. I rolled out from under the blanket I'd hunched beneath to do my lit, wiggled into my shoes, and climbed the basement stairs.

Slipping into my jacket, I stepped out the back door of the house and into the night. Snuggled into the porch's corner to dodge the worst of the clawing wind, I listened eagerly for Pietr's call.

"You'll be the death of him, you know."

I jumped at the words, wrapping my arms more tightly around myself when I realized Dmitri stood in the shadows on the porch not more than three feet away.

He lit a cigarette; the orange glow illuminated his nose and mouth and glinted in the dark reaches of his eyes.

"No," I stated firmly, hearing the wavering cry of Pietr joined by the basso profundo of Max. "I'm what'll keep him alive. After you and all of those like you try to use him and make him into whatever you need, I'll be there to pick him up, remind him who he truly is and why he is the most wonderful person I know. What you break, I'll fix."

"Some things you cannot fix." He took a long drag on the cigarette. "There are some things you cannot come back from."

"I don't believe that."

"You're young. Idealistic. But you've been gone quite a while by oboroten standards." He shrugged, the cigarette's glow barely highlighting the movement of his broad shoulders. "They feel time differently. Weeks feel like months—maybe years. They've done things. Become more than you expected they could." He turned toward the woodlot and the slender finger of forest that reached its way to the old park.

Where Max and Pietr howled again.

"He has changed since you left. You know that, don't you?"

"Of course."

"He says he killed a boy. In front of you."

"Yes." I fought to keep him from getting a glimpse of my fear. "What did you do to him?"

"We made a deal," he concluded simply. "A bargain he offered. Answer me this: When you finally see that he has changed so much—become so much different from what you thought— will you be smart enough to let him go?"

"I'll never let him go."

He dropped the cigarette, crushing it out with his boot tip and heading for the door. "That is what I feared," he said. "Some-times, girl, you must save what *can* be saved and leave the rest to men like me."

The door closed, blocking out the light from inside, and I shivered against the sharp breeze and the lingering scent of smoke, waiting for the wolves to return.

Hidden there, I heard them rush the hill. They paused by the garage, human again, movements tripping the motion sensor light. In their jeans once more, Pietr stood on the blacktop with his back to me; Max faced him.

I stood silent as a ghost. They goofed around, their cares

forgotten for a moment. Max gave Pietr a playful shove and they squared off like sumo wrestlers.

"Yeah," Max said, fingers wiggling for distraction as he lunged and slapped at his younger brother. Pietr evaded him easily. "You learned a bunch. Hell of a trade."

A skeletal leaf stirred on the porch, skittering in a slow circle as the breeze again kicked up.

"But what'll Jessie say when she sees—"

The wind whisked around me teasingly, snatching at my hair and carrying my scent into the yard.

Pietr and Max froze.

"Oh. Crap." Max looked up at the moon and then at Pietr's chest. His jaw clenched. He stepped around Pietr, blocking him from my view with his broader body.

"Go," Pietr said, still not looking in my direction.

"I guess you'll find out what she thinks now," Max muttered as he walked toward me. Silent, he took the porch stairs in a single bound, glanced once more over his shoulder at Pietr, and disappeared into the house.

"What haven't I seen, Pietr?" I called from the porch.

He hung his head; the tension in his shoulders made the muscles in his back ripple.

I went down the stairs slowly, dread growing with my every step. "Pietr," I called. "I thought I'd seen everything," I added, joking, "several times."

He shifted slightly, moving out of the motion sensor's range. I quickened my pace as he was absorbed in shadow.

"Pietr!"

My vision dulled by darkness, he caught me around the waist.

"Pietr, what—"

And I saw. The motion sensor's absence meant nothing because the moonlight illuminated the terrible truth carved into the higher reaches of Pietr's chest.

Two stars shimmered there, tattoos glowing like medals the size of my palms were pinned to his collarbones.

I swayed on my feet, realizing in a sudden flash what it all meant. The tattoos glittered. Mocking me.

Fearfully researching the day the Russian Mafia had appeared at the Golden Jumper horse competition I knew how tattoos differentiated ranks and station. How a man's life could be read in the ink coloring his body.

"Dmitri," I whispered. "He's Mafia."

"*Da.*"

"But you . . ." I twisted in his grip, my back to the house. I looked up at him. My throat burned. "The deal you made . . . was . . ." Shaking my head, I tentatively reached out to touch one of the stars, praying it was a dreadful figment of my imagination—a mirage rippling across the living desert of Pietr's burning skin. But it didn't disappear. It remained. As permanent as death. And just as stark.

"These . . ." I took a deep breath and steadied myself. "These are the marks of a captain."

"*Da,*" he breathed.

No attachments, I remembered reading what was supposedly part of the *Vory v zakone*—the *Thieves in Law*—code online. No family. No friends. No wonder Dmitri saw me as a threat. "Pietr, what did you do to earn *those*—"

He glanced toward the house, raising his eyes a moment as if to see who watched. He reached out for me.

"No. *No!*" I struggled against his grip. "Let go of me!" But as he released me I changed my mind. "Damn it!" I howled, pounding my fists against the stars on his shoulders. I choked. "You saved me, so many times. . . . You were my sanity!" I grabbed his arms to shake him, but he was a rock. "But you haven't let me save you! And now . . ."

I dissolved into tears, pressing my forehead against him, my eyes leaking salt across his bare chest. "Why would you let them do this to you?" Crumpling at his feet, my shoulders shook.

"I thought you, of all people, would understand." The words

dropped onto my head and he crouched before me, reaching to gather me back into his arms.

"No," I insisted, swatting at him. "Please don't . . ." I choked. "I don't know if I can . . ."

"If you can *what*, Jess? Forgive me?"

"There's only so much I can forgive," I croaked. "Oh, Pietr. What did you do?"

"I made a deal with the devil. But who else did I have?"

"And Max?" I snuffled. "Alexi and Cat? Are they part of this deal?"

"*Nyet*," he said crisply. "I'm the only one they get."

"The only one they *get*?" I looked up at him. "I thought your part was over. . . ."

"I did well for Dmitri. Showed speed, courage, and commitment. I was granted stars *abnormally* early."

"How?"

"Don't ask what you don't want an answer to, Jess."

"What did you expect me to say? Seeing those?"

There was a long pause, and, closing his eyes, he placed a hand on the ground between us to steady himself. "That I've made a horrible sacrifice, but it's worth it if I can free my mother—have her back for a while. I thought you, Jess—*you*—of all people, would understand."

"Because I lost *my* mother." My eyes squeezed shut, closing out the vision of stars cut into his chest. "Pietr." I swallowed, hating I'd raise the question, but knowing I must. "Will *your* mother understand?

He stood and through my tear-blurred vision I watched as he walked away. The door to the house opened and closed. He was gone. Without any further explanation.

Because Pietr knew I understood why he did it. He knew he couldn't free his mother without help. The strange and shadowy group parading as the CIA refused to comply. And if they wouldn't release her, Pietr would find someone who would.

He loved her at least as much as he loved me.

Still, I hated him for the sacrifice he'd made. Because by sacrificing himself to the Mafia, he'd sacrificed *us.* All the time I'd fought so hard to save Sarah I'd been sacrificing our happiness for what I'd thought was a greater good. Now that he was doing the same—sacrificing us for his mother—I hated him for following my misguided example.

I finally picked myself up off the ground and headed inside.

"Sit."

I looked up, seeing Alexi seated at the dining room table. He had a shot glass in front of him that he slowly rolled between his finger and his thumb, watching the liquid inside slosh at the edges, threatening to spill out.

"Vodka?" I asked.

"*Da.*"

"How much have you had?"

"None for the past week." He smiled at me. "There is that saying: *That birds of a feather flock together.* We're one screwed-up flock, are we not?"

Pulling out a chair I sat and rested my head on the linen tablecloth.

"You," he said. "You and Mother are the two things holding Pietr together, I think. Like glue. You cannot doubt his choice—this deal he's made. It would be the same as doubting he loves his mother. If you doubt he loves her, you doubt his ability to love. You doubt him and his love for you. Do you see?"

"You haven't had any vodka yet?"

"*Nyet.* Not yet. Hopefully not for a long time."

"Alexi. He killed a guy. . . ."

"In front of you. *Da.* I heard. He killed Nickolai in front of you, too." The vodka sloshed higher up on the little glass.

"But . . ."

"But what, Jessie? They both tried to kill you."

"Christian was no threat when Pietr first showed himself. And he was ready to kill him right then and there."

"Do you think the Mafia—men who taught Pietr so much so quickly—taught him mercy?" He released the shot glass and rubbed his hands across his face. "Jessie. You lost your mother, but do you understand the rest of what Pietr's going through?"

I blinked at him.

"Pietr is seventeen but older because of the oborot genetics twisting inside him. The things he wants—as an alpha, a son, and a young man are constantly kept from him. He wants his family safe and happy, but we are betrayed by some company, threatened by the Mafia, and Pietr, Max, and Mother are quickly dying thanks to the genetic time bomb shortening their life spans. He wants our mother free and cured, but she is imprisoned by the country she chose as her home. He wants *you*." He shrugged. "He needs hope. Compassion. Every wrong turn he's taken was to get back to something good. To get back to you or Mother."

"Go to bed, Alexi," Pietr muttered from where he stood, hidden by the doorway. "I'll watch now."

"You need to sleep," Alexi protested.

"Jess can't stand any more of you trying to convince her how I've done this out of love. Especially when it's a lie."

Alexi threw his arms into the air and stood. "Sometimes, little brother, you need to accept help."

Pietr watched until he'd left and then took the vacant seat, staring at me.

I turned away, trying to find something of interest to look at in the dining room, but instead I caught Pietr's reflection in the glass of the china cabinet.

His shoulders slumped. "I'm not sorry I did what I did. I cannot be sorry because it's the means to an end. Killing Nickolai, killing Christian, I saved *you*. I would kill a thousand more to save you. And by making this deal, I will free my mother." He sighed. "But it's no noble sacrifice. I am no hero for others to emulate. I am more like Koschei than you hope."

I adjusted my position to look at him, head still on the table in the cradle of my arms.

"I didn't do these things out of love," he admitted. "I did them out of selfishness. Our lives are too short. We get too few choices. I did these things for me. I selfishly want more time with my mother. I selfishly want you at my side. I selfishly want my siblings to have what *they* want. . . ."

"Do you hear yourself?"

"*Da.*" He seemed puzzled by the question.

I tried rewording. "Are you *listening* to yourself?"

"*Da.*"

"Remember how I said we don't live our lives just for ourselves? You're proving that. All you just described—that want, that desire? It's love."

"If it was love I would have made choices you and my mother could live with, too."

"Love is—love is like having a frontal lobotomy."

He blinked at me.

"It's radical. You never know how it's going to affect you, and it can make you a totally different person. You may not think as clearly, either." I met his curious gaze. "Put your eyebrows back down. What? You wanted me to say something cliché like *love is blind*?" I closed my eyes a moment. "I need you to tell me what you did."

"Jess."

"I want to understand you, Pietr. That's what I *selfishly* want. So tell me. What did you do to earn your stars?"

His eyes clouded and he pulled the chair closer to me, locking me between the table, my chair, and his own. "Can't you be more like Amy about this? Leave the room with your hands over your ears, believing ignorance is bliss?"

"It's that bad?"

He grabbed my chin, turning my face up to his. "You truly want to know?"

My mouth said, "Yes," though my heart begged *no*.

"There was a family . . . a mother, a boy, and a little girl . . ." And as his words filled my ears, I saw it play out before me.

"The mother had turned witness against someone very danger-ous. She and her family were to be made an example. And I was to be their punishment." He reached for me. "Come."

I was so scared of what I'd hear, I couldn't do anything but obey. He scooped me up and wrapped his arms around me.

"Maybe if I hold you tight enough, you won't leave once you've heard." He leaned back in the chair, holding me close. "I was sent to kill them all." I twisted in his grasp to face him. His eyes were slits, and listening, he guarded against something or someone. "Slowly," he clarified. "*Brutally.*"

My throat closed and my stomach knotted beneath my fro-zen heart. He'd killed *to protect* me . . . at what point was life so cheap you killed for other reasons? I closed my eyes and rested my forehead by his chin.

This might be it—the thing from which there was no way back. The thing I couldn't forgive, no matter what end it served. "And?"

He tightened his grip, and slid his lips across my cheek to my ear as he whispered, "Dmitri believes I did."

I whimpered and my eyes popped open. It took a minute for the words to sink in. I pulled away, eyes wide. "You di—"

He grabbed my head and pulled my lips to his, swallowing my exclamation with his mouth as he kissed me quiet. As realiza-tion swept through me, I forgot the question, kissing him in-stead.

"Stop," he whispered. "Easy, Jess, easy. You must learn to be quieter." His eyes slid toward the hallway and back. Satisfied no one listened, he sighed.

I pulled back, resting on his lap. "What?"

"I'm not innocent in all this. . . ." he whispered. "I . . ." He licked his lips. "I couldn't save them all." His eyes grew distant. "You don't want to hear *this*," he said bleakly.

My hands dropped from his face to his shoulders.

"And I-I don't want to talk about it."

For a moment there was no sound between us but our

breathing. I simply stared at him, watching the muscles in his jaw work in silent anguish. He shoved me off his lap and stood, walking to the window.

Following him, I slipped my hand into his and swallowed. "You can tell me anything," I insisted. "You know that. You were testing me, weren't you? Tell me the rest. The entire story."

He looked at me, the fear in his eyes warring with hope.

I led him back to the chair. "Sit." He fell into it and I again climbed into his lap. "Tell me."

"There was a man." He whispered so softly I had to lean forward to hear. "Not a cruel man, nor an evil man, just a plump, balding man with photos of his family on the wall. Photos of happier times. He was *cooking the books* for an organization and kept some of the money for himself."

"He said"—Pietr's breath caught—"as they broke his hand . . ."

I cringed and his arms cinched around me.

". . . it was to pay for his daughter's operation. I protested. . . . But I was not as willing to risk something of mine as you were to gamble your safety for Christian's. I wanted my mother's freedom more than a stranger's life. They shot him. . . ." His words trailed off. "I'm as guilty of murder as they are."

"Shhh," I whispered, resting my chin in the curve where his shoulders and neck met. "No, Pietr. You didn't pull the trigger."

"But I didn't stop them. I barely made a move against them—it happened so fast."

"You didn't call the hit. There's no blood on your hands," I insisted, wanting him to believe so I could, too.

"All I see is the blood on my hands, Jess," he confessed. "And all I want is to touch you with these same hands. . . ." He shuddered at the thought.

Slowly I traced the strong line of his neck with my lips, ignoring his brief protest and kissing him softly, sadly, wishing my kisses could ease the pain, erase the guilt. I kissed each of his tightly closed eyes and came away tasting salt.

"Kiss me," I requested. "Forget all that . . . just be here, with me. Now."

His eyes opened, soft curls of red teasing at the edges of his irises. He grunted and let me kiss his mouth open and whisper into him, gentle things, ways he was good and kind and faithful, letting me fill him with what he struggled to be and what I knew he could be as long as he never gave up the fight.

I pulled at his arms, still limp on either side of me, drawing his hands between us. "These are the hands of a good man," I assured him, setting one palm over my heart.

His gaze dropped to where his hand rested and his fingers twitched a second. He shifted in the seat beneath me.

I took the other hand and rubbed my thumb across the spot where each finger joined his palm and, spreading his fingers wide I kissed each fingertip so gently his eyes drifted shut and he sighed.

It was only when Dmitri cleared his throat and entered the dining room to grab the ashtray resting beside Alexi's abandoned vodka that we pulled back from each other. Pietr's hand was a heated warning wrapped around the back of my neck.

"You." Dmitri motioned at Pietr. "Keep your head in the game."

Pietr nodded and waited until we both heard Dmitri climb the stairs before he released me.

I wrapped my arms around his neck and pressed my nose to his. "You didn't kill him."

"I couldn't stop it, either."

Was one truly as bad as the other? I wondered. I didn't want to think about it. Wanted to finally claim *there was no time* to think about such things.

"*Couldn't* is different from *didn't try*," I pointed out. Looking down, I chewed my bottom lip. "The family. How did you convince . . . ?"

"Do *you* know where to buy pigs' blood?" he teased.

"No. Ewww."

"Well, Alexi does. And now I do, too. Amazing what access to pigs' blood and passports can accomplish."

"Were they all you were ordered to kill?"

"Nearly. But I only lost the one." He cleared his throat. "Dmitri wants me as his second in command, he intends to shake things up—start fresh. The idea of having an oborot as one of his men seems quite attractive to him."

"But you won't. That's what you meant: Everyone lies and breaks promises. . . ."

"*Da.* I have learned to lie to save a life here and there."

"But he wants even more from you, after we free your mother."

"I'll burn that bridge when we come to it."

"I just wish . . ." I touched his shirt at the two places I knew the stars lay hidden beneath cloth and invisible in regular light.

"They give access to things no one else will provide for—this upcoming big event," he pointed out. "They earn me trust."

"With untrustworthy characters," I reminded him, but I closed my eyes, nodding.

"Think of them as a passport."

"To a place I don't want you ever traveling to again." I rested my head on his chest and listened to the racing of his heart. "Do you think he can *hear* us?"

"Your ex?" he asked, eyes narrowing.

I nodded.

"I'm not underestimating him."

"And we know he can *see* us. . . ."

"Almost whenever he wants. But I'd bet he doesn't want to see through your eyes when you're so close to me."

"Now I hope he's watching. . . ." I twisted on his lap so I straddled him, my legs sliding through on either side of the armrests, feet touching the Oriental rug beneath us. My fingers wound into his dark hair and I set my lips to his until his heavy-lidded eyes sparked red and he grabbed me with a growl, covering my mouth with his, lips grappling with mine. I pulled away, breathless.

Pietr was panting.

"I love you, Pietr Rusakova."

"Then say it in Russian."

"I don't know how."

His voice gravelly and full of promise he began, *"Yah . . ."*

His fingers traced my lips and when I opened my mouth to repeat "yah," his eyes widened, glowing red.

". . . tebyah . . ."

". . . tebyah . . ."

". . . lyewblyew," he concluded, mesmerized by my lips as I struggled through the final word.

"Yah tebyah lyewblyew, Pietr Rusakova."

He sighed, his eyes closing, shoulders slumping. *"Yah tebyah lyewblyew,* Jess Gillmansen."

I pulled my legs back up to tuck them beneath me so I could curl up there, leaning against his chest, but he carefully moved me aside, off his lap.

I stood and stretched.

He watched.

Closely.

A smile twisted the edges of his lips up. "You'd better get some sleep—school tomorrow," he added. "And I'm supposed to be playing guard-dog."

"Okay," I agreed reluctantly. I leaned over and kissed his forehead. "Good night."

"Da," he agreed, stretching the syllable as I walked away.

"You can quit watching me," I teased as I disappeared from his sight.

He snorted, caught.

CHAPTER NINETEEN

Jessie

We attended school again the next day, according to our "Just Act Normal" plan. Amy was waiting for our bus outside and immediately grabbed Max for a quick morning kiss. "I needed some help warming up," she teased him, grabbing his hand and dragging him toward the door. Max didn't mind at all.

And I doubted he noticed what I did. Looking over my best friend, I determined to find out why she looked so tired after one night back home. But as it did so often, school got in the way of important things.

I noticed Marvin ahead of us, leaning by the water fountain as Amy walked by. He didn't straighten up, didn't say a word, but his eyes followed her the whole time she walked down the hall.

Away from Marvin. With Max.

I read those same thoughts in Marvin's eyes when our gazes briefly brushed.

Shivering, I held Pietr's hand tighter.

Maybe this watching Amy thing had always been normal

for Marvin and I'd just never noticed. I'd been gone a while—
and even when I'd been here I hadn't been tuned in. Otherwise
I would have noticed the trouble between Marvin and Amy.

Wouldn't I?

Jessie

In Miss Wyatt's psychology class we got a new assignment. "So,
because life is *ephemeral*—a fleeting and brief thing—we will be
doing a eulogy project," she said.

I swallowed hard. Dad, Annabelle Lee, and I had worked
together to write Mom's. This assignment hit a little close to
home. Looking across the aisle at Pietr, I noticed he was drumming his fingers softly on the desk, eyes fixed on the clock.
Yeah, this assignment was hitting a little too close to home for
a few of us, I realized.

I pulled out my pencil and flipped open my notebook.

"A eulogy, as you all know, is a summary of a person's life at
the end of it all. What did they accomplish, how will they be
remembered? What things made their life worth living? You
will have the advantage of looking ahead and imagining the
things you want to have said about you. How do you want to
be remembered? What will your impact be on society, whether
large or small? As Mary Oliver said: *What is it you plan to do with
your one wild and precious life?*"

She turned, her long flowing skirt wrapping around her ankles for a moment. "It's due the Monday following vacation.
Seventy-five to two hundred words, typewritten on standard
white paper. Find your partner."

Desks squeaked and chairs scraped across the floor as people
partnered up. Pietr moved his desk to face mine.

"Today you'll write your partner's eulogy without asking
them anything," Miss Wyatt continued. "Let them see how they

are reflected in your eyes now. Write it as if they are already dead. What have they done up until now? Use this as a reality check of sorts."

"Hey, partner," I greeted Pietr, trying to keep my tone light. I failed. "How are you with this?"

"I'll be fine. Better do it now, anyhow." He tapped his pen on the desk. "It may be necessary, considering."

"Don't talk like that." I grabbed his hand, stopped the tapping, and focused on playing the studious student. "So . . ." I thought a moment and scribbled some things down. "Want me to read yours?"

"You're done?" he asked skeptically, walking his pencil up and down his hand, twirling it between each of his fingers. "I must not have accomplished much if you can do it that fast."

"So you don't want me to impress you with a flowery, emotional eulogy?"

He leaned in, studying my eyes. "What do you really know about me, Jess?"

"I—" I blinked at him, suddenly frustrated. "I know a helluva lot more than most people here do. And I know how I feel about you."

His lips and jaw were tight. "Is that enough? Don't you wonder why you feel the way you do? Shouldn't I have somehow earned it?"

"You have earned it. . . ." I shook my head. "Stop. Now. Quit trying to quantify things and make everything logical. Sometimes our hearts should rule our heads."

He blinked at me. "That sort of attitude gets people killed."

I knew what he was referring to—his father had died as a result of acting out of passion. Pietr preferred cool logic and reason—the odd disconnect of philosophy and reason—to the blinding power of passion. Maybe that was why we kept having problems.

He wanted control of his heart.

And so did I.

Jessie

I joined Amy at our regular lunch table minutes before everyone else showed up.

"You okay?" I asked.

"Tired. Dad's place is a wreck. But he's off the sauce. Mostly."

I reached out and patted her hand. "Hey, what's this?" I touched the large pad of paper Amy had closed as I'd approached.

She shrugged, tapping her pencil on the cover protectively. "Just some stuff I'm doing."

"Stuff, like art?"

"Some might call it that." Her eyebrows lowered and I saw a look cross her face that I had missed for months now, the look of the self-critical artist. "It's just some sketches I've been working on." She tried to sweep the sketchpad down onto the seat beside her, but I rested my palm heavily on its cover.

"I haven't seen you do any art, except in class, since . . ." I realized I hadn't seen Amy do any art, any sketching, any photography, since she started dating Marvin. I swallowed hard. "Why did you stop drawing?"

"I didn't stop drawing."

"I mean outside of art class. You used to draw all the time. There were times we couldn't separate you from a sketchpad."

She glanced around, making sure no one else was listening before she leaned forward. "Recently I had a really tough time seeing beauty in anything. And if you can't find something's beauty, it just doesn't feel like it's worth trying to capture on paper."

I nodded. I'd gone through a period after my mother's death where words wouldn't come. A writer without words was like . . . Like being an artist starved of inspiration, I realized.

I'd been so selfish—so blind. "Can I take a peek? That one day Max took you outside he kept popping into the house to grab art supplies, and claiming you were drawing him"—I rolled my eyes—"but he wouldn't show me anything."

"Smart boy." Amy's hand slid across the yellow cover of the sketchpad, her thumb ruffling the corners of the paper as she thought. Before Marvin she had been pretty bold with her art. She hadn't cared who saw her stuff or when. "I don't know . . . They're rough, really unfinished."

"I won't judge," I said, lifting my hand from the cover to rest over my heart with such gravity I thought she'd burst laughing.

"Oh, hell. Judge all you want," she said with a snort. "I have to remember that art—like writing or music—is totally subjective. What I think is majestic, you may think is absolute crap."

"Or *unique*. That's the artist's bane. Like wishing someone an interesting life. Give it here." I motioned. "I guess everyone gets to have their own opinion about the quality of the artist or writer. Isn't living in a free country grand?"

She slid the sketchpad across the table to me, keeping a wary eye on the lunch line, tracking the movements of the rest of our friends.

Staring at me from the first page was a charcoal sketch of a young man with wavy dark hair and careful eyes. He looked like he had been caught speculating and didn't want to talk about what was really on his mind. I knew him immediately.

"Max," I said, my voice soft with reverence. She had captured him with amazing accuracy, using only lines and smudges. "God, Amy. It's amazing."

I glanced up long enough to notice she was blushing before I turned the page. "Oh!" Max again, I noticed. Shirtless and dozing in sunlight slanting beneath the back porch's roof, his saber-shaped birthmark carefully outlined on his shoulder blade. "Does he snore?"

Amy glanced down, finding something impressive to study in the chipped Formica of the lunch room tabletop. "Yes," she said, wistful. She gave her comparison some thought. "He does, but it's more like a purr." Her blush deepened.

Gingerly, I turned the page. This time a fawn peered back at

me, frozen as it stood not far from the thicket that was probably its home. "Wow," I said, stunned by the clarity of the sketch.
"Did you do this one from a photo?"

"No," Amy said with a sigh. "Max took me into the woods
and told me we should just sit still and be quiet, that remarkable things would happen. I thought it was just a cheesy line! I
laughed and told him nothing remarkable happens to me. He
just told me to be quiet. Wait." She grinned, remembering.

"Ten minutes later this little guy stepped out. It was the
slowest I've ever sketched anything. I was so scared I was going
to scare him away. But he just stood there staring at Max, their
eyes locked."

The poor fawn probably would have stood there forever,
realizing he was watched by one of the fiercest predators his
forest had ever known. Surely instinct told him that springing
away would only encourage unwanted attention.

"Max has a real way with animals," Amy said, awe tinting
her voice.

"I guess he does."

Amy glanced nervously over my shoulder.

I knew she was watching someone's approach. I flipped to
the next page. Max again. Shirtless and reclining on the love
seat. My eyebrows must have shot up, because Amy slapped the
cover back down on the sketchpad and yanked it across the table and into her lap.

Sophia sat, watching us in her quiet way. Looking at me, her
face scrunched up and she passed her hand about an inch in
front of her lips, signaling me.

I grabbed a napkin and took a swipe at my mouth.

Her lips puckered in frustration and she repeated the motion more dramatically.

I shrugged at her and returned to my conversation with Amy.
"Again, I say: WOW."

"Thanks," Amy said hesitantly. "I kept trying to get him right,
but it seemed like he'd blur and change. . . . The light must have

been the problem. One moment he had a full six-pack, and the next they smoothed into a solid sheet of muscle."

I wondered just how many abdominal muscles a wolf had.

Pietr clicked his tray down next to me, a sack of mainly meat—jerky from home—and a canned juice from the cafeteria set on his tray. Since we no longer trusted the school's food under the new lunch plan, we'd all become packers. Pietr's strange diet, I'd learned, was because he burned through things at a different rate with his strange metabolism. Consuming so much meat, he was a low-carb-diet dream.

Sophie glanced at my lips again, then looked at Pietr, focusing on his mouth. Her eyes darted back and forth between us for a moment.

Amy leaned nearly all the way across the table, wanting to finish our chat, but very aware of her growing audience. "The weirdest thing was," she whispered, "the way I couldn't quite get his eyes right. No matter what I did, they kept coming out more animal than human."

Suddenly beside her, Max set his tray gingerly next to hers. "It's because I'm such a sexy beast."

For a moment she looked like the fawn in her picture—too stunned to move. Then she blushed cherry, and milk nearly shot out my nose.

Pietr threw his straw paper at his older brother in silent protest.

Feeling Sophie still staring, I stood and looked at her. "Come on. You know the drill. Girls' bathroom."

Hesitantly she followed me and stood in silence by the sink while I checked the stalls.

I glanced in the mirror. "So what was the big freak-out about my lips?"

She rolled her own lips over her teeth, struggling like I'd so often done in the past to find the words she wanted. "You know my vision's funky."

"You could say that, what with the seeing ghosts and traces of energy."

"Oh. You know that last part, too?"

"It sorta makes sense. So . . ." My brows tugged together. "Are you seeing something else now, too?"

Her gaze skimmed over me, one corner of her mouth twisting. "Maybe auras? I don't know enough about this stuff. If it's auras, shouldn't I see full fields of color surrounding people? Up until a couple minutes or so ago it looked like you had lipstick smeared all over your mouth. When I looked at Pietr he had the same weird thing. . . ." She squinted at me. "It's fading. . . ."

My hands clamped over my mouth and my eyes widened, thinking back to my quick make-out session with Pietr right before lunch. There had definitely been a lot of lips-smearing-across-lips action. "Are you still eating the school lunch every day?" I asked, muffled by my hands.

"*Duh.* Packing's so passé."

"Okay, just pack. Trust me. You are starting to see—um—energy traces like auras. You're just seeing where they overlap first."

"What?" Her eyebrows lowered. "Oh. *Ew!* Can you two *not* keep your lips off each other?" She rubbed her forehead. "This is not a socially acceptable gift—seeing where people have touched. I'm going to get such a reputation for gawking at people . . ."

I wrapped an arm around her shoulders. "Look. I have a lot on my plate right now. But as soon as things clear up, we'll try and find a way to dial down your sight. The last thing I want is for you to be socially unacceptable," I teased.

"Yeah. You have the market cornered on that, thanks to your willingness to help Sarah and duke it out with Jenny and Macie. I don't want to usurp your title as school pariah."

"Nice, Soph. Glad to be back at Junction High so I can be the source of your amusement."

"Things aren't nearly as exciting without you around," she admitted.

Jessie

We were barely off the bus and back in the house after school when Max got on the house phone with Amy, checking up. He carried the phone upstairs, not worried at all about agents listening to the Rusakova land line. It cracked Max up knowing someone was listening to him flirt with his girlfriend—agents' ears probably burned hearing them talk.

It was pretty miraculous to see, Maximilian Rusakova—*player*—moonstruck.

I called Dad on Alexi's special cell phone and let him know Alexi's tests proved Annabelle Lee's blood had many of the same properties as mine. If he wanted, we'd find a spot for her, too, until things cleared up.

Dad explained Wanda was going to be staying over and that between the two of them Annabelle Lee would be okay. "But she'll ask some hard questions," he said. "Especially about Wanda spending more time over here. Do you think we should—"

"Should what, Dad? Tell her the truth?"

The other end of the line was quiet. "She's smart as a whip."

"What does that even mean?" I asked. "No, don't try and explain it. Okay. I'll call after dinner. You can drop her off to stay here tonight and I'll give her the talk."

"Good. Wanda and I'll prep the house in case trouble heads this way."

"Dad?"

"Yeah?"

"How much do you know about Wanda?"

"Enough to know I have a tiger by the tail."

I grinned. "Be careful over there. I love you."

Dinner was over and everything was following the plan—things looking amazingly normal and uneventful at the Rusakova house, even with "Uncle" Dmitri still lurking, and belated birthday presents still rolling in to better equip the army of mafiosos Dmitri would import.

Pietr looked at me wistfully as he stood up from the table.

Dmitri grunted, looking at him. "You need exercise—practice. Outside."

Pietr nodded. It would give him the chance to work out some frustration and would probably keep Derek's remote viewing abilities focused inside—on me—instead of realizing how rapidly Pietr's skills were increasing.

I grappled with the bookbag I'd hung over the back of my chair. "Before you three leave"—I looked at Max, Cat, and Alexi— "I need some help with a homework assignment." I turned to Dmitri. "*Uncle* Dmitri," I used the term the Rusakovas suggested to keep up appearances, "you are free to go. *Anytime.*"

He glared at me and rose.

"I need to know about Pietr—before Junction. What he was like."

Dmitri sat back down.

"Oh. Excellent. You're staying."

"Ask Pietr," Max suggested.

"He won't say. I think he wants me to work for this. I'm looking for defining moments from his youth—things you think made him who he is now."

They looked at each other a moment. "The fire," Max said.

They nodded and Alexi began. "Soon after Pietr turned thirteen and got his hearing, there was a fire in our neighborhood. Pietr was home, reading, when the fire trucks rolled past. Like most people, he followed them, stunned at the sight of flames devouring a house. The firemen rushed in, saved many young people—"

"A girl was having a party. No parents," Cat explained.

Alexi continued. "They thought they had gotten everyone. But Pietr"—he smiled with pride—"he heard someone else inside. He convinced the firemen to go back in one more time."

"And they found one more kid," Max said, "that stoner— what was his name?"

Cat *tsk*-ed at him. "That doesn't matter. The point is, Pietr helped save a life. With his special abilities."

"He didn't get any credit for it," Max pointed out. "The guy who came out of the building with the boy did."

"But that didn't matter to Pietr," Alexi clarified. "Because *he* knew what he'd done. And he was proud of what he was becoming."

There was a long pause while everyone avoided looking at everyone else. We all thought the same thing—that Pietr once wanted to be the thing he now fought so hard against finally becoming.

Cat finally broke the silence. "He used to be very popular," she said softly. "He's always been handsome, but it seemed there was some sort of inner light that glowed in Pietr, something that made him special. We had to collar him early," she said, touching the spot on her neck corresponding to where the boys wore special silver necklaces. "The girls started coming on strong at an early age," she said distastefully. "He didn't understand it—none of us did."

"Perhaps it was the alpha aspect kicking in early?" Dmitri asked.

I had nearly forgotten he was still there, intruding.

Alexi shrugged. "Does that make you proud that you are holding such an alpha's leash now?"

Dmitri glared at him. "It could be a far worse man than I."

"So he had girl trouble early?" I asked Cat.

"He made Max look like chopped liver for a while," Cat replied.

"Bad for the ego," Max chuckled.

"Do you remember Rachel?" Alexi asked the others. "I think she was, what? Were they fourteen? Freshmen."

Cat nodded. "That went badly," she recalled.

"But, when you consider defining moments . . ."

Cat picked up the tale. "Rachel had a cat she loved very

much. She kept it indoors, safe from the neighborhood dogs, very much loved."

"Spoiled," Max specified.

"Pietr and Rachel's relationship was"—Cat eyed me carefully—"heating up. They had dated steadily for a few months. They were frequently together, holding hands, kissing . . ."

"Groping," Max added.

Again, Cat gauged my expression. I stayed perfectly still except for my head, which I nodded. Pietr was still a virgin by his own admittance, so I knew things hadn't gotten too hot with this Rachel girl, but at the idea of him pawing someone else . . . my stomach twisted a little. *The past,* I reminded myself. It's *just part of his past.*

"He probably loved her," Max said, trying to excuse Pietr's past explorations.

"*Nyet,*" Pietr muttered, making us jump in our seats. He stood in the doorway, leaning against the door frame. His eyes trapped mine. "I did not love her, but I was crazy about her."

"She was very pretty," Max said in consolation.

Pietr shrugged. "One night, in the worst bit of winter, she called me, frantic. The cat had gotten outside and disappeared. No claws, bad teeth—it would be no match for the neighborhood dogs, and we were expecting more snow. Rachel was desperate. She wanted my help." He shrugged. "Her parents were out at some event and there was no one to help her look for the cat. I wanted to help her. Perhaps I wanted a reason for her to feel grateful. . . ." He shook his head, clearing his mind of the memory.

"I went to her house. It was a very clean place, everything neat and tidy. You would not know a cat lived there—not by scent or sight. Rachel had already gone into the snow and come back unsuccessful. She was crying." He looked at the floor between us. "I wanted . . ."

"You wanted to be her hero," I said with a smile.

"I had been a hero before—why not again? It seemed such a small thing, to scent after a cat. She tried to tug me out the door into the backyard to look. . . . I pulled away and went to the cat tree they had in the corner of the kitchen. I tried not to be obvious, but her mother had mopped and vacuumed and there was so much disinfectant in the air . . ."

"She saw you smell the cat tree."

"*Da*. She must have." He rubbed at his eyes. "We plunged into the snow, her hand in mine. I dragged her all over. There were moments she argued—pointed to small snatches of tracks— trails I knew had gone cold. And I pulled her away. I caught her staring at me, at my nose as my nostrils flared. I should have known. The look on her face . . ."

"But I pushed on. I found the cat. Alive and scared. I even scared away the dog that was digging at its hiding place."

"By *growling*," Max pointed out.

"*Da*, not my smartest move," Pietr said. "I couldn't carry the cat. It wouldn't let me. But I saved the snubnosed beast." No pride marked his voice—no sense of accomplishment colored his tone.

I reached out and touched his arm. "You were her hero."

"*Nyet*. Heroes don't get dumped for *weirding out* their girl-friends," he stated. "We were barely back in the house, I leaned in for a kiss—and she ended it. Then and there. She called me a freak and kicked me out."

"Oh, Pietr," I murmured. "I'm sorry."

He shrugged.

"And the next day?" Cat prodded him gently.

He glared at Cat. "Thanks for reminding me. *Da*. The next day at school I was suddenly friendless. She made up a reason we were no longer dating—the truth was too weird. So she said I'd gotten . . . pushy." He looked away, still stung by the lie.

"He couldn't get a date for the next two dances," Max said.

"I finally left my necklace in my locker out of desperation."

Cat hissed. "You didn't—" She blew out a long breath when he nodded. "Was that how . . . ?"

"*Da*. That's how I wound up with Sonja at the spring formal."

"*Dog!*" Cat declared. "Max was after her!"

Pietr grinned devilishly. "My ego was shot, but I couldn't stand seeing Max on the rise so soon."

"Do not feel guilty," Dmitri said. "Simply another alpha trait. The need to dominate."

Pietr looked him over. "You're too quick to embrace the more dangerous side of our behavior," he said. "You and Jess have more in common than you think." Glancing pointedly at my notebooks and pencil, he left the room.

Jessie

"Hey, Max, I just wanted to—" I froze in the doorway of Max's bedroom. He froze, too, picture and thumbtack in his hands, caught just before he hung it on the wall. With about a dozen other drawings.

Of Amy.

"Whoa," I whispered. "Maaax."

He hung his head, letting his hands drop and hide the drawing behind his back.

"Did you . . . ?"

"Yeah."

I trotted into the room. "Max. These are really good. I mean, really—seriously . . ."

He moved back as I reached around to grab the one behind his back.

"Come on. Lemme see, lemme see, lemme see." I hopped up and down until he grinned.

"Okay," he said reluctantly, slowly sliding the picture around in front of me.

"Wow."

Amy in her Little Red Riding Hood outfit from Halloween peered back at me in a classic pinup-inspired pose. She was absolutely gorgeous and nearly animated.

"Holy heck. You really captured her."

His smile broadened into a goofy grin. "That's when she captured *me*." He chuckled.

I examined the pieces hanging on the wall. "Wow. I mean, Amy's good in that serious art student, going to be an art major and create beautiful paintings way, but these—these are graphic-novel good."

"I'll take that as a compliment."

"That's exactly how it's meant," I stated firmly. "So what has Amy said about all these?" I handed the Red Riding Hood one back and finished skirting the room.

"Nothing."

"What?"

"She doesn't know."

"She. Doesn't. Know?"

"*Nyet*. I do these when we're not together. I wouldn't have the guts to draw her—in front of her. She's the artist. I sketch."

"Pfffft. She'd be so frikkin' flattered. . . ."

"And embarrassed."

"What? Why?"

"She doesn't see herself like this. She doesn't think she's hot. Doesn't realize she's beautiful."

"That's a common ailment among girls," I muttered. "Luckily, if you boys play your cards right it's totally curable, too. Show her these. Sometimes we have to see ourselves through somebody else's eyes before we can imagine being more than we give ourselves credit for being."

"Why did you come up here?"

"I wanted to say thank you."

"For what?"

"Two things. Trying to explain Pietr's past—*fun*—with

some other girl. Only a good brother would try to protect him like that."

"He was just a dumb kid."

I shrugged. "Aren't we all? And I wanted to thank you for Amy."

He glanced at the wall of images and looked down at the one in his hands.

"You're being exactly the kind of guy she needs right now," I confirmed. "You're doing your best. Being supportive and protective. I told you you'd grow into the title of hero."

"I'm not there yet," he admitted.

"Give yourself time."

CHAPTER TWENTY

Jessie

I found Pietr out back a few minutes later, working slowly through some sort of kata—part martial arts, part dance. He flowed more than moved through each strike and kick, testing his balance, working to perfect control of his body. Watching him, I nearly forgot my purpose for being there, but he spotted me during a sudden turn, kick, and punch combination and paused.

"*Da?*" he said, raising one eyebrow at me.

I clapped my hands together twice and called, "Time to alpha up!"

He stalked to the stairs and looked up at me.

"You're needed inside. Now. My dad should be pulling up with Annabelle Lee any minute."

His head tilted, gaze questioning.

I put my hands on my hips. "You're gonna have to show her"—I glanced around the yard; how likely was it a neighbor might overhear and if they did, was anything really still *weird* in Junction?—"your *stuff*."

He snorted.

I sucked my teeth in exasperation. "Not *that* stuff. Who am I talking to? Pietr or Max?"

He climbed the stairs to stand beside me. I pulled in a quick whiff of Pietr—slightly damp from working out—and was suddenly not thinking clearly.

"Do you want me to—" Pietr moved his hands in a quick flourish, miming taking off his clothes.

I started to nod before I remembered what I was agreeing to. "Uhm. No." I shook my head firmly, trying to toss the image of Pietr—naked—from my head. "Annabelle Lee," I recalled. *Focus, Jess.* "She's twelve. No need to see all that. If you want to show her in a less naked way, that's fine."

He peered at me.

"Like, do the wolf-head thing, or make hands into paws. But nothing that requires stripping south of the equator."

Inside, Alexi laughed all the way out the door and onto the porch.

Pietr and I blushed in matching tones and headed inside to tell my little sister that the boy I was dating—the boy who had helped us find her when we got briefly separated at the fair months ago—was a werewolf.

My normal.

Jessie

"Okay," Annabelle Lee pouted. "I don't get this. Why can't I stay at home tonight? With Dad and my books?"

"Well, there's a lot of crazy stuff going on," I started to explain.

"Dad already said that. Cut to the chase. He said you had something I need to see to believe."

I nodded. "What else did Dad say?"

"That even seeing isn't always believing. And that everything's been turned upside down because of your connection to the Rusakovas."

Pietr blanched.

I squeezed his hand. "You're on."

"It *is* because of us," he agreed sadly. "We have a strange history—"

"Oh, holy crap." I pushed Pietr aside and looked at my little sister. "You wanna cut to the chase?"

She nodded.

"Great. Pietr and Max are genetically engineered were-wolves, the result of Cold War experimentation. Cat was one, too, but my blood—like your blood, probably—is a key component in the cure. Alexi's adopted." I waved a hand in the air. "Okay so far?"

Annabelle Lee nodded her head and then changed direction with it: *No.*

"Hang in there another minute," I said. "Some company that may or may not be potentially affiliated with the CIA wants the werewolves to be their dog soldiers. The Russian Mafia wants them, too, for some scheme to eventually over-throw the government of Russia. I know, I know. It sounds like some crazy plot cooked up by a housewife-turned-author. But that saying *Truth is stranger than fiction*? Dead-on. And, because we can stop the werewolves from being werewolves, both groups would like us dead."

Annabelle Lee blinked at me. "This is unbelievable." She looked at her backpack, pillow, and stuffed rabbit on the floor nearby. "I'm not an idiot. I know what's really going on here."

"Ohhh-kayyy. Fill me in."

"Dad and Wanda want to have one night together without prying eyes and my *judgmental attitude*," she placed the words in air quotes with her fingers before returning her hands to where they'd rested before, arms crossed.

"Wow."

"I'm not so young that I don't know what goes on between a man and a woman," she announced. "I know."

"Oh, you do, do you?"

"They teach sex ed in sixth grade. Not that it kept Susie Har-rolsen from getting knocked up in seventh."

I blinked. "Pietr," I said. "Strip. Now."

He stared at me, surprised by my sudden change of attitude.

"If my darling sister believes she's so worldly that she understands all the stuff that goes on between a man and a woman—and supposes that stuff goes on between our father and Wanda . . . Well then—we might as well give her the full monty."

Pietr began to peel out of his clothes, T-shirt first, and Annabelle Lee began to blush.

Pietr's hands moved to his jeans, watching me all the time.

Annabelle Lee gasped, hands flying to cover her eyes.

I stopped Pietr before he'd even unbuttoned and leaned over to tug my little sister's hands away from her face. "Don't pull that *I'm old enough to handle anything* crap with me," I warned her softly. "I want you to stay young as long as possible. So pardon me for calling your bluff. Thank you, Pietr. Back to plan A."

Pietr's eyes began to glow and Annabelle Lee's mouth and eyes began to widen as the sounds of joints moving and slipping and bones shifting began and Pietr's face stretched and distorted into the wolf's heavy head.

Annabelle Lee screamed and Pietr changed back, blinking to clear his vision.

I brushed his arm as I went around the table and grabbed Annabelle Lee. "See," I soothed her, wrapping an arm around her shoulder. "It's Pietr. Just Pietr."

The shock on her face shamed Pietr so much he looked away. "He's a *monster* . . . ?"

The word stung.

"No. He's no monster. He's a werewolf. An oborot. But more than that, he's Pietr. Just Pietr." I stroked her hair. "Sometimes he changes, and wears a beautiful wolfskin and prowls the night. But he's always Pietr. *My* Pietr."

He looked at me, bashful and thankful all at once, eyes filled with a loyalty I'd never thought I'd have from anyone.

"Isn't he amazing?" I whispered, my eyes holding his a moment.

Annabelle Lee nodded, mute with wonder. "Pietr," she agreed, finally finding her voice, "you *are* amazing." Her face grew briefly serious. "Do it again!" she commanded, clapping her hands together.

And he did, laughing at her eager acceptance.

My alpha.

Jessie

I finally stopped the strange new sensation that seemed to be the "My Boyfriend's a Werewolf" show. Pietr had done hands to paws, stopping at the freaky in-between stage, wolf's head, wolfman face. . . . An entire repertoire. And Annabelle Lee had marveled at him the whole time.

I didn't want to take this away from Pietr—the fact that being what he was was truly remarkable, but deep in my gut a new worry gnawed. What if being accepted for this special part of him gave him one more reason to hesitate about taking the cure? If he could be loved as the oborot he was born to be—no matter how briefly—could that be enough for him to decide a short life of truth was better than a long one denying your roots?

"Okay, that's enough," I announced.

Annabelle Lee hugged Pietr tightly and confessed, "That was waaay cooler than the last gothic novel I read! Oh." She turned to me and dug something out of her pocket. "The lawyer got back the stuff they took from you at check-in. Here."

She held Mom's netsuke rabbit pendant out to me.

I hugged her so tightly she squirmed to catch her breath.

Putting the pendant on, I took her downstairs, said good night, and wondered briefly if her first instinct about Dad and

Wanda might be accurate. I shuddered at the thought. Not because I didn't want Dad happy—I did—but because it was Wanda: weird, dangerous, woman-with-a-past-I-didn't-know-yet Wanda.

As much as everyone kept trying to protect me and one another, I was also doing my best to protect them.

Climbing the stairs again with my eulogy notes in my hands, I realized that although I was already in love with Pietr, thinking about everything his family had said about his past and the way he so willingly showed my sister what he was in order to help my family—I fell in love all over again that night.

And I fell hard.

There'd been enough time for thinking and research. I needed to be able to better help protect the people I loved.

Alexi

When I heard the knock at my bedroom door I didn't expect to find Jessie. She stood in the hall, hands on her hips, back straight and chin held high; everything about her body language told me I would not be allowed to refuse her coming request.

"I need your help with something." Her words were as firm as her stance.

"What is it?"

"I need you to teach me some moves. Fighting."

"I'm no expert. You'll have a gun. Or three," I added, smiling.

"I could be disarmed."

I opened my mouth to argue.

"Even if I keep a relaxed grip." She finished the thought I was only readying to say. "Guns jam, too. And run out of ammo. But bodies . . ." Her eyes grew unfocused and I wondered if she was thinking of how far Pietr had pushed his own body to keep her from the asylum. "Bodies only give out near the end."

I nodded, noting the grim design of her expression and the

determined set of her jaw. "Ask Pietr or Max to teach you. They were always faster and more agile. Even Cat's an option."

"I don't want to accidentally telegraph what Pietr can do by seeing him in action too much. And Cat? I think I'd frustrate her. Max bulls his way through a fight. His methods require more bulk and a Hulk-like power. But you . . . you can teach the skills to a simple human because you've always been a simple human. And yet—you were a believable oborot when it mattered." She winked at me. "You got skills."

I looked her up and down, considering. She certainly wasn't some frail flower that couldn't handle a little training. She was strong from moving hay and sacks of grain and was agile from competitive horseback riding. She had a sharp focus when it was needed—that was the only way one succeeded at competition shooting.

"If I'm going to teach you anything, I'm going to teach it my way. And only the skills I think will work to your advantage."

She smiled. "I'm totally cool with fighting dirty, if it helps us out."

I stood. "*That's* my girl."

"Desperate times," she said, following me outside.

I grinned. "Desperate measures," I agreed, only waiting until her sneakers touched the grass of the backyard before I lunged at her.

"Crap!" she blurted as I took her to the ground.

Peeling myself off her, I knelt over her legs and peered down at her, catching my breath as she got hers. "First lesson? Expect the unexpected."

She nodded and her knee slid up to tap my groin as her lips stretched into a smile. "Second lesson?"

I grimaced at the threat. "Be aware of your opponent's weak points. Nice," I congratulated her, rolling up into a standing position. I reached a hand down to her.

I tugged her up to her feet, spun us a half step to narrow her stance, and took her down again, sweeping her feet out from under her and this time straddling her chest. "Third? Never trust anyone in a fight."

I popped off of her and she snared my foot and yanked me down, my ass hitting the ground. "Okay, okay." I laughed. "Time out. We could grapple for hours and you would learn very little other than basic reactions." Taking a breath, I coughed. Damn cigarettes.

Jessie climbed to her feet and shook out her knee. "Fine. Tell me how to keep my feet under me."

"*Da*. Good. We'll start with that. Widen your stance—feet shoulder-width apart."

"Like target shooting," she realized.

"Good, good. Now bend your knees slightly and lower your center of gravity. . . ."

Jessie

"I need you to read this, O, editor," Pietr whispered, coming up behind me in the sitting room on silent feet.

I turned to face him, my hands still damp from washing up after training with Alexi. I was stiff. Tired.

Probably bruised. But I knew a few more things than I had known before, so I chalked the experience up as a win.

I took the paper he offered without looking at him. That close to Pietr there was never anything I wanted to see *but* him. "What am I looking for?" I asked, shifting into editor mode. "Spelling, facts? Voice? Flow?"

"Accuracy."

"Accuracy, I can do," I promised, thinking of one hit I'd surprised Alexi with.

He leaned forward and plucked something out of my hair. "What—?" He held the dead leaf before me.

"Must have gotten that rolling around with Alexi in the backyard." I blinked and looked at him. "That sounded so wrong."

He nodded, eyebrow quirked. Waiting.

"I'm trying to learn a few things from your more experienced brother so I'm ready for our big event."

His expression didn't change.

"Yee-ahhh. Not any better, huh?" I laughed. *Our big event* could mean two vastly different things to Pietr. "Lemme just run through the other ways I could get this wrong: Alexi's teaching me some moves. He's trying to put the hurt on me. He was putting me into some positions I've never tried before. . . ." I snorted. I couldn't help myself.

A muscle near Pietr's left eye twitched.

"He's teaching me to fight!" I laughed, grabbing his wrists.

He rolled his eyes and groaned. "You," he whispered. "A school newspaper editor."

"Hey, buddy." I grinned. "Editing means we get time to improve the words. We're allowed to be pretty rough originally."

He smiled, kissed my forehead, and slipped away, leaving me with the paper.

"'A Eulogy for Jess Gillmansen,'" I read the title aloud. Oh. Our psychology project. I flopped down in the love seat, pulling my knees up under me.

> Jess Gillmansen led a life spent enriching others' lives. Friend to strays and monsters, she accepted everyone with gracious abandon and loved them well beyond what they ever deserved or dreamed. A true friend and fierce forgiver, she pulled the man in me out to face down the monster I feared and helped make me the best bits of what I am. I would follow her to Hell and back if only to protect her and let her know how much she's loved. Now and forever.

My hand shook as I set the paper on my knees. "Pietr?" And he was there, eyes dark with worry. "I—"

"Don't you dare try and apologize. It's perfect—better than I could've expected. You give me a lot of credit."

He stared at the floor marking the distance between us and I reached out to take his hand. "You deserve it."

"Although you made me go into research mode on your childhood and it appears you wussed out and went all sentimental on mine."

"I wanted to get it finished before . . ."

He didn't have to say it. I knew. Before the big fight. Tie up any loose ends, say whatever needed to be said, because who knew what the outcome would be?

"It's going to turn out fine." I tugged him over to the love seat and, pulling him down beside me, curled up against him and drifted off.

Until I heard the chair in the corner shift, I didn't realize that I'd been moved. I woke up, a soft pillow beneath my head and the scent of Pietr—*everywhere*. I sat up and, blinking to clear my vision, found him sitting in the chair in the corner, watching me.

He cleared his throat. "I thought . . ." His eyes narrowed. ". . . since Annabelle Lee's in your bed . . ."

"I should be in yours?"

He shrugged one shoulder, noncommittal, but his expression was decidedly guilty. "Tomorrow everything will change, no matter what happens tonight."

I didn't know how to respond. "Is the mirror new?" I asked, looking at the long oval mirror framed with dark cherry wood. I didn't remember seeing it before, but I seldom remembered much after I'd been alone in a room with Pietr.

"Something Cat gave me. She insists I look at myself as part of accepting who I am. It's lame."

I laughed, and, catching my reflection in the mirror with just a bit of his, an idea came to me. I slipped off the edge of the bed. My bare feet touched down on the wooden floor and I padded over to him, my brooding, silent Pietr. Pietr with so much pain and heat and hope in his eyes. So confused, so torn, so beautiful.

"You're thinking too much."

"Everything depends on my plan working. I can't stop thinking about it—running scenarios through my head."

"Come here," I commanded, my words as strong as the pounding in my chest.

One step was all it took and he was standing before me, casting me in his shadow. "Distract me, Jess," he begged. His hand trailed down the side of my face, fingers sweeping aside my hair and dropping to my shoulder.

I held his hand there a moment, moved it down, and over slightly so it rested on my heart.

"Look at us," I whispered, turning my face as I reached to turn his to the long antique mirror that stood beside us. "Focus on us. Now."

He did, his eyes sparking as he was mesmerized by the image of his hand on my chest. His fingers twitched, reaching for the buttons on my shirt, his eyes on my eyes, watching us in the mirror. He fumbled a moment with a button and then carefully opened it, separating the two sections of fabric as far as he could and tracing a tantalizing line along the neckline of my shirt until his finger brushed against the next button.

In the mirror I watched his hand on me, watched him catch my mirror image's gaze and ask a silent question.

I nodded and he undid the next button. It was agonizingly slow, this tentative torture, and I finally shook his hands off and undid the next three buttons quickly with trembling fingers.

He pushed my shirt down, baring my shoulder, and looked away from the mirror, focused with a devastating intensity on me. Something inside of me loosened, heated under that look, and I lifted his shirt, pulling it up and over him, off of his head, but stopping before I slid it free and loosed his hands. Instead, I brought his hands down, the T-shirt still binding them and held in my closed fist. I stood on tiptoes to kiss along his jaw and he growled, hands flexing against my hip, eager to touch me again.

"*Nyet.*" I nipped at his neck.

When he said my name it came out strangled, his voice breaking the word into two syllables.

And then I heard the sound of cloth tearing and his hands were free—his shredded T-shirt falling to the ground. "I liked that one," I mused.

He snarled and the remaining buttons on my shirt popped off like shots fired one after the other as he tugged my shirt all the way off, letting it crumple on the floor like a puddle of fabric around my feet. "I liked that one, too."

"Shut up, Jess," he whispered, and he bent his powerful legs and lifted me up, his hands sliding across my back and clutching me to him while he kissed me quiet. One of his hands reached behind my left leg and dragged it around so it wrapped his waist. He adjusted his grip with a grunt and did the same thing with my other leg.

His face buried in the curve of my neck, I heard him draw in a deep and ragged breath. "You're beautiful," he confessed, his breathing shallow. Pressed so tightly to him I felt his heart racing into my stomach—a mind-numbing sensation.

He set me down on the bed and, propping himself above me, he searched my face for an answer to the question we both kept arriving at.

"Yes—*da*," I whispered, and he groaned. "*Pocelujte menyah*," I commanded.

And he filled my ears with his trembling confession: "*Yah tebyah lyewblyew*, Jess."

"*Yah tebyah lyewblyew*, Pietr Andreiovich Rusakova," I replied, peppering his face with kisses.

His pants fell in a heap by the bedside and his nightstand drawer opened and closed with a squeak. I heard the rustle of a foil packet and my eyes popped open a moment, realizing *this* was it. Then Pietr's mouth was on mine and we rolled under the covers.

For a while the world fell away and there was only me and

Pietr. And a fire that burned in us both as bright as a wolf's eyes at midnight.

Jessie

It was still dark outside when I untangled myself from the sheets and sat up in the bed, carefully moving toward its foot so I didn't wake Pietr. Focusing on the mirror, I ran my fingers through my hair, trying to straighten it. I turned my face from side to side, examining my image. Did I look any different?

I *felt* different. A little sore, and a lot nervous. A bit guilty. Yeah. Definitely guilty. I'd never imagined myself here, sleeping with a guy I'd only met a few months earlier. I wasn't even eighteen. My eyes settled on Pietr's sleeping form. What had we done? How would it change things between us? I swallowed hard. What if . . .

What if Pietr had been right and we didn't really know enough about each other?

The mattress squeaked and Pietr reached out in his sleep. "Jess," he rumbled, his fingers prowling my empty side of the bed. "Jess?" He sat up suddenly, blinking. "Oh." His brow wrinkled as he focused on me. "What are you doing there?"

"Thinking."

A smile slid across his lips. "Liar. You're worrying," he corrected. "Quit that. Come here."

I nodded and flopped down beside him.

"Better," he said, his hand walking along my arm.

"This"—I looked at him meaningfully—"changes everything."

"*Da*. It does," he agreed, and he pulled me into his arms and fell asleep again, his forehead hot against mine.

CHAPTER TWENTY-ONE

Jessie

The next morning we drove together to Junction High, Pietr wrapping himself around me like the finest of coats, Annabelle Lee riding shotgun so she could be dropped off at the middle-school entrance.

Our behavior didn't go unnoticed and after Annabelle Lee had been dropped off, Max and Cat exchanged a look, glanced at us, and laughed.

Max had planned to take the group of us out to the movies after school to keep up appearances and fill my head—and eyes—with things that would keep Derek watching us and not exploring the house while Dmitri and Alexi finalized plans.

Amy told Max the night before that she'd take the bus to school. It was always earlier and she needed a few minutes before homeroom to deal with some library books she'd rediscovered in her closet.

So it surprised me when she wasn't waiting for us. "Wait—where's Amy?"

Pietr looked up and down the sidewalk. His nostrils flared momentarily. "She hasn't gotten here yet."

"No. There's her bus." I pointed.

I jogged over to it. She was nowhere in sight. I dug my cell phone out of my back pack and hit her number.

"Hey," she answered.

"God, you sound awful."

"Yeah. My throat's really killing me," she said hoarsely.

Max trotted over, his eyebrows tucking his normally bright eyes into shadow.

"So you're not coming in?"

"No." She coughed.

"Should we bring you something?"

"No. I mean . . . I just feel like crap. Can I—can I talk to you later?"

"Yeah. Oh."

"Did you tell Max?" I asked, catching his eye.

"No," Amy said. "Could you—" She was coughing again, so loud I had to move the phone away from my ear. "Sorry," she gasped. "I gotta go."

"Where's Amy?" Max asked, tossing the car keys back and forth with Cat.

"Home. Sick." I slipped the phone back into my pack's pocket. "It must be some bad bug," I muttered. "She hasn't been sick enough to skip school in . . ." The words dropped away when I saw him. Smiling, laughing, flirting with some girl—a girl who looked remarkably like Amy.

Max, Pietr, and Catherine followed my gaze.

Straight to Marvin.

Max snagged the keys out of midair and spun back toward the car, his stride so long I jogged to keep up. "Take notes for me!" I told Pietr.

Max glanced down at me, his jaw set.

"I'm coming, too," I panted. "Shotgun!"

"I may want one of those."

I felt the color drain from my face, wondering what he thought we'd find. And I worried he'd be right.

Jessie

"I'm sick," Amy protested from the other side of the door. "I don't want you to get this, too." She coughed. Suddenly it sounded fake.

"I'll take the chance. Let me in now," I insisted.

"I am absolutely unwilling to spread this contagion. Go back to school."

"Open the damn door, Amy," Max demanded.

The dead bolt slid into place.

"Nice move." I tugged at my hair. "If she's locking both of us out it must be bad. What the hell could he have done . . . ?"

Max closed his eyes and he stepped forward, one hand on the door.

"Oh . . ." Bile rose in my throat.

He licked his lips. "I can get through this." He tapped the door with a finger.

"Amy, open the door," I urged.

Silence.

"Step back, Amy," Max commanded. "Check me," he whispered.

"Coast's clear."

His eyes glowed and he grabbed the edge of the door and peeled it off the hinges, throwing it behind us like he was discarding old cardboard.

There, behind a coffee table leveled with shims, Amy stood, eyes wide, arms wrapped protectively around herself. The hem of the bathrobe she snugged against her flapped in the sudden breeze.

Hair snarled, her wrists were black with bruises. At a glance I knew her sore throat was legitimate, a handprint visible on the slender curve of her neck.

Max was inside a heartbeat ahead of me.

Something passed between them and the air electrified. Max's nostrils flared. And then his hands brushed the hair back from her eyes and rested on either side of her face. Tenderly he tilted her face up to him and he kissed her forehead so lightly his lips might have been a feather brushing her battered skin. "I have to go," he apologized. "Here." He handed me his cell phone and some cards. "Use the Visa to get a door that works."

"When will you be b—"

But he was already gone, the car slinging gravel as its tires spun.

"Visa." I flipped through the plastic options. My hands shaking, the cards tumbled to the dingy carpet. "Oh. *Crap*."

Amy's eyes widened at the sight, too. She picked them up tenderly and tears came to her eyes. "What is he planning?"

My stomach curled in on itself and I shook my head. Whatever Max was planning, it was obvious he didn't want any identification on him if he was caught.

Amy clutched his school ID and license and I rooted through old newspapers and magazines for a place to sit.

Jessie

I awkwardly nudged the door up the trailer's rickety stairs and leaned it in place to provide us with some sense of security. Coaxing Amy's old computer to crawl to a site with a phone number, I called and ordered a new door.

We sat there silently for a few painful minutes, Amy staring at her hands, and me staring at the handprint on her neck.

"Marvin." I said the name and she flinched. "I didn't think . . ."

"I didn't, either," she admitted, the words scratching their way out of her throat. "I mean. We fought. A lot," she confessed. "More than I ever wanted to think about. I mean . . . I thought he was like some prince at first. Taking an interest in me. Him with all the money and privilege . . . I thought I was being rescued. My brother Frank got out of this dive. Mom left soon after that. Dad escaped when he started drinking. Heavily. Why not me? Don't I deserve to escape?"

I reached out and rested my hand on hers.

"But he pushed me around. At first he said he was sorry."

"And you believed him," I said.

"I was stupid."

"No. He was a liar. How could you know?"

"The flowers he gave me at Homecoming? They were part of an especially big apology."

"Oh." I had thought they were beautiful.

"He wasn't what I expected. He pushed me around. He smacked me. He kicked me. He pinched me and shoved me . . ."

The words unsteady, I urged her, "You can just say it, you know." I couldn't stand to hear each way he'd hurt her. . . . The use of each cruel verb. The summary was bad enough. "Just say he beat you."

"No," she said, the word stark and cold. Her eyes locked on to mine and I saw a bit of fire—a bit of that beautiful and bold Amy sparking in their depths.

"Why not?"

"Because of the word, Jessie. It makes a difference. *Beat* has different meanings, you know? One's right for the way he treated me." She swallowed and tugged her hands out of mine to rub her tender throat. "But one relates to winning—like if you beat someone in a race. If I say he beat me, it feels like he won. And he hasn't." She swallowed hard, a tightness around her eyes at the pain. "No," she croaked. "He didn't beat me. He'll *never* beat me," she promised. Her eyes flashed open and she caught me watching her. "But he did rape me."

And then she was silent. The words all used up.

I stood, rubbing my forehead and urging my brain to kick in. "I need to make a call."

She nodded. "I need a shower."

"No," I said, aching at the look she gave me and so sorry to make her wait. "Not quite yet." I closed myself in the small bathroom and called Alexi.

Next I'd call Dad.

Alexi

"God." Words escaped me. *"Where will he go with him?"* I heard Jessie's question, but my ears were so full of the noise of blood rushing through them as my pulse pounded in anger, it took me a moment to respond. I pushed the phone more firmly to my ear. "This is Max we are talking about. He will take the fight to Marvin. *Nyet.* An audience won't be enough to stop him from grabbing him. *Da.* I know. Pietr's at school."

She rambled, doing what she always did when panic set in.

"Jessie." I stopped her. "Max has the car. *Da.* Taxi. You get her to the hospital to be checked out."

I hung up and called the cab service. It was the slowest ride I'd ever taken, knowing what I did.

Amy had been attacked and Max was out for blood.

Alexi

If doing cardio was good preparation for a fight, then I would be in amazing shape, I thought as I sprinted away from the taxi, hurling bills at the driver and racing for the main entrance of Junction High. I'd used my time in the crawling cab wisely (after cajoling and then verbally berating the man in Russian when he refused to go a single notch past the speed limit).

I'd called Jessie back and gotten a basic overview of the school's layout.

Hindsight being what it was, I realized I should have attended the parent-teacher conference about Max's flirtatious behavior when it was first requested. At least then I would have known the school's layout personally.

The place was nearly empty—the strange illness that kept being mentioned in the local papers making the high school more and more desolate. I slid to a halt outside Pietr's classroom and waved my arms wildly at him. He needed no more instruction, but vaulted out of his desk.

Behind him a man shouted about his current math grade not being mathematically impossible to lower. Yet.

Pietr winced.

"Max," I wheezed, struggling for breath. I should have given up cigarettes months ago. Hell, I should have never started smoking the blasted things.

Pietr's nostrils flared and he grabbed my arm, dragging me with him down the hall as my shoes—a decent grade of Italian leather—slipped on the linoleum tiles. This was why Mafia men were so often shown in tracksuits on television and in the movies, I thought as we rounded a corner and I scrabbled for purchase: There was running involved. Sensible shoes were necessary all the time.

Pietr, not even winded, pulled me to a stop at a door marked BASEMENT. "Down there," he said, yanking the door open. He paused, seeing the line of steps, and then, judging the distance, took them all in one stunning leap. *Show-off.* I ran down them as quickly as my feet could carry me, my goal simply to not trip to my own death in my haste.

Pietr stood in the corner, assessing things, and I leaped between my brother and his girlfriend's attacker.

"I will *kill* him—" Max's fist raised and I covered my head with my arms—the noise of glass breaking punctuated his words as he shattered a lightbulb swinging above us—like a boxer taking a warm-up swipe at a convenient punching bag.

Marvin dropped to the floor and rolled into a fetal position as glass rained down and I straddled him.

"Max—MAX!" I shouted, trying to break his focus and stem the rage boiling in his bones.

Glass stuck out from Max's bloody knuckles, but he didn't even twitch at the shards wedged there, his focus so tight on Marvin, whimpering before him.

I spread my arms. "Max, think!" I urged. "Pietr—a little help!"

Pietr jumped forward and grabbed Max's arm.

Max's shoulders rolled forward, head low, his brows brutally shadowing his eyes. The beast inside my brother fought to claw its way out and he welcomed it.

I closed my eyes and puffed out a breath. "Max," I urged, trying to find him somewhere beneath the red swirling in his eyes. "Stop this madness." This could quickly go from bad to tragic. And no matter what Max was planning, Amy would lose. Realizing we had one casualty already, I focused on limiting the collateral damage.

"Max. Calm down," Pietr said, pulling back on his brother's arm and bracing himself for a fight.

He spit. "Calm down? Whose side are you on?" His glare cut at us as deeply as the claws and fangs of the wolf could bite.

"Amy's," I answered, working to rebuild a cool façade that kept crumbling beneath the rolling heat of his hate. "We're on Amy's side."

"Then let me have him," he purred—a deceptive noise that folded seamlessly into a growl.

"*Nyet*," I insisted, my ears disbelieving, my own neck still remembering the brutal power of his enraged hands from the one day we'd had it out for top dog of the family.

He knocked me aside easily, barely flicking his wrist, but I still stumbled under the impact and plowed with a curse into the wall.

Max straightened, stretched, swaying. In one long, smooth movement, bones cracking as he raised his arms, he leaned back his head and summoned the change, relishing the beast as it pushed to the surface. His face stretched, eyes glowing the red of hot coals, hair sprouting along his skin as his fingers curled under and his hands became heavy paws.

Cloth ripped as his haunches and barrel chest burst free of the constraints of human clothing. For a moment he teetered on his hind legs, balancing awkwardly as he peered at his paws and flexed them—claws like stiletto points unsheathing with a deadly whisper.

He looked down at Marvin—impossibly small in the shadow of the wolf—and fell forward . . .

. . . to come face-to-face with me.

I amazed us both, successfully sandwiching myself between the leering wolf with its slavering jaws and its whining human victim.

I was officially an idiot.

Marvin reeled back beneath me as far as he could go, his face pressed into the floor, trembling so hard at what he saw above me his body shook mine.

"No!" I shouted, keeping as much of my back pressed against Marvin's quivering form as I could. "I won't let him destroy your future, too!"

Glass ground into us both as I adjusted my position to better cover him.

Max grabbed my arm to pull me out of his path.

I stiffened. Marvin balled up more tightly beneath me and my disgust for him grew. He was only brave enough to fight if his opponent was smaller than himself.

And I protected *him*.

"Urrgh!" I snaked my neck to catch Max's glimmering eyes with my own. Nose-to-nose he could hardly ignore me. If I stared him down—grabbed hold of the humanity in him, the part that wanted blood as much as it warred against the idea— maybe I could stop him.

"Max, don't . . ."

His eyes glowed, the red fire swirling up to consume the light that regularly sparkled in them. The cords on his neck stood out—metal rods holding his head in place—and I wrapped my hands around them and raised my legs so my knees were jammed beneath his heavy chest.

I built a wall of bone, flesh, and blood between him and his prey—a wall he could raze in an instant. His lips slid back from his teeth as his anguished snarl turned into a jagged-toothed grimace.

"He rrraped herrr," the beast within him shrieked from deep in his gut, shaking everything but my resolve.

Pietr stepped back, putting his hands up. "Tear him apart," he agreed.

"Shit, Pietr!" I snapped. "It's murder!"

"Justifiable homicide," Pietr returned.

"When did my questionable moral code start to qualify as the guiding light in this family?!" I wedged myself more firmly between the two of them. "He will pay, Max," I swore. "He'll pay. . . ." My hands on his shoulders I pushed, trying to pry him off. No good. "But if you kill him—"

Marvin shuddered beneath me, pinned and listening.

"—you *will* go to jail. There will be no way to stop that."

"I could run," Max muttered, his eyes still glowing, and fixed, on Marvin. "I could kill you and run," he clarified, looking past my shoulder at Marvin. Max's mouth twisted into a smile.

At my back, Marvin's heart pounded.

In the corner, Pietr rubbed his forehead and cursed. He stepped forward again, leaning over Max and wrapping a hand around his shoulder. "Then who will protect Amy?" he whispered to our brother.

Max froze.

Pietr closed his eyes and added, "What will happen to Amy without *you?*"

"*Da,*" I agreed, grabbing at Pietr's logic. "She will need you now more than ever."

The temperature dropped as the fire faded from Max's eyes and the light of reason returned.

Max slid back onto his heels, crouching, his eyes on my face. Reluctantly he stuck a hand out. I took it and popped up to my feet and off of Marvin.

"He has to pay," he said, eyes locked on mine.

"He will," I assured him. "God." I sniffed. "What's that smell?"

"Him." Max pointed a finger at the heap of humanity still curled in a puddle.

"Disgusting."

Marvin only moved far enough to get his eyes back on Max and then he froze again, still as a statue.

I looked at my two brothers. "Get Max some clothes and then head back to class," I said to Pietr. "You," I said to Max, "stay." I pulled out my cell phone and called the cops.

Jessie

I'd wrapped Amy in a long winter coat and dragged a brush through her hair before my father's truck pulled up. We'd been through the reasons she couldn't shower and shouldn't change and I was sick knowing that maintaining evidence of Marvin's crime meant maintaining physical proof of his contact with her.

The door was dragged aside and my father, eyes dark with worry as they scanned the damage to the door frame, asked, "Max?"

I nodded and, shielding Amy in my arms, walked to the truck with her. We rode in nearly perfect silence to the hospital; the only sounds were the wind with its growing chill as it clawed at the truck's windshield and the grinding of Dad's teeth as he worked his jaw in anger.

We were ushered into a small room, just Amy and I, and we waited behind the drawn blue curtain for a nurse and a police officer. I stayed the whole time, Amy's hand tight around mine, while the nurse collected evidence and the female police officer asked questions that swirled around my head and fed my blood with rage. Nothing but being there for Amy mattered in those long minutes between formal introductions and the suggestion she see a counselor.

There was, in fact, only one moment when I felt the need to speak.

The officer, scribbling detailed notes on a small pad of paper, looked at Amy and asked, "So this Marvin Broderick, you say he smacked you around numerous times before and you never reported it."

Amy nodded slowly.

"He beat you a lot."

Amy paled at the word and looked away.

"No," I corrected the officer when Amy could no longer find the words. "He hit her, he punched her, he kicked and pinched her. I saw bruises on Halloween night before she left him for the last time," I admitted. "And today he raped her. But he hasn't *beaten* her." I squeezed her hand and looked at her, hoping she read the determination in my eyes. "And I'll be damned if he ever does."

CHAPTER TWENTY-TWO

Jessie

Dad took it upon himself to talk to Amy's father. The trailer, now officially the last place Amy wanted to be, was quickly emptied of the few items she'd taken back to it by Pietr.

When we got to the Rusakovas' home, Amy hesitated on the stairs. "I don't . . ." She touched her throat. "I don't want him to see me like this again. I don't want him thinking of . . ." Her eyes squeezed shut at the thought.

"Shhh." I took her hand and listened. Upstairs something broke against a wall. Cat shouted. Max was working out his anger on the furnishings. "Come on," I insisted. "We'll go straight to the basement."

We did, gliding like ghosts through the foyer and down the long line of steps.

Amy froze at the sight of her bed, the blanket rumpled and Annabelle Lee's stuffed rabbit—that Amy still teased her about—peeking out from the sheets.

"Oh. She isn't going to . . ." The words didn't come at first. "I don't want anyone to . . ." She slumped onto the bed, wrapping the rabbit in her arms. "I don't want anyone else to know . . ."

"It's okay." Sitting beside her I stroked her hair and let her lean into my shoulder. "It's all going to be all right." As much as I wanted it to be the truth . . . how could things ever be all right again?

Cat brought us plates steaming with food that night instead of expecting us to eat dinner at the table, and she gave Amy a gentle hug that made tears ooze out of them both.

Above us I heard the Queen Anne's front door and back door open again and again. The noise of footsteps was frequent and I knew the werewolves—both the Rusakovas and the Mafia men who called themselves werewolves—were finally assembling.

Tonight would be the night. It was better I wasn't seeing the final preparation, in case Derek was borrowing my eyes for the evening.

Readying for bed downstairs, unwilling to risk walking past Max in the hallway before she was ready to see him again, Amy looked at the huge pile of belated birthday gifts stacked in the corner. "What are they really, Jessie?"

My mouth flapped open, but no words fell out.

"The truth," she insisted. "I think I'm ready for the truth. I've seen the way you're changing—growing a little tougher, a little faster. Friends notice. Something big's about to happen, isn't it?"

"Yes."

"Something involving the whole family here, right?"

"Yes. Tonight."

"Tonight," she repeated, eyes widening.

"Shhh. Don't worry," I soothed her. "Lie down now." I picked up our plates, mine clean, hers still full. "I'm going upstairs. But I'll be back. Soon."

She nodded and crawled into the bed, pulling the sheets and blankets high up on her body like a shield.

Alexi

Wanda and Leon had come to our party late, but I was glad when they finally arrived. They'd made it clear they'd help incapacitate threats in the bunker, but were against outright killing, except in self-defense. Looking around the table at the mafiosos I knew we had eager killers aplenty.

Dmitri had tried to take over the entire operation and we were already arguing about getting past the doors. The first one, we had a way around, but the door at the bottom of the stairs was a different matter.

Jessie walked past the group of us on the way to load her plate and Amy's into the dishwasher. For a moment everyone fell quiet.

"If he uses her eyes, why is she here?" one man grumbled.

The question continued to circle, growing in power until Pietr smashed his fist down on the table. "She is much more of an asset than a liability."

"More like a piece of as—" the same man muttered a heartbeat before Pietr knocked him to the floor.

Leaning over the other man, Pietr growled, "Her skill with a gun may just save *your* ass."

Dishes clattered in the kitchen as Jessie arranged them in the dishwasher.

I whistled for attention. "Look. Look. We don't need C-4 for the door at the bottom of the stairs," I argued. "We need stealth. We need surprise." I shoved my hands through my hair.

Jessie was suddenly beside me. She looked from me to Wanda. "Remember those files?" she asked.

Wanda nodded.

I nodded—the files Wanda had slipped out of the bunker in a ruse that they were to return to the warehouse.

"You want stealth and surprise? What you really need also starts with an S."

Wanda nodded sharply and reached around behind her to pull up the filebox she now carried almost everywhere.

"I," Jessie announced to the group, all the while focusing on Pietr, "am going upstairs for a nice, long, peaceful shower." She wiggled her fingers near her ears like rain poured down around her head. *"Lots* of water."

Pietr was transfixed, his imagination running as fast as his heart probably hammered at the thought of his girlfriend in the shower, but I knew what she was getting at and understood the message she was sending.

We'd work out the rest of our plan while she showered, blind and deaf to our plotting, with the nearly guaranteed benefit that Derek's eyes would probably be on her the whole time, following the soap's lathery trail.

To have a power like that . . .

I shook myself and looked at Wanda as Jessie climbed the stairs. "S, Wanda," I prodded. "Pietr." I snapped my fingers, pulling him back from his brief fantasy.

He blinked and refocused.

Wanda pulled out a file and slapped it down on the table for everyone to see. "S, it seems, stands for *Sophie.*"

Things only got weirder and weirder in Junction.

"Cat. This one's yours," I suggested, sliding the file to her. "It won't be a trip like your usual ones together to the mall and movies, but you can guarantee her it's bound to be unforgettable."

I considered what else needed to be done in Jessie's absence. "We need to move the presents."

Cat spoke up. "I'll go. I think . . ." She glanced at Max. "I think Pietr and I should handle this."

Max barely reacted but understood as well as he could that Amy didn't want him around. Not yet.

Cat and Pietr descended and climbed the stairs multiple times, carrying package after package of colorfully wrapped presents filled with guns and bricks of ammo while Max, Dmitri, Wanda, and I argued strategy in front of the mafiosos Pietr had paid for with a promise he was eager to break.

Jessie

I had become a prune in the interest of keeping Derek's attention away from the group plotting Mother's rescue. For my own satisfaction I focused on scrubbing my ankles, knees, and armpits and sliding a washcloth carefully between all of my toes. Even after such a long shower, I felt filthy knowing Derek's eyes had probably seen the same bits of my body as mine.

I slipped into my pajamas and walked to the basement, ignoring the debate still raging in the dining room. Downstairs Amy had been joined by Annabelle Lee. I'd persuaded my father, honest and bright as anyone, to tell Annabelle Lee she'd be tremendously helpful if she kept Amy out from under foot. Amy, Dad had pointed out to her, *didn't* know about my amazing werewolf boyfriend.

Not only had that amazed Annabelle Lee, but it thrilled her to know something about Pietr and me that my best friend didn't.

I lay down in the bed beside Amy, gently resting my arm over her shoulder as she rested hers around Annabelle Lee. Amy flinched at the contact. "Shhh," I soothed her, and recognizing her surroundings and friends, Amy fell quickly into a deep sleep.

And I did as Alexi instructed.

I slept.

Alexi

Everyone headed to bed like normal. Cat and I sat up a few minutes longer, I clicking through television channels with the remote while she clutched the popcorn bowl and picked at the kernels.

"They know to set the beds?"

"*Da*," she said, staring straight ahead at the flickering screen.

I ran through the list of precautions we were taking. The clocks were set wrong. The mafiosos had loaded the presents into several different vehicles and had already left, going different ways to get to the same place at the right time. Jessie, Amy, and Annabelle Lee were curled together sleeping—a curious enough arrangement that a horny teen boy like Derek would want to peek in several times hoping to see something more intriguing than what reality offered. Our beds would be stuffed to give the appearance we still slept while we actually raided the bunker.

"And you have made arrangements with Sophia?"

"*Da*," she said reluctantly. "It is difficult being a normal American mall-shopping girl while roping a fellow girl—with a fine appreciation of style—into assisting on a bunker raid. My social standing may suffer."

I snatched the popcorn bowl away from her and turned it over on top of her head.

She squealed and shook her hair, flinging kernels everywhere. "You are the most awful brother!"

"*That* I can live with, Ekaterina," I admitted as she stomped away, fuming. *Da*. The *most awful brother* was still a brother. And *that* I could most definitely live with.

Jessie

I woke in the Rusakovas' car, squashed beside Max in the back-seat, presents stacked around me and piled on my lap, a heavy vest—bulletproof—hanging on me, holster snug across my chest.

The car was already in motion.

Cat had hopefully gotten to Sophia. There was so much I was blind to for everyone else's safety. So much I wouldn't know until it happened.

"I need you to do something very strange," Pietr said, leaning back from the passenger's seat. "I'll be slipping around the building to sneak in with Max and I need you to play decoy in case they have Derek doing the night shift."

"He may believe you're asleep," Max rumbled beside me. "Might start prowling the house with his power."

"The clocks are set to confuse him," Alexi reminded us from the driver's seat. "Hopefully, with nothing out of the ordinary appearing to be going on, he'll start scanning for you."

I nodded, my eyes still blurry.

"But," Alexi said, "to give us a better chance, we need you to use *your* ability."

He must have seen my expression grow puzzled in the rearview mirror. "That ability all competition shooters and writers have—to focus—*visualize*—give him something creative, detailed—"

"Intense—" Pietr specified.

"To watch."

"You'll want to close your eyes in a moment so you aren't distracted," Alexi suggested.

"Think about *anything* else?" I considered.

"Feel what you're thinking strongly. It'll send up an emotional flare he should latch onto."

Max adjusted his position in the seat beside me, stretching his powerful legs. "As long as we haven't already given him something better to watch."

Alexi caught my gaze in the rearview mirror. "You'd better start now."

"Something he won't want to look away from," Pietr whispered. "Something to remember us by." His eyes glowed and I felt the smile twist across my lips as the car pulled to a stop and I undid my seat belt, leaning forward to catch Pietr's mouth with mine. I kissed him hard, my body tightening at his breathless response.

My emotional flare shot sky high.

"The mirror," I murmured against his lips, closing my eyes and pulling back. And with the experience that came from long hours of visualization practicing as a competition shooter and imagining as an aspiring author, I dropped into a memory Derek would be both fascinated and pissed off by.

Like watching a train wreck, he wouldn't be able to look away. I shivered, realizing how trains excited him.

Layering back in the details of scent and sound and touch that too easily faded, I built on the memory.

In another part of my mind, the part that kept me breathing and kept my heart pumping, my lungs going, I felt someone pull the boxes off my lap, take my arm, and tug me to a standing position.

Alexi. My arm was tugged around his waist and he pulled me along, carefully guiding me, blind as I was as my mind reeled under the power of bringing a memory to life again.

In the foremost part of my mind Pietr and I were again in front of the mirror in his bedroom in the precious minutes before we tumbled into bed together. Opening my eyes, I willed the memory to play on.

The breeze brushed by us, snaring a single tendril of my hair and pulling it loose from both my ponytail and knit black hat. I tucked it back in and scurried forward with Alexi into the thick of the aromatic plants and hedges, things planted to help cover the company's scent from the Rusakovas' patrols as they searched for their mother. Rosemary and the curled and crunchy leaves of neglected basil snatched at our jackets, marking us with desperate final bursts of scent.

Dmitri crouched ahead of us, watching me with quiet curiosity, three of his men at our backs. Alexi looked at me and carefully unwrapped my arm from around him. Even with a

Rusakova beside me, I doubted there would ever be a moment I felt safe with the Mafia nearby.

Alexi nodded sharply to Dmitri. I was back—aware—the time to go was now. Dmitri turned, pointed his fingers to his eyes, and then turned them to us, announcing a changing of the guard. Tapping the silencer on his gun, he reminded us all stealth mattered especially in this initial phase of our attack.

Two of the three men nodded understanding, looking at us.

Even in the dark I knew Alexi's jaw twitched as we nodded grimly back. A deal with the devil. That's what we'd all been thrown into.

Dmitri looked at the remaining man and signaled. The two of them moved forward, down the freshly broken path I guessed Pietr and Max had made.

Together we sprinted forward and Dmitri checked his watch. He nodded and he and his man raced around the house's front as we ran with our two Mafia men toward the front door. We paused, hugging the shadows, and I peeked around the corner.

Dmitri's man held an army blanket to the window and Dmitri whacked it with his arm as Alexi pulled me back around the corner. The sound of breaking glass was muffled, but the sound of shattered glass landing inside was still clear. Moments of difference—but we needed every moment we could get.

As Dmitri rolled inside to fire on the surprised agents, we heard the echo of more glass breaking all around the house. Dmitri flung the front door open and I felt people press in behind us.

"Jessie," Sophia whispered, "tell me this is *not* my life."

I ducked down, tugging Soph down with me and covering her head with my arms, Cat flanking us as our guards stepped around and, with Dmitri and his man, cleared out the first bunch of agents. The only cameras in the narrow hall of the Colonial farmhouse were pulled from their roosts high on the walls. "Don't look," I suggested to Sophie, and I wrapped my hands like blinders around her face to shield her vision from the agents lying dead on the floor.

On silent feet Max and Pietr raced to the second floor, quickly checking rooms and calling, "Clear!" The floorboards above creaked and I heard the distinct *thump* of a body hitting the floor.

Feet pounded up the stairs from the bunker below and I nudged one of the Mafiosos forward. "Latch that door." I pointed to the one at the top of the bunker's stairs. It wasn't much, but hearing the latch fall into place, I felt a little better. It bought us a moment more, and with the Rusakovas, every moment mattered.

By the time Max and Pietr returned, we'd backed away from the door leading down, ducking and covering as agents on the other side sprayed the door with bullets. But even guns with big clips needed reloading and every few minutes the pitch would change and one or two guns would stop for a refill.

Wanda found me. "We're going through the Grabbit Mart entrance," she explained, nodding at Dad. "Things look covered here." More bullets sprayed the door.

"Really? *This* is covered?"

She chuckled. "We'll try and hunt down Derek and his new pet." To my astonished expression she simply said, "Yeah, you've been replaced."

There was no time for me to even wonder by whom.

Pietr and Max slipped behind us and I caught a quick glance as they peeled out of their clothing and dropped to all fours. Stretching, howling, and welcoming the change. For a moment the shooting stopped, the agents surely frozen for a heartbeat.

A heartbeat was all it took.

In their wolfskins Pietr and Max charged the door, splintering its pocked surface as they bowled the agents down the stairs, knocking them out of the way of their advance. Fast on their heels, the Mafiosos made quick work of the stunned agents.

I swallowed hard and counted the steps as I started Sophie

down the stairs with me, careful of the blood slicking their surface. These agents wanted us dead—or as good as. I tried to
keep that in mind, but it was almost impossible to keep a reason for the bloodshed in my head when I witnessed it all.

The path down into the bunker's heart clear, Cat dodged
back up the stairs and outside to do a perimeter sweep and I led
Sophie the rest of the way down the stairs, careful of the bodies. "Don't look down." I glanced over my shoulder. "There," I
said, seeing Pietr, standing in human form at the bottom of the
stairs. "Look at Pietr. Not at the stairs."

Looking past me, I noticed her eyes widen. "Look at his *face*,
Soph." Despite the corpses we picked our way around, Sophie
was still surprised enough to blush at Pietr's naked body.

If only the blood streaking Pietr's face and body was a primitive warpaint, I could believe him to be a fiercely beautiful
warrior from some ancient tribe roaming Russia's most distant
steppes—or a grim god.

Gunfire snapped me back to the awful reality of our situation.

God, we were all so messed up—and this wasn't going to
help any of us overcome our trust issues or petty paranoias.

I stood her before the keypad. "Okay, work your magic," I
said, watching her lean over the keys.

She shoved her blond hair back and screwed her face up with
concentration. "I'll give it my best shot . . . but it's no magic," she
muttered in her breathy way. "Just energy impressions. I see the
colors of energy someone leaves behind like a slightly brighter
fingerprint if it was more recent. Okay. The last one to touch
this keypad had fast fingers. The difference in the traces are subtle. Huh. Backward we have . . ."

Pietr listened, waiting until she finished to tap the numbers
into the keypad in the right order.

Nothing happened. "I need a hand," Sophia called.

"What?"

"Like, literally. A hand," she balked, but held up her palm.

Dmitri dragged a corpse forward, flattening his hand to the scanner's surface, and Pietr swept us back from the doors as they slid apart and bullets rained out.

"Shiiit," Pietr snarled, hit in the shoulder a moment before he wolfed again and bounded into the fray.

I thrust Sophie into a corner, blocking her with my body. She panted and snagged her lower lip in her teeth. "This is not my life," she insisted.

I looked at her solemnly. "I'm afraid it is. But it doesn't have to be for long. Let's just get through this. Then things go back to normal for you."

"Like they keep going back to normal for you?" Sophie hissed. "Ghost of your mother, psycho ex-best friend, company agent dating your dad, psychic vampire ex-boyfriend, werewolf current boyfriend—by the way, I can't blame you for that one," she confessed, eyes round as she mouthed the word *whoa* before continuing with her list, "Trip to the asylum, attempts against your life, vigilante father . . ."

"Hey, the last ones are brand new. And the vigilante father thing? He'll revert."

"Anyhow, I'm not so keen on your concept of normal." I caught her staring at me. "Your aura's all smudgy with a different color tonight," she whispered. "Something's changed. . . ." She craned her neck around to catch a glimpse of Pietr. "Pietr's color . . . and his is all smudgy with your color, like his energy's been smeared all over yours really vigorously. . . . Oh! Ew!" She covered her eyes.

I blushed for both of us.

"I just don't know what to do with you, Jessie. Should I congratulate you or rail on you about the dangers of doing *it*?"

I just shook my head.

My normal.

In the room beyond us the shooting stopped and one final thud sounded as a body hit the floor. On the other side of the doorway, Alexi motioned to us.

"Clear," Pietr proclaimed.

We stepped through the doorway and kept our heads up, still trying to ignore the worst of the casualties surrounding us. It was impossible as the blood continued to spread in slow, slippery puddles.

A man with a briefcase set it in one of the cubicles and opened it, displaying a bunch of wires and buttons.

Bomb, I realized distantly.

"Two more doors, Sophia," Pietr called as he fell back into his wolf form.

"Actually three," I said, pointing over the wolf's thickly furred shoulder at the science lab's door.

In his wolfskin Pietr shook his head. *No.*

"The Hell! Right now there are probably a dozen smaller than average scientists in there wetting themselves while you all take out their protectors. What were you going to do, leave them in there as the bunker falls down around their ears?"

The wolf blinked.

"Pietr!" I demanded. "They've only followed orders. Why should they die?"

With an impatient whine the wolf whipped into a very angry Pietr again. "Following orders?" he retorted. "You who love your history and research so much should know that was the excuse of every war criminal during the Nuremberg Trials. Every Nazi used that excuse," he spat. "Following orders! When do they realize they're doing something awful and stand up and say no, Jess?"

"I don't know! But what if they just need a chance to realize and change? What if this could be their epiphany?"

"Stop trying to save everyone," he ordered. "Some can't be saved."

I caught Dmitri smiling.

"And when is following orders ever a good enough excuse for not standing by your principles, for not having a moral code?"

"What moral code do *you* have, Pietr, if you just let people die—unable to even defend themselves?"

He looked at me, eyes flickering for a moment, and then he said, "Two doors, Sophia," and was the wolf again, shifting as he dropped to all fours.

I crossed my arms and watched Sophie go to the door that would open on the final room before Mother's cell. She leaned over the number pad and tapped in the appropriate digits in the appropriate order. "There should really be some other way I could use this new talent of mine," she said.

A bullet zipped so close to her head her hair fluttered and Dmitri swung her back against the safety of the wall for a moment before releasing her to finish.

Eyes wide, she tapped in the rest of the code, deciding, "On second thought, I'll just use it this once and never mention it again. Then back to normal, right, Jessie?"

"Sure thing, Soph," I called. "Whatever normal is."

The door whispered open and one more firefight ensued, the werewolves rushing headlong into the broad room holding their mother's strange clear cubicle of a cage. They raced into danger like life didn't matter—like, in this moment, they were immortal.

Things changed when the last set of guards' bullets tore into their flesh.

Pietr's growl turned into a shout of pain as he flashed out of his wolfskin and skid across the concrete floor, human and bleeding.

"Dmitri!" I screamed, seeing the wisp of smoke wafting from Pietr's side. "The bullets are spiked! Poisoned!"

Shoving Sophie back, I rushed across the open space to Pietr's side. I heard Dad's yell and Wanda's reply as they gave me cover. Glad as I was they'd rejoined us, there was no time to focus on anything but Pietr. And survival.

Sitting in a pool of sizzling blood, Pietr thrashed and cursed, clawing at his side with shaking hands. I dug the Leatherman out of my pocket and unfolded it, looking at the knife and Pietr's quickly healing flesh.

"Stay still," I urged as I grabbed his arm and sliced into his side with an inaccuracy that had him cursing my name. "I almost have it—" There was a thud and the slug fell into the red puddle, spinning and spitting.

Wolf again, Pietr rushed forward, knocking an agent down and out.

In her shatterproof cell, Pietr's mother howled her joy. She pounded on the clear wall and screamed her children's names.

Grabbing Sophie I slipped back out the door and raced to the science lab. The man with the briefcase looked up at us doubtfully, rearranging the contents in his case with swift and sure hands.

"Pietr's not going to be happy," Sophie protested.

"I'm saving lives," I reminded. "Pietr will get happy again later. Press the buttons."

Sophie did and the door hissed open.

Inside, the whole staff of the lab gawked at me.

"Get out now!" I shouted. The lead scientist, Henry, reached for a box; another reached for some files. "Leave it all, or you won't get out alive."

The box hit the ground and files fell, forgotten, as people rushed for the stairs.

"Last door, Sophie," I said, and we turned back toward the room where I'd just dug the bullet out of Pietr.

"Not so fast."

Dr. Jones.

I froze, thinking about the location of the gun at my head. How fast could she pull the trigger? If I fell to the ground . . .

And then there was a shot and I felt the gun slip away and fall, clunking loose to the ground, followed by the limp body of the doctor.

"Now *that'll* require therapy," Wanda apologized loudly, lowering her gun in the next room.

Sophie glanced behind us and went a shade paler.

Pietr's eyes focused over my shoulder and I knew he saw the scientists slipping their way up the stairs and away. His gaze fell on me a moment and instead of the anger I expected to find, I caught a sense of relief shining there. Until he noticed the doctor, dead, behind me.

His face tightened.

One last agent fell to Max, the gun falling out of his grip. Guiding Sophie by the shoulders, I steered her into the last room and in front of the control panel at Mother's cage. Soph tapped in the ghostly pattern she read on the touchpad; the sirens sounded their warning, lights flashing one last time, and Pietr's mother tore into the free world. Hugs were quick embraces, snatches at arms and hands, and kisses brushed cheeks.

In Pietr's arms, Mother looked around the room at the people, fallen and still standing, and her gaze settled on Wanda. "Traitor!" she howled, lunging for her and nearly breaking free of Pietr's iron grip.

Struggling to hold her back, his eyes narrowed. "No, Mother. Nyet," he insisted. "She's helped us. She's no traitor."

"She must be confused," Alexi justified, stroking Tatiana's arm gently and speaking soft words in Russian to sooth her. But his eyes stayed sharp addressing Wanda. "Da, Wanda? Tell me she's confused."

"Yeah," Wanda agreed, keeping a wary distance. She glanced from Pietr to Dmitri and back before announcing, "I'm going for the files."

The moment she was out of sight, Mother calmed down and Pietr passed her into Alexi's guarded embrace.

Dmitri looked at his watch.

Pietr didn't need to.

Turning, Dmitri said, "To a fresh start." He shot his three nearest men. "A new way," he added, shooting another to leave only his original second. He looked at Pietr.

A chill flashed through me and I realized I couldn't read Pietr's expression.

My father squeezed my shoulders before shoving both Sophie and me toward Max, his eyes still on Pietr. "Get the girls out of here," Dad instructed.

Max nodded and Pietr paused to confer with Dmitri. "Let's go," Max said, glancing back to Pietr and his mother. "Sophia," he rumbled. "Watch where you're walking—don't gawk at anything else."

Sophie looked at me, pink as a fresh carnation.

Reentering the office spaces I saw the man with the briefcase dead in a puddle of blood, the bomb slowly moving through its countdown.

Behind us, Pietr's mother suddenly called out. I spun back toward the commotion. Mother clung to Pietr, convulsing as the wolf tried to take control and Max dropped his arms from around our shoulders and rushed back to help his family.

"Where's Cat?" Max called, racing to his mother.

I turned to look, but Dmitri's second came up behind me, one hand on my back, one hand on Sophia's. I couldn't remember seeing Cat since she'd headed out on her perimeter search. "I'll take the girls," he called over his shoulder.

Distracted and struggling to again calm his mother, Pietr simply nodded and said, "We'll meet everyone at the vehicles as soon as we're able."

We were all going to make it out. We were all going to be okay, I thought as we started up the stairs. So why did goose bumps race across my skin, chilling me to the bone?

"You did admirably, girls," Dmitri's second congratulated. "It is nearly over."

My hand slipped toward my holster at something in his tone, and at the top of the stairs I turned left to head out of the house, but, a gun nestling in my ribs, he nudged me right, his hand clamped to my holster, sealing my gun to my body.

"Here is the problem, girls. As much as we admire your bravery, we have no need of you in the new organization."

"Crap." I was tired of needing to be rescued.

"You, especially, Jessica," he continued, "are more a liability than an asset the way you yank the alpha's chain. If he would screw you and move on, we might have no problem. But he believes he loves you. He is young—naïve." He shoved us into a small bathroom. "We will help him grow up. Fast."

The lights went out.

"Well, it's about time," Sophie called out. The lights snapped back on and Sophie confirmed what I'd guessed when a whiff of wildflowers blew past me. "Your mom's ghost is here. She's pissed."

The lights snapped off and on again and in the brief darkness I shouldered the man back. Hard. His head slammed against the door, teeth biting through his lower lip and blood spilling down his chin. His gun fell and scrambling after it I drew my own gun, turning them both on him.

"I'm sorry, but as difficult as Pietr is sometimes—and as much as we argue, he's the light in my frikkin' world. And right now? You're trying to screw up that light. Let us go."

He lunged for me and I emptied both guns in disbelief.

Sliding down the door, he left a broad smear of blood.

Behind me, Sophie gagged. I grabbed her, tugging at the door and dropping the guns. No ammo meant no use. "Oh. God. Jessie," she protested. "You just . . ."

I nodded, choking the thought down as I guided her out of the ruined bathroom. "I just eliminated someone who was going to kill us both." Standing just inside the Colonial's back door I caught my breath. "Let's not talk about it."

Eyes shut, I leaned against the wall, Sophie leaning against the door.

Now we'd all be okay. And least physically.

There was a *creak*—the door flew open and Sophie disappeared.

"Sophie—?" Words blew out of my lungs in a gust as I was yanked out the back door and fell onto the lawn with a grunt.

Sarah laughed and landed with her knees beside my ribs, pulling back a hand to hit me.

"Play nice, Sarah." *Derek.* "I'm not quite finished *here.*"

Ahead of us I heard a hiss and, straining my neck, I saw Derek kick someone on the ground. *Cat?* Stepping away from her, Derek circled Sophia. I snagged Sarah's arms and twisted, rolling and shoving her so I was on top.

"Don't you touch me, you freak of nature!" Sophie snapped, winded but still able to climb to her feet.

Derek laughed. "Takes one to know one." He rushed her, tapping her head with his fingers.

"Soph!" I shouted, but her knees gave way and she collapsed.

"Pitiful," Derek muttered, looking at her crumpled form.

Taking advantage of my split attention, Sarah rolled me, snarling like a wild dog. Derek's new little pet—*she* was who Wanda had meant.

"Sarah, stop!" My hands and hers linked, she leaned all her weight on me, trying to pin my arms back. "This isn't *you!*"

"No, you're wrong. You lied to me, Jessica Gillmansen. You fed me a string of lies about who I was and what I'd been," she growled. "You tried to make me something I wasn't supposed to be. To make me as miserable and guilt-ridden as *you.*"

"Sarah, you can be whatever you choose to be—"

"Quit trying to talk your way out of this," Sarah snapped. "Get dirty, for once—Pietr likes girls with *spunk.*"

That was it. Remembering every time she had pushed herself at Pietr, every time I had helped her . . . With a shove of my hips and twist of my back, I tossed her.

She landed in an ugly heap.

"Sarah!" Derek shouted.

"What?" I demanded. "Can't you fight your own frikkin' battles?" Regretting the challenge, I sprang to my feet, looking for a weapon. If I needed to fight Derek, I needed to do it without getting into his reach—without getting touched.

Otherwise?

Over.

One touch and Derek could get in my head again, mess with my body's controls. My gaze raked the area, searching . . . There was an old greenhouse and garden behind me, probably kept up to make things appear more normal. I rushed to the garden, staying clear of Derek's hands and Sarah's limp form.

Maybe there was—a shovel? A hoe? Nothing. Didn't people leave their tools lying outside in the suburbs? I glanced toward the greenhouse. "Sarah," I called, "you okay?"

"No, you whore, I'm not!" She staggered to her feet.

Exasperated, I puffed out a breath, eyes on both Derek and Sarah to see who was the more immediate threat.

"You lied—"

"You're right. I lied. I lied about not wanting Pietr. I lied about all the moments and kisses we stole behind your back. And I hated myself for every bit of it. And I lied about the day of the accident. But it all stops here. Now. Do you remember what I told you about June seventeenth?"

"That I was in a car crash. That I was lucky to be alive."

"So true. And I wasn't just referring to the accident then. Do you know why?"

Her brows knit together and she shook her head slowly.

"Because the first day I visited you in the hospital, when you were still comatose—I had my hands on your pillow. And I sure as hell wasn't going to *fluff* it." Raising my hands, I pantomimed, remembering. "I was going to press it over your face—"

"Why?"

"Because the biggest lie I ever told was a lie of omission. And I made everyone in school take part in it, too. I told them we all deserved a second chance—that we could have a fresh start with a better Sarah if they just gave me time. . . . It took some work. I wasn't sure Jenny and Macie would keep the secret but, in retrospect, I should've known. They replaced you the moment they found out you were hospitalized!" I laughed.

From the corner of my eye I watched Derek. His eyes grew darker and I knew he was juicing up, using my anger and Sarah's confusion to feed. I exhaled and eased back from emotion.

"I even got your parents to help me convince the police to drop all charges and wipe your record clean of your real role in the accident."

"What? *Why?*"

"Because you killed my mother."

Sarah gawked at me. "No," she whispered. "Those were nightmares . . . Liar! Tell the truth, Jessica!"

Did she mean the nightmares she'd had right before Pietr and I made our relationship official? I blinked. There was no turning back now. "Your joyride cost my mother her life. She made me pull you out of your Beemer before she'd let me help her. She was all about forgiveness, redemption—she made the best parts of me—and you killed her!" Remembering Derek, I gulped down a breath and advanced on her.

"Instead of suffocating you, I did what I thought was the opposite of destroying you—but it was just as bad. I gave you a second chance—tried to make you into someone my mother would have liked . . . respected. To justify her loss."

"I wasn't driving—" she insisted. "No, your mom was . . ." She whipped around to stare in horror at Derek. "That night— you and I . . ." Clutching her head, her fingernails dug into the scar that proved she'd been part of an accident no one talked about because second chances were more important than past mistakes. "Ohhh . . ."

"Sarah—Sarah!" Derek yelled, starting toward her.

"No." Focusing on Derek, her eyes narrowed; her words became clipped. "You were there," she said. "You told me there was no way in Hell I could—" She pressed her hands together on her head and doubled over, screaming like something tried to break through her skull. "Oh . . ." She gagged. "In the nightmares, I'm not driving." She straightened, her eyes fixed on Derek, "*You* are."

He chuckled, a low, sick sound. "I've been *driving* for years," he admitted with a helpless shrug. "Just not in a physical sense."

Sarah swung back toward me, eyes wide. "I drove right in—right into her."

As outrage and horror warred in my head, I saw the same things play across her face. Everything pointed back to Derek. Happy, smiling, social manipulator, remote-viewing, energy-sucking Derek.

Why couldn't I just be justified in hating Sarah now that I finally realized that was what I'd felt all along?

Sarah's voice was a thin whisper. "I've done horrible things," she said, "but—*that*—that was—*murder*. That's unforgivable. . . ."

Unable to disagree, I shuddered. She'd been his puppet even then. There he stood, watching, orchestrator of my mother's murder and the guy who had warned the Rusakovas to save me.

Why was nothing black and white anymore?

"Quit it, Sarah," Derek snarled. "I *made* you." Rushing her, he jabbed her head with two fingers. Her eyes rolled back and she flopped to the ground. *Out.*

"What did you . . . ?"

"What did I do?" he cooed, approaching slowly. "I did whatever it took to get to you, Jess."

"Jess-i-CUH," I barked, stepping back.

"Don't you get it, Jess? I've wanted you ever since I realized the sort of power you have just under your skin. You're the best damn battery—a psychotronic generator in the flesh."

A chill spiraled around my spine, twisting through me.

"You just needed to be a little . . . off-balance? When I set Sarah—who *needs* a chauffeur—out on her little joyride, I never thought I'd get so lucky. I figured she'd maim a pedestrian and someone would freak and be a little emotionally damaged. But killing your mom? I had no idea how much energy you'd throw out."

My gaze strafed the ground while he continued—what did people call it? *monologuing*—hoping to find a rock. A sharp stick. *Anything.* I looked back at Cat, lying limp, just long enough he noticed and spun to give her another brutal kick.

Damn it.

Rolling into a ball, Cat groaned, lungs rattling as she fought to breathe. Her eyes sparked against the darkness. . . .

"I didn't even have to be in the same room with you to feed in those first months. The same town was close enough. But it was such a brilliant stroke of ingenuity and luck . . ."

"It's only ingenuity if you *really* made Sarah—"

"You have no idea, do you, Little Miss Investigative Reporter?" he teased.

"Seriously. Where was the challenge with having someone like Sarah do your dirty work?"

"Sarah was nothing when I first met her. Pretty and popular, but so much potential pissed away. And all Sarah wanted was a date with Jack. That was back when Jack was number one and I was his sidekick." He wiggled his fingers at me. "I was bored and suffering from a severe lack of attention, so I *encouraged* the situation."

Thinking back to middle school, I shook my head.

"Come on, Jess. You're bound to remember Sarah before she dated Jack." His eyes narrowed and his grin widened, watching my expression race from angry to horrified.

Before Jack, Sarah was just like Derek had said: pretty and popular. Nearly normal. Even *nice.* "What did you do to her?"

He shrugged. "I guess you'll have to ask her and put two and two together to figure it out. I think this is one secret I'll take to the grave." He cocked his head, looking at me. "Huh. You're not as *sparky* as I expected. Getting tired?" He glanced at the ground between us.

Measuring the distance? Judging the time it'd take to get his hands on me?

Beyond Derek, Cat twitched; her chest quivering.

I needed to keep her alive. Buy her time. "So you did something to Sarah in middle school. And she turned nasty. Why'd she go after Pietr? He was a Boy Scout compared to the sharks she dated."

He grinned. "Maybe deep down she thought he'd be like other guys. But he was a total gentleman—a challenge to break down and dirty up. It drove her nuts."

He shook his head. "She used to have her pick of guys. Then the one guy she wants doesn't want *her*? She had to feel that creeping doubt in the back of her brain every time he kissed her with closed lips. Every time she caught him looking at *us* together like he could kill. But there's so much you don't know, Jess—so many questions you never *bothered* asking. You were so preoccupied. If you'd stop fixating on what *unmakes* something like Pietr—and ask yourself instead what *makes* someone like *me*, you'd learn a lot."

What was taking Pietr and the others so long? Surely they'd gotten to the car and realized we weren't there. . . . As much as I hated being rescued, I was finding the alternative—*not* being rescued—sucked *waaay* more. I needed to incapacitate Derek and get to Cat.

"By the way, that was pretty crafty, distracting me with you and dog-boy by the mirror. You definitely had my attention. I guess he beat me to the punch." His lips slipped into a greedy smile. "But man, I was close."

"What?" My stomach churned at what his words implied.

"Oh, that's right. *You* don't remember."

Before I could blink, he jumped and tapped my forehead.

I gasped, blinded by the image of me sprawled on his bed beneath him, shirt up, jeans unbuttoned. . . .

"Remember now?" He laughed. "Lemme guess. Your buddy Max didn't tell you about that, did he? I'll bet he didn't even tell Pietr. That'll do some damage," he said with satisfaction.

"Bastard."

"Nope. Mom and Pops were married. Quite the arrangement, really."

"*Murderer.*"

He rolled his eyes up in his head a second as if testing out that word instead. "I'll take it," he said. Rubbing his hands together, he looked me up and down, anticipation flooding his features. "I think we should wind this up. Get ready to evacuate the area, you and me. But first I think I'll rip those memories right out of your head—make you forget Rusakova even exists." He took a sudden step toward me.

I scrambled back. The worst thing imaginable was losing the memories I'd built with Pietr. Without him and all I'd done since meeting him—who would I be? More precious than my physical safety was keeping my memories—good and bad. "Why do that? Why blot out someone's existence?"

Behind Derek, Cat's back arched up in a painful angle and I saw—fur? Her hand thrust out from beneath her and curled into a paw. Determined not to give away the strange thing going on just behind his back, I focused on Derek's face.

"The power you ooze is addictive. And the damage done here? No problem. We'll set up shop somewhere else." Grinning, the leer he shot me was worlds away from his all-American-boy-next-door smile. "I'm very valuable to the company and because I'm valuable, you're valuable. So don't worry. . . ." Stepping closer, his hand by my cheek, he said, "On second thought—*worry.*"

Cat's head raised, stretching her neck cruelly, her face blending between wolf and human for a moment. Streaked with her own blood, she collapsed again, her features fighting and settling once more—furless.

Dodging Derek's hand, I ducked around him, fear giving my feet speed. "If you feed on drama, shouldn't I keep my memories? You could try and turn me against Pietr." My heart pounded at the suggestion, my throat narrowing.

"That's what I like about you, Jessica. Always thinking."

Suddenly beside me, he nearly kicked my feet out from under me.

Nearly.

But my stance held even as things fuzzed in my head and my vision dimmed, his grip biting into my wrist. I kept my focus.

Get closer . . . keep his attention off Cat. . . .

Twisting in his grip, I landed with my back tight to his chest. Fireworks sparked at the edges of my fading vision.

"That's nice," he soothed me, smoothing my hair back. Ants marched through my head. Spiders crawled out from the dimmest regions of my mind, wrapping memories in strangling silk. "Give it up, Jess. Give in." His breath hot in my ear, my body convulsed, images of Pietr spinning loose in my head. "Where's your precious brooding hero now, huh?"

Focus. Through the thickening haze dulling my sight, I glimpsed Cat wiggling out of her clothes and prayed we both knew what we were doing. I caught my breath. Jabbing back with my elbow, I stomped my heel down hard on his instep, and tears burned hot at the edges of my eyes.

"Bitch!" he shouted, releasing his grip.

Stumbling forward, my vision cleared. I spread my feet, lowered my center of gravity and kicked, connecting with Derek's chest, the insulated rubber sole of my sneaker the only thing touching him.

He staggered back with a groan and I caught my breath.

Cat's body convulsed suddenly and the wolf ripped free, stunning me so much I fell backward into Sophie.

"Thank God you're okay," I breathed, tangling awkwardly with her for a moment. She said nothing as I shook free of her and she staggered forward, limbs loose and awkward, her eyes . . .

The smell of leather and warm horses filled my nose and I recognized someone else peering out from Sophie's eyes. "Mom?"

Sophie's head bobbed, her body on paranormal autopilot.

Cat, fully furred and snapping, drove Derek back toward the greenhouse as Sophie advanced on the pair.

Behind me Sarah groaned and stood.

Derek hesitated, his back to the old greenhouse's glass wall glittering with cracks.

Cat backed off, doing a slow semicircle to keep Derek pinned. But Sophie, awkward limbs moving, stumbled into her, spun, flailed and shoved Derek into the glass.

It looked like an accident. But so much else had, too.

An awful wail tore through the air as Derek's body slid down jagged spears of broken glass, flesh tangling with disjointed metal. He shuddered and coughed. I raced forward, grabbing Sarah and dragging her with me. Partly because I didn't trust her at my back and partly because Derek still had something of hers. Something precious.

Her past. Her truth.

His blood puddling by my shoes, I stayed just beyond his fumbling reach and whispered, "Give it back, Derek." Circles darkened beneath his eyes, color leaking from his face like the blood dripping from the corner of his mouth. "You're dying. There's nothing that can save you." I choked, realizing it was the most honest thing I could say—and the most awful.

That most primitive part of me wanted to reach out, take his hand and hold it in his last moments, giving some small comfort even though he'd tried to destroy so much.

But the part of me he'd attacked kept me back. "Give back the memories you stole," I urged. "I'm sure you still have them—like trophies in a case. Give them back and go in peace."

Sarah whimpered, and Sophia, eyes clear and her body again her own, grabbed Sarah's other arm.

Derek rolled his eyes toward me and opened his lips to speak—the trail of blood thickening at the edge of his mouth. "I'll give you what you want—"

Sarah, Sophie, and I leaned in. Would he ask forgiveness,

explain why he put us through such Hell? There was so much we didn't know about Derek. Maybe he'd share his reason for being so cruel. In all the fiction I'd read there was always a reason for a villain's actions.

People weren't *born* evil . . . evil was manmade.

"—and *more*," he promised, and with a frighteningly fast move, Derek grabbed Sophie and me, Sarah wedged between us, completing a strange human circuit. And in his death throe, he vomited *everything* out of his boiling brain and back through us.

CHAPTER TWENTY-THREE

Jessie

I woke with a pounding headache. Even trying to pry my eyes open the smallest amount made me queasy. I swayed and closed my eyes again. Warm, I was wrapped in an electric blanket turned one notch too high.

"Jess." Pietr's voice came through the fog of pounding pain. Gentle and scared.

"*Ow*," I said.

A hot hand rested on my forehead, bending my neck gently until I felt I had a hot water bottle for a pillow.

"Pietr?" I whispered through dry and uncooperative lips.

"*Da*, Jess." Words rumbled through his chest. "I am here."

"What the hell happened?"

Cat scolded, "Language!" but her exclamation was tender.

"You let him grab you," Pietr snarled. "And then you all dropped to the ground at once."

"All? Ohhh." I pulled away from the hot water bottle and the noise of the racing clock vanished. I forced my eyes open and noticed Pietr's arms wrapped around me, Pietr's chest rising and falling where my head just rested.

My bulletproof vest lay on the ground near Pietr. He made no apology for the way he skimmed his hands back over my torso, checking for wounds. "Ouch. Stop. I'm bruised. Nothing else. Sophie?" I called, finding her seated not even ten feet away. "Is Mom . . . ?"

Sophie closed her eyes a moment, her lips pressed tight. "She's still here. I'm going to totally regret this in the morning, but—come here."

Pietr watched me, worried. "I'm not letting you up yet," he said. "You're not quite together."

"The heck I'm n—" I stood, swayed, my knees betraying me, and I flopped into his waiting arms.

"Belligerent, aren't you?" he whispered, lips against my cheek. He scooped me up in his arms, walked a few steps, and sank down beside Sophie.

"This is different from seeing auras and energy fields," Sophie admitted, "but since she made herself at home earlier . . ." Her eyes popped open and roses seemed to blossom in a sudden breeze. "Jess."

I trembled hearing my mother's voice. "Mom . . ." Tears sprang from my eyes, streaming hotly down my face.

"I can't stay. And you don't need me as much now—"

"I'll always need you," I hiccupped. "You're my mom. . . ."

"Shhh," she soothed. "You're doing much better now. You've made some strange choices since my death." Her gaze paused on Pietr before returning to me. "But they've worked out well. I'm so glad you made him understand he wasn't the boy I was warning you about. . . ." Her voice grew softer, the words coming at a slightly different speed than Sophie's lips moved at, almost like I was watching a poorly dubbed kung fu flick.

"Mom?"

Sophie shook herself, straightening, her brow furrowed. "He's a good boy." Mom returned, clearer for a moment.

Pietr tucked his head against the back of my neck. His whisper of "thank you" warmed me all the way down.

"I love you, Jess," Mom whispered. "And your father, and Anna . . ." Sophie sucked down a breath, steadying herself. "I have to go."

"But . . ."

"But I'll always be with you. In your heart," she clarified. "I know. It's cheesy."

Pietr chuckled. Had Dad told him even *that* part of my message from inside the asylum?

"Where did you think she got it from?" Mom asked, her eyes finding Pietr's. "Treat her well," she commanded.

He nodded.

"And be smart, you two."

Pietr's skin heated at her words.

"Jess," Mom said, her voice thinning again. "Forgive yourself. You made the right choice. You did what I asked in the end."

"I—"

"Stop now," she commanded. "The fight? It's forgotten—as it should be."

"I was so mad I didn't say . . ."

"There's so much we never say when we should. We never know when our time's up, when the last chance comes and slips us by. But *you* know that now. That's why we need to live life fiercely—make each moment count. And love courageously."

"I love you, Mom."

"I never doubted that."

Silence stretched between us, and Sophie blinked.

"Mom?" I croaked.

She shook her head, glancing around. "She's gone, Jessie. This time, I think it's for good. She did everything she could to help us—to help you. I think you should move on now. Forgive yourself. She did."

I swallowed hard, nodding and taking a swipe at the tears still on my cheeks.

Looking back toward Sarah, I noticed Cat, fully human and fully clothed.

Not far beyond her Alexi paced beside Derek's body as if trying to determine what to do next with it.

"Leave him," I suggested, a shudder shaking my backbone.

It was over. We were all going to be okay.

Dmitri came into my line of sight and I flinched. Scooting further into Pietr's lap, I whispered, "His second . . ."

"Dmitri thought he was with us," Pietr apologized.

"With *us*?"

Pietr's arms tightened around me and in the moonlight his stars glowed, a reminder of his devil's bargain. "It's nearly done, Jess," he swore.

"We'll burn it," Dmitri said, extricating Derek's body with a sickly squeak as glass slipped free of skin and muscle.

"*It*." I shivered.

Pietr pulled me tight to his chest, rumbling protectively. "I agree," he said, and Derek's body was dragged back into the bunker to be destroyed with everything else.

"How do you feel?" Pietr asked, his eyes searching my face.

"Like my head's been unzipped and turned inside out," I admitted. "Like it's overstuffed. Worst. Headache. Ever."

Standing, Pietr lifted me and gingerly pulled me into his arms, tucking a stray wisp of hair back behind my ear. "Time to go. Max is in the car with Mother." He looked over his shoulder at Dmitri dragging Derek's body away.

Sophie rose and Sarah moved to join us.

Pietr bared his teeth at her.

"Stop," I urged. "We're sticking together for a little while. At least until we get our stories straight."

"And get cleaned up," Sarah stated, tipping her chin up.

At a slow, shambling pace, we made our way back to the car and then to the house, leaving Dmitri to wait for the explosion that would destroy the evidence.

Jessie

Back inside the Queen Anne we collapsed, an exhausted and relieved jumble of bodies stinking of sweat and gunfire and, more importantly, life. Reaching for Pietr I dragged myself to him. "You did it. Do you understand? You got her out," I reminded him, winding my arms around his neck. "You got what you wanted most."

He grinned, peeking over my shoulder to where his mother dozed. "There were two things I wanted most."

"Well, I hope I'm not wrong with what the other thing was when I say *you've got me.* Because, if I'm wrong, I just sounded really arrogant."

His laugh shook me. "You? Wrong? Never." He nuzzled my neck.

"Sorry to break up the love-in," Cat said, reaching out to turn on the radio. She adjusted the volume. "Seven a.m. news."

The announcer's voice was firm, clipped, and yet reassuring. "This morning an explosion ripped through the Colonial section of Junction, killing and wounding an unknown number of victims at this early hour. Firemen on the scene believe the explosion was the result of an underground gas leak caused by the recent construction at a nearby Grabbit Mart. The construction company responsible is currently unreachable. We will keep you updated as the story develops."

"They're going to get away with it." I rested my head on Pietr's chest.

"It's okay," Pietr rumbled. "There weren't many to get away."

"The asylum. It's the company's other campus. What if . . . ?"

"Shhh. Later, Jess. It's not a priority. Especially since Dr. Jones is out of the picture."

"Good point. The experiments should stop. For a while."

The radio announcer rambled on, "And in more tragic news, another student from Junction High was struck by the 5 a.m. train. It has been confirmed that Marvin Broderick, recently

held by local police for an undisclosed crime, committed suicide on the tracks."

"At five?" I swallowed. "Derek was occupied with us."

Cat nodded. "Definitely."

"Then . . . Marvin *did* kill himself."

Max untangled himself from our awkward sprawl. "Maybe
the bastard realized . . ." His jaw twitched and he focused his
glare on a spot on the wall. ". . . that what he did was unforgivable."

"I can't even think about it right now," I apologized.

The basement door creaked open and Amy and Annabelle
Lee crept out, peering at the pile of us. "Sophie? Sarah?" Amy's
eyes narrowed. She looked at me. "Lucy?" she asked in her best
Ricky Ricardo voice.

"I know, I know. I got some 'splainin' to do."

Amy spotted our newest addition, Mother, and smiled a moment, surely noticing the family resemblance.

"You're back," Amy stated, seeing Max.

"*Da*," he agreed, sweeping his tousle of dark hair back from
his eyes to look at her. "I'm back."

She looked away.

"Did you hear—" I pointed at the radio.

"Yes." She went pale. "I'm . . ." Letting out a huge sigh, she
caught and held my eyes. "I need to clear my head. I mean, I
guess that's it, then, right? Marvin's dead. Is that justice?"

Silent, Annabelle Lee wrapped her arms around Amy's
waist and hugged her tightly.

"Things appear to be—handled—in whatever you all were
doing . . . ?"

I nodded.

"What I need is some sense of normal," Amy admitted. "So
I'm going for a run. On my regular course."

I pulled myself up, reached for my jacket and glanced at my
sneakers, tugging the laces tight. "What you need," I stated
firmly, "is the truth." I looked at Max.

I nodded at the question his eyes asked. This was the time. Desperate times. Desperate measures.

Max stood. "Amy," he said so slowly I wanted to shake the words out of him, "we need to talk."

Something about her shut down. "After I run."

"I'm coming with you," I announced.

Although she said, "You'll just slow me down," the corner of her mouth turned up faintly, welcoming the idea.

"When I get back, everyone's going home," I said. "So showers are most definitely in order."

Outside, Amy swept her auburn hair up and into a ponytail, pulling a hat firmly down on her head. We plodded forward, soles slapping the road as we ran.

A few blocks down we turned onto Main Street, hopping onto the sidewalk and out of the sparse Junction traffic. Running in the shade cast by the old department stores, houses, restaurants, and cafés that crowded the street, we shivered as the first flakes of snow peppered down.

A cat burst out of an alleyway and Amy jumped in surprise, stumbling and cursing.

"You okay?"

"Yeah, yeah," she said, obviously spooked. A couple months back she would have seen the cat, hopped over it, and stroked its back with her trailing foot. But now? She was shaken.

I wondered what she was thinking, this best friend of mine who'd grown up rich enough—in ways most people never counted—in a trailer park until her parents started fighting. She'd had everything she wanted for a while. But things changed. Her brother escaped by enlisting—finding that some battlefields were easier to understand than others. Her mother left, and her dad lost his job.

She found Marvin.

Her prince turned rapist.

She lengthened her stride, and I pushed to keep up, as we reached the east end of Main, the spot where the redbrick heart of town became punctured with postage-stamp lawns and the street stretched into an abbreviated suburbia.

Up toward the colleges we went, feet pounding blacktop as we climbed the hill. Amy could have eased up—gone more gently with a slow jog—but she had reasons to run. And nothing would stop her today, so I fought to keep pace.

Like the friend I should have been all along.

"You know there's something different about Max," I puffed.

"Yes," she said. "He's uncomplicated. I like him because of that."

Oh boy.

"Marvin lied from the beginning. He—my dad would have called it—*sold me a bill of goods.*"

"So you like Max?" I pressed her, knowing her answer.

Something moved in the shadows and Amy hopped to the side, jostling against me, eyes wide. Recovering, she said, "So much it hurts. But . . ."

"But what?"

"Everything's changed. So fast. I don't know what to do."

"Trust me. Trust *Max*," I urged.

Off the blacktop and onto packed dirt we went. Everything was colder here: the ground, the air . . . Winter was already moving in, so cold it burned in my throat and lungs. This park wasn't as well-kept as the one by the river, but its crisp wildness felt right.

Amy slowed, watching me. "Max wants to talk," she said.

"Yeah."

She shook out her feet and legs, clapping her hands together. "Guys *never* want to talk—not unless they're breaking up with you."

"You think . . ."

"I do have a little more experience with this relationship stuff," she pointed out. "I just didn't expect the *it's not you, it's me* speech so soon."

"What if that's not it?"

"Of course that's it. And who can blame him after—"

I grabbed her arms and shook her. "No," I insisted. "Who can blame *you?* Why are *you* blaming you?"

"I had this friend," she began, "who lost her mom. She blamed herself for it. But it wasn't her fault."

"Sounds like a stupid friend." I kicked a pebble. "I know it wasn't my fault. Rationally speaking."

"Yeah," she agreed. "I know what Marvin did wasn't my fault either—*rationally speaking.*"

"So what do you want, Amy, from Max?"

"One minute all I want is for Max to hold me, kiss me—wipe out everything I remember about Marvin, and then . . ." She bent over, sucking down a ragged breath. ". . . the idea of him touching me like Marvin did . . ."

"He'll never touch you like Marvin did," I whispered, pulling her up and into a hug. "It's Max. He's an oaf, but he's a wonderful oaf."

She jumped. Something rustled in the brush not far from where we stood. Something large.

"Seriously," I assured. "He's just a wonderful oaf who needs you as much as you need him."

"There's something special about him . . . ," she agreed, but she was listening to the disturbance near the path's edge.

"Oh, he's special, all right. . . ."

"Did you hear that?" she asked.

I nodded, knowing.

"Hello?" she called.

"There's something you have to know, though. . . ."

"Not now, Jessie." She waved her hand, listening for movement in the thicket.

"Yes, now," I insisted, stepping back.

A crunch, a crash, and Max, in his wolfskin, shoved through the brambles.

I took Amy's hand, watching her as she processed what stood before us, imagining what she saw through her eyes: a wolf.

Huge, brown, broad-shouldered, and long of body, it peered at her with eyes not quite canine—somehow human. Except in color. They glowed a grim crimson. In its mouth hung . . .

Amy blinked, whispering, "Jeans?"

It stepped forward and her hand tightened on mine.

The wolf stopped, dropping the jeans at Amy's feet.

Amy turned and looked at me, eyes wide. The only monsters she'd ever known were human ones, so a large wolf . . .

I could almost see the wheels in her head turning as she watched him through narrowed eyes.

He drew back rubbery lips to reveal teeth curving in a hungry grin, and his eyes turned to me.

I nodded, and Amy jumped when the wolf fell to the ground and changed . . . fur became flesh and hair, paws lengthened into hands and feet.

Amy gasped. I let go of her hand. She grabbed mine again.

The fur disappeared, leaving smooth human flesh.

She reached toward his broad back—the tattoo, she recognized. A saber marking his shoulder. She stared at me. But only for a moment.

Head down, body still bent, he slipped into the jeans and stood slowly up, pushing raucous curls back from dramatic eyebrows and out of his sparkling eyes.

Nearly nose-to-nose with her, Max smiled, saying, "We need to talk."

Amy screamed and I dropped her hand so Max could take them both and tenderly, carefully, kiss her quiet.

CHAPTER TWENTY-FOUR

Jessie

Brighter than we often gave him credit for being, Max had brought the car. We piled in, Amy still in shock, and headed back to the Queen Anne as Max tried to pour out in words everything Amy needed to know.

And probably a good bit more. It seemed Dad and I weren't the only ones who rambled when worried. And Max was most definitely worried. At least he was doing something about it.

Back inside the house, I said, "I need to check on Dad and Wanda. We need to get everyone home."

Pietr stood behind me, arms draping around my shoulders.

Annabelle Lee called from the kitchen. "They're fine," she assured us. "They want *us* to come home."

"Now?" I whispered, looking around the sitting room. In such a very short time this had *become* home.

"First things first, Jessie," Alexi apologized, reaching for me. "We need some blood."

Cat looked at me, her eyes saying what she didn't with words: She hadn't told Alexi the cure didn't hold. That she'd changed when Derek had her bleeding in the dirt with no hope.

I looked at Mother, curled on the floor, chin propped on her fists. She looked human enough, but her body language showed just how strong a grip the wolf had. "What if it's not enough?" I murmured, peeling myself away from Pietr.

"It has to be."

"What if . . ." I searched for words, but came up empty.

"We don't know enough," Alexi admitted. "She's so advanced in the stages of this thing, what if . . ."

"What if your grandfather was so efficient in making us that nothing can save her now?" Max hissed.

"Shut up." Mother stood, rubbing at her eyes. I noticed they never lost their red glow now, the wolf taunting her from within. "I will not tolerate my family bickering." She swayed on her feet and both Alexi and Max grabbed her to steady her.

They paused, looking at each other, each holding their mother, one the adopted son with no blood ties, the other a full-blooded mama's boy when he wasn't a full-blooded player. But in this, they saw eye-to-eye.

"What is the worst that could happen?" She flung up a hand to silence me before the words fell out. "I'm dying already. How much time do I have? A week? A day? You risked enough to free me. This is *my* risk. My choice. None of you will take my choice from me. Prepare the cure. I will drink tonight and see what tomorrow brings."

We nodded and Alexi led me away to give the only thing I could other than my hope everything would be okay: I gave my blood.

Jessie

We were readying to take everyone home when Pietr caught me in the foyer. "I'm sorry."

"I understand," he said, his jaw tight. "Go home. You've done more than your part."

"Do you think leaving you is easy?" I wondered, horrified.

"You have a chance to know her. But you're going home."

"She's taking the cure. I'll have more time to know her." But my heart stuttered and raced like I was lying.

"Kiss me, Pietr," I whispered as everyone skirted us, heading for the door. "I'll come back as soon as I can."

He leaned over and kissed me, his lips hard and tight.

"Pietr . . ."

"Do what you have to do," he said, pulling out of my grip. He turned on his heel and walked away.

I sank into the seat beside Amy, who'd insisted she'd ride along. From the car's front seat Sarah fiddled with the radio as Alexi backed down the drive.

"Okay," I said to Alexi, "Sarah first."

"My parents are still in Aruba," she complained. "I doubt the maid even noticed I was gone."

I reached forward and grabbed her arm. "At least you won't have to explain anything. It'll be fine."

"How do you know that?" Amy interjected.

"Because—"

"No," Sarah agreed. "She's right. Add that to the list of things I didn't think I'd ever say," she muttered. "I don't know if I—if any of us—will be okay. I mean, what exactly did Derek do to us?"

Amy turned and looked at me in question as Sarah continued. "I get the feeling he shoved a whole file folder worth of crap into my head, but—"

Sophia picked up. "I don't want to open it."

Sarah nodded and my stomach tightened. They'd put words to the same sensation I'd noticed. Something crawling in my head, like a snake slowly coiling, readying to strike.

Alexi looked into the rearview mirror, concern clear in his eyes. "You need to keep me in the loop about this. If you start having any weird . . ." He shook his head. "Let me know if you notice any changes in yourselves—or each other."

We pulled into Sarah's driveway. "Well, that's it for me."

A gardener looked up from where he was trimming the hedges. "Morning, Miss Luxom."

Sarah nodded. "See? No welcome wagon."

Amy shrugged. "At least your dad's not sleeping off a hangover in some bar. Mine probably hasn't noticed I'm gone."

Sarah paused at the open door. "Do you truly think my father's any different except when it comes to his fashion choices and income?" She glanced over her shoulder. "He's probably sleeping it off in a hammock on a beach. No clue about me." With a flip of her hair, she headed toward her house.

Worlds apart, it wasn't a long drive between Sarah's and Sophia's. The moment Sophie stepped out of the car, the front door of the house swung open and her mother came screaming out of it, tears streaking down her face. "I was so scared—"

"Can we go now?" I asked, but Alexi was already backing up.

I was glad someone had missed Sophia. Glad she had a mother who cared enough to greet her in curlers and a terry cloth nightgown, not caring how the neighbors would talk.

I missed that. I was jealous I no longer had that.

But sitting beside Amy I felt guilty for feeling that way. I at least still had Dad and Annabelle Lee (a blessing and a curse). But Amy . . . her dad seldom made it home from the bar anymore. And when he was home, it wasn't like he knew if she was or not. He was mired so deep in self-pity he couldn't appreciate the gift he had.

His daughter.

When we pulled up our long gravel driveway, I looked around, spotting Rio, dancing on nimble hooves in the paddock. Dad and Annabelle Lee had really worked with her in my absence. Hunter and Maggie rushed the car, Maggie springing up in her bizarre black Lab way and nearly hovering in midair, ears flapping out on the downdraft. Hunter whined, wanting a pat on the head. Or snacks.

Annabelle Lee climbed out first.

Do what you have to, Pietr had said—the same thing I'd texted him from the asylum. The reason he'd captained up and risked himself for his mother. He'd done what he'd had to.

So would I.

"Wait," I said to Alexi.

"Are you sure?"

"Yes." Heading for the house at a sprint, hands out to pat canine heads, I pulled the front door open. "Dad!"

He was there in a moment, picking me up, twirling me around so my sneakers brushed the wall. "God, Jessie, we were so worried. . . ." He set me down and grabbed Annabelle Lee. "Anna, Anna, Anna," he crooned, so happy his voice cracked.

"Dad." I put a hand on his arm.

He glanced out the screen in the door, spotting the car. "You're not running off again," he protested.

Leaning against the entry to the kitchen, Wanda's eyes were soft. "Jessie. Can't you stay? Things are settling down."

"They just got their mother back and . . ." I swallowed. "They may not have much time. Pietr needs me."

"Anna?"

"I'm here to stay," she assured.

Jessie

Seated at his mother's feet with Cat and Max, Pietr looked up at me, surprised when I entered the house behind Alexi and Amy. For a moment his expression was unreadable. I wondered if it would have been easier if I'd stayed home and given him time to build up some wall.

Mother nudged him with her foot. "Go," she commanded. "You will not be able to concentrate until you do."

Cowed, he stood and walked over to me, taking my hand and leading me into the kitchen so we could be alone.

He dropped my hand as soon as we were out of everyone else's view. "You came back."

"It appears so."

"Why?"

"Because I realized something, even if you haven't. You need me, Pietr. At least as much as I need you."

He crushed himself against me, lips covering mine as he swallowed my breath and stole away my thoughts. His arms wrapped around me and lifted me, setting me on the counter's edge. "I've known that for a while."

"So you understand, Pietr Rusakova? *Yah tebyah lyewblyew*," I assured him. "I love you. Very much. I would do anything for you." I looked deep into his eyes. "Tonight, maybe we . . . celebrate?"

"Celebrate what?" he asked, intrigued.

"Being alive."

He sucked down a breath, nodding. "It's a good thing to be."

"Come on," I said, taking his hand. "You're the one who says we should make the most of our time."

He nodded, following me close as shadow to sit beside me at his mother's feet.

Telling the stories she still had to share with her children, I saw the strain on her face as she fought to hold things together while the wolf tried to work its way free.

She was a fighter. Sometimes she paused in a story, focused on odd details, a scent, a particularly round and moonlike shape, but then she'd blink, recover, and move on.

There were moments she slipped, scratched at her ear with a curled hand that seemed more a paw, or licked her lips or flared her nostrils and panted at the most exciting parts of her tales. Still, she never let the wolf overtake her.

Not in front of us.

There was a moment she suddenly stood, apologized, and headed for the bathroom. "Sit," she commanded her children.

Pietr and Max exchanged a look, and Cat and Alexi stood, anyway, all of us sensing a problem.

We heard the whimpering moments after she'd closed the bathroom door. There was scratching and yipping and the clatter of things falling onto the tile floor.

Pietr rose.

I did, too.

"*Nyet*," he whispered, unable to meet my eyes. "She's confused. She might hurt you. But she will know me."

I followed him to the stairs, letting go of his hand then.

From where I stood I could just glimpse the bathroom door.

Pietr knocked, waited a moment, and twisted the knob.

Mother stumbled out and into his arms, wholly human, her shirt buttoned wrong, her hair mussed. She licked at his face as wolves did in the wild, acknowledging the leader.

"Cat," Pietr called.

I bounded up the steps against her protest.

"He's embarrassed," she said in my ear, matching me stride for stride.

"He has no reason to be. Let me help."

Cat shook her head but didn't argue.

Mother gazed at me and I slowed my approach. Still in Pietr's arms, she tilted her head, examining me quizzically.

"Wherrre am I?" she asked.

Pietr looked over my head at Cat, blinking rapidly.

Stepping forward cautiously, I placed a hand on his back, and one on her arm. I thought of my hours at Golden Oaks Adult Day Care, of what I'd overheard the nurses and staff say when patients were confused. "You're home, Mrs. Rusakova," I explained. "With your family."

She squinted, looking at me closely. "What a pretty daughter I have."

Releasing her arm, I tugged Cat into her range of vision. "Yes, you do."

Cat sniffled.

"Ekaterina," Mother whispered, her eyes focusing.

Cat caught her breath and nodded.

"My beautiful baby," Mother said, stroking Cat's cheek.

I carefully separated Mother from Pietr and transferred her to Cat and myself, encouraging her back into the bathroom. As Cat straightened her blouse, I realized we were suddenly in a stage of something like senile dementia.

The floor was puddled with water, cups scattered across the tile. "Here we go," I said, heading back out of the bathroom. "Wait." I grabbed a hairbrush and gently pulled it through her hair. "There now." I put her hand in the crook of Pietr's arm. "Go on, Pietr, Cat. I've got this."

"No, Jessie," Cat protested. "You don't have to. . . ."

"No arguing," I said, looking pointedly at their mother. "Head back downstairs."

"Do you have her?" Pietr asked Cat as I searched the bathroom for a ratty towel.

They started down the stairs and he entered the bathroom behind me. "Please go." But my voice cracked as I pulled out a frayed green towel from the bottom of the slender linen closet.

"Jess."

I dropped the towel onto the puddle and sat on the edge of the clawed tub. "Pietr. Let me help you and help her."

"You shouldn't—"

"What? Be helping you? This confusion is normal," I said, "with senile dementia."

"Senile dementia shouldn't hit when you're thirty-eight."

I nodded. "Take the cure, Pietr."

He looked down at the towel soaking up the water. "Maybe I'm meant to be this thing. Maybe I'm meant to go this way," he said, lips curling. "What if the cure isn't what it might be?"

I looked away, remembering the way Cat had changed when pushed too far. And knowing she still hadn't told.

"If it buys you more time . . . if it buys *us* more time . . ."

"What if I wind up drinking more and more of it—because it might happen that way—perhaps because there's a tolerance level in this mix of your blood that keeps us alive?" He jammed the heels of his hands into his eyes. "How much blood will you give to sustain my family? How dare we expect you to bleed for us?"

"I would give you every last drop," I said. Standing, I crossed the floor.

"And what happens when others come and they want the same thing? Do we ask Annabelle Lee to open a vein, too? Do we deny them a chance at life so you aren't hunted and sucked dry?" He doubled over, growling in frustration.

"Why was I so stupid, so selfish? We should have gone and let you be. The morning after we botched the first rescue attempt. If I'd had any balls we would have packed up then. But all I could think of was how much it'd hurt not seeing you, not smelling you, touching you . . . I should have broken your heart. . . ."

"Stop," I commanded. "Look at me."

He refused.

"You're a horrible liar. I would have never believed you didn't love me, even if you'd just up and left. It wouldn't have mattered what you said. I would have figured out you were trying to protect me." I sighed. "I have to admit, the roundabout method you tried with Sarah nearly worked, but again—you're a bad liar and I'm a good enough one to recognize that."

I shrugged. "So here we all are. Thrown together. I love you. You love me. So we make the most of what we have. You don't get to wuss out on me. I love you too much to let you go."

I put my arms around him, holding him until he relaxed in my grip. His arms slipped around me and we clung to each other a moment before I pried him loose and said, "Now go see your mother. Let me finish up."

I turned him around and stood him at the top of the stairs. "Go," I urged. "Don't miss these moments, no matter how hard they are. Each one—it's a precious gift some of us have already lost."

He kissed me and when I was finally certain he'd gone, I returned to the bathroom to finish cleaning.

Amy's voice made me jump. "Is this how it ends for all of them? They're these proud and strong wolves—*werewolves*—and then this . . . so soon?"

"Unless they take the cure, I think this is it," I admitted. "Alexi's afraid it may be sooner for them than for her—no one knows what to expect as the generations go on." I was amazed at how coolly the words came out.

"So how do we get them to . . ."

"Take something that makes them less amazing than they're used to being?" I snorted. "No idea. I just know I'm going keep trying with Pietr. Because even if he does become less amazing than he already is, he'll still be damned amazing to me."

CHAPTER TWENTY-FIVE

Jessie

Their mother rallied in the afternoon, coming back to her senses. She chatted and played with her children as if time were not running out. Maybe that was the key to making the most of it: put the important stuff first—family and friends. Then worry about the details that made up most days.

Pietr curled me into his lap and we listened to her tell the story of how she and their father had met.

"I had only just left Eastern Europe, running through the wild remnants of state forests and national parks, driven west for no better reason than my desire to watch the sun set off the western coast. Where precisely I was and when, I do not know—what did I care for any political limitations like boundary lines? I ran most of the year as a wolf, proud and free and sometimes hunted"—she shrugged like it was only a game—"until one early morning I ran across the tracks of another oborot.

"I was astonished, and a bit frightened because the only other of my kind I had known were my parents and one oborot who had nearly killed me when I was newly changed. I decided I would sniff this one out, find his lair, and determine if he was a threat. I tracked him an entire day and night until I found a place his scent was thick as mushrooms after a rain. A place at the edge of the most beautiful forest I had seen in leagues. It no longer quite lived up to its legend as the Schwarzwald—the Black Forest—but it was shadowy and pine filled and beautiful. At its edge the oborot's scent was heavy as if he passed by frequently. And there it was. A human's house. A small but pretty cottage with flowers in the window boxes. Well maintained and wild all at once. So I slunk around the small fenced·yard, rubbing my body along the wood so he would have no choice but to catch my scent. And then I went to the forest to wait.

"That night I heard his call—a beautiful noise so much more soulful than human song. I could not help myself. I threw my head back and answered, wanting to know immediately if he was friend or foe.

"But instead of coming to meet me, his call died away and I heard nothing until the next night. Again he howled, I replied, and he fell silent. It was as if he was wondering about me, curious but afraid." She glanced at her children's expressions. "I know you do not remember your father as a plotter and a planner, but he was. That was how he had lived so long among humans without notice."

She shrugged. "He acted and lived as they did and only entered the woods out of necessity. But I ruined his tidy little life," she said proudly. "The next night he did not howl. I thought it strange, so I put up the first cry. I waited and tried again. Then I heard them. Hunters. Bumbling through the forest, they came with lanterns and flashlights and dogs. I raced away, evading them, but in the darkness I heard a whimper.

"I could not help it. I turned back toward the little town where his cottage was, listening. I heard it again. I sprinted and there he was, his foot in a trap and already trying to heal by growing into the gruesome metal teeth. As a wolf, there was nothing I could do for him, but as a woman . . . It was strange, trying to change after so long.

"I had to remember what I had been, had to remember my human face and human eyes—things I'd long ago glimpsed in streams and in the single mirror in my parents' home. It took longer than I'd hoped and my hands were so clumsy. . . ."

Cat caught her breath—she had complained before about clumsy human hands.

"But I pried the jaws apart with a stick, and yelping, he tore free. I changed and together we ran from the hunters and their dogs, muddling our scent through the pines and streams, until it was nearly dawn and it seemed safe to return to his house. I slept the day away in his bed, while he did the normal, human things that eluded me." She shrugged and stretched, yawning widely before she returned to a proper-appearing position, seated at the edge of the couch. "What shall we have for dinner?" she asked.

I looked at Pietr. Nudged him in the ribs.

"Mother, you will take the cure tonight?" Pietr tried.

She looked at us each in turn. "*Da*," she said. "I think perhaps I will. May I have dinner to wash it all down with?"

"Of course," Cat said. "Anything you want, Mother."

Jessie

We were all gathered at the table, Mother at its head. Dmitri glowered at Pietr from the table's far end—I'd heard them arguing about there being little time to accomplish certain jobs. Dmitri wanted Pietr away from his mother as much as he wanted him away from me.

No connections. No family.

"A toast," Pietr's mother suggested, noting the wineglass before her, filled with the cure. We raised our glasses in response. "To brave young men and women who give a bit of themselves so others may profit."

She looked at me.

Glasses clinked and she drank. She wobbled a moment, the remaining cure sloshing in the glass Pietr caught and set down carefully, before taking her hand.

"This may get messy," Max warned Amy.

"Mother?" Pietr asked.

"*Da*," she said, her eyes sparkling. "Have I told you the tale of how I first met your father?"

We stiffened.

"I had only just left Eastern Europe—running through the wild remnants of state forests and national parks, driven west for no better reason than my desire to watch the sun set off the western coast." She trembled.

"Pietr," Cat warned.

"Mother," he whispered, moving to stand beside her, wrapping her in his arms.

She shivered. "Where, precisely, I was, and when," she continued, her voice falling away to a whisper, her eyes unfocused, "I do not know—what did I care for political limitations. . . ." She smiled. "He was such an amazing man . . . just like my boys. . . ."

With a shudder, she collapsed out of the chair, falling limp into Pietr's arms. Her chest stopped rising and falling, the glow fading from her still-open eyes.

Pietr stared at me, mute. "Mother . . . ?" His knees gave way beneath him and he tumbled to the floor, dragging her body onto his lap.

Dmitri rose, solemn and cool. "Her time is over. Now yours begins," he said to Pietr.

Shaking, Pietr cried, "Do you not see this?" He lifted her body, her head lolling to the side, hair falling across her face. "She was as much our future as our past!"

I ran to him, my chair tipping over and clattering behind me. Wrapping my arms around him, I held on.

Around us, Cat and Max and Alexi pressed in close, crouched or kneeling.

"Oh, God," Pietr whispered, cradling her in the crook of his arm and tenderly moving the hair back from her face. "You tell them, Dmitri—tell your masters—tell your *dogs*—" Shaking free of my grip, he set his mother reverently down and took the wineglass from the table. "Tell them there are no more werewolves in Junction"—he downed a dose in one large swallow, grinning at Dmitri with bloodstained teeth. *"That* time"—he grabbed Max's mouth and forced it open, spilling the last of the cure into his mouth and along his face—"is over!"

He jumped to his feet and grabbed the stunned Mafioso. Dragging him to the front door, he shoved him into the cold outside. "Our deal is ended. I have nothing left to give you. We are all just men here, Dmitri, damaged, damned, and dangerous men. Leave. Do not come back—there is nothing to come back for. There are *no* werewolves in Junction," he repeated.

The door slammed and I watched him sink to the floor, quivering as the pain of his final change overtook him.

From the dining room I heard Catherine, sobbing, and Max as he gagged and coughed and spit.

ACKNOWLEDGMENTS

By now you all should know I pride myself on being thankful to people who have made a difference in my life and my journey as an author.

Thanks goes out to Mindy Klasky (a great author of romances), who sat me down to talk, and later, via e-mail, introduced me to the amazing Richard Curtis of Richard Curtis Associates. Mindy and Richard—you rock!

To Panayiotes Asimakopoulous for doing the Greek translation for me!

To the beta readers who helped *Secrets and Shadows* become the best book it could be and stuck with me through *Bargains and Betrayals*: Alyson Beecher and Karl (the husband). You guys know this series from the ground up.

Likewise, Robin Wright—you're one of the very first people I call when my brain's become oatmeal, or I'm freaking over drama in the publishing world—well, the drama I *can* talk about. You may never know how much that means to me, that you're around, but I hope you have a chance to make those same sorts of crazed calls to me (and soon).

Thanks to Christie Webb, the winner of Karen Alderman's

auction, which went to support both The Fisher House and Doctors Without Borders.

To the new betas who helped make *Bargains and Betrayals* what it is now: author Jordan Deen (another writer of were-wolves!), who chatted with me about broken down vehicles, dis-placed alphas, and life in general, is an absolute sweetheart, and reminds me weekly when it's Werewolf Wednesday; Lynsey Newton (the team's witty Brit), who knows my characters very well and helped give me the courage to let what happens hap-pen in this story—*so* very important; Saranna DeWylde (an author of spicy paranormal romance), who was the second Textnovel winner and is a scream; Anthony Mincarelli (the treasured male beta), who chewed through *Secrets and Shadows* and *Bargains and Betrayals* as quickly as a college schedule can allow, and fas-cinates me with the tech stuff he's doing and has gotten quite good at talking me back from the ledge. During the course of much madness, these people have become more than beta read-ers or fans, they've become my friends. MINE.

Anthony gets double the thanks because the black and white Augmented Reality marker you'll find on the next page (a paw print on a heart), which leads you to online fun well beyond this book's paper pages, was his concept, too. Check it out!

And, of course, I'm thankful to the amazing team at St. Martin's Press. Without these folks, the Rusakovas would be nothing: Michael Homler (an amazing editor who understands I occasionally freak out, and who teases me about stuff I have yet to learn about publishing—yes, there's much he can still tease me about), and Eileen Rothschild and Sarit Schneider, who help make sure my books get into your hands. Their efforts mean so much!

And finally . . . Thanks to each of you who have embraced the Rusakovas, the Gillmansens, and all of Junction—you make their weird world turn!

If you have a computer with an Internet connection and a Webcam, you now have a special invitation to explore the world of 13 to Life more fully . . .

1. Go to http://13toLifeSeries.com/ARpawprint.
2. Hold the AR marker above up to your Webcam.
3. Explore more of the world of 13 to Life!